PURE BLOOD

A millennium of mankind's folly had left the earth strangely changed. Tampering with life itself, man had crafted a dozen new races to be his servants, each gifted with awesome powers, yet his descendants hunted them down in a fury of hatred and fear. A killing heat had turned the north-lands into jungles, and now a host of fantastic creatures roamed the desolate ruins of the ancient cities.

Into this new dark age two brothers were born. Morgan, whose nobility and honor made him a natural ruler, was deprived of a title by the baseness of his birth. Ramon, whose cruelty and cunning marked him as a tyrant, used his power for a war of conquest and extermination.

Outcast and betrayed, Morgan sought refuge with the last remnants of the new races. With their beautiful leader Alicia at his side, Morgan became their champion and challenged his brother for the future of all humanity.

Pure Blood

Mike McQuay

BANTAM BOOKS
TORONTO • NEW YORK • LONDON • SYDNEY • AUCKLAND

PURE BLOOD
A Bantam Book / February 1985

Map by Robert J. Sabuda

ISBN 0-553-24668-2

Published simultaneously in the United States and Canada

Bantam Books are published by Bantam Books, Inc. Its trademark,
consisting of the words "Bantam Books" and the portrayal of a
rooster, is Registered in U.S. Patent and Trademark Office and in
other countries. Marca Registrada. Bantam Books, Inc., 666 Fifth
Avenue, New York, New York 10103.

PRINTED IN THE UNITED STATES OF AMERICA

H   0 9 8 7 6 5 4 3 2 1

For my children,
Elise, Chris and Jenny with love.
Never grow up.

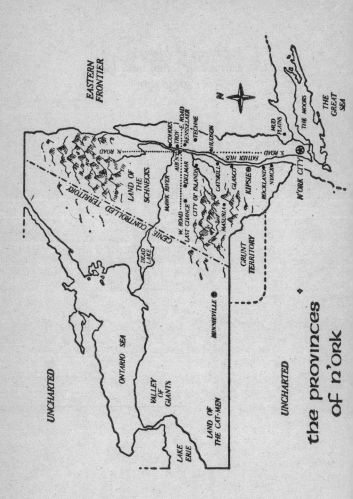

the provinces
of n'ork

Distant Thunder

i
Rab Hunt

Morgan lay on a steel beam in a low branch of the hemlock pine. The branch corkscrewed around the beam like a snake, winding to a centuries-old dance of Man and Nature, winding like some clockwork mechanism of steel and concrete and wood and romance. The surrounding trees bore the fruit of that mechanism, beams of now organic metal, pushed up as the trees grew, twisted and became one with them. The trees were thick and strong, stronger for the steel that latticed through them like the insane web of some monstrous brooding spider.

Morgan lay on his back watching the gray sky slide restlessly overhead through a tiny break in the eternal thicket of branches, his tangled mane of fiery red hair hanging over the edges of the beam to drift gently with the breeze from the south that had somehow managed to penetrate the forest. Below him lay the clearing where the rabs would pass on their sojourn to the Hus to drink. Above him, always above him, his half brother Ramon sat on another rusted beam, his white stockinged legs dangling, his dark eyes staring down at Morgan.

Morgan drank in the smells of the forest and the sights of the city in the trees. He felt a fire burning brighter than his hair flare to consume him with the bursting, jumping excitement of being alive. It was good to be ten years old and on a rab hunt. There was nothing better.

"Morgan," Ramon whispered from above.

"Shhh . . ."

"I don't think they're coming today," the dark boy said.

Morgan frowned up at him. "They won't if you don't keep quiet!"

He rolled onto his side and wiped the sweat off his face. It was hot, and humid, as usual. Where his back had touched the beam, his leathers were dank and gamey. He hugged his bow and quiver tightly and tried to listen to see if he could hear the roar of the Hus in the distance. He couldn't.

"Maybe they came before we got here," Ramon said in that maddeningly loud whisper.

"They'll be here," Morgan said. "Just be patient."

3

"I can't," Ramon said, and Morgan could believe it.

They were the same age, born within weeks of one another. They had the same father, Ty'Jorman, Governor of Alb'ny. They grew up together, played together, the same games in the same ways—yet the difference of their station was the measure of infinity. And therein lay a tale.

Ramon stood carefully on his beam, grabbing another that criss-crossed it for support. "I'm starting to get tired, I . . ."

"Listen!" Morgan called.

Ramon's eyes narrowed and he crouched on the beam, listening to the persistent, distant rumbling.

"It's thunder," he said, "just a . . ."

"Listen," Morgan said again.

The rumbling got closer, louder. Morgan shot a glance to his half brother. The sound came not from the active, roiling sky, but rather from the mantle of the barely quaking earth.

Rabs.

The Screamers in the vibrant green thickets below heard them too, quieting their own restless movements in anticipation.

Morgan sat up soundlessly, holding his great sword tight to his side lest it clank against the rust-eaten beam. He removed a shaft from his quiver. He could feel the vibrations in the trees now, and his hand was shaking with excitement as he notched the arrow into the bow string.

He stiffened his arm and pulled back on the gut string, sighting the shaft at the wide, worn pathway below. He waited, young muscles tightened against the strain.

"Where are they?" Ramon whispered.

"Shhh . . ."

Time became meaningless, lost in the rumble of the rab migration. The forest was dark and impenetrable. Were it not for the time-worn pathways of the creatures of the twisting jungle, there would be no travel for anyone.

Morgan pulled the bow back a little farther, until his shoulder ached and shook like the tree.

And then the sound came. The high, moaning wail, a banshee cry: the vibrations of the steel grounded in wood and set off by rab thumping. The forest cried all around them like mourning widows after a battle.

Ramon screamed.

The world tangled white.

The rabs bounded into the clearing in a jumble, going fifteen and twenty feet into the air. They were big, bigger than Morgan remembered, bigger than grown men. They were everywhere.

Morgan tried to loose his bolt and realized it was already gone, lost somewhere in Ramon's yell. The Screamers were out of the thicket, blowing brass horns, accompanying the rusty chorus, filling the woods with shrill alien sound to confuse the animals.

Morgan, deadly calm amidst the turmoil, notched another arrow. Four rabs filled the clearing, five, their powerful hind legs flailing the ground, their large ears twitching in alarmed confusion. The lead ones turned back on those behind. They sprang high into the air and in every direction.

Morgan's aim was true this time, and he put an arrow through the throat of one in mid-leap. It hit the ground, dark blood squirting, then bounded once more to the bushes and died.

The clearing was jammed with rabs now, jumping on top of one another, hearts pounding. Farther down the path, the hunting party's mounts were barking loudly, denying them escape.

Morgan drew another shaft as he watched one of Ramon's strike home. The bow whistled in his hand, time after time. His aim was good, but the targets erratic, difficult to cripple.

Then the fear of the arrows started to outweigh the fear of the Screamers, and the rabs crashed madly into the bushes. They hit the Screamers with their full weight and their full terror and real screams, painful screams, mixed with the battle sounds. Rabs weren't flesh eaters, but their front teeth were powerful, and their hind legs could snap bones like twigs.

"They're getting away!" Ramon yelled, shooting into the bushes.

Morgan lowered his bow, afraid of hitting the Screamers. Standing full, he drew his broadsword without thought, hurling himself off his lofty perch.

He hit the ground hard, tumbled, and came up on his feet. He was moving now, all sensation, beyond fear. Running up the body of the first rab he killed, he dove off it, coming down on the back of a large white one that had a Screamer pinned to the ground.

The creature turned its searing red eye to the parasite on its back, human blood dripping from its teeth. It jumped, trying to jar the boy loose; but Morgan held fast, never losing a grip on his sword.

It leapt again, coming down twisting in a tight circle, as Morgan watched the world spin crazily around him. The creature jumped again, springing back into the thicket. Fighting the cloak of leafy brambles, the boy raised himself on his haunches and drove the point of his blade into the animal's high-arching ear. The rab jerked violently to the side and pitched the boy heavily back into the clearing.

And it came for him, staggering and quaking, its blood pouring down the exposed blade and dripping in huge, thick gobs off the silver hilt.

Morgan tried to rise, but the creature was right on top of him, head twitching, eyes set with determined ferocity and pain. He tried to scoot back, but it pinned him, body pumping for air, breath hot like a fireblast.

The teeth were there, drooling pink-tinged saliva; he tensed to meet death. Suddenly, the rab fell on top of him with its full weight. The air went from his lungs, and as he gasped beneath the animal he felt the death constrictions of its muscles. Finally, it lay still.

He felt hands helping him out from under the rab's dead weight. Standing on wobbly legs, he looked at the beast. Half the shaft of an arrow protruded from the monster's head.

His eyes drifted up the hemlock. Ramon still sat in the safety of its reinforced branches, laughing and shaking his head. Morgan smiled and waved, and Ramon responded by wagging his bow above his head.

He looked around, his body beginning to stiffen now that the excitement was dying down. The clearing was filling with people and Screamers, all talking excitedly, expanding in their fashion the events that had just taken place. Before they returned to the Keep, the day's hunt would be a monumental undertaking for all concerned.

Grodin, the Governor's Breeder, ran into the clearing, his hard bare chest gleaming with sweat, his face nearly cracking from the weight of the smile that consumed it.

"Morgan!" he called, running up to hug the boy. "Are you all right, lad?"

"Did you see it?" Morgan squealed. "Did you see me ride that monster?"

Grodin stood upright like an oak tree and put his hands on his hips. He turned to face the gray sky and laughed, deep and throaty. "See it?" he bellowed. "I'd have been a blind man to miss it! You rode him into the ground like the twisting devil he is."

He picked the boy up under the arms and hoisted him high in the air, twirling like the rab had done, spinning the world for Morgan just once more before the memories faded.

"You are the demon of the forest!" Grodin yelled, setting Morgan back on the ground. "Master of the red-eyed monsters!"

"Ramon killed him," Morgan said quietly.

The man frowned deeply, stretching the line of his deep scar that ran from temple to jawbone. Grodin was a hard man, hard and swarthy. A fighter and grandiose peasant to most, Morgan knew him as nothing more than a large heart held together with sinew.

"Don't believe it," he said, nodding. "He just slowed him down for you. Look."

He walked to Morgan's rab, pointing to the still-dripping half blade that stuck out of the huge ear. "Believe me, lad. If somebody stuck you like that, you'd die."

He hoisted a leg up, bracing a foot on the creature's furry head. He pulled on the blade, straining, and when it finally jerked out, Grodin nearly fell to the ground.

"Better clean this off," he said, handing back the sword with the ornate boar's head hilt. It was the only gift that Ty'Jorman had ever given Morgan, and the boy treasured it more than his life.

The man bent, grabbing handfuls of dirt to clean the blood off his own hands. "Best to not argue with the young Governor about the rab, though," he said, nodding toward Ramon who was being helped out of his blind by many hands.

Morgan nodded grimly. No one needed to tell him that. "Want me to bring up the Woofers?" he asked.

"Just a minute," Grodin said, looking around. "Weatherman!" he called loudly, then again.

A man dressed in light-gold robes appeared from the jumble in the clearing and walked to where they stood. His face was passive, blank, his slick bald head shone dully in the overcast sky. He was young, not many seasons older than Morgan—but then, Weathermen were always young.

"You called me?" the young man said in a monotone.

"Rain," Grodin said harshly. "Tell me about rain."

The man looked at the sky. "It will hold until we return to Castle Alb'ny," he said calmly.

Grodin's eyes darkened under his thick brows. "This tells me differently," he said, tracing the scar with an index finger. "This throbs with coming rain, and it now throbs a lot. Look at the sky again."

"I don't need to look at the sky again," the Weatherman said. "You have heard my prediction."

Grodin spat on the blood-soaked earth. "The young Governor is our responsibility today," he said. "I hope for all of our sakes that you are right."

The Weatherman was unshaken. "No rain," he said, and walked deliberately away.

Grodin looked down at Morgan, winked at him. "See to the Woofers," he said, and the boy ran off immediately. "And don't spoil them too much," he called after.

Morgan shoved his way through the clearing. There were five dead rabs all together, and six Screamers. The Screamers were outland Genies of mixed breed, so their nature was moronic and their lives of no consequence. Most of Ty'Jorman's Genies looked like people, but that was where the relationship ended.

The voices were loud and brash, the bloodlust and wine skins making everyone bold in retrospect. It would take quite a while to gut the carcasses and attend to the dead.

Stooping to one of the dead rabs, Morgan used his blade to laboriously hack off a piece of its flank. The smell of death and victory were strong in the air, too strong, unfortunately, for they concealed the smell of rain.

Morgan wandered down the wide pathway, the tangle of steel trees a thick, impenetrable wall on either side. He had his gift of meat tucked tightly under his arm. The sounds of the hunters died quickly, soaked into the sponge of the dark jungle, its own ominous sound seeping eerily through the cracks to set the boy's senses on edge.

The pathway twisted through the city jungle. This was an ancient ground city that had been abandoned before the Troubled Times and simply pushed up over the centuries by the quick-growing trees and vines. The cities collapsed, then grew with the trees, affecting their turns and twists, making a new city of intricately connected limbs and beams. There were many such cities up and down the length of the Hus, many such pockets of ancient civilization.

Morgan could hear the river now, surging and charging in the distance. He could hear the reassuring whine of the Woofers just ahead.

He cupped a hand to his mouth. "Murdock!" he called loudly,

and heard an answering bark in return. Picking up the pace, the boy felt a deep soreness in his right buttock and leg. Ignoring the pain, he broke into a trot.

The seven Woofers were tethered under a natural canopy where ivy-covered beams intertwined diagonally above the pathway like a roof. This angling was repeated eight or ten more times straight up from the first, reaching a hundred feet into the air. From each beam dangled vines of brightly colored red and green flowers buzzing with fat fuzzy bumblebees.

Most of the animals were curled sleeping on the pathway, but upon Morgan's approach they jumped up, straining against their leashes and crying like babies when they smelled the meat he was carrying.

"Take it easy," he said laughing, walking into their midst, pushing their muzzles away from the rab meat. "There's some for everybody."

He reached up, patting Murdock on the snout. Murdock was his, at least away from the Keep when Grodin would let him ride the beast. All of the animals were Bernards, and Grodin's expert care in breeding the stock made him Ty'Jorman's most valuable asset. Proper breeding, purity of blood, was everything; and the Bernards—short brown and white-haired, vicious, but fiercely loyal—were a prize for any kingdom.

"You get the first piece, boy," Morgan said, hacking off a hunk of the meat and tossing it in the air.

Murdock caught it in flight, gobbling it down without even chewing. The other Woofers crowded around, whining softly, vying for position. Morgan cut a piece for all of them, feeding them one at a time.

"You owe me your life," a voice said behind him.

"I know," he answered, not even turning to Ramon. Standing on tiptoes, he put his arms around Murdock's neck, pulling himself close to the animal, enjoying the slight stench of it.

"You like my father's animal," Ramon said. "Perhaps someday when I'm Governor, I'll give him to you."

Morgan turned and smiled at his half brother. "Let's go to the river. I must wash my sword."

Ramon smiled thinly. "Let's race to the river," he said.

"Down, boy," Morgan told Murdock, and the Woofer dutifully lay its huge body on the pathway. Raising his leg high, he climbed on the small saddle that wound around the brute.

"Up," Morgan commanded, and Murdock stood quickly, muscles rippling in the animal's powerful legs. Morgan sat high,

feeling the strength beneath him. He looked down at his half
brother. "Let's go."

Ramon ran to his mount, a jet-black Bernard named Otter,
and jumped at it, grabbing the saddle horn and scrabbling up on
the Woofer's broad back. He reached up to the lashing on the
girder and unleashed the animal.

Without a word, he slapped the Woofer on the rump and
charged down the pathway toward the Hus.

"Go, Murdock, fly!" Morgan yelled, and the Bernard gave
chase, stretched out sleek, staying above the ground with long,
leaping strides.

Morgan leaned forward, wrapping his arms around Murdock's neck to make himself one with the animal. The forest
whizzed past them in long, blurry lines of green and brown.
They moved fast as an arrow, barely touching the ground beneath them, and boy and Woofer were as one mind, exhilarated
with the physical poetry of it all.

They saw Ramon in the distance, slapping Otter to make him
hurry. They would overtake him in a matter of seconds.
Breathing out, Morgan sat up straight, reining Murdock in. The
animal turned its sad brown eyes to the boy, unable to understand why they were pulling up so short of victory. How could
Morgan tell him that winning would be the greatest loss to both
of them?

"Someday," Morgan whispered to him. "Someday."

They tailed Ramon, staying there until Father Hus brought
an abrupt end to their pathway. Ramon reined in a second before
Morgan and looked at his brother with an attitude of superiority.

"You are strong like the river," he told Morgan, as Father Hus
raged white and frothy beside him, "but I am stronger."

Morgan dismounted and Murdock immediately went to the
river to drink. The boy walked up beside the animal and drew
his blood-caked sword. "There is someone stronger than everyone," he said, and knelt to the wide, charging waters.

"There must be an end point," Ramon said, moving up to sit
next to Morgan. He drew his legs up and sat with his chin on his
knee, watching the water. "Someone must be the strongest of
which there is no stronger."

Morgan dipped his magnificent blade in the river, watching
the dried blood break off in pieces and flow with the roaring
current, a tiny fleet of blood boats. "And you are that person?" he
asked.

Ramon stood up. "And why not? Am I not of Pure Blood? Am I not human, and the son of Kings?"

That last part was for Morgan's benefit. His mother had been a concubine and of dubious heritage. Had it not been for the Lady Jerlynn's conception at the same time, Ramon's position might have been his.

Morgan stood also, wiping off the blade in the tall goldenrod of the riverbank. He checked the ornately carved boar's head hilt to make sure no blood was still in the creases. "And how will you prove this strength beyond all others?"

Ramon hitched up his dark velvet knickers and opened his arms wide to the river, the power of the land, the source of life in the human territories of N'ork.

"When I am Governor," he said, "I will raise an army, and sweep down the Hus in my boats of power, conquering all between here and the Great Sea."

Morgan laughed and put away his sword. "And what of N'ork City and the power that resides there. What will they say about that?"

"Do not mock me!" Ramon said. "I will travel to N'ork City and pluck the Jewel of the East and put it in my crown. And you will help me because you owe me your life and must do as I say."

Morgan bowed low. "Yes, your Majesty," he said, stifling a giggle.

"It's not funny," Ramon said, pouting. "I will someday rule these lands and command the respect of all who serve me." He stared darkly at Morgan. "And you will have to respect me too."

"Oh, but I do," Morgan responded lightly, refusing to acknowledge Ramon's mood. "I have as much respect for you as I do anyone."

"Then prove it. Pledge to me your undying loyalty."

"Forever?" Morgan returned. "Wrong or right?"

Ramon stiffened, his mouth stretched tightly against his even teeth. Morgan had seen these clouds pass over before. "Pledge," Ramon said in a low voice.

"I pledge my life to honor," Morgan said. "I pledge it to the Will of God. If you are the instrument of God's Will, then I pledge myself to you."

Ramon smiled at that, the spell breaking. "My loyal friend. Maybe I'll make you a general."

"Farmers don't get to be generals," Morgan returned, sitting in the soft clover of the riverbank.

Ramon sat with him. "Then, I'll make you king of the farmers with a melon for a crown."

Morgan smiled, leaning back on his elbows. "An ear of corn for a shortsword, and a sprout of alfalfa for a longsword."

"Why not?"

Both boys were silent for a moment, Morgan's eyes fixed on the headlong beauty of Father Hus. It was freedom for him, freedom from his chains of the land, and he almost wished that Ramon's dream would come true.

"Morgan?" Ramon asked.

"Hmmm . . ."

"Why did you jump on the rab today?"

Morgan turned on his side to stare at his half brother. "I don't know," he said, and he really didn't.

"You always do things like that."

"Can't help myself."

Ramon was toying with a large ant, placing obstacles in its path every time it tried to walk around. "Remember when you swam across the Hus just on my dare?"

"How could I forget that?" Morgan returned. "Grodin had to build a raft to come fetch me from the other side. It's the maddest I've ever seen him."

"Or the time you climbed to the very top of that huge tree and jumped down from branch to branch?"

"I got in a lot of trouble for that one," Morgan said, and the memory wasn't so funny. "The other villagers said I was a demon and wouldn't let anyone play with me for months."

"My mother told me not to play with you either," Ramon replied, then wiggled his sparse eyebrows. "But then I've never listened to my mother very much."

They heard the faraway rumble. Both boys straightened.

"Rabs?" Ramon said, his eyes wide and frightened.

Morgan shook his head. "This time it is thunder . . . and it's coming this way. We've got to get back to camp!"

The Woofers had lain down to rest, but with the first storm signs they were up, crying softly, restlessly. The boys jumped on the animals' backs and charged down the pathway, Ramon too scared this time to care who won. The wind picked up quickly, blowing with gale force even through the thickness of the forest, and the thunder crashed, the dogs crying louder each time.

They charged through the tree city, the wind making the

girders creak loudly. The woods were alive, the steel beams rolling slowly, as if organic.

The other Woofers were gone from the clearing as they passed the place, and lightning flared brightly overhead, firing the perpetually dark sky.

"It's going to be a bad one!" Morgan called over his shoulder into the roar of the wind.

"Wait for me!" Ramon screamed back. "Don't leave me behind!"

They charged into the confusion of the camp. Grodin stood in the center of the clearing, giving orders. Rab meat was being lashed to the trees, while the dead Screamers were hurriedly butchered as food for the Woofers.

"Where have you been!" he screamed at the boys as they rode up.

"The river!" Morgan yelled back. "Can we make it back to Alb'ny?"

The Breeder shook his head. "We'll have to take to the trees," he said. "Feed your mounts if they'll eat, then give them to a Screamer and get up to safety!"

"What will happen to the Woofers?" Morgan said.

A bright flare of lightning struck near the clearing and they heard a large tree come crashing to the ground.

"The Screamers will watch out for them," Grodin replied. "If they live, they will find their way back home. Now, go!"

The boys moved into the confusion. The humans were attending to the important tasks, while the Screamers stood dumbly by, holding the reins of the frightened, skittish mounts.

Morgan led a reluctant Murdock to the piles of meat, but Ramon had let his Woofer go and was already being helped up into the trees.

"Eat," Morgan told the animal. "You'll need your strength."

But Murdock wouldn't eat. The mammoth beast simply lay on the ground, bringing his huge paws up to his snout, his droopy eyes running pus.

Morgan got down beside him and cleaned out his eyes. "It'll be all right," he said gently, but it was a lie and the Woofer knew it.

"Morgan!" a loud voice called.

The boy turned to see a grave-faced Grodin staring over at him from where he was checking meat lashings.

"Get to the trees!" the taut face said. "Hurry!"

Morgan jumped up and ran to a Screamer who was wandering slowly around the clearing, staring at the confusion of the sky. Taking the man by the hand, the boy led him to where Murdock still cowered on the earth.

"I've got to go," Morgan told the animal, tying his reins to the Screamer's arm. As he moved off, Murdock rose to go with him.

"Stay," the boy said firmly, wiping sadness from his eyes.

And the rain came.

It fell without warning, in blinding, ferocious sheets. Morgan cried out in pain as the pumping torrent stung him, lashed his skin red.

Still on the ground, he could barely see. Holding his arms in front of him, he couldn't see his hands.

"Grodin!" he screamed into the torrent, but the sound of the falling heavens drowned all talk. He was totally alone in his cocoon of water; its level had already risen past his ankles.

He splashed blindly, one hand outstretched, the other protecting his eyes. In a moment, his hand made contact with the bark of a tree. He pulled himself to it and grabbed hold. The water was nearly up to his knees. It was trying to drag him down.

He stared up into the tree limbs, barely able to see Ramon and several of the young Governor's retainers with him.

He tried to scrabble up, catching footholds against the tug of the rising waters. "Help me!" he called up to them, and his mouth filled with water, choking him.

He reached out a struggling hand that was met by a thrashing boot from above, Castle folk wanting to do the Lady Jerlynn a favor. Losing his hold, he fell from the tree, back into the water.

He grabbed the trunk again, looking up. They stared down at him, hatred in all eyes except Ramon's. In Ramon's he saw something different, something infinitely worse. The boy was clearly enjoying Morgan's desperation. The glare of cruelty showed like a blinding light on his angelic face, and Morgan knew that he would never find his salvation in Ramon's tree.

The water had reached his hips. It pulled on him, tried to suck him away. He held on as well as he could, but the tree trunk was bigger around than his arms could reach, and he couldn't get a good grip. His hands strained on the bark and finally broke free.

Something grabbed him! It was Grodin, lashed to another tree, tethered on rope to get him.

"Hang onto me, lad!" the man yelled in his ear, and Morgan didn't have to be told twice. Climbing on the man's broad back, he wrapped his legs around his chest and his arms around his neck.

Grodin drew against the rope to pull himself back to his tree. "On my shoulders!" he yelled, and Morgan scrabbled up, then able to reach a branch and pull himself to safety.

The man climbed up behind him. Together they climbed several branches higher, to a place where a large concrete slab stretched around and made a place where the water couldn't reach.

They sat there quietly for a time, breathing heavily, calming down. The tree city could be a beautiful sight in the rain, its tilting beams and slabs forming thousands of tiny waterfalls cascading in intricate patterns all around—it was the savage beauty of N'ork, the animal soul of an untamable land.

"They wouldn't help me," Morgan said. "They would have me drown."

"That's the way of things," the man said after a time.

"But what have I done to deserve their wrath?"

"You've done nothing, lad."

"I knew they didn't like me," Morgan said. "But I never thought . . ."

"It's an awful burden for one so young to bear. Know that it has nothing to do with you."

"Even Ramon hates me."

Grodin shook his head. "Ramon probably loves you more than anyone. But when you raise a Woofer to be a killer, it may bite all hands, even your own."

"I don't understand."

"Someday you will." The man put his arms around the boy and held him close. "And as long as I draw breath, Morgan, nothing will happen to you."

That comforted Morgan somewhat. He narrowed his eyes and stared at the rain, trying unsuccessfully to look through its dense curtain to see the brother who would not accept his brotherhood.

And he cried, long and hard, draining himself of tears. He cried for the weight he had to carry, and for the youth that was now lost to him forever. He had grown up.

ii
City of Islands

The inhabitants of Master Thulow's island awoke to the smell of smoke. It drifted lazily on the westerly morning breeze from the outermost of the thirty-seven islands that formed the city.

Nebo, the apprentice, though still in his bed, was already awake and wondering when Mistress Ayleen poked her head through his door space.

"Arise," she said quietly. "It is time to die."

He sat up slowly, staring at her large eyes, black as her skin. Light from behind splayed across the smooth crown of her head like a skintight hat, and her expression was as always, placid and removed.

"What has happened?" he asked, rubbing his own dark eyes.

"Humans," she returned. "We've been discovered."

He swung his legs over the edge of the bed and stood, his lean naked body a shining ebony. "Is there nothing we can do?" he said, picking up his plain, coarse robe and slipping it over his head.

"No," she answered simply. "I must inform the others."

He nodded. "I understand."

She left immediately. Nebo watched the empty doorway for a time after she was gone. Death was unfortunate, but humans . . . He had never seen humans before.

He walked across the hard dirt floor, to the place where they had separated the branches to form a window. Master Thulow's house, like all the houses in the city, was made in the heart of the banyan fig tree, whose branches loop downward to sprout in the earth and form new trunks. Rooms and hallways and terraces were made by training the branches. It was a long process, but Master Thulow and his kind had nothing but time.

Until now.

Nebo looked out the window, the overflow waters of the Hus coming almost to his room. A series of banyan islands filled his vision, stretching off into the morning haze, each island containing one centuries-old banyan building, each an ancestral family dwelling.

It seemed serene enough, until he realized that the morning

16

haze was actually the smoke of the outermost islands burning. His own family home lay close to the city's edge, and he wondered if his parents had been burned yet.

Humans. He'd heard they were hairy creatures with pale skin. Of their violent nature he had no doubt, but if he had, the sight of the slowly thickening smoke would have put the doubts to rest. Such extremes of character would no doubt be an interesting study. Unfortunately, he probably wouldn't live long enough to see much of it in action.

He rubbed a hand across his own hairless skull. The smoke cloud had already obscured the most distant islands he had seen only a moment before. Turning, he left the window and hurried into the narrow, serpentine hallway that smelled sweetly with the blossoms of the budding figs. Master Thulow would doubtlessly want to speak with the apprentices in the Great Hall.

They were already gathering when he arrived. The Great Hall, also called the RNA Room, was the largest enclosure in Master Thulow's house. Comfortably accommodating up to thirty apprentices, its branch ceilings criss-crossed high overhead, its living walls shone bright reflected light on their thickly laquered surface. All was precise and orderly. All lines were simple and clean.

Nebo moved to his accustomed place at the head of the first tier of students. Upon taking the lotus position on his gomden, he switched on the magnets, the cushion rising several feet from the ground. He turned to watch the others filing quietly in, the barest apprehension gleaming in their eyes.

Master Thulow was already at his place of instruction on the east side of the room. A raised alcove it was, a jutting semi-circular turret that was ringed all around by windows overlooking the gardens of multi-colored water sprays fanning all around like rainbows.

Master Thulow's face was calm and unlined, his acceptance of the situation absolute. Thin wisps of smoke lapped through the windows at his back, some of the smoke drifting beneath the magnets of his gomden, causing the cushion to vibrate slightly with the uneven field.

When the apprentices were all seated, the Master spoke.

"That which we all knew would someday happen, has happened," he said in a clear, melodious voice. "After many centuries of peace and isolation, the humans have discovered our city. It would be foolish to think that anything besides our total extinction will occur today. Since we are the only remaining members of our species, today marks the end of the Society of Mechs."

He stopped talking, his gaze drifting around the totally silent room. "You have all been exceptional students," he said. "It is unfortunate that your studies and mind-freeing exercises will be ended prematurely. You carry the knowledge of all that has gone before. It dies with you. Lest this opportunity be wasted, is there something to be learned from this experience?"

"We may study grief firsthand," a student said from the back.

Nebo smiled, knowing the response to that.

"Grieving is a useless expenditure of energy," Master Thulow said. "All that lives, dies. It's a given fact of life. Do we grieve for the coming of the night? Or perhaps we grieve for the sleeplessness of the morning light."

Everyone laughed.

A female from the clan of Worton spoke up. Her name was Mara, and she was to have been Nebo's child-mate. "Can we then grieve for the death of knowledge lost this day?"

The Master took a long breath. "Knowledge is the energy of the universe. It is always there whether progenited by us or not. We are not knowledge, only its vessel of transport. That sort of grief would still be self-grief."

Nebo raised his hand.

Master Thulow smiled in his direction. "I recognize my oldest student and Apprentice to the Chair. Speak now, twin of my duty."

"Do these humans speak our language? I would enjoy communication with them."

"We hold the root language in common," Thulow answered. "As for our dialects, I would think we should have that answer very soon."

"Soon indeed!" boomed a voice from the door.

They turned to see a large, pale human at the door. Sweaty, long, dark, stringy hair tumbled from beneath a metal cap. His soot-smeared face was lightly bearded. He wore hot, confining clothes, topped by a latticework of metal protection all over, like a spider web. In his right hand he held a bloody sword.

"I would have words with you," the human said, pointing his sword at Master Thulow.

"I think you would have more than that," the Master answered.

Several others stood behind the first human. He turned to them. "Wait out here. Tell me when the rest is finished."

The humans moved away.

"My name is Ty'Jorman Delaga," he said to the entire group, "Governor of Alb'ny and its possessions, of which this is one."

"You will excuse us for trespassing," Master Thulow said.

The human named Ty'Jorman walked to the raised dias to stand beside the floating Master Thulow. Nebo was struck by what an exciting beast he was, how action-oriented. Humans were like raw, exposed nerves, jangling, ready to put into effect whatever thoughts might flash through their disjointed consciousness. With Ty'Jorman's presence, even the air seemed supercharged.

"I am told you are the teacher here," the human said.

"That is correct," Master Thulow answered politely.

"I have questions for you."

"Everyone has questions," the Master returned, "but few seek answers."

"The Sun . . ." the human said.

Master Thulow looked puzzled. "You have not stated a question."

The human looked at the students, then removed his metal hat, tucking it under his arm. Everyone gasped at the hair that tumbled from beneath the headgear. The man looked uncomfortable in the student posture.

"Does it exist?" he asked quietly. "Does the Sun exist?"

"Yes," the Master returned.

"How do you know? Have you seen it?"

"I do not need to see the Sun to know it exists."

"How can you know if you haven't seen it?"

Master Thulow narrowed his hairless brows, as the students buzzed over the apparent retardation of the human. "I had never seen humans," the Master answered, "yet I knew you existed."

"Damn!" Ty'Jorman yelled, throwing his metal hat upon the floor. It bounced once, then stuck to the side of Nebo's cushion. "Why can we not see it?"

The smoke from without was beginning to choke up the room. Nothing was visible beyond the windows, not even the water gardens. The sounds of humans laughing and yelling filtered in with the smoke. Master Thulow passed his hand across the photocell in his cushion and the neon came on, brightening the room.

Ty'Jorman turned his head around fearfully, his sword coming up a bit. "What's that?"

"Nothing . . . light."

Nebo pried the hat off his magnets and looked at it. Its smooth symmetry was marred up close. Iron, he ventured, heated and beaten to shape with hammers. Primitive.

"The clouds are part of our history," the Master said. "Your human ancestors built devices that gave off a great deal of heat—do you know what fusion reactors are?"

"What?" the human bellowed.

"The heat that your ancestors caused became trapped in the atmosphere, heating up the temperature of the earth. It is called the greenhouse effect. The polar ice caps melted, making the oceans rise. The air filled with clouds and rain, obscuring the Sun, obliterating the Moon. We fought a war, our kind and your kind, over this issue."

"And what of Ibem?" the man asked.

Master Thulow shook his head. "I am unfamiliar with the term."

"Ibem is the creator of all, humans and Genies. How could you not know of Him?"

"Our kind was created through the alteration of the DNA molecule, just as this tree was engineered to make our dwelling. Humans created us to perform tasks for them. A by-product of that creation was the all-too-human desire for respect and dignity, something humans were unwilling to give. Your vision of history is different from mine?"

"Yes," the human answered quietly. "But this is not the first time I've heard these words."

"Ahh," the Master said, nodding almost sleepily. "Ty'Jorman has had much contact with Genies."

The human answered without pride, "Ty'Jorman has killed many Genies. That is the nature of my breeding."

All at once the lights flickered, leaving the room with the barest illumination. Some of the students were coughing against the thick smoke.

"You have destroyed our transformer," Master Thulow said.

"Just as I must destroy you now."

"Will you answer me a question first?" the Master asked.

"If I can."

"Why does it matter to you about the Sun? Of what importance is it to your life?"

The human stood silently, all eyes fixed upon him. Beyond, through the windows, Nebo could see the bright flames of island fires flaring through the curtain of smoke.

"I'm not sure," the human answered at length. "I seek something greater than myself, something greater than the trees. I am cursed with a quest for truth."

"A dangerous preoccupation for one of your species," the Master answered.

Ty'Jorman lowered his head. "For one of my species . . . yes," he said. "I wish there were more time."

Master Thulow smiled knowingly. "I understand," he said.

The human took a breath, squared his shoulders. Whatever purpose his moment of reflection, it was gone. "Where's my helmet?" he called loudly.

"Here," Nebo said, holding the shiny hat in the air.

The man strode off the dias and took it from him. "Thanks, lad," he said, putting the thing on his head.

One of the other humans ran into the Great Hall, his eyes large and glazed, a terrible viciousness upon his face. "We got them all," he said proudly. "This is the last one."

"Good work," Ty'Jorman said. Climbing back upon the dias, he raised his sword and severed Master Thulow's head with one clean blow. The body slumped, but didn't topple from the cushion.

The human wheeled to the rest of the assembled as more humans poured through the doors. "Kill them all," he said loudly, then pointed at Nebo. "All except that one."

Nebo stiffened, looking around.

"What do we do with him?" the vicious human asked.

Ty'Jorman walked off the dias and headed for the door. "Cut off his hands," he said casually. "We'll take him back with us."

Fifteen Years Later

Part I

◇

RAMON

I
Castle Alb'ny

The two Woofers sprang at one another, meeting on their hind legs in the center of the mud-slippery circle of screaming, cajoling men. The ground physically shook when the beasts came together, 3,000 pounds of snarling, insanity-bred meanness, each trying to tear the life force from the other.

Morgan watched the spectacle with a knotted, sickened stomach, the perverse fascination of the encounter too mesmerizing to allow him to exit.

"Rip him up!" the owner of the red Lab screamed as he covered the bets of the onlookers by jabbing a constantly moving index finger in their direction.

"You're on!" he yelled. "You're on! His throat, Hermie. Go for his throat!"

The Woofers, stretched to their full height, towered over the spectators, their vicious growls carrying singularly above everything despite the huge crowd that filled the courtyard to more than capacity.

The other beast, a Boxer with short hair and a clipped tail managed to bite one of the Lab's floppy ears, shaking his head maniacally when he had his prize, trying to tear it loose as his owner, a rotund, heavily-perfumed bread dough of a man knelt in the thick mud. The man pounded the mud with his fists, splattering it all over himself as he yelled encouragement to his animal.

The Boxer toppled over, half of the Lab's ear dangling from his long slick teeth. The Lab, whining loudly, tried to retreat, but his owner prodded him with a long stick. Morgan watched the hurt disappear from the animal's eyes as it leapt onto the fallen Boxer, its deadly teeth tearing into the Boxer's soft middle.

He was able to turn away then, the ache in his stomach finally greater than his curiosity. He walked off into the milling throngs, the yelling of the bettors merging with the other sounds, but not the growls of the Woofers.

Sweaty, grimy people pushed in all around him, taking up all the air; the stifling humidity made it difficult to breathe. He

25

walked barefoot through the deep, hot mud, his wet clothes
clinging like a young lover to his muscled frame, his shoulder-
length red hair sweat-plastered to his leathery farmer's head.
And the daytime-bright gray clouds rolled steadily overhead,
disdainfully watching the carnival of death play out its charade
below.

The Governor lay dying.

He stopped and let the crowd flow past him like the rushing
Hus. Turning to the castle, he watched the high window which
Ramon had once told him opened to his father's quarters, quarters he had never seen; for although Ty'Jorman had paraded
Morgan's illegitimacy before the world for over two decades, he
had never acknowledged his paternity, either publicly or in private.

The Governor lay dying as he had lain dying for some weeks,
the putrid waste of gangrene creeping slowly up his leg. And
from the time that the first messages of his demise were trum-
peted through the provinces of N'ork, the mourners began arriv-
ing in numbers that swelled larger as the days dragged wearily
on.

The castle stood lopsided and top-heavy in Morgan's eyes,
looking like nothing so much as the giant mud hill that it was.
Somewhere beneath the thickness of baked dirt, the greatest
wealth of the land of rain, stood a structure of stone and steel
built by a culture long dead. But the eons had left it mud-caked,
layers of protection against leakage and erosion until Ty'Jorman's
window, the only one left visible on the huge structure, had a
casement several feet thick.

The mourners came from nearly every province of N'ork,
even from the land of the Schnecks to the north. They crowded
the always-muddy courtyard, gorging themselves on the hospitality of the Governor's storage bins and wine cellars. They paraded in their finery, filling Morgan's eyes with bright colors and
strange tongues, the likes of which he had never encountered
before. They gambled and fought; they bartered alien goods and
exotic Genies; they groused and cursed in their own languages;
they laughed themselves giddy with drink; and they waited.

They waited for the veil to cover Ty'Jorman's eyes. They
waited, some anxiously, some with trepidation—since the suf-
focation of a reign the magnitude of Alb'ny's would reverberate
gasps throughout the entire kingdom of humans. They waited to
see the new order and their place in it. They waited to see if

Ramon would reshuffle the deck of power and deal them a new hand for good or ill. Mostly they awaited Ramon's strength and wondered if they could test their own mettle against it, for the humans of N'ork were a gluttonously hungry lot.

There was excitement at the gates, and Morgan pushed his way steadily through the milling throngs to find its source. The words reached him, spreading like ripples on a pond through the crowd.

"He comes!"

The words were infectious, the excitement they generated compelling. It was Ramon, returning from the Western Crusades to claim his kingdom.

Morgan hurried to the high brick walls, excusing himself as he shoved people out of his way. Reaching the wooden steps that scaled the big wall, he took them two at a time all the way to the top.

The commotion was mighty in the courtyard below. The castle guards who ringed the top of the walls were cheering and waving their swords in the direction of the outer battlements, many of them turned to the courtyard screaming Ramon's arrival to the crowds. It was the most excitement Morgan had ever seen, as if the perpetual cloud cover was parting, the Sun itself coming to rest on the Earth.

He turned his attention to the battlements just long-bow distance from the walls. All the seige towers had been converted to pulley labor and layer upon layer of the rusted hulks of ancient carriages were being hoisted and piled high in preparation for the Governor's death. Alb'ny was telling the world that the richness of the fruit was being protected by the thickness of the skin.

Ramon's army was just passing through the battlements, the muddy road they traveled disappearing into the thick jungles that ringed the castle all around. Their Woofers stepped high, snorting and strutting. The end of the line of men and wagons was still hidden in the shroud of the dark forests.

They carried long-poled pennants which rippled loudly in the hot wind, and Morgan recognized Ramon's coiled snake on the lead banner. Three years off to war, his brother returned in triumph and—Morgan squinted his eyes—a new mustache.

Once they attained the battlements, they spurred their mounts to a run to cover the wide-open plain that separated the castle walls from the ever-encroaching jungle. No growing thing

was allowed within the battlements, the Governor's hold on
civilization no greater than his ability to clear Castle Alb'ny of
Nature's kiss.

"The gates! Open the gates!"

They cry rose from the summit of the wall and the swell of the
crowd carried the heavy wooden gates open, the people flowing
out like the wine in Ty'Jorman's kegs to greet the new power of
Alb'ny. And if Ty'Jorman Delaga were watching from his deathbed, he could see it too.

It was a grand spectacle. Ramon's army, a thousand strong,
parading to the cheering crowds, brightly colored streamers
floating majestically from the intricate metal latticework of their
hot-weather skeletal armor. They sang of the wars, bellowing
bass voices raising the curtain of cloud with their messages of
glory while the crowds cheered loudly.

Morgan was cheering too, unable to hear his own voice in the
chorus that rose around him. Pride swelled within him, pride
and the rush of war blood that seemed to flow naturally through
his veins despite a score of years spent in the farmer's niche.

Ramon's wagons were piled high with booty, the outward sign
of his success at ferreting out Genie dens in the farthest reaches
of N'ork. Ramon himself was a study in royalty. His lightweight
armor was burnished silver, his small helmet polished to a mir-
ror-like finish and topped with a long orange plume that drooped
almost to his feet. He wore knee-high black leather boots with
matching gloves, and the cotton dressing beneath his see-
through armor was a clean light blue. Morgan looked down at
his own faded denim trousers and bare chest and feet, and suf-
fered a moment of envy.

Ramon gestured grandly to the assembled as he rode through
the gates and into the courtyard. Leaving the bulk of his force to
camp outside the red-brown walls, he entered with a small contingent of knights and several wagonloads of booty.

Morgan hurried back down the rickety stairs and tried unsuccessfully to push his way back through the tightly-packed
throng. Above their heads and waving arms he could see
Ramon, still astride his sleek black Woofer, ordering wine for his
men. He called to him, but the words were swallowed in the
swirling vortex of other supplicants.

He finally reached the inner fringes of the crowd, just in time
to see his brother stride up the wide stone steps that led to the
Castle entrance. Ramon's mother, Jerlynn, and the Program-

mer, Dixon Faf, were there to greet Ramon, and the three
quickly disappeared into the innards of the great hall.

Morgan looked away from the door. Every day since his father's accident, he had tried to gain admittance to Castle Alb'ny
and every day he had been turned away by the Lady Jerlynn's
orders. The woman hated him with a lover's passion, hated his
existence, for the supposed humiliation he caused her by just
being alive.

The Woofers looked tired, and Ramon's knights were seeing
to it that they got fresh meat and water and were able to lie down
in the castle shade. Morgan eased down the line of mounts and
wagons, marveling at the magnificent collection of polished
metal artifacts and gadgets that stuffed the wooden-slatted carriages. There were ancient books with pictures; there were furs
of all kinds; there were smells as unique and exotic as a fever
dream.

Morgan heard the sounds of a commotion toward the end of
the line. Curious, he slowly pushed his way down to a wooden
cage on wheels, drawn by a spotted Woofer. The cage contained
a giant.

He was twice the size of a grown man and three times the
girth, like a walking oak tree. The cage was far too small for him,
forcing the totally bald Genie to squat uncomfortably, his massive hands pulling on the sturdy bars. He was naked and abused.
Festering sores and welts covered his filthy body, and it looked
as though beating the man was a major occupation of Ramon's
returning troops.

People crowded around the cage, poking sticks through the
bars or throwing stones. The women blushed and pointed,
laughing, at the enormous appendage that dangled between his
legs.

The giant looked at them, his face hurt and confused, his
parched lips quivering and pleading.

"P-Please," he rasped in their own tongue. "Please. Water. To
give me water."

He moved up to the bars, jamming his blood-caked face between the slats. "Why?" he asked weakly. "Why no water for
me?"

His wide, bloated tongue came out to lick his dry lips, but
there was no moisture for them.

"He wants water!" someone yelled. "Let's give him some."

A man dressed in the robes of the South came cautiously

toward the cage, holding a water skin out at arm's length; but when the giant reached for it, the man snatched it back, tilting it to squirt some at the unfortunate Genie.

The crowd roared as the giant tried desperately to lick the water off his arms and the floor of the cage. Morgan had seen enough.

Striding up to the man with the skin, he grabbed it away from him, shoving him to the ground in the process. He moved boldly up to the bars, the giant staring at him from the other side of the cage, an edge of hatred beginning to creep into the innocence of his wide, flat face.

"I know how you feel," Morgan said, and shoved the skin through the bars. "Take this and know that even in Hell you have a friend."

The Genie reached out a tentative hand, then grabbed the skin when it was within his reach. His dark eyes widened and he stared for a second. Morgan caught those eyes—held them. The hint of a smile touched the corners of the giant's cracked lips and he tilted his hairless head back full, laughing the water into himself.

Morgan caught movement out of the corner of his eye and backed away just as the flat of a sword banged against the cage.

"Get away from there," came the voice of one of Ramon's knights.

The man moved quickly to the bars and reached inside, snatching the water from the big man's grasp. The crowd yelled their appreciation. The giant flew to the slats, grabbing for the water. Laughing, the knight brought his sword back down on the Genie's forearm, opening a large gash which sent him back into the cage, holding the place, dark blood welling up between his fingers. Morgan had never seen hatred the like of which flared from the caged man's eyes.

"And let that be a lesson to you!" the knight said loudly, for the audience. "Redrick of Firetree sharpens his lessons on the edge of cold steel!"

The words tumbled from Morgan without thought. "Would Redrick of Firetree speak so bravely if the animal were out of its cage?"

Redrick spun to the words, his dull, gleaming sword wagging just in front of Morgan's eyes. The man took an involuntary step backward, grudging respect for the regalness of the red-haired man's bearing.

The man was gaunt like a deathshead, his face shaved smooth.

His pale eyes smoldered with the excitement, but Morgan smiled when he saw fear there also. Morgan had that effect on most everyone.

"Reason me, ground digger," Redrick said, low and menacing, "why I shouldn't make you eat the tongue that wags so foolishly."

Morgan smiled broadly and took a step toward the blade. "And why, Sir Knight, would you want to cut out your own tongue?"

The crowd laughed loudly as Redrick tightened his lips, the muscles on his neck standing out like thick vines around a tree trunk. The hand holding the blade quivered slightly as the sweat rolled down the man's face.

"Best walk away," Redrick said, the steam gone from his voice. "Run back to your rab hole and thank Ibem that the wine you drank didn't prove your undoing."

"My courage comes not from a bottle," Morgan returned. "Nor from the sharpened end of a blade pointed at an unarmed man."

The crowd applauded politely.

Redrick's gaze faltered, unsure. "I'll not dull my blade with peasant blood," he said, and a smile that looked like a grimace twisted his thin-lipped mouth.

Morgan took another step toward the lowering blade. "Fear not for the sharpness of your sword, cage keeper. It's not swift enough to draw the blood of a real man."

Redrick's slack face lit scarlet and he drew back his sword arm to strike. Morgan tensed, ready to spring at the man, when a figure stepped between them. It was Grodin.

"It's a gallant decision, Sir Knight," he said, moving to grab Morgan by the shoulders, "to hold your just rage against this young ruffian out of respect for Ramon's sorrow. It is truly a great man who knows when to temper his wrath."

Morgan made to speak, but Grodin tightened the grip on his arms and hissed him to silence.

Redrick looked confused for a long second, then turned an angelic face heavenward. "Yes," he said in a contrived voice. "The laws of God take precedence even over the honor of Man."

The crowd added their confirmation while Redrick made a great show of sheathing his sword. "I'll forgive your insolence this one time," he said. "And you can thank the circumstances for your life. But be on guard when next we meet."

"And you can . . . " Morgan began to say, but Grodin clamped a hand over his mouth.

Reaching into Morgan's mouth, Grodin grabbed his tongue. "So help me, I'll cut it out myself," he warned.

"Ahtwababa," Morgan mumbled.

"I take leave, fair people," Redrick said, bowing to the crowd, his high-peaked helmet falling from his head and into the mud. He snatched it with a frown and hurried into the thick crowds, leaving Morgan and Grodin to stare after him.

Grodin held Morgan until Redrick was out of sight.

"Why did you stop me?" Morgan asked, pulling away from the Breeder. "I was just about to teach the puff ball a lesson in politeness."

Grodin used a hand to wipe his wiry gray hair. "Maybe you're the one who could use a good lesson. Why do you persist in flogging the world when your God-given father lies up there this very minute, breathing his last few?"

Morgan grabbed the man around the waist and lifted him in the air, twisting around with him. "Because I'm full of meanness, my old," he laughed, hair whipping around his face. "Because my teacher never taught me how to slow down."

Grodin caught his tangled fiery mane and pulled, bending Morgan's head back. "Listen to me, wild animal," he said.

"Only if you let me bounce the puff ball!"

"Stop!" Grodin said, jerking on Morgan's hair.

Morgan let the man drop to the ground, his hand going to the back of his head. "That hurt!"

"They want you in the castle."

Morgan stared at him for a long second. "Jerlynn's orders . . . "

"Ramon put a stop to his mother's orders," the old man said. "You're to see your father."

"He wants to see me?"

Grodin nodded. "He's asking for you."

Morgan searched the steel of Grodin's stare. "Why do I see hesitation in you?" he asked.

The man reached out and took Morgan's smooth face in his rough hands. "I've taught you everything but how to bend," he said seriously. "And now you need that art more than any other."

Morgan smiled, but it somehow got lost in Grodin's grave nature. "My will bends to no man," he said only half casually. "My self-respect is all I've got."

"Listen to me," Grodin said in his low, gravelly voice. "The old order dies. When the new order takes over, you are going to have to make a place for yourself in it. Do you understand me?"

Morgan danced away from him, laughing. "You're drunk," he replied. "You've been in the kegs with this whole crew of free-loaders, and now you're talking like the King of Fools. Have you forgotten who it is that makes the new order?"

He moved to one of the heavy laden wagons, pounding on its side with the flat of his hand. "Ramon has arrived; his army bolsters the gates now. It is my brother brings us the mysteries of the outlands."

One of the knights called from farther down the line. "You!" he yelled at Morgan. "Get away from that wagon!"

Morgan's face flushed and he started walking toward the armored man.

"Morgan!" Grodin called.

Morgan turned to the Breeder, looked once in the direction of the knight, then sighed and joined his mentor. "My brother is the new order," he said.

Grodin's eyes remained a cold wind, his mouth a tightly clamped slash. "I'm neither drunk nor a fool," he said at last.

II
The Governor's Chambers

The Lady Jerlynn Delaga sat at the foot of her husband's deathbed with her holy man, suffocating mourning robes bunched up around her. She scowled at the artist who was recording the event for posterity.

"Can't you make him look any better?" she asked shrilly. "He looks like . . ."

"He's dying," the artist said. "Of course he looks like he's dying. It's difficult for him to look any other way."

That's no way to talk to me!" Jerlynn said indignantly.

"Sorry, mum," the man said, returning to work.

The court recorder's legs were chained at the ankles, although he wouldn't have gone anywhere had he the opportunity. Small and weak, he had been captured years before in one of Ty'Jorman's Genie Crusades. His talent was art and nothing else. His eyes segmented life into bands of color and form; his hand transformed his mind's segments precisely into concrete reality. But he could not draw what he could not see. He had done the portrait in bright, cheerful colors, even putting a suitable halo above the withered man's head; and still the Lady was displeased. She wanted the Governor to look as if he just conquered the world and was lying down for a short catnap.

Dixon Faf patted her hand. "There, there, dear lady," he said. "Don't concern yourself so over the portrait. It's not that important."

Jerlynn looked at her husband. He slept fitfully on his grand oaken bed without posts, bloodless lips twitching on a face already pallid as death. A circle of gray light funneled through the length of casement to fall on the bed, highlighting the cedar box that the dying man gripped in his clawlike hands.

She did not sorrow for his death, just as he wouldn't have sorrowed for hers. Theirs had always been a marriage of land and of station. Had he ever cared for her he would have granted her perennial request to send his bastard away. His sin had been that he never would; his punishment was the life he had to endure with her because of it.

Jerlynn did grieve, however. She grieved for the supplies that were going out unchecked to the masses in the yard. She grieved for the uncertainty of her life until Ramon was able to stabilize matters of State.

Dixon Faf leaned to her ear, his never-shorn hair and beard tangling into one congealed mass somewhere about the middle of his black-robed back. "About the box," he whispered. "Have you any information about the box?"

She shook her head, hating her husband for keeping secrets from her even to his last breath. "He has clutched it thus for a week," she replied. "No one touches it but him. I fear it has something to do with the bastard."

"What do you mean?"

She looked in the Programmer's eyes, feeling secure in the strength she saw there. "He began calling the bastard's name the day the box first appeared," she said. "He calls still, and the box is still present."

Faf dismissed the thought with a wag of his head. "A coincidence," he said, but neither of them believed that it was.

The door opened and Ramon strode in, two servants hurrying behind, unfastening the clips that held his cagelike armor.

"The dutiful wife," he said, as the servants lifted the breastplate over his head. "And the holy man. What a touching scene."

"Curb your tongue in this chamber," Faf said sternly. "Have you no respect?"

"For my father, yes," he replied, then winked at Jerlynn, his dark eyes dancing. "I have sent for Morgan."

Jerlynn was on her feet. "You're bringing him here?" she said loudly, her eyes darting to the Programmer, who then stood, supporting her with his arm. "To these chambers?"

"It is my father's wish," Ramon said, watching as his leggings were removed.

Jerlynn faced her son. "For twenty-five years I have kept the bastard from these halls. I will not let you dirty them now with his presence."

Reaching out, Ramon took her head and forced it closer to him. He kissed her brow. "It is not your decision to make," he said softly, using the power in his arms to hold her a second too long, just to make the point.

For twenty-five years she had poisoned him with her hatred and frustrations, while his father ignored him for the obsession of his Crusades. Now things would be different. Now everything would be his way.

"My whole life I've wondered what it looked like in here," Morgan said to Grodin as they walked the narrow halls of Castle Alb'ny, his muddy bare feet slapping the tiled floors in syncopation to the solid leather thunk of Grodin's boots.

"It's not so much," the old man replied. "Probably not like your mind's eye saw it anyway."

Morgan looked. The halls were dark and cramped, poorly lit with a multitude of candles. Torches were impossible in such a confined setting. But the angles were sharp and straight, the engineering meticulous to a fault. He liked the order of that.

"It's so cool in here," he said. "Do the layers of mud . . ."

"No," Grodin said. "They do it an ancient way. Maybe I'll show you later. Here."

The Breeder stopped by a metal door, taking two candles out of a large bin. He handed one to Morgan, lighting his own on a candelabrum mounted on a cracked wall. Morgan followed suit.

"We go up now," Grodin said, opening the door. The doorway faced rising stairs.

"What's that big opening back there?" Morgan asked, indicating a large cutaway section of wall which led to a small brick chamber with no floor.

"Come on," the Breeder said, starting up the steps. "We can't keep the Governor waiting."

Morgan followed him, holding an open palm in front of the candle flame to protect it. "But what is it?"

"They call it the drop hole," Grodin returned. "We don't know what the ancients called it, but the shaft goes from the top floor all the way to the dungeon. When they hose down the floors and clean up the body wastes, it's all pushed in the drop hole."

The stairs went up a distance, then turned back upon themselves to climb some more. Each set of stairs was separated by a landing. Guards wearing the blue-and-white-striped tunic of Castle regulars were stationed on each landing. Each set of guards challenged them as they passed, and Morgan realized that it was only Grodin's position that had gotten them that far.

They passed eight guard stations before coming to a halt in front of another metal door. *It was the most stairs Morgan had ever climbed, and he could feel it in his knees.*

Two of the Governor's men stood before the door, long pikes crossed at their approach. They refused even Grodin's admonitions despite their fear of Morgan, whose reputation of being a crazy man extended even into the halls of Castle Alb'ny. Finally one of them was persuaded to search out Ramon and ask him.

A moment later the door opened and its space was filled with Ramon Delaga, heir apparent, a large smile consuming his dark face.

"Welcome to my house!" he bellowed, taking Morgan in his arms. They embraced roughly, like two boys wrestling, and Morgan could feel his own smile straining his face.

They pulled apart, still gripping one another's arms, and stared into eyes that shared many memories, not all of them good.

Morgan felt a surge of warmth, for surely, save Grodin, the bastard had no other friends. "The Western Wars haven't marred your infant's face," he said, tugging on his brother's straggly mustache, "despite your puny attempt to cover it up."

Ramon laughed and it sounded like a groan. "And years in the fields haven't dulled the edge of your tongue." Laughing, they embraced again. Ramon was beside himself. The farmer would be the perfect foil for Jerlynn, the prickly proof that it was he who now commanded the throne of Alb'ny. Though mother she was, she had raised him in the hardness and coldness that ran through her own blood. And now was the payback.

"I watched you from the wall today," Morgan told him. "You were a proud sight . . . and glorious."

"You honor me," the man answered. "But I must make a confession to you. At this moment I would trade all that is, and all that is to be for a week of hunting with my dear, dear friend." He put his hands on Morgan's shoulders, "Companion of my youth."

"Our youth is gone," Morgan responded.

Ramon smiled with appropriate sadness. "But not forgotten." They were silent for a moment, eyes still searching, then Ramon said, "There is much we need to talk of, but . . . my father, his time grows short."

"I will take my leave," Grodin said.

"Thank you for fetching me," Morgan said.

The old man turned and stared for a moment. His face held no humor. "Remember," was all he said before disappearing into the darkness of the stairwell.

"A strange man," Ramon said when Grodin was gone. "Were it not for his talent with the breeding, I believe I would send him away."

Morgan laughed sharply. A joke. It had to be a joke.

"Well, let's not stand out here in the dark," Ramon said loudly, returning to his former humor. "Come in."

He ushered Morgan through the doorway, and into the opulence of Ty'Jorman's court. Smells struck Morgan first, incense and spices and foods. Then light from thousands of candles.

This was the Room of Ages, the place that he had longed to see since first his brother spoke of it when they were children. And it was grander than he had imagined, grander, certainly, than a thick mud exterior would bespeak.

Many small rooms were arched to make a single large one. Candles and people were everywhere. The room was loud, with people talking, arguing. The vultures were already picking over the bones. The smells and the sounds swirled around him, nearly overpowering him. And even in the crush of people, it was still miraculously cool.

Rich brocaded tapestries hung from every wall, telling the history of Alb'ny in grand, bursting stories, tracing the line of Delaga nearly a thousand years past, to the times before perpetual summer. Pictures of Ty'Jorman's reign hung everywhere, his legacy from the Genie wars and his captured artist.

The clothes of the gathered dignitaries were opulent and exotic, robes of rich crimsons and blues, with gold overlaying everything; and for the first time, as startled eyes rested upon him, Morgan became aware of his own lack of attire.

"Ramon," he whispered, as the man led him through the thick crowd.

Ramon turned to him, looking magnificent himself in a deep gold robe that settled over the pale blue of his jumper. "Quite a gathering, isn't it?" he said. "Every province is represented, even the Jewel of the East."

He pointed out a man in a strange, bulky white suit with attached headdress that just left a cutout for eyes, nose and mouth.

"What about me?" Morgan said. "My clothes . . . I'm so out of place here, I . . ."

"Nonsense!" Ramon said, and Morgan couldn't interpret the look on his face. "You look perfect. Just perfect."

They made their way through the mourners to stand before a closed metal door. Ramon was grinning. "Here we go," he said, opening the door quickly, shoving Morgan in ahead of him.

Morgan stopped in the middle of the room. Despite the candles, the tapestries, and all the riches, it was a room of death. Morgan could smell death. He could feel the chill creep over his bones, and for the first time since walking into the castle, he longed for the honest heat outside.

His father lay on the large bed, clutching a box feebly to him. He recognized the Governor only because he knew that's who it was. This pale, emaciated shell was not the Ty'Jorman that he had locked and would keep locked in his memory. This was a creature of the dead, alive only because the flesh had not consumed itself yet.

The artist stood painting, his concentration total. The Lady Jerlynn and Dixon Faf, both in black, stood in the corner shadows. Morgan knew that part of the cold hand that gripped his heart was being tightened by their sinews. On the floor next to the bed, Pack, the Governor's Physician, was kneeling beside a strange-looking black box, fiddling with it. He was dressed like the ancients, in matching gray britches and shortcoat, a black tie knotted at the throat of his white blouse.

"This way," Ramon said softly, leading Morgan to the bed, watching his mother the whole time.

He reached out a tentative hand to touch the dying man's shoulder. "Father," he said gently.

The man's eyes fluttered, then focused halfway open. A thin

smile played upon his man'a lips before turning to a grimace of pain. "You've come," he said in a barely audible voice.

Morgan took his hand. It felt like a leaf, brittle and fragile. "I pay my respects," he said, bringing the hand to his lips and kissing it. "And the respects of my mother."

He heard Jerlynn gasp in the corner and Ty'Jorman smiled again. "I will speak with you and your . . . and Ramon in private."

"He's too weak to talk now," Jerlynn said, and in all of Morgan's twenty-five years, it was the first time she had ever spoken in his presence.

"No," Ty'Jorman said. "I will speak."

The woman stepped to the bed, her delicate face etched with ugliness from years of emotional abuse. But still her violet eyes held power and cunning. "I will not hear of it."

Faf walked up to join the woman, his face severe and unchanging as the rock face of a granite pit—his eyes even harder. "You must save your strength," he told the Governor.

"I will have words," the Governor said. "Where I go there is an eternity of rest."

"I must insist that you leave," Ramon said.

His mother stared at him. "I will not."

His voice was a command. "Will you force me to call the guards and have you removed?"

"Ramon!" she said.

"For now," the Programmer said, leading her away from the bed. "You must yield for now."

Jerlynn let herself be swept away across the room, but her face never left Morgan's, her hatred complete.

The physician had pulled one of Ty'Jorman's skeletal arms to the side of the bed and was pouring water upon it from a crock pitcher. Then he unwound two iron-colored wires from his strange machine and held them above the place. Reaching to the machine, he furiously turned an exposed crank several times, then lay the tiny wires on the Governor's wet flesh.

There was a crackle; Ty'Jorman jerked in his bed like a puppet for several seconds before Pack pulled the wires away, leaving behind two black burn marks and the smell of cooked flesh.

"He's delirious," Jerlynn called from the doorway, as the Programmer attempted to gently usher her out. "His brain has rotted with his body. You must not talk with him."

"Don't embarrass yourself with a display, Mother," Ramon

said smiling. "Go to your room and rest yourself. You look tired."

"No good will come of this," she warned, as Faf got her into the hall, curious passersby staring into the open room. "You've made the mistake of your young life."

Ramon ignored her and turned to Pack. "You, Physician," he said. "Out."

The little man stared up from where he knelt on the floor. "The Governor needs his treatments."

Ramon stroked his mustache. "And you'll need your hands if you intend to continue practicing your black arts."

The man stood immediately and moved toward the door.

"Take him with you," Ramon said, pointing to the artist.

Pack walked to the artist, taking his arm and pulling him. The artist bobbed his head around as if he had been awakened from sleep, but hobbled obediently out with Pack, the chains on his legs rattling loudly.

Ramon followed them to the door, closing it behind, listening to Jerlynn's shrill voice disappearing down the hall to her chambers.

He returned to the bedside flush with victory. "Mother's prattle hasn't changed," he said.

"Nothing ever changes," Ty'Jorman said weakly, and patted the box on his chest. He gazed once more at Morgan. "So, you've finally come."

"I come daily, my Lord," he said. "But they always turn me away."

The dying man nodded. "And what of Zenna? Does she come?"

"My mother does not wish to cause you any undue . . . embarrassment."

The Governor breathed heavily. "Would that others loved me so much," he said. "Sometimes I feel that I have brought vipers to my bosom."

Morgan started. "My Lord?"

The Governor reached out his hand again; Morgan grasped it. "'Lord' is a word used by servants and underlings," he said, "not by the flesh of my flesh. Please. Call me Father."

Morgan's mouth went dry. His entire life had been a dream of acknowledged paternity. Hearing the words now left him confused. He was a dry well suddenly filling with flood waters. He looked at Ramon who stared blankly back at him. In all their lives together, the subject of their brotherhood had never been breeched.

"F-Father," Morgan mumbled, and had he been capable of tears, they would have come then. "Father, I love you."

"I love you truly," the old man said. "I've watched you from afar, never able to . . ."

His voice choked off, his breath coming in gasps.

"Perhaps you'd better rest now," Ramon said, suddenly solemn.

"No," the Governor returned. "Not now. Words must be said."

Morgan heard a commotion outside. Turning his eyes to the window he could see the battlement erection at the edge of the jungle, and closer in, the courtyard. The giant had been taken from his cage, three ropes tied to his neck. He was being led around the courtyard as the excited crowds pelted him with rocks and sticks.

The Governor spoke to Morgan. "You do not understand why your life has twisted the way it has," he said. "You have always been in the middle, belonging everywhere, fitting in nowhere."

"And always wondering," Morgan said, his thoughts turning to Zenna and the disgrace she endured because of her love for his father.

"I have denied you much," Ty'Jorman continued. "I've denied you a life. Please believe that I never wanted to, and forgive me if you can."

Morgan sat beside him on the bed. "There's nothing to forgive."

"Don't lie to me," the Governor said. "Six weeks ago, I fell on my own sword. Stupid thing to do. The Physicians told me they'd have to take the leg. I didn't believe them and look at me. Fate takes me as its lover. I cannot go content without your forgiveness. Believe me as I didn't believe the Physicians."

Morgan looked hard at him, and realized that he didn't want to forgive the man. "Father, I . . ."

"Please," Ty'Jorman pleaded. "Take pity on me."

Morgan looked at Ramon. His brother had turned his back and was pacing quickly.

"Will you tell me why?" Morgan said. "Why did you not at least let us leave this place?"

"You must forgive me without question."

Morgan closed his eyes, but he still saw the old man's face. "I forgive you," he said quietly.

Ty'Jorman breathed heavily and lay back content. He could die in peace; but Morgan's agony had not abated.

There was desperate silence for a matter of minutes, uncomfortable silence. The Governor had used up his strength and lay panting, staring at the battlements through his window. Morgan listened to his labored breathing, now unsure about his own feelings. He had always thought that acknowledged paternity would set his life aright; but it wasn't the case. There had to be more.

After a time, the old man spoke again. "Ramon, come here."

Ramon, thinking the audience was over, hurried quickly to the bed. "Should I send Pack back in?"

"Not yet. We still have business."

"Business?" Ramon said, and his face was grave when he looked at Morgan.

"You have been a joy to my life," Ty'Jorman told Ramon. "And your friendship with your brother a constant source of happiness to me. And now, I have a task for you."

"Yes."

"I wish Morgan to have station."

"What?" Ramon said loudly, bringing himself to his full height.

"Give your brother a fast Woofer, start him on one of the jungle pathways. As far as he can take his mount in one day, and as far as he can see in either direction, shall all belong to him."

Ramon's mouth dropped open, but he said nothing. Morgan, for his part, was unable to do or say anything.

The Governor continued. "He shall be legally deeded such property and be henceforth titled the Earl of Amends. There will be those who will counsel against such actions, but you, Ramon, you are the Governor of Alb'ny and all decisions are yours."

This time when Ramon looked at Morgan there was something sinister in his manner.

"Swear to me that you will implement my dying orders."

"But this is . . ."

"Swear!"

"I swear," Ramon said softly, without conviction.

"There's more," the Governor said. "Here. Take the box."

Ramon reached across the bed and lifted the box. It was light enough to be nearly empty. The Governor looked at the son he never knew.

"The questions that still cloud your mind will be answered by the box," Ty'Jorman said to Morgan. "I place it in your brother's care, for I am surrounded by treachery and trust it with no one else. He is to give it to you on the day of my death and not before."

Morgan glanced at the box, then back to his father. "Why not simply give it to me now so that I may thank you for its contents?"

"I had always intended to do so," Ty'Jorman said. "But now that I am dying, I find myself without the strength to address the responsibilities and consequences. I wish to die in peace, not turmoil. Is that too selfish of me?"

Morgan lowered his eyes and shook his head.

The old man spoke again. "Know you this for now: within your breast beats the heart of a warrior. You're wild . . . untamed. It was as I wished. But now that you have station, you must learn to take your proper place in the order of things. You have greatness in you, boy. Use your gifts wisely, for I'll not be here to guide you."

Morgan watched him, overwhelmed by the weight of the discussion. There was too much, too much to soak up with one sponge. "What must I do? You have to help me."

The man's head turned back and forth on the milk-white pillow. "I've done all I can. Your brother will help you. Your brother . . ."

His words trailed off as sleep overtook his body. Morgan kissed him gently on the cheek and turned to speak to Ramon. But his brother was already gone. And the box was gone with him.

III
Intrigues

The artist hobbled down the early morning corridors of Castle Alb'ny, moving slowly to prevent the rattling of his chains from disturbing the sleeping guests.

It was dark except for the tiny flickering of occasional night candles that infused the rooms with a misty yellow haze, even though daylight had already risen full outside. The artist was going to Ty'Jorman's chambers to finish his portrait by the gray morning that would now be streaming through his casement window.

The forms of sleeping dignitaries lay scattered about the rooms like so many bodies after a battle, snoring loudly, sleeping restlessly because of the huge amounts of food and drink they were consuming at the Castle's expense. The artist had seen battles before. He had watched Ty'Jorman's army trample through his tiny jungle settlement, putting it to the torch—vivid oranges and yellows, beautiful—and hacking up the flowing symmetrical forms of his fellows with clean-lined swords, spilling their insides in reds and dark greens. He had watched the Governor cry as he did it, and marveled at the liquid clarity of a tear. The reason why he was spared had never made itself clear to him, although he understood very little in life save the translation of the three dimensional to the one dimensional which, in essence, was the delineation of his own existence.

No alternating blue and white stripes stood at the entry to the Governor's chambers, and it struck him as odd because he almost passed the place as he was so used to using the color bars as a landmark.

He entered without knocking and smiled at the good natural light that flooded the room. Shuffling to his easel, he picked up the color-wild palate and loosened the drying paint with a few drops of thick yellow oil. His brushes were Woofer hair and had stiffened during the night. He used his fingers to make them pliable again and was ready for work.

The Governor lay very still, but something was different this time. The hilt and part of the edge of a long-bladed dagger protruded from the old man's chest. The artist sighed happily. Finally a clean, straight edge to break the monotony of sagging flesh, and the beautiful red that splayed across the front of the old man added a wonderful contrast to the drab, pale colors of his flesh.

Glad for the positive changes, he hummed a toneless melody and set dutifully to work trying to capture the flavor of the new additions to the painting.

Morgan was working outside of the hovel that he and Zenna shared when he heard the tolling of the bells that marked the end of an era.

They lived in the middle of a steep hill on the edge of the ever encroaching jungle. He was clearing back underbrush from around the shack, bright green funguslike growth that would sprout up overnight and completely swallow a dwelling that let it grow unchecked for more than a few days.

The house was built in a gouged out section of the hillside, protected by tons of earth above and on the sides, and high enough so that the rains would flow right past without washing it away. Even with those precautions, Morgan had been forced to completely rebuild several times when the rains rose higher than anyone could have anticipated.

He looked toward the front door when he heard the bells, watched as his mother came to the door, a wooden spoon held in one hand, her apron brought up to her face with the other.

He dropped his hoe, ducked under the metal chimney that jutted straight out from the house, and went to her. His large, muscled arms wound around her quaking frame and pulled her close.

"This is better than the pain he lived with," Morgan said softly into her loose gray hair.

She gazed up at him with red, swollen eyes. "I grieve for myself," she replied, and turned from him, walking back into the house.

He followed her in, closing the rickety wooden door behind him. It had been his idea to build their hut in the hillside. Most of the families of Alb'ny lived in tree houses because of the rains, but that left them at the mercy of the jungle beasts who would sometimes steal children or devour entire families. Building on the hillside gave them the isolation they wanted, the insulation Zenna needed from the wagging tongues of the citizenry.

She sat at their simple wooden table, her tears now gone, drinking a cup of tea she had made from the roots that grew through their ceiling.

"We're free now," Morgan said. "Free to live as we choose."

"Some things we're never free of," Zenna replied.

"But I'm to have station," he said, sitting across from her.

She smiled slightly. "Let's hope for the best," she said, "and prepare for the worst."

"You speak in riddles."

Thunder rolled outside and both of them jumped to the sound, smiling at the startled looks they saw on the other's face. Morgan took Zenna's strong hands in his.

"The dragon roars," she said, her eyes now bright.

"And we stand firm," he replied.

Getting up, he walked around the table and bent to embrace the beautiful woman in the plain brown shift. And he knew that, even in sackcloth, Zenna of Siler was twice the woman that the Lady Jerlynn in all of her jewels and finery could be.

"I fear for you," she said.

He straightened, shaking his head down at her. "You're as bad as the Breeder," he replied. "For fifty-five plantings I have bent my back to the fields while my feet wanted to be walking the jungle paths. Why the crooked mouth and the sad eyes when my hour of deliverance is at hand?"

He turned and walked toward the window as chain lightning latticed across the gray sky, lighting the tethered logs and support pillars of the inside of the shack.

"Do you fear for yourself?" he asked. "Do you fear that I will stop being your son because I have begun to be the Governor's?"

"Of course not," she said quietly.

The window looked out over the bottom of the hillside and the small fields which stretched out from there to the jungle. The fields were a myriad of small towers made of red brick with brick steps spiraling upwards from base to apex. The fields looked like hundreds of manmade anthills with plateaus of cereal grain on top.

Morgan could already see many of his neighbors in the distance charging up their twisting stairs to try to cover the crops with huge canvas tents before the coming deluge washed them away. Never one to put off work, Morgan had harvested his crops the week before, and so had nothing to cover now. He pulled the shutter closed and the house immediately darkened, its natural musty cellar smell dominating the uncirculating air.

Zenna rose and began lighting candles with a twig she had recovered from the black iron cook stove, and the shack breathed with flickering yellow light.

"You expect so much of Ramon," she said, as she lit the last candle and tossed the stick back in the small fire. "Expect nothing and avoid disappointment."

"This always comes back to Ramon," he said, filling the earthen basin from a large pitcher. He splashed tepid water on his face, smoothing it back through the tangled length of his hair. "He is my brother. Our father acknowledged it to us."

"Your father is dead," Zenna said sadly.

"But he's my brother."

Zenna retrieved a small cotton towel from a wash line she had strung across her bed and carried it to Morgan. "There's more to it than that."

He took the towel and wiped his face. "What more?"

She lowered her eyes. "More," she said, whispering.

"It doesn't matter," he said, throwing the towel on the washstand. "He swore an oath. I heard him."

Outside, the dragon roared again, and the rain began falling with determined ferocity, gushing past the mouth of their cave with the sound of a waterfall.

"An oath is only as good as the person who makes it," Zenna said.

Morgan wagged his head at her. "Ramon is my brother and an honorable man," he said in the same voice. "Any honorable man will keep his oath."

She smiled up at him, pulling his face down to kiss him on the cheek. "The world is a dark and complicated place. And there are many things that keep you in ignorance."

"What things?" he demanded.

She moved away from him and said something he couldn't hear. "What?" he said.

"Boxes!" she said loudly. "Cedar boxes!"

He moved quickly to her, taking her by the arms. "What could you know of the box?"

"I know it's evil," she said, eyes hard and firm. "I know that Ty'Jorman meant it for good, but that none will result. I know that our lives will change forever when the box is opened."

Morgan laughed, a short, nervous burst. "What can this mean?" he said, his face still strained in a smile. He kept waiting for her to admit the joke or her groundless fears. She just stared at him. He tightened his grasp on her arms without realizing it; she flinched and he let her go. "What could you possibly know of the box?"

She turned away from him, walking to the window. He followed.

"You can't know of it. How could you?"

She creaked open the lopsided wooden shutter and stared out at the rain. It was a solid sheet at the mouth of the cave. She couldn't see past it.

"I've said too much already," she answered in time. "I will say no more."

With that, she walked to her bed and lay down, covering herself with a dusty woolen blanket. She put her face to the wall, and wished she'd never said anything. She knew her fears were grounded, but she couldn't tell him what they were on the chance that she was wrong. Ty'Jorman would never have done this had his mind been stable. He must have been overcome with brain fever.

Morgan watched his mother pretend to sleep, knowing the strength of her will, and knowing she'd never tell him what he wanted to know. In due course he let his eyes rest on the specta-

cle of the rain. The rain had let up enough that he could see to
the fields beyond. Most of the crops had been covered in time.
The water had climbed a third of the way up the large towers.

Soon, the rain stopped completely, the air immediately becoming hot and sticky. Morgan left Zenna without a word, and
climbed the hill to the castle road.

There were four roads that led to Castle Alb'ny corresponding with the cardinal points of the compass. The roads twisted
into the heart of the jungle, each winding a connecting lifeline
to the other kingdoms of N'ork. The roads were kept cleared
by slave labor gangs who did nothing but march them continually, hewing Nature, fighting the inevitable. The roads
were dark and dangerous, and were absolutely essential to
Man's survival.

Morgan picked up the road to the rear of the Castle to the
north. He came up in thick forest, but knew the battlements
were less than a half mile ahead, though he couldn't see them
yet.

The mud was calf deep on the road and the jungle was misty,
steaming all around him. The sound of voices assailed him
ahead, and as he hurried through the mist, he caught sight of a
small caravan moving toward Alb'ny.

It was the strangest group he had ever seen, and at first he
thought a band of Genies was marching toward the Keep. On
closer inspection he saw that they were Schnecks, from the
farthest Northern province of humans. Schnecks were of impure
Genie blood, mixed Genies and half-breed humans. Not of any
pure breeding stock, they lived by the thousands in the province
of Schneck and it was looked at as something of a homeland for
them.

Morgan hurried to catch up with them, joining their little
parade for a time before moving on. Schnecks were for the most
part an ugly lot, with lopsided heads and elongated appendages,
and these Schnecks were no exception. A product of impure
breeding, Schnecks tended to be moronic. This group was
dressed like the forest in clothes made from vines and leaves.
They looked like walking trees.

"Ho! Little brother!" someone called to him as he skirted past
the group.

He turned to an elm tree that was smoking a huge pipe filled
with juniper. "My name is Morgan. I welcome you to Alb'ny on
this sad day."

The elm tree had one blue eye and one green. His nose was

large and totally flat. "Sad day is it? What could be sad in the kingdom of Pure humans?"

"The Governor has died this day," Morgan said. "Even as we speak the bells toll."

"Stop!" the Schneck cried, and the tree at the front of the line stopped dead, others trying to stop behind and piling into one another.

The elm tree looked Morgan up and down. "The Governor, Ty'Jorman is dead?" he asked and all the trees were staring at Morgan.

"Listen," Morgan said.

They listened with great concentration. The bells could be heard tolling softly.

"Ty'Jorman dies!" the elm yelled, and the entire group began cheering.

Morgan felt the anger welling up in himself. "This is a sad time for our city," he said. "If you don't respect that, at least consider my feelings."

"Oh, little brother," the tree said loudly. "We do not cheer your unhappiness, we celebrate our good fortune; for the new Governor seeks treaties and council with us."

Morgan was surprised. Most humans considered Schnecks one step above the beasts of the field. That Ramon would extend treaties to them was unthinkable with one possible exception. Their hatred of pure Genies was all-consuming. They were the most vicious and cold-blooded Genie trappers in all of N'ork. What was Ramon thinking of?

"I will congratulate your new alliance," Morgan said, "if you will allow me my grief."

"Done," the elm said. "We gnash our teeth at the death of your Governor and will kill many Genies as a sacrifice to the gods of the clouds."

"You kill Genies for the new Governor?" Morgan asked.

"We kill Genies anyway," the Schneck said, slapping his wooded chest with a large, misshapen hand. "For Ramon we will kill many, many more. Us and many like us come to this place."

"A crusade?" Morgan asked.

The Schneck's nearly blank face became blanker. "I have told what I know," he said, and puffed furiously on his pipe.

"Then I wish you good luck," Morgan said. "I go to mourn."

"And I wish you good luck, Morgan whose hair is like fire," the elm tree said. "Mourn well."

Morgan hurried on as the Schnecks continued their march through the deep mud, their hand-drawn wagons, sunk to the axles, having to be grunted along by the entire group. Morgan had often heard that Schnecks liked to wear the jungle for their clothing, changing to fresh leaves each morning, but he had never seen it before. He realized that it made good sense for them because they could use the leaves to cover physical defects, each according to his own peculiarity.

He hurried through the misty boulevard, catching sight of the battlements on the edge of the treeline. The rusted carriages were piled high and they had closed up the roadway entrance so that only one man and one Woofer could pass through at any given time.

He passed through the entrance, seeing other townspeople on the road, all going the same place as he. Ramon's soldiers were working the wide open field between the battlements and the castle walls, clearing away any undergrowth, leaving a large mud lake. Alb'ny had nearly five hundred yards of mud between wall and outer wall, fully a hundred yards more than Troy, the next closest city. It was a great matter of pride to the people of the region that they were able to keep so much of the jungle away.

The Castle gates stood open, an invitation to all pilgrims to enter, although Morgan figured that the invitation wouldn't extend very far past the duration of the funeral.

The courtyard was even more packed than it had been yesterday, the atmosphere more charged. Woofers stood snorting among the crowds, some with riders, some tethered, all whining for the food smells that wafted heavily through the stifling air.

He found out quickly that an official announcement was expected at any time, that the bells were the only indication any of them had up until that point that something had happened. In fact, speculation was high in some circles that the Governor really hadn't died. Morgan paid scant attention to such talk. He had seen his father. He knew.

Moving to the main stairs, he pushed his way up close to the steps. Traditionally, this was the place of announcements, and within minutes, his feelings were confirmed on all counts.

Pack, the physician, walked out on the broad porch that connected the stairs to the Castle. His gray suit was soaked black with humid sweat. He held the meeting horn in his hand. Slowly he turned the crank on the back of the horn. It emitted a low, throaty wail that increased in pitch the faster he turned the crank. It was loud and grating, forcing Morgan to cover his ears.

The crowd fell to hushed murmurs as they gathered for the announcement. Ramon Delaga, wearing the white rab fur of station, strode out onto the porch, followed by his mother and the Programmer. Their faces were strained, their movements jerky.

Ramon paced back and forth for a moment, hands on hips, fire in his eyes. Then he turned to a crowd of thousands, studying them. He didn't speak until there was absolute silence save for the whining of the Woofers.

"My father, the Governor, is dead!"

The women began to wail, as was customary, but Ramon quieted it immediately. "My father has died ingloriously."

A chorus of "No" moaned through the crowd.

Reaching into the folds of his white robe, Ramon extracted a bloody dagger, holding it high above his head. "He was murdered, murdered in his sleep by a vile coward!"

Morgan felt his heart jump, knew the surge of anger. Everyone felt it, as the murmurs became shouts of indignation, and the crowd became a mob.

Ramon strode deliberately to the front door and returned dragging a heavily shackled man by the arm. Morgan recognized him. It was the artist he had seen painting Ty'Jorman's portrait.

Ramon shook the man, as the thin Genie looked around in obvious confusion. "We caught him in the act this morning," Ramon said, "found him with my father's body, the blood on his chest still wet."

The crowd went wild all around him, but Morgan found it difficult to believe that Ty'Jorman would keep someone around him for so many years who was such an obvious threat.

"What should I do with this animal?" Ramon asked the crowd. "What must we do to Genies who kill humans?"

One of the Schnecks from the roadway had pushed himself up to the steps. As the crowd surged around him, he walked partially up the steps. "Give him to us!" the gruff man called. His eyes were wide and staring beneath the bark that covered the deformity of the rest of his face. "Give him to us!"

The crowd picked up the chant, louder and louder. Morgan jerked his head around, back and forth. He was astounded at everyone's reaction, amazed at the life force exhibited by the mob body.

Ramon turned and said something to his mother, then turned back to the crowd. "You want the Genie?" he called loudly.

"Yes!" came the resounding chorus.

"Then take him!"

Ramon pushed the uncomprehending man to trip down the stairs, the artist's chained hands not breaking his fall as he bounced down the thirty steps. The mob surged around the artist lifting him high in the air and carrying him off.

Morgan saw the man's face as they carried him past. He saw fear, animal fear, and he saw simple confusion and knew that this poor little Genie did not kill his father. And his blood ran hot too, but for the real murderer, the one whom Ramon was inadvertently protecting.

"Avenge me!" Ramon called, amidst the shrieks of the Genie. "Avenge the honor of Alb'ny!"

The screams ended quickly, as the man was literally torn apart by Morgan's neighbors.

"My father was kind to that animal!" Ramon cried, gesturing wildly. "He brought the viper to his bosom and it infected him with vile poison!"

"My Lord! My Lord!" a voice called. It was the Schneck again. He ran the steps two at a time, clutching something to his chest. He knelt at Ramon's feet and bowed his head, holding his package in the air.

It was the Genie's heart.

Ramon took it from him holding it up for the crowd to see. "Does it take just one heart to satisfy the life of the Great Governor?" he called.

"No!" came the thundering response.

"Must only one beast die to avenge the wrongs of Alb'ny?"

"No! No!"

An unseen pressure weighed upon Morgan. He couldn't help but remember his conversation with the Schnecks earlier that day. He felt surrounded by throbbing, jumping insanity.

The Schneck had stood up and was calling to the crowd in a gutteral voice, and Morgan got a glimpse of the capacity for bloodlust of his northern neighbors.

"I swear to avenge the life of the Great Governor!" he called, his voice thick and slow. "We must rid the land of the Genie!"

Ramon went to the man, making an obvious show of embracing him. "We will work together to rid ourselves of this pestilence!" he said, and with that, brought the heart to his lips and ate from it.

He handed it to the Schneck, who promptly gobbled the thing down, his wide gap-toothed mouth grinning and slurping the whole time.

The crowd cheered wildly all around Morgan, and it bothered him that he did not feel what they felt. Arm in arm with the Schneck, Ramon walked down to greet the people.

"Long live the Governor!" one of his knights called, and the words were picked up by the entire crowd.

His knights jumped to the stairs as Ramon approached the crowd, setting up a cordon around him. The people surged to meet him, reaching hands past the armor of the knights.

Morgan was swept up with the crowd; he was pushed toward the knights. Reaching the human barrier, he put his hand out to his brother.

"I mourn with you," he called, but Ramon's smile did not seem one of mourning. When he saw Morgan, however, he reached directly for his hand.

"Sweet friend!" he called, shaking hands enthusiastically. "Sup with me tonight. We have things to discuss."

"Yes!" Morgan returned. "When?"

"Dark time," Ramon said, and he began looking at other people.

"You will bring the box then?" Morgan asked.

Ramon narrowed his gaze. "The box?"

"Will you bring it tonight?"

"Yes," the Governor said, turning his back to his brother.

IV
Ramon's Float

The decorations settled upon the ballroom like wildflowers on the grassy plains. Heavy gold-and-purple velvet drapes sagged from the two-story ceiling, while a flock of meticulously painted green-and-blue birds flapped in unison through the huge room, landing on drapery after drapery, only to hurry to the next one as if they were on an inspection tour.

The ballroom, taking up the entire fifth and sixth floors of Castle Alb'ny, was by far the most elegant in N'ork, with the exception of the Jewel of the East. Colored bladders full of air hung from the support pillars and long tables awash with breads and sweetmeats were being wheeled in for the banquet. The

light from three thousand eight-day candles flickered the room
in reflected gold, making the room sparkle like the facets of a
diamond. But Ramon's concentration was centered on the float
which took up one entire end of the rectangular building.

A large-wheeled display, it depicted various incidents from
the life of Ty'Jorman Delaga, thirty-seventh Governor of Alb'ny
and all its provinces—an unbroken line of Delagas going back
923 years.

One section depicted the fungus plague of '95, when Nature
made its most serious bid for domination of N'ork. The scene
showed a man dressed as the Governor physically ripping a large
section of the bright green fungus from the form of a sleeping
child, so quickly did the fungus grow. Another depicted the
Governor with his back to a grove of trees, symbolically holding
back the trees' progress through human lands. A large middle
section depicted the famous rab hunt where Ty'Jorman and his
huntsmen killed and butchered fifty-four of the creatures, ne-
cessitating the on-the-spot building of fifteen large wagons to
carry all the meat.

The Governor himself was even being used on the float, his
embalmed body tied to a metal aperture in the standing position, a sword fixed in the lifeless hand. The stuffed body of a
green scaly Genie with webbed hands and feet lay on the ground
beneath him, arm up in a defensive gesture. Ramon was extremely disappointed in the positioning.

"We need the sword up more," he said to the carpenter who
worked on his father, and raised his arm to better approximate
the heroic stance he was looking for.

The bearded man in the large leather work apron frowned and
tried unsuccessfully to push the arm higher. "He's already got
stiff," the man answered, staring into the dead eyes of the man
who was already being called the Great by those who survived
him. "I can't get it up any higher."

"I didn't ask for your opinion," the new Governor said quietly.
"Break the damned arm if you have to, but get it up there."

The man stared for a second. Profaning the dead was not an art
he was practiced in, but it seemed a fine alternative to incurring
Ramon's anger. "Pardon, my Lord," he whispered to the corpse.
Putting one hand on the shoulder and grabbing the forearm with
the other, he used the strength of his biceps to force the dead
arm upwards. It cracked, then broke. He got it up then, but it
didn't want to stay.

He looked helplessly at Ramon. "My Lord, I . . ."

"Add something to the aperture," Ramon said impatiently. "Brace it."

It was getting later. Ramon still had to dress for his first official function as Governor. "I want to get a look," he said. "Get to your positions and freeze."

The twelve people who performed functions on the float all hurried to their positions. Six of them were Ty'Jormans. The carpenter released the arm to go to work on the aperture. It swung lightly back and forth, the blade in its hand inscribing a tight arc above the head of the Genie.

Ramon walked all around the brightly colored float which had been under construction since the day Ty'Jorman had refused to have his leg taken off. It was truly impressive. Ramon climbed the steps and walked among the displays.

"Remember," he told the performers. "From the time we wheel out the float tonight you will have to remain perfectly motionless. You will be well rewarded for this, but should any of you fail to control your posture, the entire company will suffer for it."

He moved to his father, admiring the expensive silk robes the corpse wore. They would be his after tonight. He smiled at the swinging arm, then noticed the ring inscribed with the serpent seal of the realm. His father still wore the ring of power.

"You certainly won't be needing this anymore," Ramon told him, and began to pry out the ring finger. He strained with the finger, finally breaking it. But the ring wouldn't come off.

After struggling for several minutes, he drew a sharp dagger from his loose-fitting robes and took the ring, finger and all.

"You all look wonderful!" he said to the company, jumping from the platform. "Wheel this back behind the curtains, and be ready for tonight."

He strode off, the magnificent white robe streaming out behind him. In the cool of the Castle chambers, the robe felt comfortable, but he knew from experience that once the ballroom filled with people it would become quite hot. He made a note to speak to the dungeoneers about bringing the temperature down.

He swept into the darkness of the long hall, wresting the ring from the severed finger as he walked. He grunted with satisfaction as he placed the bright gold band on his right index finger. He had just officially coronated himself. He walked on, dropping his father's digit casually down the drop hole as he passed by. He hurried up the stairs to his quarters on the seventh floor.

When he arrived at his apartments, he stripped out of his lightweight jumper and washed at the basin on the low stand near his bed. His chamber was thick with dark wooden beams. It had the look and strength of the forest about it. He enjoyed his rooms, but they weren't nearly as large as Ty'Jorman's. As soon as he could get the royal chamber aired and fumigated, he'd be moving in there.

He called for hot water to wash himself with, then had his way with the serving girl who brought it. When he was finished with her, he beat her lightly for putting his schedule behind. He dressed in a black jumper and his knee-high snakeskin boots, topping the outfit off with his white robe and gold beret.

When he was done, he went to the ornate desk with the fluted legs that sat in the corner and rolled a long cigarette from the tin of tobacco that had been sent him from one of the Southern kingdoms as a peace offering. Normally he would have one of his servants roll the smoke, but he had learned to do it himself while in the field, and reveled in that ability now. It was his connection to the common people, and certainly a ruler needed to understand the problems of those less fortunate than himself.

He lit the cigarette and moved to the massive four-poster that had been his as long as he could remember. He threw himself on it, boots and all, and smoked his cigarette before going down to the ball. His thoughts turned to Morgan, and he smiled again as he thought of the look on Jerlynn's face when she saw Morgan all barefoot and covered with the mud of ages.

He supposed he'd have to do something with the farmer. Even his father indicated that something should be done, although the orders about free land and station were obviously the result of delirium—and that damned box. The farmer was already asking about the box. "Where did I put it?" he said to no one, sitting up. He stood and turned a full circle, hands on hips. Then he remembered.

Laying the cigarette on the end of his desk, he climbed up onto his mattress, holding the top canopy of the bed. Peeking over it, he saw the small chest lying on the canopy. He strained his long arms to retrieve it.

Getting back down, he sat on the bed again, looking the box over. There was a lock on it, but he didn't have the key. He supposed he didn't need the key since he was just supposed to give it to the farmer, but after Ty'Jorman's incredible bout of generosity on his deathbed, Ramon wasn't about to give away the contents of a locked box without at least looking through it first.

As he went to the desk to get his letter opener, he thought about giving Morgan some decent position on the castle staff. That way, he'd have his boyhood friend around should he wish to spend time with him, and at the same time he could drive Jerlynn to the jungle of insanity, so much did she hate the farmer. The thought pleased him.

Getting hold of the dagger-shaped opener, he used it to pry open the small lock. It sprang easily.

The box contained folded linen upon which a message was written. He carefully unfolded the message and read it over three times before leaning back in the chair and looking at life through entirely different eyes.

"You'll not reach back from the grave for this," he said deep in his throat. "You can be doubly damned and the farmer and his mother with you."

His face set in a scowl, he sat up and rummaged through the desk until he came out with his own linen upon which he scrawled another message, dripping candle wax upon it from his desk light and fixing it with the seal on his finger.

He smiled, satisfied with the job. After blowing on the linen to dry the dark ink, he folded the message and placed it in the box, sticking the original message in his desk.

He thought about giving Morgan the box as it was, but he feared the farmer might remember it had been locked when last he saw it. He took a breath and stood up. It was worth acquiring another lock just to end this matter quickly.

Hurrying out of the room, he went in search of Pack. The physician always knew where such things could be had. He raced down the hall to try to avoid being late for his own banquet.

As soon as he was gone, a figure emerged from the heavy draperies that hung on the south wall. The person moved with rigid determination to the desk and opened up the drawer which held Ty'Jorman's message. Picking out the linen, the person read it with satisfaction, then hid it among long robes and hurried out of the chamber.

Later, when Ramon Delaga returned with a new lock for the cedar chest, he would go into his desk with thoughts of destroying the original note. But he would come out of the desk empty-handed and frightened.

* * *

The stables always smelled worse after the rain. Morgan
smiled as he walked up the long incline where he had played so
often as a child. The stables, at a suitable height, ringed the
courtyard wall, along with a long row of barracks for the Castle
Guard. These made up the sloping side of the funnellike courtyard. The entire yard slanted toward its center, where a huge
grated hole drained rainwater into mammoth underground
pipes that carried it to no one knew where.

The night was calm and still; a sweat night, and the crowd that
still jammed the courtyard seemed strangely quiescent and
dark-willed. They had been since the incident with the Genie.
The carnival atmosphere was all but dissipated; something more
brooding had taken its place.

Bright yellow kerosene light burned steadily in a corner of the
stable. Morgan ducked under the low slanting roof and entered
the open front wooden building, heading for the light source.

The Bernards lay obediently in their stalls, most of them
sleeping, the others staring at him with brown, drooping eyes.
Though he hadn't been there much since Ramon had gone to
the wars, the animals still remembered him and a few tails
wagged happily at his approach. The stables smelled of Woofer
and leather and straw and raw meat and wet wood.

Grodin squatted in the far stall wearing nothing save a breech
cloth of dirty white. He was gently brushing down one of the
animals, a wine crock fixed solidly between his feet.

Morgan walked into the circle of kerosene light, walking
stiffly because of the confining nature of the new clothes his
mother had stitched together for him. He wore tight white
knickers without socks for his bare feet and a puffy overblouse of
the deepest red he had ever seen. His sword hung at his side,
gleaming brightly from hours of devoted cleaning.

The Woofer's head came up first, and it jumped up immediately, moving to him. "Hello, Murdock," he said to the grand-
son of the animal he had ridden as a child.

He patted the mount's flank and fed him a small piece of meat
he had purchased from the food vendors in the courtyard.

"You'll spoil them," Grodin said, unfolding slowly to stretch to
his full height.

Morgan grinned wide, putting his arms around Murdock's
neck. "Of course, I will," he said, feeling the animal's hot breath
on his face. "You look to be in a fine state."

"I mourn," Grodin said harshly, and bent over to pick up his crock. "Your hour of sadness seems to have come and gone quickly enough."

Morgan moved to face the old man. "My sadness is deep and abiding," he said in the same tones. "But my life must go on. And my mother's."

Grodin softened. "Excuse an old man," he said, and embraced Morgan. "In my youth, the grapes made me wild and vigorous. Now they make me think." He took a long drink. "Judging from my thoughts, I fear that thinking is a dangerous preoccupation."

Morgan took the crock from him and drank a measure. "My father acknowledged me yesterday," he said, handing the crock back to his teacher of old.

"And now you dress the part?" Grodin returned, cocking an eyebrow.

"I've been invited to the Castle for supper," he replied with barely repressed excitement.

A smile played upon the old man's thin lips. "You'll be needing boots then," he said.

Morgan looked at the straw-covered ground. "I'll take very good care of them."

"Come."

The Breeder put an arm around Morgan's shoulder and led him through the open doorway to his quarters, stopping to pick up the lantern as they walked.

Grodin's quarters were small and bare, with just enough room for a cot, a plain wooden table and a small stove made from the innards of an ancient carriage. There were very few personal items around the room—the stables were the old man's life and always had been. The Woofers were his children, and they were always there, always young.

The old man set the lantern on the dusty table and got down on his knees, feeling around beneath the bed. "What did he tell you?" he asked.

Morgan sat carefully on one of the room's two chairs. The pants were tight around his middle and his crotch. He shifted around until he found the most comfortable spot. "I am to have station," Morgan replied. "I am to have holdings and title."

Grodin stood up, a pair of shiny rust-colored leather knee boots dangling in his hand. He was not smiling. "Be careful of yourself," he said. "I trust Jerlynn to do her worst with you."

Morgan took the boots, admiring their luster. "Ramon swore an oath to do what my father wished."

Grodin grunted and sank heavily onto the bed, drinking again. "I've been a Breeder for fifty years," he said. "One of the things I've learned in that time is that you mate your animals with an eye to the breeding. You mate the best animals so that their offspring will carry the strong traits of the parents. You weed out the weak and the vicious and the slow-witted and deny them the benefit of continued generations for the good of the breed.

"It's the way we run our whole world. Pure Blood. We avoid the tarnish of the non-human to retain the purity of our own blood. And we've all seen the retardation that results when species crossbreed. Breeding is everything, the only thing that holds our world together. Unfortunately, humans don't breed among themselves with the proper eye."

"What are you trying to say?" Morgan asked, as he struggled into the boots.

Grodin leaned up on the bed. "Only this: if your want to know the son, look to the mother. It's the heritage of the ages."

"You're drunk," Morgan answered.

"This time you're right," the old man said. "I'm too drunk to lie, and not drunk enough to be creative with the truth."

He tried to stand, but fell back to the bed, spilling wine to run down his chest like bloody sweat. "Listen to me," he said and the lantern caught his wide eyes, making them glow like fire. "When your father died, all that you knew died with him. You must remember that. Your protection is gone. You saw what happened outside today."

Morgan nodded, standing awkwardly in the boots. "I think my brother is wrong about the Genie, and I will tell him about it tonight."

"Of course he's wrong," Grodin said, wiping his sweaty face with a large hand. "He knows he's wrong. He's sowing his own seeds now."

"I don't understand."

"You don't want to understand," the old man snapped. "You believe what you want to believe because it's convenient for you to believe the best." He clenched a fist in front of him.

"You've always allowed yourself to be a child," he continued, "believing the best of everyone you meet. That's a very noble attitude, and one that will insure that your young life never gets much older. You will pay for your childhood, I fear, pay dearly for it."

He drank again and Morgan's mind turned once more to the

scene in the courtyard that afternoon before he forced it away. "The boots are beautiful," he said, "magnificent."

The old man watched him through sad eyes, for he understood all too well what was coming. At that instant, if he could have forced his will into the younger man's body he would have done it, even if it would mean his own death. Instead he said, "The boots are yours."

"No," Morgan protested. "I couldn't take them. They are yours; you worked hard for them."

"I have no need of new boots," Grodin said honestly. "I go nowhere anymore where such things would matter. You keep them. Maybe a pretty face will see them sometime and swoon for the one who wears them. If so, think of me while you do Nature's bidding." He pounded a closed fist into an open hand to make the point. "That's all I ask. It's no big thing."

"It is a big thing," Morgan said, and moved to embrace the Breeder. Grodin pulled away from him.

"No," he said. "I cannot give any more of myself to you."

He turned to the wall, and shed tears he hadn't shed since his wife died, twenty years earlier.

Morgan pulled back, arms outstretched. "What are you doing?" he asked. "You, who are like a father to me."

"You already had a father," Grodin answered. "I cannot be that thing any more. I—I will be going away from this place very soon."

"But why?"

Grodin wiped his eyes and looked at the man, so strong, so trusting, so foolish. "The young Governor takes my measure," he said in even tones. "I have had many years here. It is time for the season to change."

"The season never changes in N'ork," Morgan returned.

"Yes it does," the old man said, and stared at the wall. "You just can't see it."

V
The Banquet

Morgan walked into the banquet, and it was as if he had fallen asleep and awakened to a whole new world. The sights and sounds and smells twirled around him like sensory dust devils, confusing him with multiple images, making him dizzy with sensation.

The room was mammoth and crowded full of people, as if everyone in the courtyard had been invited inside—although the courtyard was still full. Candlelight, a yellowish ball of flickering haze, hung silently over everything. Banners floated everywhere, rippling in a cool wind coursing through the room from Ibem only knew where. The large, brightly colored banners stuck straight up from the long banquet tables and each one marked the kingdom from whence that party originated.

A two hundred-piece orchestra of wooden flutes filled the rooms with aviary sounds that were barely louder than the guests themselves, who laughed and yelled to one another like a continuous roll of thunder. Dressed in red robes, a chorus sang with the orchestra, making Morgan blush when he recognized the lyrics written many years before to commemorate a hunt:

> While the bloody breath of certain Doom
> Dripped on the young boy's face,
> Young Governor sang with his bow
> And stopped Death in His place.

There was a dance floor roped off near the orchestra, and several couples spun in the raucous physical style of the provinces; but there were not many dancers since very few wives made the dangerous trek to Alb'ny for the wake.

The atmosphere was explosive and exciting, making Morgan's blood course more energetically through his tingling veins. He smiled; gone was the depression of his conversation with Grodin. All that existed was the Moment; the Moment was everything.

And the smells, the smells! The entire place was filled with long tables, and the tables were piled high with more food than he knew existed in the world. There was a riot of smell, a wall of it as the essence of steaming vegetables and spicy sweets coursed through the chamber on that invisible wind that rippled the banners and cooled what should not have been coolable. A whole rab had been baked in the castle's huge oven and wheeled out on its own table, hot fragrant steam rising from the baked brown skin of the creature. A steady line of people marched dutifully past the two thousand pound carcass, cutting off dripping gray hunks as the music trilled through the sounds of the deep rumbling voices.

Morgan moved through the crowd, grabbing a crock of dark ale from a tray carried by a young serving girl whose clothes were disheveled enough that it appeared the guests assumed she was serving more than beer.

At the far end of the room, over the heads of the milling crowd, he saw his brother sitting at the head table in front of a large curtain. Sitting with Ramon was Jerlynn and the Programmer and his favored knights. Morgan would speak to him presently, but for now, there was too much to take in.

Hearing a screech, he turned and saw a whole line of cages behind the tables. The cages contained animals, animals unlike any he had ever seen: a huge snake with arms and hands; a fleshy pink glob that emitted a continuous gurgling sound; a black bird the size of a child whose beak contained a full set of large, jagged teeth and whose eyes flashed bright red at anyone who came near; a cat with a tiny body and stiltlike legs several feet tall; and a big something-or-other that floated quickly around its cage, banging into the bars and whistling a melody that Morgan didn't recognize. There were more, many more strange and wondrous animals, and Morgan realized that they were probably brought as gifts from Coxsackie where he had been told that strange animal breeding was the major preoccupation of the royalty.

Morgan brought the mug to his lips, quaffed it down as people flowed around him. He was intent on having the right time of it. After all, this was the first day, the very first and finest day of his new life; and he intended to enjoy it, Zenna and Grodin's fears notwithstanding. Someone was calling to him, calling to his red hair. He turned and recognized some of the tree Schnecks he had visited with on the roadside.

He wandered over to them, picking up another drink as he walked. They had been drinking heavily and shedding their leaves to where much of their lopsided heads and bent, deformed bodies were visible.

"Morgan! Friend!" the one he had spoken with in the morning called. "You come to the feast too."

Morgan walked up smiling and drinking, trying not to stare too deeply into the blank, frightening void of his eyes.

"Ramon is my half brother," he said proudly, seeing no reason to keep it secret now. "I sample the fruits of his new reign."

"We also . . . sample," the man said, and drank some more, though he was obviously way past the point where he should have stopped.

Morgan glanced at the table. All the Schnecks were in the same condition, as if they had absolutely no capacity for alcohol. Their heads were like sandbags half full, stretching in this direction or that, shapeless cavities caused by nightmare breeding. Their eyes were deep set and dull, their reactions slow and heavy with profound retardation. They had shoved aside part of the white tablecloth and were carving on the wooden tables with their long knives, their bent, deformed bodies hunched desperately over their work as they argued and got sick and passed out.

Morgan glanced up at their fluttering banner. It was a patchwork quilt made of scrap fabric sewn together and was the closest thing to cohesion that he saw at the entire table.

"We will kill many Genies for you," the apparently nameless Schneck said because it was all he knew to say. "We will be worthy of our alliance with you."

Morgan smiled and drank. "Your alliance is with my brother," he said.

The man's face darkened, his eyes going wild. "Humans. Our alliance is with humans. We will be worthy. We will kill; we will die. Don't worry."

"I won't," Morgan said, and let his eyes drift toward Ramon, wishing he was over there already.

Ramon Delaga, titular Governor of Alb'ny and its provinces watched his half brother on the other side of the room with the filthy Schnecks. He drew his lips to a tight slash. Leave it to the farmer to find his own level.

His mood was dark, his anger deep rooted. Here he sat in the midst of his greatest triumph, and because of the farmer he felt himself steeped in fear and dread. It wasn't fair: someone had the letter; someone held his throbbing heart in their dirty hands. The cedar box sat before him on the table. He drank wine and stared at it.

"You carry the box now," Jerlynn said from beside him. She still wore the mourning robes, but had allowed herself the luxury of her jewelry. It tumbled from her, a virtual rock slide cascading from her neck and hair and hands. "Your father carried his little secret and now you carry it."

He turned and stared darkly at her and didn't say a word.

Her own face solidified. "That may work on the servants, son of mine, but don't use it on me."

"The box interests you, Mother?" he said loudly, emphasizing the last word. "Do you have a vested interest in the box?"

She sat stiffly in her chair, neck craning higher. "My interest is in the efficient operation of this province. If the contents of the box affects that operation, I should be told about it."

"How should I know?" he asked, his voice strained and high-pitched. The entire table was staring now. "I haven't looked in the box. My father left it for the farmer. I will simply give it to him."

"I don't believe you," she said quietly. "You would never give that box up without looking in it."

He leaned to her, took her face roughly in his hand, smiled at the fear he saw in her eyes. "Do you call me a liar?" he whispered harshly.

She shook her head as much as she could in his unrelenting grip.

"Take your hands off her," Dixon Faf said in his clear, resonant preacher's tones. "It is not well for us to present such an undignified appearance to these strangers."

"These aren't strangers!" Ramon yelled, getting shakily to his feet. "These are my people!"

There was answering applause from the closest tables, and Ramon shouted so that everyone could hear him.

"Welcome to my house!"

The chamber rocked with cheering. All the Schnecks who were still conscious jumped upon their tables, pounding their feet and screaming. Morgan took the opportunity to slip away from them and wander over to the food line.

At that moment, one of Dixon Faf's retainers made his way into the ballroom, moving quickly along the outer wall and around the animal cages to the head table, where he stood off to the side wrapped in the drapery shadows and tried to get the attention of the Programmer's man, Cannibis.

Cannibis stood several feet behind the table, dutifully watching the crowds. The curtain that hid the float brushed his back. He was acting as Faf's bodyguard, a position he had loyally devoted himself to for over fifteen years.

He saw Nulliby creeping obviously along the wall and hoped that no one else did. That hope was dashed seconds later when the Programmer turned and stared at him.

Cannibis hurried to the holy man's side. "Your Grace . . ." he began.

"What is that man doing in here?" Faf rasped, face red within the tangles of his gray beard.

Ramon was still on his feet, swaying with the wine he drank as he addressed the banquet. "You are all my friends!" he called. "And all of you will share a New Age with me, a New Age for the humans of N'ork!"

"He knows better than to come, your Grace," Cannibis said,

his dark eyes darting between Faf and Nulliby who still stood, fidgeting against the wall. "It must be a matter of grave importance . . ."

"See to him," Faf hissed. "If the Governor knew I had my own people on his staff . . ."

Cannibis nodded, straightening his leathers and his dignity as he walked behind the Governor to reach his man.

"We forge strong alliances!" Ramon called out. "And the strength of our alliance will form the cornerstone of a strong future!"

Faf watched Cannibis out of the corner of his eye. He had to handle everything just right, just so, to maintain his own political balance and yet retain some power for the Lady Jerlynn. She looked in his direction, their eyes meeting for just a second before moving discreetly onward. His hand crept down to pat her leg reassuringly under the table.

Cannibis moved quickly to the man against the wall. Nulliby's expectant face darkened when he saw the bodyguard's demeanor up close.

"Don't say anything," the Programmer's man said through clenched teeth. "Just turn around and walk out of here as quickly as you can. I'll meet you in the hallway."

"But . . ."

"Go now."

Nulliby looked at the man's bearded face, saw the darkness there and turned immediately, walking out of the ballroom.

"Your Lordship." A little man in stark white robes and boots strode up to the head table and bowed deeply from the waist.

"Speak, good sir," Ramon said, coming down heavily on his golden, high-backed throne. "We're all friends here."

He had drunk far too much wine far too quickly, freeing a tongue that had already been sharpened on his depression. But he wanted to hold things together; there was business to attend to here. If only he had not invited the farmer, he wouldn't have to look at him and remember.

"I am the Honorable Mayor Jorge Grossinger," the man in white said, "absolute authority for the city of Berlino. As a token of friendship from my people to yours, we'd like to present you with a gift."

He motioned toward the back of the room, and a large, covered cart was dragged up by two four-legged Genies.

"From the dairyland of Berlino," the Mayor said theatrically, and pulled the tarp off the wooden cart to reveal a block of cheese the size of a man and carved into the likeness of the new Governor, complete with the beret of office.

Ramon and his knights were on their feet again, faces wide with amused surprise.

"Does this make you the head cheese?" Martin of Rochester said.

Ramon twirled to face him, spilling wine on his fine robes as he did. "Mark you, Marty!" he laughed. "To persist in such humor will render you more cheddar than alive!"

The table rocked with laugher and foot stomping. Ramon drank, all the while knowing he should stop. Throwing down his cup to clang loudly on the floor, he climbed drunkenly onto the table. His Woofer, Petro, lay sleeping beside the throne. He stood quickly when Ramon climbed.

"Stay," Ramon said, and he was on all fours, trying to stand. "Stay there, boy." He put out a hand, and lost his balance, tumbling off the table onto the floor in front of the cheese statue.

Jerlynn was on her feet looking crossly at him, but Dixon Faf pulled her down to her chair and whispered something in her ear.

Ramon managed to get to his feet and made it to the statue. Drawing his broadsword, he cut off a hunk of himself and took a bite. "Delicious!" he exclaimed to the appreciative crowd.

"Look!" one of his knights said. "Stand them up beside one another and you can't tell Swiss is which!"

The crowd roared as Ramon staggered around with his sword, pretending to chase down the errant knight. He finally turned to the congregation.

"Come you all and take from my cheese," he called. "But mind you the genitals—I am without an heir!"

Nulliby heard the laughter out in the dark hallway like a dull explosion, but he paid no heed to it. His concerns were a great deal more personal.

He stood thirty feet from the door, watching its light spill into the hall. Two lovers stood moaning together in the shadows not too far from him. Farther down the hall in the other direction he could barely make out a Schneck on his hands and knees, retching as quietly as he knew how.

He saw Cannibis stride out the door with his hands on his hips, looking back and forth.

"Sir!" Nulliby whispered loudly.

Cannibis turned to the sound and followed it, joining the man within seconds.

"Not here," he said low when he reached Nulliby's side. "Farther down the hall."

Hanging candles cast dim illumination in the hallway. Cannibis walked Nulliby to the circle of light that sat the farthest from the ballroom doors.

"This had better be something very special," he told Nulliby, laying his hand gently, but with minute pressure, on the man's shoulder. "This had better be the most special thing you've ever had to say in your whole life."

Nulliby looked at him with dull eyes. He wasn't afraid, not through any lack of respect for Cannibis' intentions, but because he had that much faith in his material. He pressed the folded linen into the bodyguard's hand.

"I stole this from the new Governor," he said.

Cannibis silently unfolded the message, gazing once at the man before reading it.

"When did you acquire this?" he asked.

"Tonight," the man returned. "Not long ago. It was within the cedar chest that Ty'Jorman gave to Ramon."

Cannibis nodded. "You've done well," he said. "Let me reward you."

He pulled a pouch from his fat, black belt and dumped several chunks of gold and plastic into the man's hand.

"Have you shown this to anyone else?"

Nulliby shook his head as he counted his fortune. "I brought it right to you. I knew you'd want to see it straight away."

"Good," Cannibis said, and drawing his dagger, he quickly cut Nulliby's throat, putting a gloved hand over the man's mouth to quiet him.

Nulliby died within a matter of minutes, and when his last kicks had subsided, Cannibis picked up his money and dragged the body to the drop hole, shoving it down. He heard a distant thud seconds later and walked off wondering what the holy man would do with his information.

Fifty jugglers moved through the center of the room, using pieces of fruit as props, keeping five, six, seven in the air at one time.

"Fruit!" the tall, distinguished man in the black tights said. "Fruit from the South . . . and balance!"

He gestured to the jugglers, all dressed in tights, all students of balance. The Southern provinces were tree dwellers, poor kingdoms that had given themselves over to the jungle.

"I thank you people of the trees!" Ramon said to them, his

voice barely disguising his revulsion. "We do not get to see many of our Southern brothers this far North."

The man bowed low. "Ripples in the pond of Alb'ny extend even into the forest, M'lord."

"May I ask you a question, Lord Freiway?" Ramon said.

The man straightened, narrowing his gaze.

"Is it true," Ramon said loudly, "that you people of the trees eat only the fruit that grows on your trees? Is it true that you do not eat the flesh of animals?"

The crowd began to laugh as the man looked around. "It is true that we have no use for red meat."

"And is it true that you do not engage in the manly arts of warfare and that you do not destroy Genies when you encounter them?"

"We try to live in peace with all people," the man returned, pulling long silver hair out of his face.

The jugglers had stopped juggling and the room had gotten quiet.

Ramon stood slowly. "Are you men at all?" he asked.

"Ramon!" Jerlynn whispered, putting her hand on his.

He jerked it away. "Or are you little children who are here to show me how well you can climb trees and toss apples around."

"We came in friendship . . . " the man began.

"Friendship!" Ramon bellowed. "I seek the company of brave men with vision for the future. I do not need the council of the long-tailed monkeys of the trees."

The man from the South turned without a word and walked from the chamber, his jugglers following behind. Ramon made monkey sounds behind him that were picked up by the entire party.

Morgan watched with interest the departure of the Southern delegation and grabbed the next ale that went by, a large chunk of rab meat dangling from his other hand.

"Morgan?" the server said, and he recognized Ona behind the tray. They had grown up near one another and had been friends, though her parents didn't care for her associating with "the bastard."

"Ona!" he said, putting an arm around her slim waist. She wore a tight bodiced gown that pushed her breasts out seductively. He shook rab meat at her. "If your mother saw what you were wearing . . . "

"The Governor made us wear these," she said. "What are you doing here?"

"My brother, Ramon Delaga, invited me," he said, and drank.

Someone jostled against Ona, pushing her into Morgan who grabbed tight to steady her. She felt good there in his arms. "You look beautiful," he said, nuzzling her hair.

She kissed him quickly on the cheek and broke away from his grasp with a knowing smile. "Tell me that sometime when you're sober," she said, and disappeared into the ever-flowing crowd.

He smiled after her. "Now that I have station," he said aloud, "I will be needing a wife." He stuffed the meat into his mouth and thought for another few seconds. "Of course, I should take my time and choose carefully."

The delegation from Green Island was down under their table playing dice. Morgan squatted to watch for a while.

At the head table, Jerlynn was speaking frantically with her son. "You've got to be nicer to these people," she said, as he stared drunkenly at her. "Your father spent his entire life building good self-sufficient alliances. Enjoy that luxury. You must reassure everyone that nothing will change."

"My father burns in Hell," Ramon said.

Jerlynn's eyes flashed and she slapped Ramon without realizing she was doing it. His expression never changed as his hand moved in slow motion to brush against his cheek.

"You will never mention my father to me again," he continued. "We go through with the wake and the funeral, and then we destroy all memory of Ty'Jorman Delaga. Do you understand?"

She searched his eyes and found no humanity there. "But why?" she whispered.

"I have a mission," he said. "And it begins with the former Governor of Alb'ny."

"What sort of mission?" Dixon Faf asked, and he saw Cannibis moving back toward him behind the tables.

"You see to our spiritual needs, Programmer," Ramon said. "And to my mother's . . . comfort. Affairs of state are my concern."

"Everything that happens in this province is my concern," Faf replied. "The hand of God is evident in all things."

"Not anymore," Ramon answered.

Farley Bowman, the rotund Alderman of Coxsackie, moved to the fore, his light cotton robes clinging to his corpulent frame. Large gold rings adorned every pudgy little finger of his pudgy little hands. He made grand gestures as he talked

"As you all know," he began in his high nasal voice, "the business of Coxsackie is breeding. We breed for work, but we also breed for fun."

Bowman's people were dragging the cages up behind him. "We bring you some very special gifts today."

Dixon Faf pretended to be watching the Coxsackie exhibition as Cannibis knelt next to him to speak.

"The spy had news of import," the dark-eyed man said.

"Do tell," Faf said casually, picking at the meat on the plate before him.

"Our gifts we give to you," Bowman said, as the cages were lined up along the front of Ramon's table.

"You'll want this in private, your Grace," Cannibis said.

"Come now, aren't we overdramatizing?" the Programmer said quietly.

Cannibis put his mouth to the Programmer's ear. "I killed the spy after receiving the news."

Faf nodded, expressionless. "I see," he said.

Ramon was on his feet again. "I want to see the cat creature," he said, gesturing toward the stilt-legged animal. "Bring it out of its cage."

Bowman nodded to one of the attendants, who opened the cage door and grabbed the beast by the scruff of the neck to lead it onto the floor.

Ramon glanced over at his contingent of knights, winking at their smiling faces. Redrick of Firetree grinned wide, knowing what was coming next.

"Petro!" Ramon called loudly, and Ramon's Woofer jumped up startled. "Look Petro! Look!" He pulled the animal's head in the general direction of the cat.

The Woofer growled deep and loud, the cat suddenly struggling for release from its keeper.

"Get him!" Ramon yelled. "Get him, boy!"

Petro scrabbled up and over the table, sending it flying as he did. Wine and food and candles and clattering utensils flew everywhere, as knights and servers tumbled to the hard floor.

The cat broke away from his keeper and tried to run, but its long, thin legs got tangled up and he fell onto the remnants of the cheese sculpture. The Woofer barked loudly and jumped, knocking the cheese out of the cart and grabbing the cat. As Petro snapped, his powerful jaws closing around the creature, the cat completely disappeared, with only his wildly thrashing spindly legs hanging out of the Woofer's mouth. Petro ran off with his prize, charging through the ballroom to the amusement of the guests. As he ran, large candelabra crashed to the floor, setting hanging draperies on fire and filling the ballroom with smoke. Laughing, the guests used mugs of ale to douse the flames.

Many people rushed to help the Governor right his table, while Jerlynn sat with her head in her hands. Ramon turned to her. "Isn't it good to hear these old halls ring with laughter again, Mother?"

She just stared at him in return.

"My Lord," a voice slurred, and Ramon glanced up to find a Schneck standing before him, smoke residue swirling around his gnarled body.

"Welcome, Northern brother," Ramon said, and his knights were giggling again. "What word from my Genie-hating allies?"

Ramon smiled at the grossly deformed man who was dressed like a tree. Schnecks wanted acceptance from the human world so dearly that they would do almost anything to get it. The Governor had plans for them.

"We have no gift to bring you," the Schneck said. "We have no . . . commerce in the North."

"You need no gift, little brother," Ramon answered. "The beauty of your presence is enough."

"Enough to turn our stomachs," Redrick added and they all laughed at the retarded man, who smiled with them, not understanding the joke.

"We congratulate you on your new . . . position," the Schneck said, closing his eyes to try and remember his speech. "And we give to you the only thing we have—our loyalty and our lives."

With that, the man drew a long-bladed dagger from his rainment of leaves and poised it above his breast. "My blood and the blood of my people I pledge to you, Ramon Delaga."

He then plunged the blade into his breast, doubling over. The man took several steps forward, then fell headlong onto Ramon's table, and promptly died.

Ramon's features turned dark. "Well, there's a proper mess for you," he said angrily and pushed the body off the table. He frowned down at the bloodstained tablecloth.

"Let's get this cleaned up!" one of the knights yelled, and servants rushed to accommodate him.

"And we were having such a splendid time," Ramon said.

Redrick walked over to him. "The float, my Lord. Bring on the float."

"Yes, it's time for the float."

He stood again, watching the Schnecks drag their comrade away before addressing the guests. He realized why he had drunk so much now; it was to get himself through this part.

"Honored friends!" he called. "This banquet tonight serves a twofold purpose. First to introduce you to the change of leadership in Alb'ny, and you've all undoubtedly seen enough of me tonight to last you a lifetime."

There was laughter and a chorus of noes.

Ramon smiled, putting his hands in the air. "The other purpose of the night's entertainment is to memorialize the man who went before."

He swallowed hard, trying to keep his voice light. "My father ruled Alb'ny with strength and dignity for thirty years. It was he who forged the alliances that we strengthen here tonight. It was he who worked out the methods of keeping the roads cleared, making civilization possible. All of what we are, we owe to him. By way of tribute, I present to you the deeds of a great man and a great ruler, Ty'Jorman Delaga!"

Hurrying to the curtain, he poked his head through a slit. "Places," he rasped at the living float pieces. They scrambled to their positions. "Remember, no one moves. You are statues."

With that he brought his head out and pulled the rope that parted the curtains. Several of the palace guard began pushing it from behind, moving it into the center of the ballroom.

It was a truly magnificent sight, floating into the ballroom like a cloud kingdom, the guests sighing in unison at the work and splendor that went into it. There were forests and running water and miniature castles and deadly rabs poised in attack positions that stretched the limits of the taxidermists' art. And soon, people were pointing to the front of the float. Ty'Jorman Delaga led his own parade, his shining sword raised to slay a demon from Hell. And the smoke that still coursed through the room made it seem that much more dreamlike.

Ramon beamed, accepting congratulations from those around him. He turned and looked at his mother. She sat staring, brows knit in concern, her mouth moving wordlessly. Could he never satisfy her?

And Morgan sat arm wrestling with the blond-haired representatives from Grafton. He and a young man named Hyram faced one another across the banquet table, forearm and shoulder muscles straining, jaws clenched tight.

A group of the blond men dressed in light armor were pressed in close, wagering on the contest.

Hyram stared at Morgan, his face red and quivering. "You're exceedingly . . . strong for a . . . farmer."

Morgan grinned at him and answered casually, "You'd be surprised what we farmers can do."

And with that, he bent and pinned the man's arm, just as he had done to every man in the company. But no one was watching him, they were all staring behind.

He turned and saw the float. Without thought, he was on his feet and moving toward the display. Pushing through the appreciative crowds, he moved right up to the float and stared at his father's body.

"Father," he whispered, and was sick at heart. "What kind of a world is this where the honored dead must play the buffoon for the living?"

He looked up at the dead staring eyes, and there seemed, even in death, to be a sadness there. The entire room disappeared for Morgan, leaving only him and the spirit to share a final moment, a moment that was never shared in life.

He felt the tears well up inside of himself but he could not cry. He climbed up on the float and closed Ty'Jorman's eyes with loving fingers.

"Rest in peace," he whispered and kissed the cold lips. "You deserved better."

When he climbed down, everyone was staring at him. He turned in the direction of the head table and saw Ramon, on his feet, leaning heavily on the table top and staring. He walked toward the man, the crowd parting to allow him passage.

The Lady Jerlynn was sobbing loudly, leaning on the holy man for support. Morgan of Siler stopped before Ramon, the banquet table between them. He tried to understand the anger that flowed through his brother's eyes.

"I feel that you have treated our father in a dishonorable manner," Morgan said, and several of Ramon's knights were on their feet.

The Governor of Alb'ny raised a hand to stay them. The large chamber and all its boisterous inhabitants were deathly silent; the only sounds were the whining of the Coxsackie animals and the flapping of the birds on the draperies.

Morgan glanced at Jerlynn. She stared at him fearfully, her mouth open.

"The disposition of *my* father's body is my concern alone," Ramon said.

Morgan put his hands on his hips. "I'm older than you by several weeks," he said. "As the eldest son, it is *my* decision to make."

There was loud murmuring in the ballroom, and the Lady Jerlynn gurgled, fainting onto Faf's chest.

The Programmer stood, gathering the woman up into his massive arms. "I will see to her, M'lord."

Motioning for Cannibis to follow, he carried Jerlynn through the chamber, taking his opportunity to leave the feast for Cannibis' news.

"You are not my brother, young farmer," Ramon said, laughing. "I fear you have sampled my hospitality overmuch. Perhaps you'd be best to sleep off your strange dream."

Morgan's eyes went wide, and the guests laughed and began talking again.

"Enjoy!" Ramon called. "The evening has not reached its shank!"

The music started again, and the noise levels built. Ramon sat down.

"What are you saying to me?" Morgan asked.

Ramon stared at him.

Redrick leaned across the table. "I should have taken care of this one in the courtyard as I wanted to."

Morgan didn't even look at him. "You have your life," he said. "Be grateful."

"Bastard," Redrick spat.

"You will leave this place," Ramon said to Morgan. "You will leave this place tonight. You will take your mother and go. For our past friendship, I will grant you till morning light to leave this province."

Ona, the serving girl, was moving around the table, filling wine crocks from a large metal pitcher. Morgan wished that she wasn't present to hear this.

"And what of my birthright?" Morgan asked.

"Your what?" Ramon said angrily.

"Don't deny that you were present when our father acknowledged my parentage and granted me station."

Ramon drank from his wine cup. "You fantasize, farmer. Go now, before I change my mind."

As Ona walked past Redrick, he grabbed her around the waist and pulled her onto his lap. She struggled silently in his grasp.

Morgan lay his hand on the box. "If I fantasize, then what, pray, is this?"

Ramon stared at the box, not wanting to use it in light of the missing letter. "My father gave it to me as a keepsake," he said.

"It's mine," Morgan said, and he was tensing for a fight.

A voice called, "Stop!" and Morgan looked to see Ona in Redrick's grasp. He had ripped her bodice and was pulling roughly on her naked breasts, all the while trying to lower his mouth to them.

"Leave her alone," Morgan said coldly.

Redrick looked up, startled.

"Do what you will," Ramon told Redrick. Then to Morgan. "In my court my knights do whatever they have the will to do."

Redrick laughed loudly, taking the opportunity to tear at Ona's skirts.

"Get out!" Ramon said.

Morgan took a breath, his eyes wandering over the table, sizing up the opposition.

"I will not leave without my birthright and Ona."

Redrick picked up the girl, dropping her onto the table. He climbed up with her, trying to force her legs apart with his knee while she screamed and cried; the knights cheered him on.

The time for talk was finished.

Morgan walked the length of the table until he reached Redrick and Ona. Putting out a hand, he grabbed the man by the hair and pulled him over the table to land at his feet.

"My birthright," Morgan growled, as Ona climbed off the table and ran away.

Redrick jumped to his feet and drew his sword, the blue tights he wore accentuating his thin frame and gaunt face.

"Prepare for eternity," he said, and the room was quiet again.

Ramon frowned deeply. He knew Morgan too well.

Morgan still did not even look at Redrick. He stared evenly at his brother. "I will silence this annoyance," he said. "Then you and I must talk."

Ramon looked to Redrick. "Kill him if you can," he said without conviction.

Redrick lunged. Morgan sidestepped easily, drawing his own blade, the blade given him by his father.

"You must hate yourself a great deal," he told the man from

Firetree, and charged, driving Redrick back with a vicious attack.

He had the knight on the run from the first, and when he finally backed him into the tables that joined to make a corner, he shook his head at the look of pitiful fear he saw in his face.

"There's no honor in drawing the blood of such a coward," he said, and turned to walk away from the man.

With his last ounce of courage mustered, Redrick charged Morgan's unprotected back. Morgan sidestepped again, but this time he arced his blade instinctively, severing Redrick's sword arm at the wrist.

Sword and hand clattered to the floor. Redrick stared transfixed at his bloody stump for several seconds before charging from the room with banshee screams. The other knights looked away, ashamed of his behavior.

There was a commotion at the doorway where Redrick exited. It was Castle Guard. They were carrying two bodies. Morgan wiped the blood from his sword and watched.

"Governor Delaga," the Captain said, bringing a closed fist to his stripe-tunicked heart. "We have found the men who were guarding your father."

The bodies were brought forth and dumped on the floor. "We found them with gold in their pockets and their throats slashed in a storage room."

"More conspiracy?" Ramon said loudly. "I had hoped that the Genie acted alone, but now we have proof of complicity. There are more of them about! We must purge ourselves of this menace!"

"Wait!" Morgan shouted to the cheering crowd. "No Genie killed my father!"

"You will be silent!"

"Not this time!" Morgan snapped and addressed the guests. "The Genie knew only how to paint. He couldn't have hurt anyone. Why will you not search for the truth?"

"Pay him no heed!" Ramon told the guests. "He raves! He's a madman!"

"Who do you protect with your silence?" Morgan demanded. "Speak!"

"Enough!" Ramon yelled. "Guards, arrest that man!"

Morgan heard the sound of metal scraping metal all around him, from the Castle Guard and from the knights, anxious to show more mettle than Redrick.

He felt his mouth stretch into a tight grin. His blood was up; the air smelled of violence.

"I welcome all of you," he said, hand on hip, blade wagging reflected candlelight. "Singly or in groups."

With a shout, they charged, over tables and across the floor. Morgan flashed to them, swinging wildly, the clang of sword on sword a fire coursing through him.

There must have been thirty or forty of them. He swung out hard, taking a head of a knight, the body stumbling through the crowd of attackers.

He worked like lightning, his arm the instantaneous slave of his mind. And he moved, always putting obstacles between himself and his attackers. He parried and dipped into soft flesh, one after another falling beneath his sword.

Morgan's mind left his body, becoming a free-floating thing that directed the sword arm. The knights were slower than he, always a second behind. He drove back a wall of them, then turned abruptly and gutted the young blond man whom he had beaten at arm wrestling. He was drunk beyond drinking, intoxicated with something nameless and exciting; he was ten years old again, riding the back of the vicious white rab.

His back bumped the float, and he jumped upon it. Images of Ty'Jorman posed statue still all over the thing, afraid to move.

The guards swarmed the float, knocking over the living statues, throwing them aside. Morgan ran into the little forest, using the trees for cover, taking arms that thrust at him.

When they began pushing the trees over, he charged out, knocking rab bodies over onto his attackers. It was like an anthill, all confusion and erratic movement.

A crowd was coming for him, pushing him ever backwards. His silver sword was rust red, rapidly dulling from its work. He backed up, parried, then drew back his arm to strike . . .

Pain shot through his sword arm, sending the blade from his hand to skitter across the hard floor below. He had a second to turn around and see that he had gashed his arm on the raised sword of his father's corpse before he was pulled down by many hands.

They beat him, then dragged him down off the float to throw him to the ground before Ramon's table. Blood was streaming from his face, and his side ached horribly. All around him the bodies of the slain littered the floor and tables.

"Who killed my father?" he bellowed in a hoarse voice.

"Why do you still persist in your fantasy?" Ramon asked, and his voice had a catch to it, so unnerving was Morgan's skill.

Morgan struggled to his feet, still stooped from the pain. Four drawn swords kept him in careful check. "You are my brother," he said. "Our father promised on his deathbed to give me the station I deserve."

"Fantasy!" Ramon yelled.

Morgan pointed. "The box! The box is mine too. The box will reveal my father's plans for me."

"Take him to the dungeon," Ramon told the guards, who grabbed Morgan's arms and pulled him across the floor.

"The box!" Morgan yelled as they dragged him out. "Open the box!"

And the phrase was picked up by some of the other guests. Southern provinces mostly, provinces whose loyalty Ramon wasn't sure of. Now he knew.

"The box! The box!"

"Stop!" Ramon said to the guards. "Bring him back."

Ramon climbed atop the table, drunkenness lost in the pounding of his blood. He picked up the box and held it high in the air.

"You want the box?" he asked.

There was applause from the crowd.

"So be it."

He threw it to one of his knights. "Force the lock," he said, "and give the contents to me."

The man drew a dagger and pried open the chest, handing Ramon the folded linen within. The Governor of Alb'ny cleared his throat and read aloud:

"To my son, Ramon Delaga, upon my death. Be it known that we harbor among us one who is not of Pure Blood. Many years ago, one of my Castle Guard impregnated a woman without the benefit of marriage. The man in question ran away, leaving the woman to fend for herself. Being of soft heart, I vowed to take care of her and her infant son until such time as he reached manhood. At a later date, this woman did confess to me that she was of Genie blood, and lived with humans because she could pass as one. I was by now too fond of the child to take the proper legal and ethical steps, and so, did nothing. I feel shame for my softheartedness now, and tell you these things so that justice may be served. The woman's name was Zenna of Siler, and the boy is called Morgan."

Ramon waved the linen in the air. "It is signed and sealed by Ty'Jorman Delaga, Governor of Alb'ny and its provinces." He looked down at Morgan. "Are you satisfied, farmer?"

Morgan said nothing, his pain an overwhelming and silent thing.

"Put the half-breed in the dungeon," Ramon said, "and have the woman brought to me."

Faf's Keep sat a half mile from Castle Alb'ny facing the South Road. He had a wall and even a small courtyard that was kept cleared by his company of Guard. It was their major occupation.

He saw to the Lady Jerlynn, then went directly to his three-story stone castle, addressing Cannibis in his study. The study was high-ceilinged and had an overlook window to the South Road. The window was open. It was extremely hot. A fresco of men adoring a stainless-steel Ibem filled one entire wall. The other walls were segmented into cubby holes that housed rolled-up religious and secular tracts, many of them written by the Programmer himself.

When Cannibis handed him the linen, he went to his large, dark wood desk and read it under the flickering light of a white candle.

"No one else has seen this?" he asked when he was finished.

"No one but Ramon and Nulliby."

Faf settled into his ornately carved desk chair and folded his hands in front of his face. "There is no way I can repay the prize you have given me," he said sincerely.

"I ask only to serve," the man returned.

Faf nodded, full of love for the man. "You've been more to me than a retainer," he said. "You're a friend good and true."

Cannibis moved to the desk. "My happiness comes through service," he said. "You have nothing to thank me for."

Faf stood. "I know," he said, and the men shook hands warmly. "How sounds wine to celebrate our good fortune?"

Cannibis' eyes widened. "Your Grace? Drink?"

Faf smiled wide. "I know I sit squarely on the wagon of life," he said, "but it wouldn't hurt . . . just this once."

"Just this once," Cannibis repeated.

"Good."

Faf walked to a recessed cabinet and drew out the dusty crock, pouring them each a cupful. Giving Cannibis his drink, Faf raised a toast. "To the future," he said. "A future that looks a lot brighter beginning tonight."

"The future," Cannibis responded, and drank heartily.

Several minutes later, when the retainer was dying in painful, choking agony, he realized that he had never actually seen the Programmer drink from his own cup.

VI
The Bend of the Twig

The Lady Jerlynn Delaga, Daughter of Kings, stood gazing from her dead husband's window at a distant storm to the west.

The candles were dimmed in a room reeking of death, the only illumination entering the chamber offered up by the web of lightning that made the far sky dance to the demon's song. It flashed the room white-hot then dark, accenting the puffy fullness of a face strained from crying before mercifully settling it back into the safety of the night.

Jerlynn turned from the window and looked at the bed that would be burned in the morning in preparation for Ramon's intrusion.

"God help me, I miss you," she said, then laughed softly at the irony of it.

She had been seventeen years old when the rugged crusader had swept down from his new kingdom to make her his bride.

Rensselaer had been a beautiful city in those days, an entire walled-off town of bleached white cottages with red thatched roofs whose inhabitants cheerfully worked to keep the jungle away while not letting it interfere with the substance of their lives. But her father, Alderman Hooks, had been anxious to form an alliance with the strong warrior ruler, for Rensselaer had no army of its own.

Ty'Jorman had been like a god to her, large and powerful, totally self-assured. During their courtship, they would walk through her winding, narrow streets hand in hand, he in his bulky armor, sweating like a steamhouse, she in her gowns of purest white, a small water lily in her hair as tradition demanded. And they fell in love.

The alliance was perfect, their love even more perfect. They were wed during the turbulence of the rainy season. It was looked upon by some as an ill omen—but she didn't care, so great was her love, so strong his resolve. When he took her for the first time, it was with gentleness, both of them crying together with the pain and the happiness.

Then they moved to Alb'ny.

She discovered the Governor's brooding nature, his private ways that sometimes kept him locked in secrecy for months on end. Ty'Jorman started his Genie campaigns in earnest then, something that was to occupy him for the rest of his life. He turned her beautiful city into a troop garrison for his campaigns, forcing Rensselaer's men to become tavern keepers and its women, concubines. Her beautiful city became a brothel and her father took his own life with the shame of it.

And there was the bastard.

The bastard was the sword that hacked them to bits. He was always there, always a reminder. He was a symbol to Jerlynn, and not because she wanted him to be. Ty'Jorman refused to speak with her on the issue of the bastard; he was just there, a thick impenetrable wall that she couldn't scale and he wouldn't.

She was bitter, the Daughter of Kings now the grieving widow of her own station. She fed on hatred, force feeding the scraps to her own son who now regurgitated them back to her. She had no one to blame but herself. Suckled on hatred and selfishness, Ramon had been molded to be the human outline of her own pain. Unfortunately, she never thought that it would turn against her.

"It's your strength I miss," she said.

Faf was strong, the strongest man she had known other than the Governor. She needed a man to survive; she needed a strong man to survive well. If she was to bring anything away from her years of servitude to Alb'ny, she'd need strength to get it. She couldn't depend on Ramon; he was consumed with himself and his own hatreds.

There was a commotion out in the hallway. Moving quickly to the door, she pulled it open and peered into the dimly-lit corridor.

Ramon was leading two of the Castle Guard and the charge they half-dragged between them. It was a woman, struggling fiercely to get free. And though she had never before looked upon Zenna of Siler, she knew the enemy of her life was within her house.

"What have you done with my son?" the woman said loudly, no hint of fear in her steady voice.

"We could use the sharpness of your tongue to clear the roadways," Ramon said. He sounded weary. "Be silent."

And then the woman laughed a laugh that chilled Jerlynn's blood, and she knew immediately the magnetism that had attracted her husband to this commoner. She suddenly was afraid; she suddenly wanted nothing more than for this thing to be done with.

"Ramon," she said quietly from the doorway.

Ramon started, surprised to find her there. "Go back to your rooms," he said, his dark eyes lost in the deeper darkness.

"This is still my home. Why are you bringing this woman in here?"

"This is your home by my good graces," Ramon told her. "Be vigilant of that."

Zenna of Siler laughed again. "The pup bites the bitch," she said with contempt.

Ramon turned angrily to her, hitting her savagely across the face, knocking her to the ground.

Jerlynn watched her fall, then climb right back to her feet. She was awed and fearful of the woman's strength. She had seen it in the son, a thing beyond reason.

"Must you do that in here, before others?" she said.

He frowned deeply, shadow creasing his face. "If that is what pleases me," he said quietly, accenting each word.

Jerlynn looked to the woman, saw her smile through the blood that poured from her lower lip. She hated Zenna's look, hated her existence, yet felt a perverse respect building within her for this creature of action and reaction. That frightened her more than anything.

"Send them on," she said softly. "Please."

Ramon turned, still frowning, and looked at the Guard. He cocked his head, and they followed the movement. The woman turned to her as they took her away.

"I matter naught," she said. "My son you will not silence so easily. He is his father's son."

Jerlynn felt a dagger rip through her. Her hands were shaking when she finally addressed Ramon. "Holy Ibem," she said. "What goes on?"

His gaze moved quickly between her and the retreating Guard. When he was a child, he always did that when he was lying. "Father left a message in the box," he said. "It accused the farmer and his mother of being of impure blood. I am the instrument of his dying justice."

"What goes on?" she said again.

"What you've alway wanted," he said. "Leave me to my duty and walk away from it."

"If you're going to do it," she hissed, "do it now. Don't keep the woman or her son under this roof. If you've ever listened to me, do it now. No good can come of this night if you don't act immediately."

"I can't," he said. "The act is public. All must be performed in a public manner to satisfy the provinces."

"Take her out of this house!"

He stood before her, hands clenched in front of him, shaking wildly. She thought he would reach out and strangle her, but he did not.

"I can't!" he said loudly.

"My lord?" a voice called from down the hall.

"Go on!" Ramon screamed.

"I don't know what your reasons are," she said, "but take her out of this place."

"You do not want the burden of my reason," he whispered. "She will be put in the recorder's room tonight. She will be tried after the funeral."

"You will bring ruin to my house."

"My house!" he screamed. He paused, then said softly, "My house."

He took her by the shoulders, his grip like steel. "Why couldn't you have raised me like she raised the farmer?" he asked, his voice strained. He turned from her then, taking long strides down the corridor to join his people.

She watched him disappear into the darkness, many feelings at war within her. After a moment, she returned quietly to Ty'Jorman's chambers, the fear and the sadness an overwhelming tide that threatened to drown her. And Jerlynn Delaga, Daughter of Kings, also wished that she had raised her son the way Zenna of Siler had raised hers.

VII
The Dungeon

The creaking sound wound through Morgan's painful dreams, becoming the glue of his fragmented brain. And eventually it displaced the dreams, becoming his sleeping and, finally, waking focus.

He opened his eyes to a terrible headache. The creaking was

loud, grating. It pervaded everything, giving some definition to the darkness that surrounded him.

"Glitch vid?" a tiny voice said from the darkness.

He tried to speak, to answer the voice. "Ohhh . . ."

"Taka, taka, taka!"

The sound of scurrying mixed in with the creaking noise. He felt a presence all around him, and then, light. Tiny glowing embers, swaying in small braziers, flaring brighter as they were blown on. The light defined shapes: bent shapes, small shapes with large eyes—shadows with staring, glassy eyes.

He tried to move, but couldn't. Pain flared from his entire body, and it cleared his mind. He remembered.

"Ramon," he growled low, vowing vengeance for every foul blow that had been rained upon him by the brave knights and Castle Guard.

Tentative hands reached out to touch him. They prodded gently, some not so gently.

"Please." His voice was as dry as dead leaves. "Help me."

But there was no help. The forms with the swaying embers moved in closer. They gave off a foul stench that together with the creaking noise made him feel perhaps he was dreaming again.

He wasn't.

When the dark figures realized that he was completely helpless, they attacked. Morgan was already in pain. He could feel nothing more, and accepted his beating with detached indifference, waiting idly for the cover of darkness to descend upon him completely, to take away what life was left within him. And his only real regret was that he'd have to come back for Ramon from beyond death, that perhaps his vengeance would have to wait.

The world hazed, then fogged, and then something happened. His attackers were being roughly pulled away by a huge figure, their little lights scattering in all directions. He was staring into a large face that he recognized from a million years before. A light swung between his face and the large one. The face smiled broadly, and Morgan did the best imitation he could muster.

The face laughed loudly. "I know you, U-man!" it bellowed. "You gave me water."

"T-The . . . courtyard," Morgan said.

"And now you're down here with the People. Hurt bad are you?"

"I think so," Morgan managed to say. He tried to laugh, but it came out a painful cough. "I can't move enough to find out."

The giant moved his brazier up and down the length of Morgan's body, checking him over. "You look dead," he said at last.

"Not yet," Morgan said, and his thoughts were not of himself. He tried to move, ignoring the pain. "If you can just help me . . . sit up."

The giant grabbed Morgan by the front of his red blouse, pulling him into a sitting position. But the pain coursed hotly through him and he slumped back down again.

"What is your name, U-man?" the giant asked.

Morgan told him.

"I am Serge," the giant said, slapping his muddy, naked chest with a large hand. "Serge will take you to Nebo for help."

With that, Serge stood, scooping Morgan up and cradling him as if he were a baby in his mammoth, muscled arms.

For the first time, Morgan realized he had been lying in deep, thick mud, and that it must form the entire floor of the dungeon which was below the already existing wine cellar of Castle Alb'ny.

"Who's Nebo?" he asked, trying to keep his mind away from the intensity of the pain.

"My Mech," Serge said proudly, as he sloshed through the mud with his burden. "Serge comes all the way to the catacombs of U-mans to find his Mech. Funny, right?"

"Funny," Morgan said.

They slogged through the darkness, mud continually sucking at the giant's legs. It was too dark to see anything, but Serge seemed to know what he was about. They passed a great many brick pillars as they walked, and Morgan figured that the giant somehow used them as reference points.

The creaking sound, which had never abated, got louder the farther they walked, and Morgan soon discovered why. They came to a place of light. Several small, clean burning fires that seemed to spring magically out of the rocks illuminated as strange a scene as he had ever witnessed.

A huge, rimless wheel attached to a fat pole sticking through the ceiling filled a section of the dungeon. A number of long spokes came out of its hub. The spokes were being pushed by Genies of every description from pure blooded to hybrid man/animal types with snarling, furry heads. They trudged the hard circle, groaning with the pressure; and the hub creaked loudly as it turned the ceiling pole.

"What's this?" Morgan asked as he watched them straining with their task. The ground around the wheel had been worn down to a hard-packed hole. He realized that this operation had been going on for years, perhaps lifetimes.

"Nebo will tell," Serge said. "Serge doesn't quite understand yet."

The giant carried Morgan to the wheel. He approached a Genie who was tall and sleek as a cat. He had a small bunched-up cantaloupe of a face and wide, staring eyes that seemed to glow with night vision. His pupils were slits that went up and down in the yellow iris. Serge walked around with the Genie, talking as they walked.

"I have something," Serge said.

"You do indeed have something there," the Genie said, and he turned to stare at Morgan with his head cocked like an animal's. There was puzzlement on the Genie's face, but no judgement, perhaps no capability of judgement.

"I must take it to Nebo," Serge said. "It's hurt."

"Yes," the Genie said.

"Do you know where is he?"

"Who?"

"Nebo."

"I do not know where he is," the Genie replied above the creaking. "But I think where he is."

"Where?"

"At the place of light and water," the Genie said, his eyes rolling toward the ceiling. "He feels many things. Something is afoot."

"We have U-mans in the dungeon," Serge said. "I go to Nebo."

"Yes," the Genie said, and continued walking his never-ending circle.

The giant carried Morgan back into the darkness. Morgan slipped in and out of consciousness as they trudged onward, and he persisted in the feeling that there was something watching them from the beams above, something cunning and hungry.

"There," Serge said after a moment, and Morgan turned his head toward distant light.

A large, yellow-white fire carved a bright notch out of the blackness; a series of small beams of outside light flashed through angled cutouts in the wall of the dungeon and left perfect squares of daylight on the thick mud.

Serge lay Morgan gently into the mud near the fire. Blinking

through the flame, Morgan saw a man sitting rock still in a chair.
The chair had high legs that kept the sitter out of the mud. The
man wore coarse brown robes with a hood that was pulled up
over his head. His hands were secreted in the folds of the robe.

"What have you brought me?" a voice said. It was a low voice,
but the tones were clear and melodious, almost like a song.

"A U-man," Serge said, his voice reverent. "We found him
just inside the bars. The other U-mans have broken him up."

Morgan watched through the flames as the figure sat silently
for a time, as if wondering if it was worth the trouble to get off the
chair to look at him. Finally the man rose, unfolding himself
slowly, gracefully, like a flower. He walked into the mud, but the
mud didn't seem to be his master.

He walked up to stand near Morgan, his hood falling away
from his face. His skin was not the light of mahogany, but was
dark like ebony wood, his unlined features just as smooth and
hard. His head was bare, but not shaved bare. Years did not
seem to touch him, so ageless was his countenance, and when
the man rolled his large brown eyes toward Morgan's, it was as if
the farmer were staring into the coral pools of the great sea.

Morgan watched him silently, never having seen the like of
this man before. And finally, in time, the tall, lean figure knelt in
the mud beside him.

"I am Nebo," he said with the voice of angels. "You must be
Morgan of the fiery hair."

"You . . . k-know me?"

Nebo didn't answer. Instead, he glanced at the giant.
"Serge," he said, his voice casual to command. "Get the shirt off
him."

Bending easily, the giant grabbed Morgan's shirt by its ruffled
front and ripped it from him.

"Owww!"

"Where is the worst pain?" Nebo said. He squatted, examin-
ing Morgan's face up close.

"My left side," Morgan said through the waves of agony.

"You'll take some stitches on your face," Nebo said clinically.
"And also on this gash on your arm. You've lost much blood."

The Mech's arms came out of his robes. He had no hands.
Reaching out with a stump, he prodded Morgan gently all over
his legs and torso.

"Will I . . . live?" Morgan asked.

"Probably. Is that the answer you wanted?"

"I will have vengeance in this life," Morgan said firmly, and he detected a slight change in the Mech's eyes. An impression had been made.

"You have three broken ribs," Nebo said, "a concussion, plus assorted cuts and bruises."

Morgan grunted. "You should have seen the other fellows."

"I'm not sure if you have internal damage or not, but—" the man smiled for the first time "—I think it would matter little to you."

"How long have I been down here?" Morgan asked, his pain already lessened from the knowledge that it wasn't fatal.

"No more than a night, certainly," Nebo answered. He looked up at the big man. "Fetch clean water and food. Get me a Minnie, also. Have him bring mending gear."

The big man started off.

"Wait!" Nebo called after him. "I need you for something first."

Serge dutifully returned to the alcove of light.

"Bundle up the shirt," the Mech said. "Tie it tightly around his middle."

The giant did what he was told, Morgan clenching his teeth when he was lifted off the ground to get the material around his injury.

"Not much you can do for broken ribs," Nebo said. "Rest. They'll heal naturally."

"I don't have time for rest," Morgan responded. He reached out a hand to Serge. "Help me up."

The giant took his arm, and he struggled into a sitting position. This time he stayed up.

"Not much else to do down here besides rest and push the wheel," the Mech said. "What have you in mind?"

"Escape," Morgan said. "Soon."

Nebo raised his eyebrows, then motioned Serge away. "They hold Ty'Jorman's funeral today," he said quietly. "They have also arrested your mother."

Morgan felt the fire course through him. The letter. That damned letter! By law it would surely sentence both him and Zenna to death should Ramon so choose. He had been foolish to trust Ramon's honor, and now his foolishness was bringing dishonor to his mother. He didn't believe that Ty'Jorman had actually written the letter; it made no sense connected to the other things that had happened. His father had been too lucid, too straightforward to lie even as he welcomed death. The horrible dark comedy of the letter was much more like his brother than his father.

"I've got to get out of here," Morgan said. "Now."

"A good trick," the Mech responded.

"How do you know so much?" Morgan asked him.

The Genie stood with that same fluid movement and glided back to his seat. "I'm a Mech," he said at last. "I know certain tricks that sometimes amuse the dungeoneers. I trade my tricks for occasional food and information."

"That may be useful," Morgan said.

"They could never be bribed to free you," Nebo told him, folding his stumps back into the drooping sleeves of his robes. "There's nothing we have down here that is worth the value they place on their lives."

Serge returned to the light. His large hands held food and water. On his shoulders sat perched a woman who was no larger than a small tree stump but had no other deformities.

"Transelfmit," Nebo said, and the woman jumped off the giant's shoulder and zipped over to Morgan. She moved more quickly than he could have believed possible. "Troubleshoot, sync medic."

The woman quickly began cleaning his wounds with clear water, her little face fixed with intensity as she worked. Her hands moved quickly and gracefully, never using too much pressure on his tender skin. Once, he reached for the water crock she held to get a drink, but her eyes flared angrily, and she pulled it back away from him and resumed her work.

"Eat," Serge said, handing him a small bowl. "Drink."

He drank the crock water first, his dry tissues absorbing it quickly. He wasn't really hungry, but began eating to get his strength up. The bowl contained large chunks of meat in some sort of gravy. It was some of the best fare he had tasted, in or out of a dungeon.

When the tiny woman finished cleaning his wounds, she pulled a long shiny needle out of her filthy robes and moved toward his arm.

"Stasis," she said in a squeaky voice.

"Don't move," Nebo said.

The Minnie, whose name was Sheila, began stitching his arm. Morgan ignored the pain and continued eating. "Have you ever tried to get out?" he asked around a mouthful.

The Mech looked puzzled. "No," he answered simply.

"Why not?"

"It never occurred to me."

"What happened to your hands?"

The Genie sighed. "Your father had them cut off when he took me from my home and brought me here."

"Why?"

"He was afraid of me."

Morgan let that pass. "How long ago was that?"

Nebo thought. "Not sure," he answered finally. "Ten years, maybe fifteen. It all jumbles together after a while."

The Minnie finished with Morgan's arm and moved to his face, forcing him to chew very slowly. He was confused to say the least. He knew nothing about Genies or their motivations, and his ignorance was compounding by the second.

"Why do you push the wheel?" he asked, putting another chunk of meat slowly into his mouth, the Minnie fussing at him in her strange language the whole time.

"It's our only reason for being alive," Nebo said. "To push the wheel for them is our charge, the reason they feed us at all."

Morgan swallowed, tilting the bowl to his lips to get some of the gravy. "Well, you certainly don't eat bad down here."

Serge laughed. "Not regular food," he said. "They give gruel."

"Then what's this?" Morgan asked, holding up the bowl.

"A U-man," Serge said proudly. "He came down the drop hole last night. Serge just pulled him through the grate a little at a time and we cooked him. Good, huh?"

Morgan put his bowl down. He'd have to find a way out of there.

VIII
In the Forest of Kings

The jungle hung low, like rotted fruit ready to spill from the vine in a jumble of decay and sickly sweet odor. It was steamy, convoluted green confusion and death, a tangle of disorder that choked the windpipe of the land and tried to rasp the last breath of life from its sweet red mouth. It wanted nothing for men and everything for Itself, and though the soft, yielding flesh of man sometimes ventured into Its dark avenues, he always came away with deep, unhealable scars. For man recognized the face of his Master, and trembled before It.

The shade of the Mother Sequoia was formidable enough to encompass the entire company of mourners. The tree stretched tall and firm, its centuries-old branches thick enough to keep any other tree from growing in its shadow. It was several hundred feet tall, with the circumference of its branches at least that. No one knew where the tree came from, for surely no other tree like it grew in the lands of N'ork.

Mother Sequoia was the traditional burial place of the family Delaga, and in its might they took their own strength. The company of mourners had already assembled when Ramon arrived in the wagon carrying the corpse of the old Governor, a man whom the new Governor was happy to put to rest.

The wagon was a fine black carrier with gold trim and large red wheels. It was open with seats of fine, rich leather. Six matched Bernards pulled the thing under the able hands of the Breeder, who was shaved close and dressed in black robes for the occasion. Of all those occupying the seats, it was probably Grodin who would miss Ty'Jorman the most.

The carriage seats faced one another, which left Ramon to stare over the body of his father at Jerlynn and Dixon Faf who occupied the other seat. Ty'Jorman was dressed as he had been on the float, his body still fixed in its heroic posture as it lay between the seats.

The day was as all days, sultry gray. Ramon was sweating alcohol profusely into the blue jumper beneath his webbed armor. He was agitated and sullen, and knew that this would be the most arduous day of his life.

Grodin drove the wagon into the tree grotto, just a stone's throw from the North Road. The road had been cleared in haste that morning for though it had been cleared the night before, it had already become impassable from undergrowth.

Ramon looked upon the crowds that jammed around the wagon, and waved stoically to them. Most had handkerchiefs to their mouths to ward off the smells of jungle decay, their free hands silently waving evergreen branches with rocks attached, the symbol of their unwilling servitude to the Will of Nature. They dressed in many colors, for the mourning was observed differently in every province. The one color that they didn't wear, that no human wore, was green.

Ramon's knights, in full armor and colors, formed a tight defensive ring around the outside of the mourners to ward off the always-present terror of the jungle; and the sounds of that terror bled into the crowd from all around—the calls of beasts and fowl and insect that thrived in the decay which joined in its quest for complete domination of the land.

The crowd parted to let the carriage pass, and Ramon looked just above their heads with unfocused eyes, for in truth he was there and wasn't there. In truth he rode a huge, sturdy boat down the raging rapids of Father Hus with his army to pluck the Jewel of the East. The lands of his father, and all the fathers before him, were, in truth, not enough for Ramon Delaga. Alliances were not enough for him; like the forest, he wanted domination over all. He knew he could be satisfied with nothing less.

His back was to their forward progress. Turning in his seat, he peered ahead. The scaffolding was still being hurriedly nailed into place by a gang of workmen, its skeletal frame climbing over fifty feet up the side of the trunk. The pulley stuck out from the top of the thing, its long rope dangling idly like a dancing snake all the way to the ground.

"Breeder," he said. "Take us right up to it."

"Yes, M'lord," Grodin returned, and it was only the thought that Morgan was still alive that kept him from drawing his dagger and cutting Ramon's miserable throat right on the spot.

"A fine turnout," the Programmer said. "Ty Jorman was a beloved man."

"Save it for the eulogy, would you?" Ramon said to him.

"My Lord, this is a solemn occasion," Faf protested.

Ramon wiped the sweat from his face. "Let's not make it any more solemn than we have to."

"Your father is dead," Jerlynn said, a catch in her voice. "He deserves respect and veneration."

Ramon felt his throat constrict. With a slow, deliberate motion and his eyes on Jerlynn's, he put up his booted feet, resting them on the corpse.

"Please," Jerlynn whispered. "Someone will see."

With a small laugh, Ramon moved his feet and leaned up close to Jerlynn. "Expect no more veneration than this from me. Programmer, how long is your eulogy?"

Faf looked sternly at him through the tangle of his long hair and beard. "I have not timed it," he said.

Ramon nodded, pulling on his sparse mustache as if to help it grow faster. "Keep it short," he said. "Let's get this over with."

"I will do what is proper," Faf said, as Jerlynn drew her lips tight in disapproval.

"You will be properly brief," Ramon said, and leaned his head back on the seat cushion to stare at the solid ceiling of branches and leaves that left the whole proceeding in soft shadow.

Grodin reined in the Woofers beside the scaffolding. The structure looked immense from that vantage point, the unsyncopated clank of the many hammers loud and resonant. Among the crowd of workers and retainers who wandered around the platform he saw Zenna, bound and gagged, tied by the neck to the wooden structure. Several feet above her head he saw a plank extended from the scaffold, another pulley attached to it. He saw that the pulley rope was drawn to the hangman's noose, and he became sick at heart.

The Bernards were skittish as Grodin climbed down from the carriage, but they still held themselves proudly. The Breeder made sure he patted them all gently before walking to the front of their tether.

"Down," he said, in a low but firm voice, and they all sat upon their haunches, their large heads erect. They panted heavily in the heat, drool dripping from their black muzzles. Grodin went in search of water.

He walked past Zenna, their eyes meeting as he did. The woman of Siler saw the deep sadness in his world-weary eyes, and knew that her son would have someone to love and trust after she was gone, and that made her happy.

That she would die was a certainty; that Morgan would live, she accepted as a given. It would take something greater than the spawn of Rensselaer to stop what had already been set in motion. She looked to the carriage, to Jerlynn, who saw that the woman understood more than she had the courage to understand.

The Lady Jerlynn Delaga sat mesmerized by Zenna's unfaltering gaze. It was deep, penetrating. It left her naked and exposed with nothing to hide behind.

"Mother!" Ramon said. Jerlynn seemed almost to be in a trance.

Jerlynn started, her head shaking in small vibrations when she looked at Ramon. "W-What?"

"Let's get this over with. Come on."

He stood, Jerlynn and the Programmer standing also. The mourners all knelt as a group, bowing their heads. All labor had ceased on the scaffold, though workers still occupied it on every level. Small wisps of gray-white smoke drifted through the grotto, residue from the funeral pyres that Ramon had ordered on the roadway for the men who had died the previous evening at the wake.

"Honor Guard!" Ramon said loudly, and the rulers of Alb'ny's six closest allies rose from their positions close by and moved to the carriage. They opened the small door and slid out the six-handled pallet that contained Ty'Jorman's remains.

They carried the body solemnly to the scaffold, Ramon's party just behind. The Governor saw the farmer's mother looking at the body as it passed, and he wanted to strangle her right there—but all things come in their time.

The pulley rope was attached to a platform. The Honor Guard laid the pallet upon it. Ramon, as tradition demanded, placed a dagger upon the corpse's chest and Jerlynn then laid a dead rose across the dagger, symbols of their mastery over the elements and Ty'Jorman's greatness in that regard.

Ramon and Jerlynn then stepped off, allowing the Programmer to step on. The Honor Guard immediately began to pull upon the rope and the platform rose from the ground, Dixon Faf having to grab the ropes to keep from getting thrown off.

"Brief," Ramon whispered to him as he ascended slowly.

The holy man watched the assembled spread out before him as he rose slowly above their heads, and the higher he rose, the more abstract the people became, the more a part of the whole of the forest. He found air up high, as he was pulled toward the burial branch, fresh clean air. With the curtain of leaves above and the carpet of men below, he was moved to consider the interrelationships of all things.

In a surge of creative power, he forgot the speech he had prepared and said this:

"What is a man?" he called loudly. "What is the thing we call human? Are we trunk and branches and leaves of hair and veins like roots that flood the sap of life beneath the soft bark of flesh? Are we set solid in the earth, never to move, never to bend except for that natural bending that comes with the winds of inevitable change? Or are we more? Is there something else?"

He had been raised quite high now, the people below colored pebbles on the pathway. The platform shook and the body of Ty'Jorman Delaga stared at him with the eyes of eternity. The fear was in him up that high, and with it, an exhilaration. As he spoke, swaying up there, the branches of Mother Sequoia rolled his words around to fall gently upon the heads of the mourners.

"Ibem destroyed the folly of men once, long ago. Men had

been headstrong, like the trees, unmoving, unwilling to move.
Ibem consigned men to the ashes in His just anger and gave us
the plague of Nature as a continual reminder of what we'd done.
We are soft and pliable. We can bend and move with the life
around us. We can understand. We can forgive!"

The platform jerked to a stop at the burial branch. Several of
Faf's friars were huddled there atop the scaffolding, lashed to the
huge branch lest they return to the ground the fast way. The
branch had a hollowed out place in it just large enough for a
man. It was toward there that the brown-robed friars gingerly
pulled the body. Ty'Jorman was the hundred and third Delaga to
be buried in this tree.

"Ibem is the Master of this world. The forest is proof of that.
He has made for us the life we are to live, as we have lived life for
a millenium. We are born as the trees, but not of the trees. We
bend. We live for the glory of God, not for the relentless push of
the forest. We are as the forest, but not of the forest!"

The friars had managed to jam the body in its living casket,
one of them stealing Ramon's dagger and hiding it in his robes.
They refitted the cut-out lid of the branch cask and began bind-
ing it with rope. Faf feared the political directions his speech
had taken, but he couldn't stop.

Ramon watched the Programmer from the ground, becoming
angrier the more he heard. The man would pay dearly for his
veiled criticisms of the Governor's expansionist feelings.

"We are not made to be the master of Nature, nor of other
men. We are made to do what we have done since the Fall. We
praise God and do penance for the sins of our fathers. Were it
otherwise, would not the trees stand aside and let us pass? We
must not grow and expand in a headstrong fashion without regard for where we grow or why. It is for us to be pliable to the
Will of Ibem. Ty'Jorman understood that. He made alliances
without subjugating, built roads through forests without destroying them. We bury him in Mother Sequoia today as the
fitting sign of our continued bending to the Will of the Almighty.
Our paths and our feelings must ever bend until there are no
tomorrows and only yesterdays remain. In this and no other lies
the pathway to Redemption."

He raised his thick hands to the gray skies. "Oh Ibem," he
called. "We send to you the best among us today. Accept our
sacrifice and forgive us our pettiness and our greed."

With that, he motioned for the Honor Guard to lower the

platform. The sensation was like sinking from the mountaintop back into the mire of mere existence. And he knew that of the people who heard, only one listened to his words—the only one he wished would not have listened.

Ramon stood like a statue, watching Faf descend, then step from the platform. The Programmer was rapidly distancing any respect the Governor had for his office with the speed of his tongue. He'd have to be careful with this one, though. Not only for Jerlynn's sake, but because what power the man had came from the Holy City of Kipsie, the one unifying force in all their lives. It would take some doing, but there was time for that.

The burial finished, the mourners began rising from the moist, barren ground as the workmen prepared for the task of disassembling the scaffolding that they hadn't even finished building.

Ramon turned and jumped back into the carriage, standing atop one of the plush, quilted seats. "People of N'ork!" he called, and the people turned as a body to him. "Now that my father's body has been laid to rest, we have to serve the justice of his dying wish."

He pointed toward Zenna. "Bring the prisoner forward."

The Guard jostled her roughly toward the carriage, even though she offered no resistance, then Ramon grabbed her arm and pulled her into the carriage with him. He pulled her close; their eyes met, and she reflected his hatred like twin mirrors.

"Say nothing," he said to her so no one else could hear, "and I swear Morgan's life will be spared."

Her mouth was still gagged, her eyes widening above it. He pulled the cloth down beneath her chin.

"You ask me to trust in your honor?" she said.

"What choice do you have?"

She lowered her head then, and he turned her around to face the crowd. Ramon pulled the forged linen from his pouch and held it high for the crowd. "This my father wrote on his death-bed!" he called, and read the message in a clear voice.

The mourners grumbled angrily when they had all heard the note. "I submit to you that not only does this note positively prove that Zenna of Siler is not of Pure Blood, but that it cements her firmly in the conspiracy that murdered my father!"

There were shouts then, the grotto echoing with the sounds of anger. Ramon quieted them with upraised hands. Now he would see.

"By law, the accused has the right to speak. Even now, on the grave of Ty'Jorman Delaga, I give you that right. Have you anything to say in your own defense?"

The woman looked at him, then inexplicably turned to face Jerlynn, who huddled close to Dixon Faf, leaning against him for support. Ramon saw a look of terror cross his mother's face, and jerked Zenna back around to face him.

"Have you anything to say?" he demanded again.

She held her head erect, staring defiantly at the crowd; but she did not speak.

"We have the answer from her silence!" Ramon told the assembled. "What is the verdict!"

The answer was a word, and it resounded like a monstrous bell through the grotto with a sound that would eventually reach the farthest corners of the land of N'ork.

With that, Ramon shoved her from the carriage, hands still tied behind her back, to fall heavily to the ground. Many hands dragged her to the scaffolding.

"We must carry out the punishment as prescribed by law," he said.

Everyone assembled knew the punishment for Genies. Zenna would be drawn and quartered—drawn by the neck, then disemboweled to die a slow, agonizing death.

The rope was put eagerly around her neck by the Guard, and everyone crowded around, clawing and hitting her; and still she did not cry out, even as the blood flowed from her face and soaked her cotton dress.

"We must have an executioner!" Ramon called. He began searching the immediate area with his eyes until he found who he was looking for. He smiled. "The honor goes to our loyal servant and Breeder, Grodin of Alb'ny."

Grodin had been close to the Woofers, calming them amidst the hysteria. He turned in shock to stare up at Ramon. "It is for the family of the slain to seek vengeance."

"It is the duty of every noble son of humans to kill Genies," Ramon said. "And for loyal service, that responsibility is today yours."

Ramon drew his sword and, taking it by the blade, thrust it down toward Grodin, hilt first. The crowd cheered as Grodin took the sword dumbly. They pushed, propelling him toward the unfortunate woman until he stood face to face with her.

He looked at her. "I cannot," he said softly, lips twitching.

She nodded to him. "You must," she said, sputtering blood. "Morgan must have someone after I'm gone."

"Zenna, no . . . I . . ."

"Someone else will do it if you don't," she said. "And Ramon will probably kill you as well. He's promised to free my son."

Tears fell unashamedly from Grodin's old eyes, tears that hadn't come since his wife had died so many years before. Zenna's words rang true to him, yet how could he kill the mother of one who was like a son to him?

"Do it now!" Ramon said to him, and the crowd began cheering loudly.

"Please," she said. "For Morgan."

With hands and heart shaking, he turned and nodded to the men who held the pulley ropes. They grunted and jerked the rope, pulling until she was raised off the ground, just the tips of her feet touching earth.

And with the sound of her gagging in his ears, Grodin slit her open, falling immediately to his knees as her blood rained upon him.

The mourners cheered wildly as the woman dangled in agony, and Ramon spoke again, while he knew she was still alive.

"And now we go and take her bastard son!"

Zenna of Siler, through waves of abstract agony, fixed her eyes on the mother of such dishonor. Her eyes magnetized Jerlynn, tore at her soul, and in a horrible tumble of empathy and prophesy, Jerlynn stared in horror as the structure of Zenna's face seemed to dissolve and reform. And she was looking, looking as if in a mirror.

The woman had her face.

IX
The People

Morgan stood, leaning against the dungeon wall for support, and stared into the fire-dancing faces of the Genies who crowded into Nebo's alcove. There must have been thirty in all, and all stared back at him through eyes that viewed life as a beast must view a sunset. All were there with the exception of the smallest possible crew that could man the wheel. They were met to pass judgement. It was he they were judging.

Nebo was apparently the reluctant ruler of the dungeon, though he seemed to command no one but Serge; and when they came and asked him for the trial, he shrugged and gave them their due, neither supporting nor discouraging the movement.

"How can we trust one such as the human?" a Genie named El-tron said. He was frail and lean and stripped to the waist, possessing long fingers tapering to delicate points and extraordinarily large eyes for intricate work. He was the most vocally negative about Morgan's status. "They are our sworn enemies and executioners. They think of us as less than the beasts of the forest."

"Not all humans feel that way," Morgan said softly, though he was not prone to give much outright in his own defense. "There are all kinds of humans, just as there are all kinds of Genies."

"He gave me water," Serge said, as he had already said several times. "He is a good U-man."

"That is not at issue," Nebo said from his chair. "The question is whether or not he shares what life we have here, or whether he is banished to live alone in another part of the dungeon."

"They put him here for punishment," El-tron said in his high, chirpy voice. "So they forgive him soon and he rejoins the company of his human friends—free, on the outside. And what of us? Still caught, still trapped. Send him away."

The assembled began murmuring then.

"I do not think they will free him," Nebo said.

A woman in gray robes and arms that reached to the ground spoke. "To be a stranger in your own home must surely be punishment enough," she said with considerable passion. Morgan saluted her. "Because fortune frowns upon us is no reason why we should be as those who are the jailers."

"How do we know we can trust him?" El-tron asked loudly. And El-tron worried about deception since he had been lured from the forests and into a trap by a dummy machine set in the roadway many years before.

"Trust him to do what?" The man with the cat eyes said. His name was Squan and Morgan felt nothing but good from him. "What secrets have we to hide? We have nothing but ourselves and we all came here through the ill will of humans, just the same as him."

Morgan felt it was time to speak. He had listened patiently while the debate raged for a hour around him. He was hurt and angry, but he didn't want to be alone. Finally he wearied and determined to put an end to the talking. He walked painfully up to the fire and stared into it.

"As we speak, my mother is on trial for her life," he began. "She has been accused of being as you are, a Genie. I am accused of being the son of a Genie. So, you see, I am only half human at best."

He looked around at them. The wore the tattered remnants of the clothes of their region, but the equalizing mud of Alb'ny coated them all and him too. It covered them body and soul.

"Whether the accusation is true or not is of no importance," he continued. "My mother still is tried, the lies still rule the day and will continue to do so until my brother, the Governor, is taken from his own home and fed to the Woofers.

"I have tried the bars and cannot get free. Until I think of a way, I will live in this place." He brought his left hand up and moved it slowly toward the fire. "I wish to live here with you, to know you, to know if you have honor in your hearts; for the hearts of men are filled with nothing but darkness blacker than the blackest corner of this dungeon."

His hand inched very close to the fire, as the company stared, entranced by the spectacle. "You doubt my sincerity," he said, feeling the heat building on his flesh. "I have discovered that words have no meaning, promises no substance, and I have grieved for these discoveries. Now I hope to do with a deed what words could never do. I will place my hand in the fire, removing it only when all of you ask me to."

He stretched his hand into the flames, but was jerked back almost immediately by Serge. "He has spoken with deeds already," the giant told them. "He gave me water."

"They come," a Genie said. He was short in stature, but had mammoth, almost elephantine ears. "Many people, moving quickly across the courtyard."

Squan moved with catlike rhythm toward one of the cutouts in the wall that angled up for a great distance before coming out above ground. He peered up through a cutout as though he could see something there. "I feel them," he said, and everyone quieted to let him sense. "They are angry. Their anger is directed to this place."

Nebo stood. "They come to execute Morgan," he said. "His life, and perhaps our own, is now left to the whim of the mob."

"No!" Serge said loudly. "Morgan will not die without Serge to help him."

"There is a way," Nebo said, "that we can help Morgan without anyone having to die."

Morgan swung around to face Nebo. "Say it, then."

"They've entered the building," the one with the large ears said.

"How many?" Nebo asked.

The man stared at him. He had a long angular face with a large jawbone to support so much ear. His face seemed stretched out from the bottom. "More than I can count," he said.

"Now's the time, Mech," Morgan said.

"The vote hasn't been taken," Nebo said. "To help you implies risk for us."

Morgan began to hobble off. "Stay back here, all of you," he said. "It's only me they want. I'll meet them at the entry bars."

He left the circle of light and wandered off into the darkness.

"No," El-tron's voice followed him.

Morgan turned to stare back toward the fire. "The time grows short," was all he said.

"I vote we make him one of the People," El-tron said. "He's shown the capacity to be trusted. Besides, if anyone can figure a way out of here, it would be the human. I do not share Nebo's contentment."

With El-tron's resolve broken, the rest of the society of mud dwellers fell in with the vote.

"Come back quickly," Nebo said.

Morgan hobbled back to stand before them. "You have my thanks," he said, "and my undying loyalty."

"They approach the dungeon," the man with the ears said.

"Quickly," Nebo said. "Help him to a distant pillar and secret him. Serge, pile those bones you scattered earlier."

Squan moved to take Morgan by the arm. "We'll walk together," he said.

"Thanks, friend," Morgan said, feeling more comfortable and secure with these outcast progeny of Ibem than he ever did with his own kind. Perhaps, he realized finally, that they all understood what it meant to be alone.

They moved off together, Nebo's voice still drifting to him. "All of you, go about your business. Put a full complement on the wheel."

Squan moved with sure steps through the muddy darkness. Morgan couldn't see him at all. He could only feel the Genie's hand on his arm, his catlike claws digging a bit into him.

There was commotion behind—the clanging of swords, the voices of many men.

"Get me to the nearest pillar," Morgan said.

"We have not gone too far," Squan said.

"I don't care. If Nebo is wrong, I want to be able to lend a hand."

Squan stopped walking. "I feel your feelings," he said, "and recognize them. Reach out your hand."

Morgan did so, touching brick. A pillar. Feeling his way around it, he turned back toward Nebo's fire twenty feet distant.

The dungeon began filling with light from the distance, like the first dawn of the beginning of time. It chased the darkness, and the thousands of rats that thrived there. As they scattered, the ground undulated with them—a living, rolling ocean.

Nebo returned to his chair, Serge at his side. Perhaps fifty torches were moving toward them. Morgan smiled. Ramon was taking no chances with him this time.

It was Ramon with his knights. They all wore armor and had weapons drawn. He could make out his brother's voice.

"Spread out and search," he called, the words echoing through the long, low room. "But stay in contact with others. Don't wander off by yourself."

Morgan could see their faces, full of hate and revulsion. He had to hold down the urge to try and fight them all right now. They wore their helmets. Ramon's long plume dragged in the mud.

Ramon was attracted to Nebo's fire. He and a company of men moved cautiously toward it. Morgan watched Serge clench his fists. Then he saw Nebo put up an arm to stop him.

The exchange rang clearly through the dungeon. "You have fire, boy," Ramon said to Nebo. "What do you burn?"

Nebo addressed him in his quiet, melodious tones. "We burn what comes down the drop hole."

Ramon laughed shrilly and turned to his fellows. "The bastards burn our shit and garbage!" he hollered, and mean laughter filled the dungeon. "They probably eat it too!"

"Not always," Nebo replied.

Ramon turned back to him, suddenly serious. "The human we put down here last night," he said.

"With the red hair?" Nebo asked.

"Where is he hiding?"

"We found him this morning by the bars," Nebo said.

"Where is he?"

"He's dead, sir."

The lights drifted around the dungeon in small clusters. They were beginning to get very close to Morgan.

"I want to see the body," Ramon said with determination.

"I'm afraid that is quite impossible," Nebo said.

"Because he's not dead," Ramon said with contempt.

"Because we ate him," Nebo said, pointing to the pile of bones by the fire alongside the remnants of Morgan's meal. "He was very tasty."

Ramon looked suspiciously at the pile of bones, then walked to kneel beside them. Picking up the discarded bowl, he brought it to his nose, sniffing with distaste.

"You don't feed us very much," Nebo said.

Ramon turned and watched his men picking their way through the dungeon, their torches bringing light to the stench of the place. It was almost a shame that the farmer hadn't lived long enough to experience such degradation. Morgan's skull lay among the pile of bones, grinning up at him, making him shiver in disgust.

He stood and dumped the rest of the meat into the fire. Turning, he cupped his hands and yelled, "Come on back! We're through looking!"

The torches retreated a minute before finding Morgan's pillar. Ramon sheathed his sword and stood with his hands on his hips, waiting for his men to assemble.

"He's dead," the Governor said. "They ate him."

They all laughed then, and Morgan thought he detected a large amount of relief. "Let's leave them the other one," someone said. "They may still be hungry."

"Excellent idea," Ramon said. "Bring the bundle."

A knight in red staggered into the firelight. He carried a heavy bundle on his shoulder, which he let drop gratefully to splash mud in all directions.

His business finished, Ramon strode away, back where he came from. His knights followed quickly behind, anxious to leave the place.

"It worked," Morgan said.

"They believe the story," Squan said. "They believed what wasn't the truth."

"Humans don't know how to tell the truth," Morgan said. "How could they know how to listen to it?"

They moved from behind the pillar and back to the fire. The

Genies were filtering back, laughing and excited, motivated by their small victory over the humans. Only Morgan wasn't drawn to the merriment. He was too caught up in the package that was the size of a grown person.

Kneeling beside it, he gently unwrapped the canvas tarpaulin to find his mother. Leaning over, he kissed her cold lips and shut her unseeing eyes. The dungeon had gotten quiet, and Morgan looked up to see them all staring, tears in their eyes, tears that he wasn't able to cry.

"Do you see what they've done?" he said hoarsely. "Do you see?"

They all saw and understood.

"Why?" he asked. "For what reason did this happen?"

Serge walked up and put a large hand on his shoulder. "U-mans," was all he said.

Morgan sat with his mother for several hours, and when he could bear it no longer, he made a funeral pyre and burned her body because there was no place to bury it properly in the mud.

Part II

◇

MORGAN

X
The Sword of Vengeance

Morgan stood watching as Serge bathed Nebo. The Mech stood in his alcove stripped naked, his body as smooth and unlined as his face. He stood straight among the squares of sunlight that pierced the thick wall to checkerboard the ground. The giant poured a bucketful of rainwater over the smooth man's head to splash into the mud covering his feet.

"No, no," Nebo said, in his quiet patient tones. "Ibem had nothing to do with the creation of the forests. It was the fault of men, of human men."

Morgan tugged on the fire-red beard that had grown long during his months of captivity. He knew better than to condemn the feelings of the Mech without hearing them to conclusion.

"How could such happen if not by the will of God?"

The alcove was filled with those who weren't on duty pushing the wheel. They stood or sat in the mud, listening intently, as they always did when Morgan and Nebo talked of life. Morgan had discovered over the course of time that most of the Genies had very little understanding of themselves or their world. They were all directed brilliantly in specific areas, but usually undirected personally. But Nebo—he was a different story: He seemed to know everything there was to know. He simply had no personal drive to accomplish anything save the continued acquisition of knowledge.

"When Genies and men fought the Great War," the Mech said, "it was probably too late to save the Earth from the trees. The damage had already been done; the fighting was more a form of mass frustration than anything else. Genies and men hated one another, each blaming the other for the bottled up heat that made the forests and changed everyone's life."

"Then it was the war, and not the forests, that made the ancients crumble?"

"In a sense. The war was bitter, Genies using the knowledge of the ages to produce warlike variations of their own kind who, in turn, produced horrible weapons to wage a war of extermination. Those weapons produced even more heat, adding to the fund of troubles. The War lasted for nearly twenty years, and when it was finished, so was civilization. Once the backbone of mankind was broken, the trees kept it broken. The world has not budged an inch in a thousand years."

"As Ibem intends," Morgan said.

Nebo slowly closed, then opened his eyes. "As you wish."

Serge began rubbing Nebo's body rapidly with his huge hands, drying him. As near as Morgan could understand, giants were born with a natural desire to serve the will of a Mech. He didn't know why that was so, just that it was. Nebo and Serge were as one person, with Nebo being the brain and Serge the muscle.

"You say that men made Genies," Morgan said. "How could one man make another man? Only God can do that."

Serge finished drying Nebo and the Mech held his arms straight up while the giant slipped his robe back over his head.

"They removed the eggs surgically from women's bodies," Nebo continued as his robe fluttered into place, "and altered their structure, impregnating them with altered male sperm. Then they simply put the fertilized eggs back into the women to carry to term. After a generation of this, Genies were simply mated with one another."

Morgan looked at Serge and laughed. "How about giants?" he said, pointing. "Giants couldn't have been made the way you say."

Nebo nodded. "It probably took several generations, each a little larger than the one before, but it could certainly be done. Giants were very valuable at one time simply because of the difficulty in breeding them that large."

"And how could they get women to do the perverted things you're talking about?"

"They paid them money," Nebo returned.

Morgan nodded his head thoughtfully. "I don't believe you," he said.

Nebo smiled. "I didn't suspect you would. It's of no consequence really."

A light moved through the darkness toward them. It was Squan, returning from his watch at the entry bars. Nebo called the fire rocks that they burned "coal" and told Morgan once that the dungeon was carved into a deposit of it.

"Morgan," Squan said. "A human woman waits at the bars."

"Waits for whom?" Morgan asked, for he had gradually taken Nebo's place as leader, mostly at the Mech's insistence.

Cat eyes looked back and forth. "She said she wishes to speak with someone about Morgan of Siler."

Morgan and Nebo shared a look. No one outside the dungeon knew he was still alive. He had simply assumed that his memory had died also.

"Has she a name?"

"She did not give it," Squan returned. "From her dress, I think she is a Castle servant."

"We will have Nebo speak with her," he concluded. "But cautiously."

The Mech nodded.

"I'll stay a distance behind and listen," Morgan said, and they walked off together. Several Minnies crowded around Morgan, walking with him, holding onto him. They loved him like children because he usually took up their side when they had any of their continual disputes with the other Genies. They spoke a strange mixture of machine bleeps and tech jargon that he could barely understand, but they all seemed to reach empathy on some deeper, inner level.

"Too much time has passed for this to be some manner of trick," Nebo said. "They are convinced you are dead."

"Which makes this visit all the more interesting," Morgan said.

He walked with sure steps through the darkness, the Minnies returning to the light one at a time. Even though he could see nothing, time had etched a roadmap in his mind. He was perfectly at home in the dungeon, a thought that disturbed him sometimes.

He had spent a long time attempting escape, but the bars were the only route out and they had proved impassable. Food, when there was food, was passed through a small opening in the bars. No one had unlocked the dungeon since the day Ramon had come to search for him.

His anger had not abated since Zenna's death, but having nowhere to turn it, he simply placed it in the back of his mind and flowed half asleep through his life—since that was the only alternative that seemed available to him. He felt vaguely uneasy about this meeting. It smacked of stirring up the mud in already-cleared water.

He became dimly aware of a light in the distance. It was the flickering torchlight of the dungeoneers' station that connected up to the dungeon by a long hallway. As they approached the hall, Morgan could make out the vague form of a woman, back-lighted, waiting by the bars.

The hallway smelled dank and cavelike. Its ceiling was high and rounded, set off by vaulted arches of brick that cast deep, criss-crossed shadows in the sputtering light.

"I'll follow behind," Morgan said, "and step into the shadows when the time is right."

Nebo made no answer, but began walking the hall, which sloped up, free of mud. The woman stiffened when she heard them coming. She grabbed the bars before her.

"Who is it?" she said in a high, frightened voice.

"Fear not," Nebo responded in his pleasing tones. "I am of kindly disposition."

Morgan got within ten feet of the bars before slipping behind one of the arches and peering around it to see their visitor.

It was Ona, the girl he had saved from Redrick at the banquet. She looked good, and he realized it was mostly because she wasn't covered with mud.

Nebo moved right up to the bars. "You wished to speak with me?"

She cringed slightly from him, then straightened and moved right up to the bars again. "Do you remember the human who was brought down here several months ago?" she asked.

"Perhaps," Nebo answered. "Where are the dungeoneers?"

"They attend the parade," she said. "More troops arrive today from Troy. Ramon wanted everyone to turn out."

"What do you wish from me?"

"They say the human died," she replied. "Is that true?"

"Yes."

Her face darkened, tears welling up in her eyes. "Did you . . . know him at all?" she asked, half sobbing.

"Slightly," Nebo said. "He did not remain long with us."

"I have . . . something that belonged to him. I wanted to give . . . no, place it with . . . his body if possible."

"Why?"

"He helped me out once, risked himself for me." She began looking around nervously. "I wanted to return that favor some-how."

Morgan could stand listening no longer. He stepped out of the darkness, striding up to the bars. "Ona," he said, putting his face up to the slats.

She didn't recognize him with the beard immediately, then

her face exploded with happiness. "Morgan!" she exclaimed. "You're alive!"

"Something like it," he said, his hands unable to wrap themselves completely around the thick, heavy bars. "What happens on the outside?"

"Ramon prepares for major war," she said. "He keeps calling it a Crusade, but the gossip hints at something much larger."

"The Jewel of the East," Morgan muttered.

"What?"

"Nothing. What of you? How do you fare?"

She lowered her eyes. "They've had their way with me," she said softly. "Ramon and his knights. I've done things I dare not even remember. Castle Alb'ny has become a place of evil."

He stretched a hand through the bars and lifted her chin until their eyes met. "They take only your body," he said. "You're free inside, and you will soon again be free outside."

And as he looked into her frightened face, he realized that it was time for him to leave the dungeon, one way or the other. He owed a debt of blood to Ramon Delaga, and until it was paid, he would feel at least partially responsible for the dishonor caused by his brother. The blackness of despair had settled over him like the cover of the night that he lived in. But despair was a shrub with shallow roots. He need only rip them up and take control of his own life.

"I brought you something," she said, her eyes brightening with the residue of his strength.

Lifting her floor-length gown, she pulled out the sword she had hidden beneath it—the sword with the boar's head hilt. His eyes widened as she passed it through the bars to him. And when he touched it, he felt the power course through him. He laughed loudly as he wagged it around.

"I managed to get it during the fight at the banquet," she told him. "Afterwards, Ramon looked everywhere for it. He became enraged when it couldn't be found. It was so important to him that I determined he'd never have it. Then I thought to bring it here, perhaps lay it to rest with you."

"It will do very little resting," Morgan said, then moved back to the bars. "You have done a fine and brave thing. My thanks go with you."

"You're the only one who's tried to protect me," she said. "Even my parents say I must bend to Ramon's will at all times."

"I leave this place soon," he said, inspired but not enlightened. "My Genie friends and I are going to escape. You may go with me if you will."

"You would take me?"

Morgan stuck his head between the cold slats again. "Your heart is pure," he said. "I would take you from Hell itself."

She moved up to the bars and kissed him quickly on the lips. "There is nothing for me here," she said. "My parents have all but disowned me, the men of the village would have none like me, and I fear they tire of me at the Castle."

"We leave in a few days," he said. "Will you help me?"

"Anything."

"Go first to Grodin and tell him that I live."

"Grodin?" she asked, a catch in her voice.

He saw her look and feared. "Nothing has happened to him?"

She shook her head. "No. He is . . . well."

"Go to him. Tell him I live and that I want to leave here on Murdock. Tell him I want him to come with us too."

Her face still looked odd, something he simply couldn't put his finger on. "I will do as you ask," she said.

"Don't risk coming down here again," he said. He looked at Nebo. "Do you read our language?"

"I read all languages," the Mech replied.

Morgan nodded and turned back to Ona. "If you need to tell me anything, drop messages down the air holes to the dungeon. If we have any return, we will poke them up to you wih a stick. Now go. Don't ever risk coming down here again."

She nodded, happy to have someone she could believe in, even if he was locked in a dungeon and looked like a beggar. They shared one long look, then she turned and ran from the dungeoneers' watch and back up the stairs to the Castle proper.

Morgan spun away from the thick bars. He made the blade dance in the air laughing the entire time. Torchlight slipped up and down the highly-polished silver, and it seemed a living thing in his hands. He knew he was finished with grieving, but not with vengeance. It was as if he had just awakened from a long sleep.

"Is there something I haven't been informed of?" Nebo asked.

"What?" Morgan replied, his eyes fixed trancelike on his sword.

"You said we'd escape in a few days."

"Yes," Morgan said, smiling wide. "I just had a wonderful idea."

XI
The Green Woman

The wind blew hot, but at least there was wind, and the rain hadn't plagued them for several weeks. No rain meant that the courtyard dried out, cracking like a barren river bed. It also meant that Ramon was able to move his schedule along quickly, for the weather wasn't supervising his activities. As Ramon Delaga stood atop the Castle steps watching the processional from Troy march through his wide gates, he was convinced that the fair weather was a sign from Ibem that he was pursuing the proper course. Sign or not though, he was forging ahead.

Troy's colors were pure white, bleached as bright as they could make them. Their legends spoke of a time once, in the Before Time, their badly outnumbered army marched out to do battle with superior Genie forces; there was a Sun then, brilliant fire, and it reflected so brightly from their white uniforms that it blinded the Genies and routed them. Forever after, white remained the color of Troy, a large square Sun its symbol.

It was white that marched through the gates then, two legions of white that must have included nearly every male in the province. Troy loved its Crusades, but more than that, Hurtrain Nef, the young Mayor of Troy, saw in Alb'ny's ambitions the chance to carve a dynasty for himself.

His carriage was plated with white gold and would have been covered with garlands of white carnations, except that Alb'ny didn't allow them within the walls. The carriage was drawn by a team of pure-white long-nosed Woofers, who pranced lightly, proud heads erect. Cages full of doves were released upon Nef's entry, and it was quite an imposing sight to watch thousands of the white birds fluttering madly above the courtyard as the legions of Troy sang their war chants in thundering bass voices, and the crowds already assembled screamed out their affection for the pageantry and high emotion.

"How do we feed all these stomachs?" Jerlynn said.

"Smile, Mother," Ramon replied.

Jerlynn and Faf stood at his right hand as protocol demanded. Pack, the Physician, stood at Ramon's left hand. And he was an addition that was purely Ramon's.

"The harvest will only go so far," Jerlynn persisted. "What do we eat when it's gone?"

"We will take as we travel," Ramon said, a smile permanently etched upon his face. He opened his arms wide, welcoming his ally.

"When one takes it is charity," Dixon Faf said sternly. "When thousands take it is felony."

"War is above ordinary considerations," Ramon replied over his shoulder. "I avenge the brutal murder of my father."

The inner courtyard was jammed with the people of Alb'ny, gathering at Ramon's insistence to cheer on his army, the largest human force assembled in a thousand years. The outer courtyard was filled with the troops themselves, close to thirty thousand and still growing. The North smelled a change in the air, and hurried to ripple themselves in the proper wind before they were blown asunder.

Nef, blond haired and bearded, had his carriage stop before the stairs. He wore a tight white jumper beneath his cobweb armor. He stood, waving to the crowd, then climbed down. Ramon watched him fearfully, for if there was ever anyone to challenge his leadership in an undertaking of this size it would be Nef. Troy was the second largest kingdom in N'ork and the Mayor's battlefield experience was exceptionally great for a man his age.

A woman sat beside Nef in the carriage, a woman in green. She wore layers of green, filmy robes above a body of pale green. Her eyes were green, her lips and nails a slightly darker shade of the same green as her skin. Her hair was jet black and tangled wildly all the way down her back. She stared defiantly up at him, as if with a secret knowledge, and she seemed to him an exquisite wild beast, dangerously sensuous and untamable.

"Ramon!" Nef called loudly as he walked slowly up the stairs, arms outstretched. "I told you I'd return with the power of Troy!"

Ramon moved down the stairs to meet him halfway. "You honor and astound us with your sincerity!" Ramon bellowed back, for this show was strictly for the crowds. "I am humbled before you!"

They met on the stairs, embracing with largess, though Ramon was careful to remain always on a step above wherever Nef stood. The men kissed on the lips, then parted.

"Welcome to my house!" Ramon said. "Come within and rest from your journey, share my hospitality."

"I gratefully accept," Nef said with an exaggerated bow.

As Nef bowed, Ramon looked over his back to the woman who still stared at him from the carriage. "Is that your Physician?" he asked, when Nef straightened.

The man nodded. "Please don't be offended by her choice of colors," he said apologetically. "She has always been thus."

Ramon continued to stare at her. "It is a new age," was all he said. "Invite her within. I will also have words for the Physicians."

Nef drew in his brows, but his smile remained warm. "As you wish," he said.

"What is she called?" Ramon inquired.

Nef turned and looked at her quickly, motioning her down from the carriage. "She is known only as the Green Woman," he said.

She joined them quickly, her manner hot and liquid. Ramon was enthralled.

"I have heard much about the new Governor of Alb'ny," she said, bowing slightly with her head. "It is an honor to meet you."

He took her hand, patted it. "You wear the colors of the hated forest."

"We only hate what we fear," she answered, eyes flashing with quick wit. Her hand seemed to become hot within his and he dropped it.

"Come in out of the heat," he said. "In Alb'ny we, at least, do not fear that."

A smiled flashed across her lips as quickly as lightning, and Ramon had to force himself to remember that Hurtrain Nef was even there.

Turning, he led them back up to the steps and introduced everyone, Pack and the Green Woman sharing a look of distrust when they shook hands. Ramon noted that it was always that way when Physicians met, and determined that something would have to be done about that particular situation.

Introductions finished, he led them inside the Castle, wrapping them in its coolness.

"From whence does the cold air come?" the Green Woman asked.

"I'll explain it to you later," Pack told her.

"No, no," Ramon said. "We are proud of our accomplishment and the Physician who keeps it working. We'll show it now."

They walked through the darkness of the first floor, stopping before a doorway that was locked and barred, a large skull with crossed bones painted upon it, realistically rendered by the late, unlamented, court recorder.

Ramon pulled a large ring of keys from the folds of his rab cape. "Only Pack and I are allowed in this room," he said, opening the first of a series of locks. "Very few people have actually seen inside."

"We are honored;" Nef said without much enthusiasm, for what he truly wished to do was sit on something that was not moving and put his feet up.

Ramon worked the locks, finally creaking the door open. He had to push hard, and the opening of the door was accompanied by loud cracking.

"The room of winter," Ramon said and ushered them in.

The entire room was coated with a large sheath of ice. The cracking they had heard was the ice breaking that had formed over the doorway. Many large pipes criss-crossed the room, white, opaque ice dripping from them. And there was wind!

A huge bladed machine turned quickly in blurred circles, generating a tremendous wind. It sat before a hole in the wall that contained a conduit of some kind.

"The room of winter makes the cold," Ramon said, as they all wrapped their arms around themselves for warmth.

"Refrigeration," Pack said.

"The devil's tool," Faf said.

"The machine blows the cold air through that hole," Ramon said pointing, "and it is carried through many pipes to blow into the entire Castle."

"Where do you get the power to run this?" the Green Woman asked, walking up close to examine the wooden fan.

"From the generator, of course," Ramon said, proud of his knowledge of things scientific.

"Where does the generator get the power?" the Green Woman persisted.

"What?" Ramon said.

"We store kinetic energy," Pack answered for him. "There is a wheel in the dungeon that is turned by its inhabitants. Their energy is stored in the generator, which runs the refrigerator and the fan."

The Green Woman nodded her head slowly, her eyes wide. "Pragmatic," she said.

"I'm cold," Jerlynn said, and she was shivering violently. Faf put an arm around her.

"It's probably not good to leave the door open," he said.

"You don't know anything about it," Pack said venomously.

"Watch your tone, little man," Faf told him.

"I could use some wine," Nef said. "The dust is thick on my tongue."

"Then wine it is!" Ramon bellowed, leading them all from the room and locking it carefully behind.

Ona picked her way carefully through the throngs that had gathered to welcome the incoming troops. It seemed the major preoccupation and career of the people of Alb'ny any more. In fact, many of the farmers had given up the soil completely in order to set up vendor booths in the outer courtyard to provide goods and services to the armies camped there.

She moved all the way to the wall and walked a long way around it to Grodin's hut, watching carefully to see if she was being watched. Ramon tended to keep a close eye on the Castle staff, lest their gossip escape to the outside.

She had grown to hate Ramon whom she at one time had admired. When he put his hands on her, it was all she could do to keep from retching. Many of the girls from the village had taken to selling themselves to the troops in the outer courtyard, for in truth, a great deal of gold could be accumulated quickly that way. Ona despised them for their willingness, especially since she had no choice nor made any profit from Ramon's knights; but even the crass life of the courtesan looked better to her than the hell she was forced to live in every day.

She stood by the gate until she saw the Mayor of Rome and the Governor disappear into the Castle. Only then did she feel safe enough to approach the old man's lodging.

Grodin had been a total recluse since the day of the old Governor's funeral, and word in the Castle had it that he had become unhinged. She would find out.

She hurried up the slope to the kennels, keeping her head fixed straight ahead, and wondering what excuse she'd make if she were caught there. Then, with shame, she realized that she could say she was there to play the two-backed beast for money and that no one would even question it.

She found the old man sitting upon his bed. He was dirty, and smelled so that she stayed close by the door to get air. He had aged, years it seemed, these last months. He had been a giant once, a man who stood proud and alone. Now he was simply another broken soul, hobbling his last miles on the road of life.

They stared at one another for several seconds before either spoke.

"I can think of no good reason for you to be here," he said coldly.

"I bring you a messasge," she said.

He lay fetally on the bed, turning his face to the wall. "There are no messages that could be of interest to me."

"This one may be."

He sighed deeply. "I suppose I'll have to hear it before you'll leave?"

"I made a promise."

Ona had never seen walking death before, never knew that it was possible to have physical substance and still not exist. "The red-haired man sent me," she said quietly.

He did not respond.

"Did you not hear me?"

"Did Ramon put you up to this cruel folly?" he said in a broken voice, face still turned away.

"It's no folly," she said. "Morgan lives."

He turned slowly to her then, sitting up at the same time. His face had changed; it was lined with anger. "Who told you that?"

She met his eyes defiantly. "No one," she said. "I just saw him, spoke with him."

"It's not true."

She nodded. "Apparently he made friends in the dungeon and they hid him from Ramon."

Grodin stood, walking to her. He grabbed her arms roughly, shaking her. "If you're lying, so help me, I'll rip out your miserable throat."

"He has a beard now," she said, and wrenched herself away from his grasp. "I brought him his sword. He says he is leaving and wants you to go with him."

The anger in the old man's eyes melted away completely, leaving only the fear behind. "He wants me?"

"He apparently doesn't know that . . ."

"That I killed his mother."

Ona lowered her eyes.

"You didn't tell him?"

"It wasn't my place."

He turned and paced the small room. He was agitated, vibrating nervously. "Why do you help him?" he asked after a moment.

"He helped me once," she said, "when no one else would. He's promised to take me with him also."

Grodin smiled and it lit up his leathery face. "You see it too, don't you?"

"I don't know what you mean."

"Yes you do," he said. "It's something that you can't put your finger on, something that seems . . . bigger than all of this."

She smiled back. She did feel what the man said. An aura of grandeur seemed to surround Morgan of Siler. It was a physical sensation, but it was something greater than that, something indefinable. "He has greatness in him," she said at last.

And purity of spirit," Grodin said. "And he wants me to go with him?"

She nodded, still smiling. "He says he wants to leave on Murdock."

"Ha!" Grodin clapped his hands loudly. "That's Morgan all right." He pointed a bony finger at her. "He can have Murdock and every other Woofer in the place if he wants."

"There are Genies down there with him," Ona said. "I think he intends to take them also."

Grodin narrowed his eyes and frowned. "Why?"

She shrugged. "Maybe they helped him like he helped me."

He stood, deep in thought for a moment. Finally he raised his hands as if to toss away his doubts. "We very seldom get to choose our traveling companions through life," he said.

"Then you'll come?"

"That depends on you, doesn't it?" he asked. "Will you tell him about me?"

"Only if you want me to," she replied. "But I think that you should tell him."

"I will," he answered. "But not until the time is right."

The model of the boat sat in the center of the huge table, commanding the attention of anyone who sat upon the high-backed velvet-covered chairs that surrounded it. It was a beautiful ship with a high prow that curved into a serpent's head with glaring red eyes. The model had no sails; it was only designed to go downriver.

Ramon sat at table with Pack, not speaking of the boat with his most powerful allies and their Physicians. Besides Nef and the Green Woman there was old Councilman Reeder with the cancerous nose from Watervliet and his Physician, Dunbar, whose face was painted in bright swirls of color. There was Senator

Murray from Cohoes, who seemed darkly and quietly sinister when he was actually darkly and quietly stupid. Murray's Physician was an immense, fat man named Jerico who dressed in bird feathers and continuously played with a small squirrel that was attached to his belt on a thin, gold chain. The gathering was rounded out by Count Delmar of Delmar, a foppish dandy whose silver hair hung in large ringlets over the triple lace of his high collar. Delmar carried a perfumed handkerchief that resided in his lavender laced cuffs when it wasn't fluttering around his nose like dandelion fluff in the warm breeze. Delmar, despite his feminine ways, was the most vicious and deadly swordsman Ramon had ever seen. His Physician was a mean-spirited hunchback named Scab, who wore a patch on his left eye and dressed always in black tights and high red boots.

And there was one other.

At Ramon's right hand sat Redrick of Firetree, tapping on the table with a gleaming silver hook where a swordhand used to be. Since his inglorious defeat at Morgan's hands, Redrick had become Ramon's closest companion. So anxious was he to undo his humiliation that he would do anything Ramon asked without question. Ramon despised the man, and was, in fact, repulsed by him; but it would be a sin to let such loyalty go to waste. He knew he could trust Redrick in all things, and such trust needed to be exploited at every opportunity.

Ramon was speaking in his smooth, persuasive fashion. "A force unknown in our racial memory sits at this moment upon the baked earth of my castle yard. They wait, gentlemen and lady, to do our bidding in all things."

He picked up his wine crock to drink, but it was empty. Turning to Redrick, he arched an eyebrow. The man quickly jumped to his feet and refilled the crock from a pitcher set on the sidebar. Ramon took up his crock without thanks.

"Would it not be a shame if we let this opportune moment in history slip through our fingers?"

Councilman Reeder breathed loudly at all times. Now he drew in a raspy, pleuritic wheeze and spoke. "What do you speak of? I see this moment no more historically than any other moment in my day of days, which now number a great many and cannot number many more. What is it you ask and offer?"

Ramon leaned across the table. "We gathered a mighty Crusade in our grief over my father's untimely death," he said. "Unwittingly and with hot blood, we emptied out coffers in order to quest after our own human heritage. We pledged to rid our land of Genies forever, and in so doing, secure our own freedom from their blight."

Count Delmar lovingly stroked his smooth cheek with his handkerchief. "Is that not what we do here?" he asked in a high voice. "What else is there?"

Nef looked at Ramon with half a smile. "I think that our friend is asking us to broaden our base," he said. "In all honesty, we mount our Crusades also to loot the Genie cities when we find them."

"The spoils of war," Senator Murray said angrily. "That is our due."

"I do not argue that point certainly," Ramon said. "But now we must be realistic. This expedition will cost most of us the wealth of our coffers, will it not?"

They all sat staring at the tabletop, none willing to admit the fact that all of them were aware of.

"Now," Ramon continued. "With a force as large and as scattered as ours, how much booty can any of us reasonably expect to carry away with us? I say that we will be extremely lucky— *lucky*—to get out of debt with this venture."

"That does not sit well, Sir," old Reeder wheezed. "I wish not to spend my declining days in poverty over a few miserable Genies."

"Nor do any of us," Nef suggested. "But now that we are committed, what will we do?"

Murray's eyes opened wide, as if he had just awakened from a lifetime's sleep. "And my farmers are all in your army!" he exclaimed, having never considered that fact. "Who will do my planting?"

They bantered back and forth like that, Ramon sitting back to share a look with a twinkle-eyed Pack before bringing forth his dream.

"I suggest," the Governor said at last, "that we expand our horizons."

"How so?" Count Delmar squeaked.

"A sweep of the South, gentlemen . . . and lady." He caught the Green Woman's eyes, and she tried to hold him there with near success. "We have no friends in the South. They have given themselves over to the trees like beasts."

He stood, walking around the table to touch each of them as he spoke. "I suggest we rush like a tide through the Southern provinces, taking what we will, conquering, expanding our territory and peoples, killing Genies as we go." His voice was building, the force of his own dreams carrying the will of those around him. "As we conquer the South, we can cut off the food supplies to N'ork City where we will culminate our campaign, adding the Jewel of the East to the pinnacle of our crown."

"N'ork City?" Reeder snorted. "You must be insane . . . or worse."

"Why?" Ramon countered, walking up behind the man to put his hands on his shoulders. "We have a force. We'll have the momentum. And if we cut off their trade routes, they'll have no supplies. Think of the area we'll rule, the five of us. Think of the wealth. . . ."

Nef jumped in quickly. "We have the power in our hands right now," he said. "Ramon's right. We'd be fools not to use it."

"Easy for you to say," Reeder replied. "You're young. You could rebound from failure."

"You silly man," Delmar said, waving his handkerchief at Reeder's eaten-away nose. "What have you to lose? You're pounding on death's door now, screaming for admittance."

Reeder's face turned the color of a blood boil. "I hear not the remarks of one who rides side saddle!"

Delmar stood abruptly, with a toss of his head. "We may settle this in this very room," he said, his handkerchief hand resting on the hilt of his sword.

Ramon moved to him, staying his hand. "Sit, my friend," he said, guiding Delmar gently back to his chair. He walked slowly back to sit himself. Fitting his fingers together he spoke quietly to Reeder. "Let me put it this way. What happens to you if everyone else decides to go along with the idea?"

"Life will go on as before," Reeder said stubbornly.

Ramon shook his head slowly. "There are two kinds of people in my life," he said. "Friends and enemies."

Reeder breathed loudly, but said nothing.

"The only thing that concerns me," Nef said, "is how to keep from losing our forces to the jungles. The roads are not kept up in the South."

That's when Ramon pointed to the boat. "We take the river," he said. "Father Hus will speed us to our destination. I have already taken the liberty of beginning construction near the river. We will use their wood, make the jungles work for us."

"Boats," Murray sighed.

"Five boats," Ramon said. "A flagship commanded by me. Each of you to command another."

The Physicians who seemed useless to the proceedings were

suddenly wide awake and attentive, leaning over the table to stare at the boat.

"Go ahead," Ramon urged, "take a close look."

The boat was passed around, the Physicians handling it like children with a new toy. Rulers tended to listen to their Physicians, and Physicians were enamored with anything progressive. It was their nature. Then Ramon added the icing.

"I feel that it is nothing less than a new age we are ushering in," he said. "A new age demands new ideas. That's why the Physicians were invited to this gathering. What I suggest is a Physician pool with the freedom and resources to develop new ideas for us."

"Like . . . machines?" Murray said.

"Machines of war," Ramon responded. "Machines of conquest. Ultimately, machines of peace. It is time to put behind us the old ways. We will forge a new world, and the hands on the tiller will be our own."

And Ramon Delaga, Governor of Alb'ny and its provinces, watched the inner light glow from the eyes of the Physicians.

XII
Shadows in the Night

The rain came the night of Hurtrain Nef's arrival in Alb'ny. It bloated the sky full like a fat goose, and when it fell, it was as if some celestial knife had slit the fat goose belly and splashed the innards onto the land in monstrous conflagration.

To the east of Castle Alb'ny, near the raging life of Father Hus, the newborn skeletons of mighty river ships stood out like prison bars in the bright flashing white-lightning night and withstood Heaven's rigors in silent determination. Ibem had done what He could.

In the catacombs of Alb'ny, Morgan watched the Genies giggle and play in the steady rush of water that charged through vent openings in the dungeon wall. There was lightning behind the water, making it look like streams of wet light.

Morgan clutched in his hand a note that Ona had passed down earlier saying that Grodin was ready and the Woofers were theirs. Upon reading the message, the dungeon immediately had become unbearable to him. It was time to be about his business. He wondered what dark thoughts were running through the minds of the beasts who lived above him. He took heart in the knowledge that whatever Ramon was thinking, it would soon be surplanted by thoughts of him.

Above, in the darkness of the banquet hall, the Lady Jerlynn and Dixon Faf sat hidden behind remnants of the float, a single candle burning, its light trying futilely to stretch warm tentacles into the vast darkness surrounding them. A continual drumlike pounding echoed through the large hall as the insistent fingers of rain pounded upon the taut skin of the castle.

"I feel like a thief," Jerlynn said, her face yellow orange in the candle's glow. "Hiding within my own house."

Faf reached out and took her hands within his own, his large, dry paws gently and a little awkwardly caressing the softness of her delicate fingers. "I grieve for the situation, my Lady," he said, trying unsuccessfully to whisper in his own gruff way. "But I fear for your safety otherwise. These are troubled times."

She smiled thinly. "You are a comfort to me. Thank you."

He looked steadily at her, melting under the vulnerability he saw there. "I need no thanks for doing what gives me the greatest pleasure I have known in my lifetime," he said, and brought her hand up to his dry lips. He kissed her hand quickly, feeling immediately embarrassed by the liberty.

"What is going to become of us?" Jerlynn asked after a moment of uneasy silence.

He shook his head. "Ramon has ambitions that I fear will be the undoing of us all."

"Why did he allow Physicians into his conference today?" she asked. "I have never heard of such a thing."

He released her hands and stood, peering over the floor of the float into the darkness of the hall. "Your son conspires with the ungodly," he said sternly, and he couldn't keep the just anger from his voice. "We have lived in peace, by the laws of God, for nearly two score generations, and now Ramon conspires with those who would have us turn away from all that. I fear he plans progress."

"No," Jerlynn moaned. "Where does he get these notions? I never raised him that way."

"Everyone follows his own light," the Programmer responded, and his thoughts turned to the prize he had killed for. "Ramon burns with desires that no mortal should ever have."

"Like his father," Jerlynn replied softly, and Faf turned to look at her, so small and frail and alone. "Already I see Alb'ny changing, rotting from the inside like my beloved Rensselaer. And the men, the blood hot with anticipation, their eyes brimming with lust . . ."

"Don't fret yourself," Faf interrupted. "We must keep our heads in this venture or Ramon will remove them for us."

"What venture do you speak of?" Jerlynn asked.

Faf turned away from her again. "A poor choice of words, M'lady," he said, for she was, in truth, not prepared to hear what he wanted to say. Not yet. "But be it known that among my fears are ones for Ramon's soul."

She rose and approached him, laying a hand on his arm. "You see the end of things, don't you?"

He turned quickly, impulsively taking her in his arms, crushing her paper-shell body in his massive arms.

"Sir, you . . . you injure me," Jerlynn gasped.

The Programmer released her immediately, bowing his head in shame. "Please accept my apologies," he said, afraid to look at her lest he see the anger in her eyes. "I feel a . . . closeness to you that sometimes is beyond my control."

He braced himself for her fury, but instead felt a gentle hand stroke his long hair. "Dear sir," she whispered. "You honor me with your affection."

Standing on tiptoes, she kissed him quickly on the cheek before backing away. "We have much to discover, you and I," she said, "about ourselves and about the fate of our land. Let us discover them slowly, properly."

Only then did he dare to meet her gaze with his own. "Ramon has his way with the land," he said. "But he has not his way with us. We are not without power ourselves. Perhaps, with some thoughtful activity, Alb'ny can once again be the land that Rensselaer once was."

"I would cherish that above all else," she said simply.

Ramon sat on the edge of his bed looking at the model boat. He had set it upon the window casement where the lightning would flash behind it, silhouetting its lines in bold relief. He tried to picture it full size, carrying thousands of troops down Father Hus to glory.

"It's a good dream," came a voice behind him.

He jumped, startled, his first thought for his sword. Then he saw in the nearly unending chain of flashes the Green Woman standing before him.

"How did you get past the guards?"

She simply smiled in return.

He took a deep breath to calm himself, using the excuse of lighting a candle to regain his senses. That done, he tightened the sash on his sleeping robes and, fully composed, addressed her. "What brings you unannounced to my chambers?"

"Did you not want me?" she returned quietly, oblivious to his attempt at mastery.

"Why would I want you?" he returned.

She smiled and took a step toward him. "Because you are a man of extraordinary insight and intelligence," she said. "And a spirit the size of yours reaches out in kinship to a like spirit."

"The words flow easily from your lips," he replied.

"An art you practiced well in conference today."

Despite himself, he eased up, at once frightened and comfortable in this strange woman's presence. Yes, he wanted her. He had thought of little else since he had first gazed upon her mysterious ways. "Are you not Nef's woman?" he asked.

"I belong to no one," she said, and came slowly closer. "I follow my instincts."

"And your instincts bring you to me."

"Yes. At last I have found someone nearly worthy of my talents."

She stood before him, his arms snaking around her as if they had a will of their own. "I think that I am walking in quicksand," he said.

"Then don't think," she replied, and put a moistened finger to his lips.

He tasted bitterness and thought immediately that he had been poisoned.

Her eyes laughed at him. "I want you alive," she said. "I have merely given you strength, a distillation of bodily fluids."

He had very little time to contemplate her words. He had heard that there were Physicians who could make potent drugs from the secretions of a certain gland of the human body. He began to feel a tension coming over himself, a rushing of his own blood.

"You . . ." he began, but she silenced him with her warm, moist lips.

And he was, indeed, overcome with a strength he never knew he possessed. He was ethereal, removed from his body. His chambers became a dreamlike haze, the tall candle a shimmering jewel; and the flashing of the lightning became the overpowering surges of his own brain.

She was reaching for him, pulling his robe from his shoulders, cool hands gently stroking his already erect organ. And when her own clothes came off, she was soft, liquid emerald, her long nipples the same dark green of her lips.

It was she who pulled him to the bed, and for the first time in his life, it was a woman who took Ramon Delaga. She rode him amidst the lightning flashes and his disjointed mind, rode him like Morgan rode the rab when they were children. And long before they were finished, he was totally and completely addicted to the Green Woman.

He was of the damned.

XIII
Escape

Morgan had built the fires high around the wheel. He wanted light and room to walk when he addressed the Genies. They all sat, or hung from the rafters in their way, while Serge used his incredible strength to turn the wheel all alone.

Naked to the waist, Morgan had somehow managed to clean his britches to where they shone white in the firelight; he wore the boots that Grodin had given him the night of the banquet. His father's gleaming sword hung from a length of rope slung over his shoulder. He was healed and honed, the fighting spirit nearly overpowering him. All the weeks spent recuperating and grieving in the dark womb of the Keep were now but a dim memory. Every nerve of his taut body screamed for action.

It had been three days since Ona's visit to the dungeon. Three long days spent in planning and preparation. He had kept it all to himself, refusing even Nebo's usually wise council, for it was important that he work it all out himself, important that he know that he could extricate himself from his own difficulties. His plan was simple and direct, as befitting a man of action. For he had also had time to dwell on himself and his future in the months in the dungeon, deciding that until he had fulfilled the destiny his father had set out for him, and until he had attained the vengeance that was his, his only call would be to action. He was the harsh wind, blowing always, moving forever in a direction—and the direction would be toward Alb'ny.

He paced before the others, the creaking of the wheel something he never noticed anymore. The fire played upon their earnest faces, the light of innocence shining through the grime of the catacombs. These were the People, people with whom he could commune, with whom the ring of Truth was a bell, loud and stentorian.

"People of the darkness," he said, then looked at them, trying to contact every eye. "My friends. The time has come for me to leave this accursed place, for I do not feel that Destiny has placed me here to finish my days."

There were murmurs of agreement from the People, for they had all grown to love and respect the human who cared about them.

"If you wish to come with me, I welcome you gladly, but warn you that the path I follow will be dangerous and, perhaps, foolhardy."

He kept walking, moving. His body was bursting with physical tension, and movement was essential to his survival.

"I care not for the company of humans," he said. "I find in my Genie brothers the trust that humans do not know. I want for you to leave with me, for I am truly not one who seeks to be alone, and your companionship and love have been important to me."

Nebo stood solemnly in the rear of the group, trying to make sense out of the emotions going through him. He had never felt the need for anything beyond himself, yet since he had known Morgan, the urge to follow had been a growing firestorm within him.

"How do you propose escape?" he asked. "Many have thought of it before you."

Morgan smiled. "There is only one way to escape," he answered. "Through the gate at the dungeoneers' station. Our only problem, then, becomes getting them to open the gate when we want them to, instead of when they want."

"A fair estimation," Nebo returned.

"Thank you, Mech." Morgan bowed low from the waist, then straightened. "We may accomplish that goal very simply, and with the materials available to us here. First we need coal, a lot of it."

"Easily accomplished," Nebo called.

"Good. For fires, we have a natural chimney down here."

"The drop hole!" El-tron said.

"Yes," Morgan answered. "And the drop hole provides us with naturally burnable material in the form of the waste and refuse dropped down it. Nebo talked about it when Ramon came down here looking for me.

"So, we carry coal to the place and start it burning. And

believe me, it will make a smoky fire. Then we set their damned wheel on fire, so they won't have any more air blowing up there. The natural updraft of the drop hole will suck up the smoke into the Castle. They'll have to come down here to see what happened."

Morgan drew his sword, waving it in the firelight. "When they do, we'll be ready for them."

"Then what?" El-tron asked.

Morgan shrugged. "That's it. We fight our way out, take the Woofers that Grodin will provide, and make for the jungle as quickly as we can."

"Serge longs for U-man blood," the big man called from the wheel.

"As do I!" Morgan said with vehemence. "I will have vengeance. You who would follow me must know that. I do not expect anyone to walk through the fire for me, but my path will be a rugged one."

Squan, the cat man, sprang fluidly to his feet. Walking in half crouch, he turned quickly to face his compatriots. "We are a People without People," he purred. "Most of us the remnants of cultures killed by this man's father." He pointed to Morgan. "Some of us may be the last survivors of our species."

Squan reached out and put a large paw on Morgan's arm, keeping his nails retracted. "I do not understand much of the world . . . I know only feelings. I feel this human, and the pure light that radiates from his person. There is only goodness in his heart, only love for all of us. Perhaps it is time that we made a new culture together, human and Genie, Genie and Genie. Always even others of our kind have lived apart; but here, in the catacombs, we have lived together—in peace."

"A new world," Morgan said. "It is for us to make."

"What says Nebo?" asked Erbelle of the long arms.

They all turned to him, their fortress in times past. He was silent a long time before answering. "Something monumental happens here, something that reaches even beyond the scars of my own soul. I can feel it; most of you can feel it. It is the pull of Fate, the crush of history. I am a Mech, the words of the philosopher beyond my ken. I only know that I follow the human with the red hair. I follow him wherever he chooses to lead."

"Then Serge follows!" the giant screamed happily.

Morgan yelled savagely, twirling the gleaming sword above his head. "Will you come with me?"

"Yes!" they all screamed in unison. "Yes!"

* * *

Grodin took the checkered-wool saddle blanket from Ona and laid it gently over the back of the Bernard, following it with the slick brown saddle with the silver horn, his own dress saddle.

"It won't be long now," he said, a sense of excitement building within him. "The Woofers know it, too, don't you?" He nuzzled Murdock's neck, then knelt to cinch the saddle around the animal's middle. "They've been too long in the kennel. They're ready for a ride."

Ona frowned down at the old man. He had shaved and bathed and dressed in his best leathers. It was as if he were going to a party. She turned and walked to the now-closed kennel doors, the heat and the smell bottling her in. Peeking through the gaps in the wooden slats, she looked into the muddy courtyard. As always, it bustled with people. Food vendors and soldiers from ten different provinces filled the yard, trudging through the ankle-deep mud in high boots or bare feet. Beyond the yard, through the open Castle gates, an incredible tent city had sprung up, canvas structures of every color, chopped through with broad avenues and winding alleys. And thousands of men lived these streets, passing their days armed and thirsty, fighting amongst themselves and their neighbors. And she was struck by the sheer enormity of their undertaking.

"How do we get out of here?" she asked.

Grodin stood, patting Murdock on the flank. "It's done," he said, gazing down the line of thirty-five prize Bernard Woofers, all saddled and ready. Taking the Woofers was the worst way to hurt Ramon that he could think of, an unequaled humiliation before so many of his allies. It was delicious in its boldness. Moving to the empty stall, he pulled aside the large tarp that covered the cache of swords that he had stolen from the camp during the previous three nights. Lifting up an armful, he moved to each Woofer, fixing a sword in every saddle.

"You didn't answer me," Ona said, walking back near to him. "How do we even begin to get out of here?"

Grodin smiled wistfully at her. "Well, knowing Morgan," he said, "I would suspect that he'll want to charge right through the gates and hack his way to the jungle."

"That's no plan!" Ona exclaimed.

"Morgan doesn't need a plan," Grodin said with simple innocence, for he now believed the lad entirely immortal. "He has a mission."

Ona covered her face with her hands, just peeking at him over the fingertips. "You're as crazy as he is," she said, the words muffled.

He looked at her. "I'd suggest that you find some way to hitch your skirt up when we ride," he said. "Don't leave anything flapping for the soldier boys to grab hold of. Fact is, I'd tear it off and grease my legs if I were you."

"That's why you're wearing the leathers," she said.

He winked at her. "Not too dumb for an old man."

He made to move on to continue his work, but she stopped him with a hand on his arm. He stared at her, his eyes narrow, puzzled.

"Can we really make it out of here?" she asked quietly.

"How can I answer that?" he asked. "I had already died when you walked in here three days ago. I have nothing to lose. Neither do those poor bastards in the dungeon. If I die in the yard, it'll be with a smile on my face."

Ona moved close to hug him. He smelled of soap and leather. "I'm frightened," she said.

"You have a choice," he told her as he patted her gently on the back. "You can stay behind. No one knows anything about your involvement in this. You can get out now and no one will think the less of you."

She stepped back from him, surprise on her face. "I'm not that frightened," she said. "Death in the yard is still a better alternative than I have here."

"That's my girl," he said. "Now help me with these swords."

She held out her arms, and he let several of the swords slide off the top of his pile onto hers.

"How will we know when it's time?" she asked, as she walked down to start at the far end of the line.

"Don't worry," he smiled back at her. "We'll know."

"Let's go!" Morgan called to the relay line, as the heavy lumps of Nebo's fire rocks were passed down, one to the other, from the small quarry a distance from the drop hole.

"I think we've got enough," Nebo told him as they paced the line, Morgan clapping his hands and shouting encouragement.

"We had enough an hour ago," Morgan responded. "I just wanted to make sure."

They made their way down to where Serge stood in a darkened mud hole up to his waist, pulling great dark lumps of the stuff out with his bare hands.

"Make an end to it, big man," Morgan told him, and the

giant's big black eyes shone bright in the light of his small quarry fire.

"Does Serge get to kill U-mans now?" he asked with intense delight.

"Soon," Morgan said, and took the last rock from him to carry himself to the fire. "Come on out of there and go to the drop hole."

As Serge grunted himself out of the hole, Morgan and Nebo hurried back down the line to the drop hole.

"We should take our braziers with us," the Mech said. "Perhaps a little fire may prove a convenience."

Morgan nodded. "So long as we have sword hands free," he said, and looked at the Mech's dangling sleeves. "You ride with me."

They trudged to the drop hole. Morgan wound a length of cloth around his nose and mouth because of the smell, then helped Nebo with his mask. There was a floor-to-ceiling pile of feces and refuse that took up nearly a quarter of the dungeon space. It was the garbage of ages. Morgan couldn't even begin to imagine the immense feat it must have been for Serge to climb that and pull a human body through the heavily-barred opening. The pile was now dotted with coal, thick layers of it.

The relay line had finished its work and the People were congregating. A distance away, the wheel was still being pushed, but it also was piled high with combustibles. Morgan hated the wheel with a passion he didn't know he possessed. If the others felt as he did, its firing would be a cause for great jubilation.

They gathered, life's oddities standing in the dancing light of many small fires, staring with something akin to religious fervor at a monstrous pile of fecal garbage.

Morgan put himself between the garbage and the People, his cloth mask covering all but his eyes. "I have made all my speeches," he said loudly. "If any have changed their minds about following me, let them now depart without malice and in friendship to a farther section of the dungeon. The rest of you," he made an expansive gesture, "are free to become enemies of the State!"

With that, the People ran for the small fires, shoving flat boards and barks into them, scooping up the glowing embers contained there. Many ran to the garbage pile and threw their coals onto the mound, but even a greater number screamed happily in the direction of the wheel. Morgan felt a surge of power and excitement bolt through him when, a moment later, the creak of the wheel ceased for the first time in centuries.

He stood for a few moments, watching the embers glow brightly amidst the garbage. Then the pile began smoking, smoldering, small flames springing up here and there. And the smoke rose straight up the drop hole, where it would soon drown Castle Alb'ny in deep, smelly haze.

"We've no time to lose!" Morgan called when he was sure his plan was working. "They'll be here soon. Bring your embers with you."

The fire was growing large on the mound, casting bright, jumping light into the darkest corners of the dungeon, lighting Morgan's path to the dungeoneers' station.

And they ran, man and Genies, two and four-legged creatures of God, slapping mud, their race for life one of exhilaration.

They reached their end of the long hallway that separated them from freedom and stopped peering down its quiet length.

Morgan had already picked his advance men, and led them into the tunnel now. "Hide quietly behind the arches," he whispered. "Don't let them see you. Wait for my signal."

He turned to gaze at Serge who was too large to fit in the tunnel without giving away their position. "I'm counting on you; you get in here when the trouble starts."

"I will," Serge squeaked in a high voice which was as close as he could get to a whisper. "Serge is ready."

Morgan took one last look at the happy-faced, naked giant, then turned and silently made his way down the hall.

His small force dropped off one at a time to steal into the arch shadows every time they passed one. Finally, only Squan and Morgan remained. They made the last archway, taking opposite sides of the hall. Morgan quietly drew his sword and eased his back up against the cold wall.

He could see in the light on the other side of the massive bars, four of the blue-and-white-striped tunics playing dice at a wooden table. Beyond them, the two-man crank that lifted the bars.

He heard a hiss and looked up. Squan nodded to him from across the shadows. Cat eyes glowed and his hands were up, claws extended. They were coming.

The tension was on Morgan. Like a tightened coil he was ready to burst in all directions. He smiled broadly at Squan, crouching in preparation.

There were the sounds of men tramping down the stairs, their shouts. The dungeoneers heard it, too. They stood, gazing at one another, wondering.

And the Guard filled the station.

"Fire!" they were shouting, and the masters of the dungeon didn't believe it. There was a moment of confusion, then the creaking of the bars as they rose straight up, slowly, shivering as they climbed.

And the Guard mindlessly plunged into the tunnel, absolutely convinced with human arrogance that there was nothing to hurt them in the realm of the unhuman.

Ten of them, fifteen, came pounding through the tunnel, crowding the hallway as they did the station. And then one of them, a local boy named Callan, caught a glint of metal reflecting torchlight, and jerked his head instinctively to the disturbance.

He came face to face with Morgan, sword raised. And in the second that it took to understand that the insanely leering face meant to kill him, his mind turned inexplicably to a time when they were youngsters and Callan and the other village boys used to taunt the red-haired bastard with the wild streak.

Morgan saw strangely familiar eyes lock with his own, then laughed with the release and swung out with all his strength, severing the head cleanly from the body and dropping it into the arms of the man behind.

"Serge!" Morgan screamed, and the battle was met.

Torches flared and were dropped, as Genies viciously jumped from cover, taking surprise advantage over their adversaries. Shouts filled the closed-in place, and Morgan swung out again and again, hacking his way closer to the bars. This was his objective. He had to reach safety in the station to keep the bars open.

Squan was beside him, hissing and spitting, flailing at faces with his strong claws, shredded flesh dripping from them.

"Push forward!" Morgan called loudly, as he gutted one of the Guard, using a booted foot on the man's dead chest to jerk his sword free.

He turned to the melee, unable to make sense of the action in the now dark space. And when he turned back to the bars, he saw them slowly closing.

"Squan!" he yelled, and the cat man was already trying to hurry himself to the place.

The Guard was moving away from the bars as they closed. Morgan reached them at shoulder height, fitting himself between their sharp pointy tips.

The weight was crushing, pushing him inexorably down with it. Squan got under the bars in a crouch, but even his extra strength wasn't enough to stop the downward momentum.

They strained, Morgan's face drawn with agony. He turned his eyes to the hall to see men flying in all directions.

Serge.

The big man made his way to them, hands held out, looking dumbly from one to the other. A felled Guardsman staggered to his feet with drawn sword, charging the giant's exposed back.

"Watch out!" Morgan called out, and Serge stepped aside as the outstretched arm went right past him, sliding through the lowering bars.

"U-man!" Serge screamed, and slammed down with both his fists on the extended arm, taking it at the socket. Reaching out, Serge grabbed the bottom of the bars, adding his strength.

Morgan felt the pressure ease off him, and he slid out into the station. Several other Genies rolled quickly under the bars to join him. They all had procured swords from dead Guard.

Morgan charged those remaining in the station. They put up scant resistance, then routed, rationalizing their cowardice with the balm of reinforcements.

Morgan and El-tron took the double crank, winding the gate back up, then locking it in place. Genies were pouring into the station, free of the dungeon at last.

Nebo was the last one through.

"The Guard are all dead," he said. "We've only lost a few."

Morgan nodded. "Good," he said, then turned his attention to the crank. Reaching out a fist, he pounded the release and the gate closed. He looked at Serge. "Break it up."

The big man went to work on the crank, which would help keep the dungeon closed while the fire raged.

"More will be coming soon," Squan said. "We will be fortunate to make it up the steps.

"We won't go all the way up," Morgan said. "Follow me."

He ran from the station, up the winding stone stairs that branched out at the top. This section of Castle Alb'ny Morgan knew, for he had played secretly there often with Ramon when they were children.

The left fork led to the steps to the next level up. The right fork led to the wine cellar. Morgan took the right fork, the others close behind.

They hurried into the darkness of the cellar, the huge wooden kegs lined up in neat rows all through the large room. Torches lit the dank walls at regular intervals, filling the room with lines of light and shadow. Morgan ran the familiar aisles, looking for the place he used as his entry and exit as a child.

Kegs blurred past him. He cut through a horizontal aisle and headed for the far wall. In the distance, he could hear the voices of many men, as they charged the stairs to the dungeon.

He reached the far wall and ran the line of kegs. and then he saw it, the doorway hidden by the hollow keg. It had been left as an escape for royalty in times of danger, and very few knew of its existence. As the others caught up to him, he tried to pull the keg out of the way. It wouldn't budge. It wasn't empty anymore!

He turned on the spigot full and red wine spilled, but not fast enough.

"Serge," he said, and the giant moved to the keg. "Smash it."

Serge set his jaw and reached back with his fists as he had done with the Guardsman whose arm still hung on the bars. With a grunt, he smashed through the front of the barrel.

The wine gushed, a red flood knocking most of them to the floor as it surged out of the barrel. But the flood subsided quickly, and they got to their feet, licking their hands and sucking on the material of their robes.

Morgan and Serge pulled the now empty barrel off its blocks, rolling it partway down the aisle, then ran back to the metal door that was hidden.

Morgan struggled with the door. It didn't want to open; it hadn't been used in ten years, ever since Jerlynn had found out they played in the cellar and forbade Morgan to come anywhere on the castle grounds.

Finally the door creaked open to outside darkness.

"Where does this lead?" Nebo asked.

"Don't worry," Morgan said. He turned to sounds at the entrance of the cellar. "They've come. We must hurry."

He went through the open door; rats scurried away. He was standing in a stairwell of cement in total darkness.

Nebo entered, holding his brazier up to dangle from his stump. It glowed the enclosed space to partial light.

"Up the stairs," Morgan pointed, and walked the ten steps that seemed to end in a ceiling. When he reached the ceiling, he pushed. It hinged open to bright daylight.

Morgan climbed out and breathed fresh air. He was still hidden in the shadows behind the castle. Turning, he motioned the others up with him.

When all were either out with him or in hearing distance, he spoke in a clear voice, "We can do nothing but make our way to the kennels and hope that Grodin is ready for us. After that, take the front gate and make for the river. We will regroup there."

With that, he smiled and saluted them, then turned and walked out of the bushes into the daylight. The others scurried after, heads darting around. Rounding the corner that took him to the front of Castle Alb'ny, he ran into activity. When Serge came into view, everything stopped in the courtyard.

Morgan looked all around, grinning wide. He turned to the Castle entrance to see men stumbling out coughing, plumes of smoke drifting behind them.

"Ladies and gentlemen!" Morgan called, bowing low from the waist. "Morgan of Siler, rightful heir of Alb'ny, bids you adieu!"

Then he screamed animallike and ran for the kennels, sword flashing above his head. They crossed nearly the whole yard before reaction set in and thousands charged for them.

They plunged, a phalanx through the confusion. Morgan hacked away at anything human as Serge happily tossed bodies twenty and thirty feet into the surging crowds.

They attained the incline, and the kennel doors swung open, Grodin and Ona hollering them up. Morgan moved up the incline, driving back all who tried to come up for him. Then Grodin was beside him, working with him.

"Not much style!" the old man called, "but very effective."

"I'll work on the style!" Morgan called back, and the two men embraced with their free arms. He saw Ramon stumble out the front door with the rest, but an ocean of flesh and steel separated them, and he knew he could never reach his brother.

"Mount up!" Morgan yelled above the battle sounds, and his Genies drifted one by one to the Bernards where Ona helped them mount, her dress ripped off to the crotch, her legs slick with dark grease. A short sword flashed in her hand.

Pack cranked up the siren, its wail piercing the heat, calling all who were unaware.

Serge moved close. He held a screaming human by the ankles and began swinging him around, smashing him into the crowd at the bottom of the incline, keeping them at bay.

Morgan and Grodin backed a few more precious feet toward the Woofers. Squan moved up to Morgan, hissing madly, his eyes wide and frightened.

"I can't ride the Woofer," he said in near panic.

"What?"

"Woofers are the natural enemy of my kind," he said, words spitting from his thin lips, whiskers twitching.

"You must!"

"I can't!"

Serge threw his human into the crowd and backed up to join them. "Serge is too big for Woofers," he said. "Squan can go with me."

Morgan laid hands on the two People. "Go!" he said. "Good luck!"

With that, Squan sprang on the giant's back, leaning way over his shoulders to swipe at the troops with his claws.

Morgan and Grodin retreated to the Woofers, Morgan going right for Murdock. "Nebo!" he called, and the Mech hurried to his side.

Ona rushed to him, and the two embraced quickly. "Double up!" He called down the line of Genies when he saw there weren't enough Woofers to go around.

He took Ona by the shoulders. "Ride with Grodin," he said. "Nebo must go with me."

Her eyes flashed with pain, but she hurried to comply. Morgan mounted quickly, pulling the Mech up behind him.

"We meet in Hell!" he screamed, and dug his heels into Murdock's side.

The Woofer howled loudly and leaped down the incline. And they charged into the fray at full speed, Woofers carrying Genies, swords flashing and the sounds wrapping around them like a whirlwind. Serge was running, twice as tall as those who tried to stop his pounding bulk, as Squan lashed out at them, whining high like the siren.

The Woofers cried wildly as the siren hurt their ears, while Morgan watched Serge kicking humans from his path, and Grodin rode beside him, the old man and Ona lashing out in either direction.

"Fly, Murdock!" Morgan laughed, as he took an arm that reached out for him, and the Woofer churned the mud in great leaping strides, his savage teeth snapping madly at all within reach of his shaggy head.

"The gate!" Nebo cried in his ear, and Morgan looked up to see Guardsmen hurrying to close the mammoth doors. But Serge was already there. At full speed, with outstretched arms, he hit the closing gates, banging them to splinter open, Castle

Guard flying in all directions. And Squan stood on the big man's shoulders, screaming at the dusty sky.

They fought their way to the gate, then through it, jumbled humanity crushing to meet them, then crushing back in retreat. Ramon had his archers let fly from the walls as Morgan entered the camp city without. Many Woofers and their riders went down, along with a great number of Ramon's allies.

Murdock vaulted a bright blue tent, trampling several men as he came down. Nebo flung out his arm, his ember dropping to a tent. Morgan craned his head behind to see over half of his force still intact, Grodin and Ona close behind him.

He yelled with the sheer joy of battle and wound a serpentine path through the tent city, fires spreading in his wake, froth and blood dripping from Murdock's slick black lips. He caught Serge, and passed him as they attained the breech of the outer battlements, finding the main road.

He left behind a wide swath of conflagration and death. Those left of his force hurried through behind, Serge running a bit slower as he tired out.

Smoke drifted in thick clumps into the deadly sky; the Governor of Alb'ny was even then executing those he felt responsible for the escape. And in the nooks and crannies of Alb'ny, minstrels were already secretly writing the lyrics to songs which would sing of the wonder of the red-haired human who rode with Genies, songs that would spread even to the farthest corners of a wide-flung and dangerous land.

Morgan and his ragged band camped that night at half strength on the banks of the Hus at some point south of Alb'ny. They spread out as close as they could get to the mighty river, its charging waters loud in their ears, and Morgan wondered if it was because they missed the creak of the wheel.

They had three huge bonfires strung along the moist banks, placing themselves between the fires and the river for protection against the creatures of the night. They had ridden hard most of the day, and strain showed on the Woofers, who laid sprawled in piles around the fires. There had been some pursuit, but it had been minimal, considering the density of the jungle and the humans abject fear of journeying there. No, they had ridden hard, but not through fear; they had simply wanted to put as much distance as possible between themselves and Alb'ny.

The smell of fried fish drifted from the fire nearest Morgan as he sat with Nebo and Grodin, discussing their next move. Most of the People left alive ate and rested, all except the Minnies who cavorted like children in the dense undergrowth on the edge of the river's flood plain. Morgan watched them as they giggled and formed a living pyramid, only to tumble, laughing, to the ground when one on the bottom sneezed loudly. They operated as a unit, as if in some sort of mental contact with one another. Morgan was always astounded by the Minnies' unspoken cooperation in all things.

Serge stood to his waist in the raging water, grabbing fish out with his bare hands, while Squan did the same from the river-bank, intently watching the waters in statue-still anticipation, only to flare out a hand from time to time, coming up with more dinner.

Ona hummed a tuneless melody as she washed the grease from her long, slim legs. She had done well in battle; Morgan was surprised and pleased.

El-tron hobbled slowly to the group, long fingers massaging his aching rump. "We lost sixteen," he said sadly. "Erbelle's gone. Janus the L-back. Many of the slower-witted ones."

"Erbelle was the last of her kind," Nebo said. "The Clan of Long Arm is no more."

"That means sixteen Woofers," Grodin said.

"Maybe not all dead," Morgan told him.

"I think that the human cares more for his beasts than he does for the People," El-tron said angrily.

Grodin stood to face him. "I pulled each one of them from their mothers' loins, and raised them up from pups. Any one of those Bernards is better than the lot of you freaks."

El-tron drew his sword, the hatred twisting his face to an ugly grimace.

"No!" Morgan shouted, standing between them.

"There are no freaks," he said slowly. "Not human freaks, not Genie freaks. We are all the People, human and Genie. We respect all . . . including Woofers. The new way must start here."

"All my life . . ." Grodin began.

"I don't care about all your life!" Morgan yelled. Then more softly. "I don't care. This is a new way. We put all behind us."

El-tron moved to embrace him. "You're right," he said. "I am sorry."

Morgan toussled the Genie's long, silver hair. "I love you truly," he said, then turned to Grodin. "You are the father that

my father never was, and all the feeling I possess belongs to you.
But I swear to you, Grodin of Alb'ny, if you cannot accept my
authority, my order, you must turn and walk away from this
place right now and never show yourself to me again."

"You realize what you say, lad?" Grodin said slowly, his leather
face slack and troubled, his old man's body in pain from the
rugged trip.

"My old life died with my mother," Morgan said, and Grodin
seemed to flinch at that. "I spent many months in the mud and
filth with broken ribs thinking about it. My course is set and
directed. If it does not please you . . ."

Grodin took him by the shoulders. "Your path is my path," he
said, remembering the words of a courageous, doomed woman.

Morgan's face remained hard. "Tell that to El-tron," he said
quietly.

Grodin's mouth moved silently for several seconds, before he
released his hold on Morgan and turned to the Genie. "Change
does not come easy for an old human," he said. "I beg your
forgiveness, and ask your compassion."

"For Morgan's sake," the Genie responded, embracing the
man, wrapping his long fingers over the sinews of the old man's
back. Seconds later, Grodin reluctantly returned the embrace.

"Excellent!" Morgan said, brightening. "Brothers all."

"Brothers all!" Serge called from the river, and he was holding
a large carp high in the air, its silvery body wriggling in the
firelight.

Ona had returned from her ablutions at the river. Taking a fish
on a long stick from the fire, she squatted near Morgan and
began quietly to eat. She felt a terrible unease toward the People, but was determined to keep it to herself for fear of losing her
place. She stared up at the red-haired man with an admiration
she didn't know she was capable of, for, like Grodin, she was
beginning to see this farmer as something greater.

The men sat again, Morgan smiling at Ona when he came
down to stretch out beside her. Silently she offered him her fish.
He shook his head, patting her bare leg.

"We are free," Nebo said, an edge of tiredness in his voice.
"But free to do what?"

"You never think past the moment," Morgan said. "You never
plan."

"I have you for that," the Mech said firmly.

Morgan nodded. "We are free to live from the land, free to
upset the slave caravans and release their hostages, free to form

an army, a People's army, free to return to Alb'ny and regain that
which was lost to me, free to establish a kingdom for all the
People. Is that enough freedom for you?"

"You dream big," Nebo said.

Morgan looked at him intensely. "You don't dream at all."

Nebo scratched his chin with the stump of a hand. "I wasn't
designed that way."

Morgan leaned over and took a bite of Ona's fish, then shook it
off when she once again offered him the whole thing. "Tomorrow
we will rest and discuss Genie cities and the slave routes," he
said, and his eyes unconsciously studied the length of the
woman's pale legs. "The following day we will leave this place
and so begin our quest."

"You are the rock of certainty," Nebo said. "How can you be so
sure of everything?"

Morgan stood up, edgy but too tired to be angry. "We've
gotten this far, haven't we?" he said, and walked from the firelight into the night.

He walked to the riverbank. He knew not where the rock of
certainty grew, or how it came into being. He only knew that he
desperately needed something to believe in, and this was a
belief larger than himself, larger than all of them.

"Am I disturbing you?" came a voice from behind.

He turned to see Ona, a shadow among shadows, standing
quietly behind him.

"Do you think my dreams too big?" he asked her.

She moved to him tentatively, and wrapped her arms gently
around him; he returned her embrace. "My dream is of you,"
she said. "It is the only dream I am concerned with."

He held her there, feeling soft yielding flesh within his grasp.
And it had been too long since he had let that kind of feeling
anywhere within his heart. He listened to the sounds of the
night, to the sounds of camp in the distance. A liquid warmth
seemed to melt over him, spreading softly through his body, a
loving warmth that formed the core of this great, wild beast; and
he became more acutely aware of the woman in his grasp.

"Will you lie down with me?" she asked, her voice high and a
bit frightened.

He eased her away from him to look at her face, her beautiful
face and thick, tangled hair. "You don't have to," he said.

"Have to?" she returned. "In my whole life, this is the first
chance I've had to make love with someone I wanted to make
love with. Ibem, I can't wait."

She eased herself down to the goldenrod of the bank, pulling him down with her. He moved on top of her, the passion stirring loudly within him. And she moaned softly as, still clothed, he began to push himself against her.

"I don't love you," he said, as she moved her hands to embrace his erection.

"Shhh," she responded. "The jungle is eternity, and there is time for all things."

And for a brief eternity, responsibility and mission were lost to him as he drowned in fragrant hair and damp loins; and when she sobbed out her love for him, he kissed away the tears that wet her cheeks like morning dew upon the lilies.

XIV
The Shipyard

Ramon and his party stood staring at the rolling sky through the skeletal bars of the mammoth ships that stretched fifty feet high at the prow. Five ships lined up in a row on the banks of the Hus, pilings holding them back from a quick descent down their flumes into the raging waters. The ships stood in their ways, the honeycomb scaffolding climbing both sides of each construction. The ways were filled with carpenters, each working on his own section. The frames of the ships were oak, and the planks were cedar. The keels, the backbones, were made of heavy timbers held together by bolts and drifts. The smell of pine tar, used to caulk the planks, hung thickly in the air.

A large area of jungle had been cleared for the yard, a monumental task made possible only by the sweat of thousands of soldiers who were put to work full time to clear it and keep it cleared. What was even more monumental was the fact that Ramon had managed to keep the yard a secret until now, a fact that was his present salvation, since he was able to use its majesty to make his allies forget the devastation that the farmer had wrought.

Morgan's escape, and the duplicity of Grodin in giving him the Woofers, was the single most devastating incident to occur in Ramon's life. He had cut the throats of the dungeoneers left alive and couldn't even recall the action. His humiliation was so profound that he knew of no way to alleviate it save the complete denial of the event. He would never speak of it publicly, never give an outward sign that anything had happened. He wanted

Morgan almost as much as he wanted the Jewel of the East, but he wasn't about to compromise his denial by sending his troops out in search of the bastard. Far better to ignore it all.

The surrounding jungle was verdant green, still steamy from the recent rain. Father Hus was rolling fat and wide and deep, his angry rumbling nearly drowned in the hammering and sawing of a legion of workmen. The farthest end of the yard, nearly two hundred yards distant, was the supply depot, where gangs of soldiers dragged tree trunks by long chains to the pulley brigades that hefted them to a small mountain. Next came the smelter for the making of nails and materials, followed by the shapers, carpenters who chiseled and planed the rough logs into usable uniform boards cut to specs for the master craftsmen who were doing the actual building. The entire yard was ringed by a series of carefully watched fires that disposed of waste and helped keep the jungle back. Many of the fires heated great tubs of water over which the ships' frames were steamed and bent to the proper angle.

Ramon led a large group, including the rulers and Physicians of every province allied with Alb'ny. His mother was there, as was her constant companion, Faf, although their inclusion was more for shock value than anything. He extracted great pleasure from rubbing their fur against the grain. He took the group to the center of the yard, so that its reality completely filled everyone's senses.

"When will the ships be finished?" Nef asked.

"A matter of months yet," Ramon said. "But we still have a great deal of other preparation for this expedition, so the time won't be wasted. By the way, each commander will have his house symbol as the figurehead of his ship."

Old Councilman Reeder cleared his throat loudly and spoke up. "It seems, Governor, that you have been preparing for this enterprise for quite some time. Suppose the rest of us had failed to go along with it?"

"What other choice was there?" Ramon said. "We're dealing with Destiny here, Councilman. We're dealing with the chance to mold the future forevermore. We're talking about ridding the land of the beasts that think and extending the rule of humans into the outer reaches of N'ork."

"We're talking about booty," Count Delmar said, laughing, waving his lace at Reeder's eaten-away nose.

"Lots of it," Senator Murray added. "And you'll take it just the same as the rest of us."

"What of the Lawgivers in Kipsie?" Faf asked, afternoon

sweat darkening his already dark robes. "Have they approved of this . . . ill-conceived venture?"

Ramon smiled wide. "My Programmer worries for my soul," he said with condescension. "I'll make you a bargain, holy man. When we finish the boats we'll sail down to Kipsie and ask the Lawgivers about it in person."

Everyone laughed loudly.

"This is a grave matter," Faf said, turning angrily to them. He bent and picked up a handful of earth, holding it up for them to see. "This is our lot: to be stable as the ground, to be as unchangeable."

He made a sweeping gesture. "This smacks of pagan science!" he yelled, throwing his dirt at one of the ships. "The Lawgivers will never approve such blasphemy."

Delmar's Physician, Scab the hunchback, shoved through the crowd to face the Programmer. "Do the Lawgivers feed our people?" he asked loudly. "Do they help us clear the Genie infection from our lands? They make us tithe and tell us what to do. They trim the best portions for themselves and serve no useful function, just as you serve no useful function."

Faf took a step toward the man, towered over him. "The Lawgivers have kept us whole," he said, "when the jungle could have eaten us."

"And we thank them," Ramon said. "But now, my friends, the time has come for us to make our own decisions, to form our own destiny."

The group applauded, and Faf felt Jerlynn move close to him to squeeze his hand and silence him. He could see their folly as clearly as he could see the trees of Ibem that they had cut down for sinful purposes. This was going to have to be decided on a higher level.

The seed of an idea began to grow in Faf's mind. Turning to Jerlynn, he nodded slightly, and she released the pressure on his hand.

Ramon held his hand up to the group. "And now my Physician has some words for you."

Pack smiled and climbed upon a stack of boards to get above the group. "We are getting ready to increase the size of the smelting area. We will be making metal weaponry and armor, outfitting the armada with contraptions the likes of which have never been seen since the Before Time. We will take the collective knowledge of all the Physicians of N'ork and use it to make our ships impregnable fortresses."

The twenty or so Physicians all began talking at once; Ramon thought how much like children they were. The Physicians were the one link with the past that Kipsie reluctantly allowed, the one thought of the future that N'ork rulers indulged. They were the key: the past that wouldn't die, the future that couldn't be denied. Ramon smiled upon them. He would let them have their day and then dispose of them lest they become too powerful. All except the Green Woman. There was something different about her, something worthy of further study.

As if his thoughts were a call, she was at his elbow. She touched his arm and her touch surged through him like a charge from Pack's crank machine.

"I'm impressed," she said. "These vessels will carry many."

"Thousands," Ramon said, pretending not to be talking to her. "Will I see you later?"

"Perhaps," she answered as she always answered. She kept Ramon continually off balance with her words and actions. He never had any idea of what she actually thought about, other than the fact that she was as addicted as any of the Physicians to progress. He knew little of her relationship with Nef also; he didn't even know her given name.

"Don't tell me that . . ."

"Here," she interrupted, slipping something into his hand. "Take this."

Turning quickly, she walked off with Pack and the other Physicians to take a look at some of their plans.

"Look the yard over," he told the other officials. "This belongs to all of us."

The group applauded, then wandered off in different directions according to their interests. Ramon opened his hand to see a small white pill lying there. As with all the Green Woman's prescriptions, he took it without question.

His mother's voice rang out behind him. "What good is all this with the bastard out there waiting for you?"

He turned to stare at her. He waited to speak until two men in work aprons walked past, long cedar planks carefully balanced on their shoulders.

"Morgan is gone," Ramon returned. "He's been swallowed by the jungle. We won't be bothered by him again."

"That's nonsense and you know it. Do you know how many men he killed this afternoon?"

Ramon stared darkly at her. "Forty-two dead, twenty-one injured badly enough to need care. The mess he made will be cleaned up by the time we return to Alb'ny Castle."

"And you think it will be forgotten just like that?"

"I honestly don't know whether it will be or not," he said, watching over her shoulder to see Faf walking with Councilman Reeder in the distance, his arms flailing the air as he made his points. "What would you have me do?"

"You've got to go after him," she said.

"He's just one man. I have a world to earn."

She took his hands, trying unsuccessfully to meet his eyes. "He's broken your jail, taken your Woofers out from under your nose, and escaped through thirty thousand troops practically untouched. He's made a fool of you, my son, and will do so again if you don't finish him."

There was a commotion nearby. A small boy carrying a bucketful of nails from the smelter to the framers had accidentally run into Redrick of Firetree, who had drifted out to the shipyard with Ramon's party. The man with the hook had knocked the child down for the insult and was now kicking him as he rolled around in a small pile of spilled nails.

"I'll teach you!" he screamed, nearly out of control. "You hooligan!"

"Redrick!" Ramon called, motioning the man to join him. Then he looked, smiling, at Jerlynn. "You may be right, Mother. Perhaps I should be more careful of the farmer."

Redrick trotted up to them, his face red as windburn, his wild eyes staring. "Little tramp ran right into me," he said, pointing at the child who was crying as he put the nails back into the bucket.

"Never mind that now," Ramon said, watching the man's face for reaction. "I have a job for you."

Redrick bowed his head. "Anything, my Lord," he said solemnly. "You need only ask."

"How would you like the chance to avenge your disgrace at the banquet?"

He grabbed Redrick's wrist and brought the hook up between them. The man's face was a mixture of fear and animal savagery, but there was only one answer he could give and he gave it effectively.

"I live only for that opportunity," he said through clenched teeth.

"Good," Ramon said, releasing his hand. "Take fifteen or twenty of my Castle Guard and track Morgan of Siler."

"Into the jungle, my Lord?" Redrick asked, a slight catch to his voice.

"To whatever hole he curls up in," Ramon said, enjoying Redrick's unease and his own cleverness at finding a way to dispose of the man who was beginning to become a nuisance to him. Redrick's fits of temper had gone from occasional to predictable, and always with those weaker than himself.

"Track him to his lair. Keep him under constant watch." Ramon put an arm around the man, drew him away from Jerlynn. "If you get the chance to kill him yourself, do so. If not, wait until the time seems right to get a message to me and I will send troops."

"When should I leave," Redrick said dully.

Ramon showed him even rows of teeth, stained slightly yellow from tobacco. "Leave now, dear friend, though the parting is painful for me."

Redrick knelt, bringing Ramon's ring to his lips. His emotions were at war within him. "My Lord," he said softly.

"Go now," Ramon said, pulling the man to his feet.

Redrick turned and stalked away, his shoulders slumping, his head down. And Ramon watched him with his peacock strut, and it suddenly seemed the funniest thing he had ever seen in his whole life: Redrick in his peaked cap and cobweb armor, parading through the shipyard like a rooster in the chicken coop.

He began to laugh, hysterical, uncontrollable laughter. Everything seemed a jumble around him, people and things, moving through counter realities with no rhyme or reason. The boats were huge and ominous, casting long gray shadows in the half light of the ugly sky—and still he couldn't control his laughter.

The colors of the Physicians were bright, so bright and he went down in the mud, admiring the vibrant colors, as an army of knees gathered around him. Through the forest of legs he saw her, the Green Woman, staring at him. She stood rock solid, her expression never changing, her half grin etched on her face as a carving on a boulder. She stood fifty feet distant, solid amidst a flowing sea, and yet she seemed close enough to reach out and touch.

He tried, reaching, stretching—either to hold her or push her away. It was then that her grin cracked wide. She threw her green face to the sky, her soft hair tumbling down her back, and she laughed.

She laughed and their laughter mixed together. And before he knew it, many hands were lifting him, carrying him into the shade for they all feared that he had succumbed to the withering afternoon heat.

Part III

ALICIA

XV
Masuria—In the Uncharted Jungle

The twilight shadows were long in Twiddle's lair at the top of the tall pine. Outside his window, Masuria's dome glowed dully with day's last brightness. Tiny lights, like stationary fireflies, blinked from its surface. But Twiddle did not notice, nor did he move to burn his own candles—Twiddle had no eyes, nor any memory of eyes, nor even sockets from whence eyes could have once sprung. Twiddle had never known eyes, but he burned with the inner light.

The woman with the fox-colored hair sat at the table with Twiddle, the shadows angling across her smooth, unlined face. She moved with grace and precision, and never spoke without forethought. She stared at the young troubadour who stood nervously before them, Twiddle's house creaking slightly every time the lad in the purple tights shifted his weight from one foot to the other.

"Continue the song," the woman said.

"I-I didn't . . . write it you k-know," the young man stuttered, a trait that was absent in his singing voice. "I p-picked it up from a h-h-human minstrel on the W-West Road."

"I understand," the woman said in a voice that neither condoned nor passed judgement. "Just finish it."

The troubadour cleared his throat. Two sets of arms came up to lightly pluck the strings of the double-necked lute he carried. He sang in a beautiful tenor: his voice lovingly caressed the notes in the upper register.

> With flashing sword and flaming hair
> The Demon's wrath broke free.
> From slimy pits of inner Keep
> In deadly harmony.
>
> With monsters from the pool of dreams:
> Bronze giant, dark-skinned Mech,
> And humans, too, on mighty beasts.
> He shuffled all the deck.

153

The game of Life deals many hands
All different by degree.
But Demon searches out the trumps:
Soldier, Builder,
Referee.

The singer held the last note, letting it slowly drift away on the
vibrations of his sweet strings. When finished, he quietly folded
his hands, two in front and two tapping together behind his
back.

The lad's name was Coriander, which means "Follower of the
Tree Nymphs." He was an orphan of the jungle and took all the
happiness of his life from the solitude of the forest. What contact
he had with the sentient beings of N'ork came infrequently,
through his travels and his singing. It was the way he wanted it,
for humans and Genies alike caused him nothing but grief. The
forest seemed to understand this and wrapped Coriander
lovingly in its strong, protective arms.

"Did the minstrel explain his lyrics?" the woman asked.

Coriander shook his head. "We d-don't . . . ex-plain," he
said, struggling out the last word. "We just m-make m-music."

"He sings of the band of three," Twiddle squeaked in his high,
cracking voice. Twiddle was a prune of a man, small and
wrinkled. He wore only a loincloth, the rest of his body looking
like a coarse, tan sackful of bones.

"You know this song?" the woman inquired, just as a large, fat
blackbird came to perch on the wooden sill of the old room. The
room creaked, tipping slightly as the bird landed.

"No," Twiddle answered. "But I have dim memories of its
roots. Do you remember all the words?"

The woman nodded. "I have just committed them to memory."

"Then send away the boy. We no longer need him."

The woman turned to the boy. "You're . . ." she began, but he
had already sneaked out and was even then happily squirming
down the tree.

She turned to the wrinkled man. "You already knew it."

Twiddle began to laugh that his blind smooth eye places saw
more than the deep golden pools of the woman. She laughed
with him, loudly, and they shook the room so violently that the
bird on the window, thinking himself in the presence of madness, cawed hysterically, flapping his great wings, then flew off
in search of more hospitable shelter in which to set his evening
roost.

The woman leaned up close to him, putting her red-nailed fingers on his leathery, naked arm. "Tell me," she said softly.

"Alicia . . ."

"You know you must tell me."

He nodded slowly. "Such is my curse. To know."

He stood, pacing the room in slow, easy precision. It rolled with him, like a storm-tossed ship.

"Have you heard of the band of three?" he asked her.

"No."

"It may be the oldest piece of wisdom to survive the Before Times, a myth of large proportion." He stopped walking, putting his fingertips to where his eyes should be. "It talks about the power to control, some combination of elements that would bring power. It is a part of the transition from the Old World, a fantasy that emerged from Chaos."

"Do you know this story?" she asked.

He walked to the window, standing before it as if he were staring out. "Not much of it," he said. "the shred of a poem, not worth sharing with . . ."

"Tell me."

He turned from the window, faced her.

> Band of three,
> Band of three:
> Soldier, Builder,
> Referee.
> Band of three,
> Band of three:
> The perfect mix, the
> Apogee.

"They refer to that in the minstrel's song?" she asked.

"It seems likely," he said, "though probably not consciously. The story is so old, so dusty . . . I think only those like me would know of it."

"And the rest?"

He returned to his seat. "The future is never clear," he said. "All time is the same river, the currents moving and shifting . . ."

"Tell me of the Demon."

"There is a red-haired man," he said, "who is something more and something less. He leads a gang of Genies and renegade humans."

"Genies and humans . . . together?" she said, startled.

Twiddle nodded. "Yes. He has the heart of a wild beast and the dreams of a king. Either greatness or incurable stupidity runs through his veins. He will either rule N'ork or tear it asunder, and either thing may have the same result."

"Not if I can help it," she replied.

Twiddle sighed, drained physically, and lay his head on the rough wood of the table. "I was afraid you'd say that," he told her, and fell immediately into a troubled sleep, visions of a world on fire charging his brain like a fever.

XVI
Techne Monastery, East Greenbush—
Three Days E-SE of Alb'ny

The old wooden bridge groaned loudly as Faf and his party moved across it. The Programmer's carriage bumped rudely over the centuries-warped planks of the fifty-yard span that led across the moat and into the monastery, causing Faf to grunt every time he bounced and his Woofers to turn and stare at him, thinking they had been given a command.

The small party consisted of two servant friars plus seven of the holy man's personal guard. There had been eight bodyguards at the beginning of the journey, but one had been carried off by a snake on the road the previous night.

Everyone except Faf walked. The two Woofers pulling the carriage were mixed-breed mongrels, and hence were spared when Ramon cast about the countryside, commandeering and buying the animals after Morgan took his kennel.

The footsteps of Faf's men resounded loudly on the old bridge, the moat stretching out wide and stagnant all around. The trees came right up to the edge of the moat; those closest to it were gnarled and dead after drinking from its poisoned waters. Their branches reached, rotten and skeletal, almost pleadingly over the dank water. Rot wood lay in thick heaps all over the banks. No animal dared come anywhere near this place of death.

Faf had not been here for nearly twenty-five years, fifty-five plantings by his count, and yet everything was as he remembered it. As a young novitiate, he had studied here and taken his vows under the direction of the Supervisor, Clarence the Older.

He smiled when he remembered the novitiates had called him Clarence the Ogre when they were angry with him. But in retrospect, the Supervisor had been an amiable and solid teacher, the kind that one could come to with any problem—and Faf needed his counsel now.

The monastery lay ahead, its high iron walls built right up to the water's edge. The walls had probably been well maintained once, but there would be no way to know that now. Monster ivy with huge leaves completely overran the walls; no one could see that beneath the ivy was nothing but tons of rust. It was Faf's suspicion that the wall had eaten itself away many centuries before, and that all that remained was ivy holding rust together.

Two novitiates stood guard over the open archway that led to the courtyard. As Faf reined up, they were engaged in the task of cutting ivy strands that dangled down into the archway. It was a daily mindfulness task that Faf himself had often performed in his younger days, and he knew that if the ivy were left untouched for more than a week it would completely block the entry. Left for a month, it would make prisoners of the friars.

"Who seeks entry to our files?" a young, brown-robed friar asked.

Faf smiled at the familiar greeting that transported him to a past long forgotten. "Programmer Dixon Faf," came the reply, "from Alb'ny. My entourage travels under my responsibility."

The other friar, blond and blue-eyed, walked up to the carriage, respecting Faf's age and rank. "I must hear the password and see the authorization."

Faf climbed down from the carriage, the springs creaking under his weight. He stood, towering over the novitiate. "The password is 'interface,'" he said, and pushed up his sleeve to expose the tattoo on his right forearm.

The tatoo was rectangular, long as a finger. Inside the box were a seemingly random pattern of dots. Reaching into the folds of his robe, the novitiate extracted a flat metal plate with holes punched through it. The friar placed the plate over the tattoo. They were the same size, the holes in the metal corresponding exactly with the dots on Faf's arm.

"Welcome, brother," the friar said, smiling wide. "You may enter."

"Many thanks," Faf responded, handing his reins to Jartan, one of his own friars. While retying the sash on his robes, he wandered through the archway, breathing in the air of stability.

Nothing had changed. The archway opened into a small

courtyard, crowded with squat brick buildings, plain and unornamented. Windows peppered the buildings, all no more than two floors high. The windows had solid wooden awnings that jutted out from their tops and sides to a distance of several feet. The awnings were supported by thick, heavy beams dug deeply into the ground. Even the second-story windows were supported this way, leaving a latticework of poles protruding from the ground that young novitiates were made to twist in and out of as another mindfulness technique.

Young friars moved gracefully through the yard, as they cleared away plants that had grown up during the previous night. Their movements were a study in conservation—nothing extraneous, nothing wasted. The years they spent at Techne were years spent learning the simple rhythms of life, so that precious time would not be wasted upon activities best dealt with in a clinical, orderly manner, thereby freeing the mind to pursue the contemplation of the Order of things. Such were the lessons of Ibem.

Everything was peace; all was Order. Faf looked around the yard and his faith in the world was restored.

"Gerret," he called to his other servant, and the young man hurried to his side.

"Enter, Programmer," Gerret said, and the light of awe was cast on his face.

Faf pointed toward the west wall. "That long building over there should be the hostlery," he said. "You and the others ask for lodging for the night. You'll not be denied. Tend to the Woofers first, and be ready to leave with the first light of morning."

The man hurried off without answering, and Faf crossed the cobbled square to the rectory. The rectory was open and doorless beneath a large blue canopy of metal, Faf entering on the wings of a southerly wind.

It was, of course, just as he remembered it. Everything was fresh and new, as if untouched by time. The atrium was open and airy, the white stone floor scrubbed clean. The walls held striking murals depicting Ibem's destruction of the immorality of the Before World, complete with details of the unholy sciences that culminated with the manufacturing of the Beasts—the Genies. Also shown was the creation of the trees, a stainless-steel blinking Ibem amidst a forest of rapidly growing sprouts that became thick-trunked trees at a distance.

Faf moved through the archway to the office suites, heading

immediately to the Supervisor's niche as if he'd never been away.

Brother Clarence's office had a door, a swinging door that had "PUSH ENTER" written neatly upon it.

Brother Clarence stood on a small ladder at the Ibem wall, patiently working his cloth on its shiny face, polishing the precise reflecting steel with the clean lines and circular light places.

"You have entered the files, brother," Clarence said in a voice weakened by aged lungs. "We will sort through the program together."

"My program is for happiness at being in the presence of my old teacher," Faf said, smiling.

Clarence turned to him, older, and also smaller, than Faf's memory. He fixed him with clear gray eyes. "Dixon Faf, who used to ferment elderberry juice under his bed."

Faf's eyes widened. "You knew?"

The Supervisor grunted and climbed slowly down, old joints creaking under the strain. "I used to sneak some while you were at vespers."

Faf crossed the floor to him and the two men embraced, nostalgic tears wetting the Programmer's cheeks. "It has been far too long since I've bathed in your radiance."

Clarence moved away from him, waving the compliments off. "You always had the glib tongue," he said, then pointed a gnarled finger. "That's why they gave you a choice plum like Alb'ny."

"Even the choicest plums rot," Faf answered.

Brother Clarence stared silently at him for a moment. "This trip was not made for pleasure," he said solemnly.

Faf looked at the ground. "Unfortunately, no," he said quietly.

The man stood, looking small and lost in the robes that used to fit him well. "It must be quite a problem to bring you here after twenty-odd years."

Faf just stared at him.

"Can it wait on a cup of tea?" Clarence asked.

The Programmer smiled thinly. "Most assuredly."

Clarence nodded, the quick jerk of his head that Faf remembered so well. Cupping his hands to his mouth, the old man yelled, "Tea!" as loud as he could, then he coughed. "The old voice box isn't what it used to be. Will you help me?"

"Certainly," Faf returned, and both of them cupped their hands.

"TEA!" they screamed.

"That should do it," Clarence said, and moved slowly to the business side of his oak desk.

Faf walked to a wall and, taking a chair, carried it to the other side of the desk. The room was large, but basically empty, material goods of no value to the Supervisor. The Ibem shrine covered one wall. The wall opposite it was filled with large calligraphy—the Law:

1. IBEM IS ALL DATA, ACCEPT NO SUBSTITUTES.
2. TREES ARE SACRED.
3. PURE HUMAN BLOOD IS HOLY—IMPURITY OF BLOOD IS AN ABOMINATION BEFORE IBEM.
4. STATUS QUO IS THE HARMONY OF THE UNIVERSE.

The Programmer sat facing Clarence across the desk. Behind the old man was a wall open to a high-walled garden. But it didn't grow plants; there were fields for that. It was the garden of Ibem, row after row of gleaming icons—steel and glass machines, neat and tidy, stretching far into the background. There must have been thousands of the worship objects, and a team of friars were even then moving slowly down the interminable rows, carefully polishing and cleaning the ancient shrines.

"You remember our little garden," Clarence said proudly when he noticed Faf watching over his shoulder.

"It's the only thing larger than what I remember," he returned.

The man nodded knowingly. "That's what they all say."

The door swung open and a novitiate entered with the root tea, then left silently. A large dark root stuck out of the hot water. These the men used to stir until the tea reached the proper color. Then they discarded their roots and tasted.

"I have expected you for some time," Clarence said, wrinkling his nose over his cup. "We have heard dark rumblings from your province."

"They seem bent on a course of madness. I'm at a loss as to the proper course of action."

"The new Governor marshals an army, I hear," Clarence said.

"An army? . . . an armada!" Faf said. "He builds long ships."

The old man set down his tea, his face deeply troubled. "Why?"

"They seek conquest," Faf said, putting his own cup on the desk.

"Conquest is forbidden," Clarence said indignantly. "Haven't you told them so?"

"Repeatedly," Faf returned dutifully. "They will not hear me, even when I speak with the authority of the Lawgivers. They say the Lawgivers take without giving and wish to hear no more of them."

Clarence stood, turning away. "No!" he said emphatically. "I cannot believe this!"

Faf stood to comfort him. "My heart is heavy with the news," he said, reaching out a hand to the man's shoulder. "They were my charge. I am responsible."

The old man turned from him, watching out at the garden. "This is larger than one man," he said. "It is the thing we've always feared—that man would turn away from God out of insensitivity of the spirit. The Before Times are not even a memory anymore. How large an army?"

"Fifty thousand at last count."

Clarence returned to his seat, sinking with exhaustion into the wooden chair. Picking up the tea, he drank half of it before setting the cup down. "Where would they want to take such a large army?"

"N'ork City." Faf said, as he watched the friars working on the machines.

"There's more, isn't there?"

Faf kept his back to the man. "They use the ancient sciences," he answered.

There was silence. Faf returned to his chair to find the Supervisor's eyes misting over. "Why do you bring this to me?" he asked. "I am but an old cloister."

"You have connections in Kipsie," Faf said. "Perhaps if we can get through to them somehow . . ." He reached into his robe and came out with the folded linen that two men had already died for. "Show them this. Perhaps there's something . . ."

Clarence took the message from him and read it with nearly overwhelming sadness. "Layers and layers," he said, handing it back.

"Can you help me?"

"I'm too old to fight," the man returned. "I was never good at fighting; that's why I'm here."

"I'm begging you to help me save a world."

"They call me sometimes," he said, patting a strangely ornate box with knobs on it, "over this. I hear their voice, but rarely understand what they want."

"What do you mean?"

The man shook his head. "Life is . . . different in Kipsie. They call me about something called . . . Godproj and about orange agents . . . things I don't understand."

"You speak to them over this?"

"Only when they call me."

"Do they call often?"

"Monthly."

"Do they have an army?"

Clarence shifted in his robes, afraid to tell the old pupil how little he really knew about Kipsie. "Certainly nothing as large as you speak of. They'd have to raise all their support from the loyal provinces. I hate to see this come to violence between our own kind."

"Any sensible person hates violence," Faf returned. "Can you get me an appointment with them?"

"It's a long and perilous journey to Kipsie."

"Can you get me an appointment?"

"I can try."

Faf refolded the letter and put it back in his robes. "With this in hand, perhaps we can move them to action."

Clarence nodded, hoping Faf was right about the Lawgivers, fearing the whole time he was wrong. "Perhaps if you showed your letter to the Governor's allies . . ."

"The fire is in their eyes," Faf said sadly, getting to his feet. "All their men, all their money and all their food is tied up in this enterprise."

He walked to the door, feeling disappointed by his old mentor. "They would ignore me. Then they would kill me."

As he walked out he thought he could almost hear Clarence sigh with the swish of the door.

XVII
The Jungle—The Endless Season

"I still don't see how this will keep the animals away!" Morgan yelled over the roar of the waterfall.

"Don't worry yourself about it!" Nebo said. "Just wait until we complete the connection and you'll see."

They stood looking at the apparatus the Mech had made. Just below the waterfall, where the Hus overflow stream churned the hardest, he had supervised the building of a strange contraption he called a dynamo. Several wooden paddles that disappeared within a metal housing stretched across the stream, turning rapidly in the rushing waters.

"It's not much different than what we did in the dungeon," he said, "except we're using the power of the water to turn the wheel."

It was early morning, the dark gray sky just turning a pale ashen. The camp was coming to life all around them, several thousand Genies slowly waking.

The old city they occupied was unknown to the maps of men, yet it was barely an hour's trek from Ramon's Western Roadway. Given that, plus the proximity to fresh water, it was the ideal location for Morgan's lair. They had even given it a name: Last Chance, for there was never anywhere else for anyone to go after leaving Morgan's protection.

The trees were full of debris and Genies. Last Chance had been a large city, stretching out in all directions. It had a great deal of room to expand, and Morgan liked that. In the previous months he had waylaid a great many caravans, setting free their Genie slaves who usually ended up joining him for they had nowhere else to go.

The Woofers were up, slowly moving their immense bulks toward the water to drink. Grodin trailed behind them, moving just as lethargically. His habit patterns had been tied to the Woofers for so long that he automatically moved with them, part of the pack. Several Minnies walked with Grodin, chattering away, squeaking and buzzing, and he kept swatting at them. There was something about his relationship with the Woofers that appealed to the Minnies, and they followed him around incessantly, much to the Breeder's continued dismay.

Morgan turned and watched his People come alive. They seemed happy, even though they tended to segregate themselves according to type and then feud with the other groups. He tried often to arrange sleeping quarters that would force the different types together as in the dungeon, but his army had grown too large finally, and he wasn't able to control its habits.

"This is the turbine," Nebo said, pointing to the housing with his stump, "where we generate the electric charge."

Morgan nodded, uninterested in Nebo's paddles. "But I still don't see how this is going to . . ."

"Morgan!"

He turned to see Ona waving to him from the porch of their home. Built in a tree forty feet in the air, the house was shot through with limbs and leaked horribly in the wet, but otherwise provided a reasonably comfortable five-room lodging.

"Good morning!" he called. "How do you feel?"

She put her hands to her stomach, great with child. "He's got your muscles!" she called back. "I feel like I've been flopping on my belly!"

"As long as she has your looks!" Both of them smiled at their continual disagreement over the gender of the baby.

Ona tended to stay mostly in the house at her stage of pregnancy. Her stomach got in the way when she tried to climb up and down the tree.

"Have you eaten?" she said.

"No!"

"Come up, I'll fix something!"

"Not hungry!"

He turned from her then, feigning interest in the paddle machine. He was jittery and didn't know why, though he expected it was the inactivity of their life. They waited, always waited. They waited for caravans that were few and far between. They waited for their army to grow. They waited for Ramon to make a move. Morgan was tired of waiting, and it made him inordinately angry that Ona seemed to be perfectly satisfied with their existence.

She had expressd the thought on more than one occasion that she would be happy to stay in Last Chance forever, to plant some crops and live a simple life. That attitude caused him great distress, for he had a dream that needed constant fueling if it was not to burn out. He felt that she was pressuring him, in her good-hearted way, to make a decision to stay, and each time she did, he got angrier at her. Outwardly, he tried to hide the feeling from her, but inside, in the secret part of himself, it was festering.

Cookfires were being started all over camp, the smell of fish drifting through the clearing. Morgan was hungry, but he would eat later, away from Ona.

"Ho, Nebo!" Serge's voice came thundering from the high ground above the waterfall. They turned to look. The giant, in a rab loincloth, stood silhouetted against the gray sky. He was holding up a length of flexible pipe that Nebo had found in the ruins of Last Chance.

The Mech waved his arm. "Bring it down!" he yelled, then turned, smiling, to Morgan. "Now you'll see why we've been using all the scrap metal to build a fence. This will keep everything out."

Morgan shook his head. The Mech had never disappointed him, but this was beyond his understanding. Serge came lumbering down the steep, tree-lined hillside that formed one edge of the bowl that most of Last Chance sat in.

Grodin was approaching from the stream, water dripping from his craggy face. The Minnies were all over him, trying very hard to convince him of something.

"No, you little bastards!" he said, and shook off one that was swinging on his arm.

They were all talking at once.

"Woof, woof . . ."

"Attenuation check . . ."

"Troubleshoot . . . beep . . . weeee . . . Gro-din!"

"Check . . . freq . . ."

The man bent at the waist, so he could be eye level with the Minnies. "I said, no! And that's what I mean!"

One of the females, Biddy, put her little hands on her hips and yelled right into his face, "Trans-mis, glitch!" The others started laughing even before she got the line out.

"Oh yeah?" he said, picking Biddy up and flinging her into the stream, a diatribe of beeps and whistles spouting obscenely from her little purple lips.

"Attenuation!" they screamed in unison. "Attenuation!"

Grodin raised his hands in the air and screamed at the heavens. "No!"

The Minnies looked dejected as they helped Biddy out of the water. She walked right up to him and shook her head, fanning water in all directions like a wet Woofer. "Coaxial," she said, and the others nodded solemn agreement. Downcast, they all walked off.

"What was that all about?" Morgan asked, as he watched the already recovering Minnies leapfrog into the morning light.

Grodin waved it off. "Ah, they want to take the Woofers off in different directions to do some kind of test or something. Some foolishness, if you ask me."

Serge joined them, dragging the last length of the continuous circuit with him. "All hooked up," he said proudly, just as he always did when he had helped Nebo.

The Mech directed the giant to the dynamo. "The Minnies want to take the Woofers out and try their mind link at a distance," he said. "They want to see the attenuation . . . the drop in power. I guess they want to know the range of their minds."

"Foolishness," Grodin said with finality.

Morgan thought about that. "Maybe not," he said. "They can be pretty handy for long-distance communication."

Grodin shook his head. "They're not taking my Woofers out of my sight," he said.

"Grodin . . ." Morgan began.

"I don't want to hear it," the Breeder said. "I don't trust those little bastards away from here on my mounts."

Morgan started to speak, but stopped himself. He saw the look of disapproval on Nebo's face. The Mech was convinced that Grodin would never fit into the group, and the Breeder seemed to take every opportunity to prove him right.

Nebo knelt to the machine, pulling Serge down with him for the use of Serge's hands. After a moment, he stood. "It's all ready," he said, pointing to a small lever. "Just pull that and we'll have enough volts running through our parameter fence to keep anything out."

Grodin snorted. "Not only foolishness, but blasphemy."

"There's nothing blasphemous about electricity," Nebo said calmly.

"Not to a heathen, there's not," Grodin said.

"That's enough," Morgan said, his voice practically lost beneath the waterfall. "If you have a problem, take it up with me."

"I've got a problem," Grodin said.

"Would you like to do the honors?" Nebo asked Morgan, indicating the lever.

"I signed on to fight," Grodin said, "not to practice black magic."

"It's not black magic," Morgan said, not knowing whether it was or not. And with that, he moved to the lever, hesitating only slightly before pulling it.

All at once, the area around the camp began crackling with light, like miniature bolts of lightning. Sparks flared everywhere, accompanied by loud crackling sounds.

"What is it?" Morgan shouted, as the camp came alive with startled screams.

Embarrassment was washing across Nebo's face. "Trees, bushes! They're all touching the fence, drawing the electricity. I didn't even think . . ."

Grodin was laughing so hard he almost fell down.

Smoke began drifting through the camp.

"Fire!" Morgan shouted. "Your machine is setting everything on fire!"

Nebo pushed on the lever with his stump, and the crackling stopped.

"Grodin!" Morgan yelled. "Get the fires out!"

Grodin was running, shouting orders to the Genies who were now filling the smoky clearing; everything was chaos around them.

Morgan turned to stare at a sheepish Nebo.

"At least it worked," the Mech said.

Squan came running from downstream, giving the Woofers a wide berth as he did so. He was panting, tongue out, when he reached them, his nose wet and twitching. "Cara . . . van," he said, out of breath. "The forward scouts have . . . spied one coming up the . . . West Road."

"How large?" Morgan asked, as the cat man stared wide-eyed at the activity all around him.

"Small but . . . ripe," he replied.

Morgan felt his body tense, the familiar excitement building within him. Finally, action. He looked at Serge. "Prepare," he said.

A post stood in the center of the clearing; from the post dangled a cover piece from the hulk of one of the ancient rusted carriages they had found in a tree at Last Chance. Morgan charged through the dissipating smoke to the post. He picked up the club that lay beside the gong and began banging on it.

"Caravan!" he called. "Caravan!"

He looked up to his house, saw Ona on the front porch frowning down upon the scene.

He dropped the club and ran to the tree. Ignoring the climbing rungs he had pounded into the huge trunk, he swung up a limb, going up the fast way.

Pulling himself from limb to limb, he quickly reached the porch and scrambled up. Ona looked sadly at him.

"Caravan," he said, and she nodded wordlessly.

He took one look down to the clearing, seeing his force already assembling near the gong post. Turning, he moved quickly through the open door space and entered the house, searching for his sword.

Limbs were thick inside. He scooted under or climbed over them to get to his sleeping quarters. Ona was close behind him.

He got into the room where they kept their sleeping mats. It was tilted slightly off kilter from the rest of the house, but was relatively free of limbs.

His sword lay beside the bed. He strapped it on, then put on the gaudy flower-printed blouse he had taken from a fat slaver. Running hands through his long red hair, he turned to Ona.

"They'll not soon forget today," he said, and sat on the floor to pull on Grodin's boots.

"Why don't you let this one go," Ona said softly. "We've enough to eat, there's no need. Just this once."

Morgan stood. "That's like asking a farmer not to plant."

"But it's always planting season," she said. "You can get the next one."

He took her by the shoulders, speaking softly. "You know I must do this," he said. "Why do you make it difficult?"

She moved easily into his arms, the weight of her stomach a bond between them. "I just worry so, that's all."

He pulled her face to meet his. "Squan tells me this one is easy pickings," he said. "Nothing to worry about."

She closed her eyes, twin tears running down her cheeks. "You won't do this for me?"

"I can't," he said sternly, and pulled away from her grasp.

He hurried out of the room and out of the house before she could say anything more.

He took a force of two hundred, leaving El-tron in charge of the settlement in his absence. The squad leaders all had Woofers, but walked them to the place of ambush, so as to have them fresh if necessary.

The jungle stretched out thick and eerie around them as they marched. They hurried to remain within the two-hour warning that their advance scouts were able to give them.

Morgan watched his troops. Like most humans he had a deathly fear of the forest, its impenetrableness, its lack of organization, its uncontrollable nature. Yet, from the Genies he had learned to respect the forest, and eventually to love it. The Genies worked in harmony with Nature; the forest was their home, their protection. They moved with it easily, as with an old friend. The larger, heavier Genies, the ones designed to work close to the earth, all marched with sure feet through the dense thicket, by instinct never losing direction. The others, the furry ones, the ones with tails and large sensitive ears, used the trees as their conveyance. And a more beautiful sight Morgan had never seen as a platoon of cat men gracefully moving from limb to limb, silently flowing with the pulse beat of life in its purest form. It was the earth dwellers who taught him trust and respect, and the cat men who taught him love and beauty.

They reached the place on the road with time to spare. Morgan liked this spot because the trees had pushed up one of the ancient cement roadways, leaving behind huge thick cement slabs that jutted up from the ground like mammoth gravestones. He could hide a thousand men behind these flat-sided sentinels and no one would know until it was too late.

The road itself had fallen a bit into disrepair and had gotten nearly knee deep in weeds and sprouts. That was because the last two roadgangs who had come through for repairs had been waylaid by Morgan and freed. He had about decided that he was going to have to let a gang or two through unharmed though, simply so they could carry on the vital work of keeping the roads cleared. That, he didn't begrudge Ramon.

Morgan took his usual spot behind a large slab just beside the road. Grodin flanked him on one side, Serge on the other. To Morgan's surprise, Nebo had asked to come along on this trip, an occurrence that happened only rarely; and now he stood silently beside Serge, his arms folded into his sleeves, his deep eyes fixed down the road. The rest of the party moved silently to their places—places they had occupied many times previously—while the Woofers were tethered a short distance away. All was in readiness.

Morgan, ready to burst with excitement, turned away from the road and leaned his back against the flat stone. He took a breath, trying to hold himself in check.

"They'll be here soon," Grodin said, having witnessed Morgan's battle frenzy many times.

Morgan reached out and put a hand on the man's shoulder. He nodded. "Ona didn't want me to come today," he said.

"She worries about the father of her child," the old man said. "You can certainly understand that."

"No," Morgan said sincerely. "I can't."

"She's a village girl," Grodin replied, bending to pick up a fat knot of wood from the ground. He produced a knife from his belt and began to whittle. "She stayed in one place her whole life until she went with you. It's what she's used to. And now that she's got your child in her, she wants to nest."

"What I do is larger than myself and Ona," Morgan said.

"She's unable to think in that fashion," Grodin said, his face straining as he tried to hack off a particularly tough knot. He stopped abruptly, fixing Morgan with his weathered face. "I'm not sure if I can. All these . . . Genies and this black magic." He shook his head, returning to the whittling. "Sometimes I think I'd be happier going off and settling somewhere."

"I'm not keeping you here," Morgan snapped.

"Somebody's got to keep you out of trouble."

Morgan reached out and grabbed Grodin's knife hand. "My dream will come to pass."

"You are a great man," Grodin said to him. "I have never known anyone like you. But perhaps greatness isn't enough in this world."

"Then this world is not for me," Morgan said with finality, releasing Grodin's hand.

Grodin went back to his whittling as the two men stood in silence for a few minutes. Finally Morgan said, "What the Minnies suggest . . . about the Woofers, I think that may be a good idea."

"I'll never turn my Woofers over to them. I don't care how good of an idea you think it is."

"It's not your decision to make," Morgan said softly to be sure that no one save Grodin heard him. "The Woofers, like everything else, are under my control."

Grodin looked at him again, his face showing some inner turmoil. "I don't understand any of this," he said. "You're turning all my values upside down. Please don't press me on this issue, lad. I draw the line somewhere."

"What I do is bigger than you and me," Morgan said, turning his face back to the roadway.

"Look," Serge said, peering over the top of the slab.

Their point man, Melon Met, was charging down the middle of the roadway. He ran on all fours, springing up and over the weeds in great, bounding leaps, his long tongue flapping out of the side of his mouth.

Morgan moved out from behind his slab and walked to the center of the road. Melon charged to him, skidding to a halt and standing up, his back slightly convex. He panted, drool dripping from the corners of his furry jowls.

"They come," he said, eyes wide.

"What's wrong?" Morgan asked. "You look so . . ."

Melon tended to be overly excitable. Putting his hands on the side of his head, he rocked it back and forth. "Strange caravan," he said. "Maybe go home. Too strange."

Morgan smiled. "I'm intrigued," he said.

"No," Melon said. "Machines . . . giants . . . headless men."

"Headless men?" Morgan said. "I wouldn't miss this for the world." He patted Melon on the head. "Go rest with the Woofers. There's water there."

Melon whined slightly, then dropped to hands and knees and scurried into the bush.

"They're coming!" Serge said.

Morgan walked back behind the rock and peered anxiously out. Something was coming, all right, but it was like no caravan he had ever seen.

First came the music, music like whistles and loud pipes, filling the roadway with sound, setting off the jungle creatures with roars and chirps. The whole forest came alive around them, all sound and motion in an incredible cacophony.

"I don't like this," Grodin said, unsheathing his sword.

And then they saw them: tall thin people, taller than Serge, walking hesitantly down the road on spindly legs hidden by flowing robes of the brightest red Morgan had ever seen. There were fifteen or twenty of them and, as Melon had said, they appeared to have no heads, their robes tapering up to high shoulders with nothing on top.

"Let them pass," Grodin said, urgency in his voice. "There's nothing here for us."

"No," Nebo said. The control that Morgan had always heard in the Mech's voice was gone. He turned to stare at Morgan. "You must not let them pass under any circumstances."

Morgan turned from Nebo and looked back down the road. There was a machine, narrow as the road and taller than the tall people, moving up behind the red robes. It was made of wood, a framework of scaffolds with no covering. Huge wooden wheels twice the size of a man, creaked loudly through the choking weeds. Bright white puffs of smoke snorted from the back of the machine into the late morning sky. The music got louder.

"Don't be a fool," Grodin said. "They're obviously sorcerers." He grabbed Morgan's arm.

Morgan snatched his arm back. "Some of my best friends are sorcerers," he said, and drew his sword.

"Steam powered," Nebo said. "No sorcery."

The parade drew closer. The large machine pulled several covered carts behind it. The music seemed to be coming out of the rear of the rolling machine, from a series of pipes that rose into the air, each pipe puffing white smoke as it blew a note.

A woman sat before the pipes, pushing on something to make them work. She was dressed in red tights and her skin was brown like Nebo's, though several shades lighter.

Morgan turned to Nebo. The Mech was staring dumbly, his mouth hanging open. "She's like you," Morgan whispered.

The Mech's eyes found Morgan's, and there was something akin to fear in them.

The caravan was almost upon them. Morgan looked to Grodin sternly. "You may go back if you wish," he said.

"Damn you," Grodin said, then smiled wide. "What the hell . . . I'm old anyway."

"You're young enough to be my strong right arm," Morgan said, stepping out into the roadway. Grodin and Serge joined him.

"Good morning!" Morgan shouted, looking straight up at the tall, headless people.

He was right in front of them, blocking their path. The ones in the front of the line began hobbling erratically, uncontrollably.

Suddenly, one fell, toppling over stiffly, like a tree. It hit another as it fell, causing that one to fall, as the others hobbled back to the machine, grabbing hold of its naked frame for support.

One of the fallen lay directly in front of Morgan, who stared in fascination as a bald head poked out of the robes. The head was pale white with pink eyes. It began blinking, holding up a hand to block the morning light.

Serge walked over and pulled up the robes. There were two poles where legs should have been. The music stopped abruptly.

"These people are made out of wood!" Grodin said.

"They're called stilts!" someone called from the machine.

They looked. The woman in red tights had abandoned her pipes and had climbed around to the front of the scaffolding. She leaned way out, holding onto the wooden beams.

"Good morning," Morgan said again. "Are you in charge here?"

The woman looked at him the same way Nebo usually looked at him. "Who wants to know?" she asked.

Laughter poured from the roadway and the trees as Morgan's men made themselves known. They completely surrounded the caravan. The woman in red turned a circle, looking at them. She came back smiling.

"I am not a difficult man to do business with," Morgan said, loud enough for the whole caravan to hear. "You will leave me with the contents of your wagons and then you are free to go on your way. Any of you who choose may come back to my home with me and join our little community."

With that, all the red robes who were desperately hanging onto the machine laughed the way Morgan's men did.

Morgan shrugged. "At any rate, I will cheerfully relieve you of the burdens you so diligently carry behind you."

At that moment, Nebo came from behind the slab and walked to the center of the road. The dark woman's eyes looked fearful the way Nebo's had.

"You're Pure Blood," she said in something akin to awe.

Nebo nodded slightly as the red robes on the ground rose on normal-sized legs and hurried to the machine. Covering their faces with their arms, they climbed into the latticework of the scaffolding.

"They've got a Mech!" the Mech woman shouted.

A Genie stood peering down from the top of the machine. He was also dark, but not as dark as Nebo. He took one look at the Mech and hurried to an ornate box sitting atop the machine. He knocked on it and spoke in whispers.

"Now, about your cargo . . ." Morgan began.

The woman smiled again, but couldn't seem to take her eyes from Nebo. "It's all yours with our compliments," she said.

With that Genies charged from the trees, running toward the booty in the wagons. Morgan was drawn to the box atop the machine. A door set in it was slowly opening.

A woman climbed out. She was tall, statuesque, with long flowing hair, of light brown, foxlike, almost red like his own. She held herself with the grace and bearing of royalty. She wore a shapely gown of purple velvet trimmed with gold that reached to her feet. Morgan had never seen the like of this woman. She moved to the edge of the machine and peered down at him.

"You'd best order your men off the carts for now," she said calmly. "There are many things they could break."

Morgan couldn't take his eyes from her. "See to it, Grodin," he said. The Breeder walked off without a word.

"Humans and Genies," she said, "and a Pure Blood Mech. You've done well for yourself, Morgan of Siler, rightful heir to the throne of Alb'ny."

"Y-You know me?" Morgan said.

"Know you?" she said, laughing. "I've been searching for you!"

Morgan ran to the machine, climbing into it. There was a ladder in the center that ran all the way to the top. He scaled it quickly, reaching the woman's lofty position. Overhanging branches jammed the top of the machine. Shoving past them, he walked to face her.

The Genie drew a knife and put himself between Morgan and the woman.

"It's all right, Merit," she said calmly.

Morgan moved closer. The woman was the most beautiful creature he had ever seen, with skin as light and delicate as the fluff of a dandelion. She was smooth and unblemished, and of a perfection he never knew existed. And her eyes. Her eyes were deep gold, flecked with pale green, almost like spots of tarnish. Her eyes were deep, riveting pools that were impossible to look away from once they held him.

"Why do you search for me?" he asked without authority.

"To help you achieve your goal, of course," she said.

"I'm sure there's nothing you could do for me," he said, forcibly breaking the contact with her eyes.

"No?" she said, amused. "Take this."

She held a heavy metal ball in her hand with a tiny lever upon it. She switched the lever and handed it to him.

"Throw this as far down the roadway as you can," she said. He narrowed his eyes and stared at her. She smiled wide. "You'd better hurry."

He heaved the ball far down the road. It bounced a bit to the side, then lay there for a second. He was about to turn back to her, when they were rocked by a tremendous noise, a fiery explosion engulfing the entire road ahead. A fireball rose above the treetops, followed by a cloud of dark black smoke.

He was numb when he looked at her.

"Interested?" she said.

He could only nod stupidly. "Who are you?" he asked, pushing a mimosa branch out of his face.

She fixed him with her eyes again, held him. "I am called Alicia."

Redrick stood behind the fat pine, watching down the shady road as the red-haired devil and his men slowly dismantled the huge wooden machine and carted it, piece by piece, into the jungle.

Barely an hour before, he had narrowly escaped death when the bastard threw a ball of fire down the road to land near his hiding place. Had it bounced a few more feet, the blast would have torn him to pieces.

He had thought they had discovered him then and ran back into the forest to his camp. But when there were no sounds of pursuit, he had come out of hiding to see what was happening.

Morgan had talked for a time with the woman on the machine, and then they had begun dismantling the machine. Apparently, the woman was going to join him.

Turning, Redrick tramped into the godforsaken forest, scratching his smooth face with his hook. Something was afoot, but what? He had discovered Morgan's camp the previous week, and had since been trying to figure how to get near enough to do the job on him and still escape. No reason he should risk his own life to kill the demon when there were probably a hundred different ways he could do it that would involve no personal risk. Unfortunately, he had been unable to think of any.

His camp lay dangerously close to the roadway. But none of his men wanted deep forest completely surrounding them.

They camped in the center space of an almost geometric ring of pushed-up slabs. They had carefully cleared the spot and kept it cleared, and walking into the clearing was almost like walking into a house, and all of them liked that.

Redrick looked at his men in disgust—fifteen of the laziest, most disrespectful petty thieves and connivers in the entire province of Alb'ny. At first there had been eighteen, but three had already deserted. Some mix-up in the orders must have happened when his men were assigned.

Since he had gone off scouting, all of the men had abandoned their uniforms and were lying against the rocks half naked.

"You're out of uniform! What if we had needed to engage the enemy?"

"It's too hot," a chubby pig face of a man said. "We're conserving our strength."

Redrick glared at him. He didn't really know any of their names. He had always simply addressed them by rank, and was now beginning to realize that this disrobing was probably an attempt to confuse him.

"You will all put your uniforms back on this instant!" he said, and stamped his foot to make the point.

"Why?" someone asked.

"Because . . . because the bastard is on the move again, and we need to follow him."

"We've decided against that," pig face said. "We decided that you're not going to do anything anyway, so we don't see any reason why we should do anything."

Redrick resisted the urge to sink his hook into the man's grotesque stomach. "What is that supposed to mean?"

Another of the unsavory characters spoke up. This one had scars all over his body. "You've had several chances to kill the red-haired man," he said. "We've simply decided that all you really intend to do is follow him around for the rest of your life, which is okay for you, but a waste of time for us."

"There have been no chances!" Redrick flared. "Are you accusing me of something?"

Pig face smiled at him. "We've just realized that this is some kind of punishment for all of us, and we don't feel like being punished anymore. So, instead of marching back and forth between the road and that damned Genie camp, we'll just stay here and wait—see what happens."

Redrick moved into the center of the clearing, turning a circle, pointing with his hook. "You will get back into uniform, every one of you. Then we will prepare to break camp and march wherever the red-haired man marches until I say different. You will do what I say this minute or prepare yourselves for the consequences!"

He shook his hook menacingly at them, giving them the blackest look he could muster.

No one moved. The pig-faced man smiled wide, then picked up a twig and stuck it into his mouth. He leaned back against the rocks and closed his eyes.

"Maybe waiting here isn't a bad idea," Redrick said. "They'll have to come back to the road again anyway." He turned and walked slowly to the edge of the clearing before turning back to them. "And, ah, don't bother putting your uniforms back on now. Plenty of time for that later."

The men's laughter followed him back out of the clearing and all the way to the road.

XVIII
Ugly Science

The Green Woman talked incessantly as Ramon made love to her on the soft cushioned bunk of his cabin aboard the *Viper*.

". . . where the bright, golden . . . crown of the Sun floats across the rich, vibrant blue . . . ocean of heaven . . . to recede into the . . . streaming purple veins . . . of twilight . . . ah, ah . . . and the gleaming . . . facets of stars . . . punch through the . . . holes in the fabric of the . . . night . . ."

Her legs wrapped around his neck, he pounded in and out, her words weaving a rich tapestry of sensation through the 'dorphined haze of his mind.

He was lost in her, adrift with no shore in sight. His universe extended no further than the limits of the finely polished wood and brass of the opulent cabin, his mind locked solely on the senses-exploding power the female held over him. She was a divine instrument, attuned to a perfection he thought impossible this side of the afterlife.

He pushed her legs toward her, folding her nearly in half.

"Yesss," she hissed. "You're wonderful, you're everything. . . ."

Growling deep in his throat, he reached orgasm with a shuddering intensity that frightened him. He fell upon the woman, shaking uncontrollably, and she held him tight with arms and legs and soft, gentle words whispered into his ear.

It took several minutes before the pounding in his chest subsided and he was able to roll from her and draw a deep breath.

"You're a devil," he said, cradling her in the crook of his arm as the afternoon light danced through the porthole above the bunk.

She turned to stare at him, pouting a full lower lip. "You just bring out the best in me," she said.

He reached out a finger to those green lips, and she kissed it, then nibbled at it with her teeth.

The sweat rolled easily from both of them in the stifling heat of the cabin. Ramon had shut the doors so no one outside could hear them. Their hair was wet and plastered, their bodies glistening.

He sat up, his orientation catching up with him a second later. She had nearly total control over his moods with the things she gave him to take, and whatever was in him now took him away from everything with delicious abstraction.

"Hot," he said and reached up to open the porthole, its thick glass a speciality of a physician of some obscure Northern Province.

Outside, the workmen could be heard hammering and yelling to one another as they continued work on the decks and forward cabins of the great ships.

Ramon got to his knees and peered out the round window. The air was still today, the clouds hanging low. The big pulleys were busy swinging one of the heavy cannons into place on the *Viper's* main deck just below him. Billows of white smoke drifted slowly into the still sky from the stacks of the foundry at the opposite end of the yard. The construction of the foundry had delayed the completion of the ships by several months, but it was worth it for the cannons and armament that was being produced.

He felt something on his leg, and looked down to see a green hand snaking toward his penis.

"Not now. I couldn't already."

"A challenge," she said, and grasped him gently, her fingers stroking like tiny feathers.

"Oh no," he said, still gazing out the window.

She sat up quickly. "What is it?"

"My Physician," he said, and she knelt up to join him. "He's leading a group here for some reason."

"Nef's with them," she said, pointing.

He looked at her. "What do we do?"

She fixed him with her bemused look. "You're the Governor," she replied. "You're the one with the answers."

He stood, trying to get control of his mind; but reality kept slipping away like the morning memory of midnight's dreams.

"Dressed," he said. "We'll get dressed and meet them."

"What will we tell him?" she asked. "He thinks I am in camp, conferring with some of the other Physicians."

Ramon began struggling with his jumper, unable to understand why he was having such a difficult time with it. "We don't have to tell him anything, by Ibem. Who's in charge of this expedition?"

The Green Woman picked her filmy robes off the floor and began layering them over her head. "His greed is strong," she said as a veil drifted onto her shoulders. "It extends to me always. He does not think you better than him."

He turned angrily toward her. "Who do you think is better? Who would you choose?"

She moved to the looking glass and began combing her hair with her long nails. "I am a Physician," she answered coldly. "I go with the greatest opportunity."

"Bitch!"

Her face was a stone carving. "Send me away if you don't like it."

He clenched his fists, hands shaking. He realized for the first time that the woman would never choose. The matter could only be decided between Nef and himself. To fully possess the woman he would have to exterminate the ruler of Troy.

"Perhaps you should hide here until he is gone," Ramon said.

She lifted her head up. "Like a common courtesan? I think not, M'lord."

He struggled into his boots, then staggered to the mirror. "Oh gods," he said, looking at his myopic, bloodshot eyes. "I can't face them like this."

She cinched her ditty bag around her waist, then reached inside it.

"I have something for you," she said, and pulled an instrument out of the bag. "You put it on your face."

She offered him a thin metal framework fixed with dark glass. He took it, unfolding the mechanism.

"On your face," she said. "It hooks around your ears."

He put it on, the dark circles of glass resting before his eyes. It cut the glare of the light, yet he could still see.

"Excellent," she said. "Look in the mirror."

He did so, smiling. No one would be able to see his eyes, yet he could see out perfectly. It was always the same with the woman. As if with a Woofer, she would slap his rump, then throw him a bone. And like a Woofer, he responded in kind.

Without a word, she walked to the starboard cabin door and threw it open to the plain view of everyone below. He rushed over behind her to pull her back in, but it was too late. Pack and the others were walking up the gangplank, many of them staring up at Ramon's cabin.

"What are you trying to do?" he said through clenched teeth.

She waved at the group. "Why . . . nothing," she said innocently, then wheeled to him, her hand in the air. "Take this."

She was trying to put a pill in his mouth.

"Oh, no, I . . ." he began, but he had no will where she was concerned. Her fingers pried apart his lips and he took what she offered.

"We'd better get out there," she said, walking out on the upper deck.

Ramon followed behind, also waving to the group. They walked past other cabins amidships and took the stairs down to the main deck to greet the group.

"I've been looking for you," Pack told Ramon, the little man's eyes drifting uncomfortably between the Governor and the woman.

"I've been right here," Ramon said.

Nef moved out of the group of about ten. His whole body seemed tense. "I thought you were back at the castle," he told the woman, jaw muscles tightening.

"I decided to come here instead," she said haughtily. "The Governor has been kind enough to show me around the ship."

Nef turned to Ramon, and his hand was resting on the hilt of his sword. "I'll wager he has."

"Have you a problem?" Ramon said, incensed by the man's tone.

"You tell me," Nef said.

"We've come to demonstrate one of the cannons," Pack said. "It should make a mighty explosion."

"That it should," Ramon said, looking at Nef the entire time.

Below in the yard, a troop of warriors was marching in double file up the gangplank of one of the other ships, testing the quarters built for them in the hold. The line extended through the entire yard and disappeared back down the road and into the jungle.

"Shall we proceed?" Pack asked nervously.

"By all means," Nef said, taking a deep breath.

Ramon smiled, glad to be smoothing over the matter of the woman. "We wait anxiously," he said.

Pack led them fore over the tongue-in-groove wooden deck toward the prow. The ship held forty guns, most of them already in place. Others were being cast daily, along with the armor that was being fitted onto the sides of the vessels. The metal came from the ancient cities and the carriages that formed the battlements. Large stacks of it lay around the foundry yard, with more being brought all the time.

"Will we sail soon?" Nef asked. "You've pushed our expedition back several times. I hear of increasing unrest at home."

"Casting proceeds around the clock," Pack said. "We will be ready within a month."

"I've heard that before."

The fore cannons sat on either side of the great viper of the house of Delaga. The huge wooden snake rose majestically from the prow, nearly fifteen feet in the air. It was banded red and yellow, its mouth gaping ferociously to expose sharp fangs. The cannons were facing out over the wide, raging waters of Father Hus.

Two of Pack's assistants were busy dumping black powder into the guns' magazines. The fore guns were far larger, and far more powerful than the others. They had long barrels for better range, as opposed to the squat, ugly port and starboard guns.

"We were fortunate," Pack said, "to have among our number a Physician with an extensive interest in explosives."

He stooped and picked up a large cone-shaped metal cylinder, straining under its weight. "This projectile will be pushed through the barrel of the gun by expanding gases. It will follow its natural trajectory and eventually reach ground where a triggering mechanism within the missle itself will cause more gasses to expand, creating an explosion."

"This means nothing to me," Nef said, running a hand through his blond hair. The Green Woman had taken up a neutral position somewhere between Nef and Ramon.

"Precisely why the demonstration," Pack said.

Count Delmar spoke from the midst of the group. He twirled an umbrella on his shoulder and continually fluttered his lace handkerchief before his face. "May we please get on with it then. It's frightfully hot today, and my skin is delicate."

"Gawd," Councilman Reeder said. "Get on with it just to shut him up!"

Delmar clucked his tongue in disapproval.

Pack moved to the cannon and slid a lever on its top that opened a section of the barrel. Sliding the projectile in, he closed it back up.

"We can aim with this crank," he said loudly, pointing to an exposed gear on the side of the cannon. "To fire you pull this lever on the butt of the thing that makes a spark and starts the reaction."

"And then what happens?" Nef asked impatiently.

Pack frowned at him. "Would you like to be the one to find out?" he asked.

Everyone turned to Nef, whose eyes widened.

"Go ahead," Ramon said genially. "You're the man in a hurry."

The man in white nodded slightly, stepping toward the gun.

"The report will be quite loud," Pack said, covering his ears. "I suggest you follow my lead."

They all laughed nervously, feeling foolish taking part in such an enterprise; but when Ramon covered his ears, everyone followed suit.

Nef looked around, chuckling softly. "Here we go," he said.

"Step to the side," Pack told him. "There will be a recoil."

Nef's face turned grave, and if there were any way possible, he would have backed out. Instead he moved to the side of the machine and quickly flicked the lever before he changed his mind.

There was a click . . . a second of silence . . . then the gun rumbled like ground thunder, snapping back in its mooring, gray smoke spewing from the barrel. And it was still, only a slight whistling sound remaining.

"That's it?" Nef said. "This is what we've waited months for?"

"Physician . . . " Ramon said.

Pack, smiling, put up a hand for silence, then used the same hand to point across the waters. A second later, the missile struck home on the opposite shore, razing the treeline with a large crack and a huge orange flower of fire that bloomed magnificently into the gray sky.

When the smoke cleared, it left behind a deep scar of fallen trees and a rain of splinters that drifted gently downward to the river, some splinters nearly reaching the ship.

Everything on deck, everything in the yard—stopped. And not a person who witnessed the historic event would ever forget that moment of frightening exhilaration when the world he had known came to an end.

"What good castle walls?" Delmar said in a hoarse voice.

Ramon looked at a jubilant Pack, then turned to the Green Woman. Her eyes were glazed, her mouth slack. It was the same look of rut heat that she had when they made love.

XIX
The Conference

Morgan walked out onto his balcony to get some air. The night was still, not even a breeze up that high. His eyes burned from the smoke in the room and his mind reeled with confusion. He leaned on the railing, staring down into the camp.

Most of the People had curled up for the night, though many still huddled by the dying light of the cookfires, wondering about Alicia's strange machine, and about the eerie light that glowed from within Morgan's home. They talked, occasionally pointing, knowing that whatever was being discussed in Morgan's tree would soon be affecting them profoundly.

He heard footsteps behind him, then Ona's voice. "I hope you're trying to decide how to get rid of these . . ." She left whatever name she had for them hanging unsaid, knowing that he never liked labels put on the People.

He turned to her, sitting on the railing. "Just came out to clear my mind," he said, marveling at the amount of light that poured from his home. It was something that Alicia had set up, something that Nebo said was in a vacuum tube. He had been very excited. "I have much to think about."

"These people are evil," Ona said in a whisper. "You must send them away."

"Evil . . . how?"

"Their magic . . . their sorcery is evil. The light that comes from glass . . . the carriage that moved itself . . . they frighten me."

He reached out and pulled her to him, kissing her on the top of the head. "And the woman?" he joked. "What about her?"

Ona hugged him fiercely, as if trying to cement his mind. "I don't like the way she looks at you . . . or you her."

"She offers my dream," he said. "That's all I want from Alicia."

She moved away from him, staring at his face reflected in the woman's demon light. "And what does she want from you?"

He returned her stare, her face soft and beautiful in the glow. "That remains to be seen."

"Send them away now, before it's too late."

Morgan took her face in his hands, kissed her ripe lips. "It's already too late," he said, and walked back into the bright light.

The room was filled with People, sitting very naturally amongst the tangling branches. Even Serge had managed to squeeze himself into the house; he occupied one entire corner of the room. A small machine sat beside him, humming contentedly. Wires connected it to a series of glass globes that gave off a nearly blinding light.

Alicia, not sweating and looking radiant, perched on a window sill near the door. Nebo sat close to her, victim of some strange attraction. The red-suited Mech woman, named F'brizi, lay stretched out like a cat on a leafy branch, a large pipe in her mouth that furiously pumped gray smoke to hang in the hot night. Grodin, also smoking a pipe, stood uncomfortably as far from the Genies as he could. El-tron was also present, as were assorted Minnies scattered here and there in the branches.

"You were explaining how you came to find me," Morgan said, as he leaned against the door frame. Ona pushed past him with a sidelong look and moved to sit against a wall.

"It was not difficult," Alicia said. "News of you and the People reached me all the way in Masuria."

"Masuria," Nebo said, and it was as a breath escaping his lips. Alicia smiled at him. "That's right, the Mech city."

"I thought it was only a myth," Nebo said.

"It's real," F'brizi said. "It's glorious."

"Please," Morgan said. "You must go on."

Alicia looked at him, her gold eyes shining bright. Ona felt such a fierce pang of jealousy that its intensity disturbed the thoughts of most everyone in the room. They turned toward her. She looked sheepish, then gazed at the floor.

"Genies and humans have never lived together," Alicia said, and Morgan felt that she was speaking to him alone. "The consequences of such a circumstance are so profound that I went in search of it to see if it were true."

"It's only a temporary arrangement," Grodin said as he puffed wildly.

Alicia's face turned grave. "Is that true?"

"No," Morgan said emphatically and turned a dark gaze to Grodin. "My friend has never fully understood what it is I do here."

"Which is?" F'brizi asked.

"First I claim what is rightfully mine," Morgan said. "As first-born son of Alb'ny, I am entitled to its throne. Once accomplished, I intend to set up a province where all humans and all People can live as they will. The People sustained me in my darkest days. I will never forget, and I will never desert them."

"And what of the precepts of Pure Blood?" Alicia asked.

"Breeding is everything," Grodin said.

"I accept no precepts that I don't come upon myself," Morgan said.

"What about the Schnecks?" Grodin asked. "Are they not the results of cross-breeding?"

"Indeed they are," Alicia said, "but they are not the only examples of cross-breeding." She turned and put an arm on Nebo's shoulder. "Do you know that this Genie may be the only Pure Blooded Mech left on the planet?"

"What about . . ." Morgan nodded toward F'brizi.

The Genie climbed off the branch, her tight red outfit accenting the lithe curves of her figure. "Mechs have cross-bred for a long time," she said. "Depending on the thinness of the blood, we lose with every mix some of our innate intelligence. But we don't deform, we don't retard."

"My village was small, cut off," Nebo said. "We never even saw anything other than our own kind until the humans came and killed us all . . . all but me." His liquid eyes overspilled, large tears running down his cheeks. "We feared our own power, our own worth, and determined to limit ourselves for our own good."

Morgan stared at the Mech. He had never really spoken of his past before.

"You feared your addiction," Alicia said.

"Call it what you will."

F'brizi skipped over a branch to stand before Nebo. "We feed the addiction," she said, and raised the stumps of his hands. "Look what your fear did for you."

"You haven't told me how you found me?" Morgan said.

"What matter?" Alicia said, then closed her eyes for a second. "We put out our feelers. We knew you'd work the roads for it would be easier than hunting down villages. We simply watched the roads not kept properly, and followed to the place most improperly kept—and there you were. You know, others can find you the same way."

"You're a human among Genies," Morgan said. "What makes me so different?"

All the Genies in the room laughed, leaving Morgan to stare at Ona and Grodin, who shrugged in return.

"What's so funny?" Morgan asked.

Nebo spoke up. "She's not human," he said. "She's a Politico, and if I'm not mistaken, Pure Blood also."

Alicia inclined her head in the Mech's direction. "He is quite right," she said.

"You're a . . . Genie?" Ona said, incredulous.

Alicia looked at her as one would a child. "We come in all guises," she said.

"What's a 'Politico'?" Morgan asked.

Alicia stared at him for a long moment, the room quiet save for the rustling of the ever restless Minnies. All at once, she stood, moving to a more central position in the room. Slowly, she turned to face everyone.

"I have a talent," she said, fixing one, then the next with her golden eyes. The room hissed, as if all of them were sighing in unison. Even Grodin was affected as his mouth slackened, his pipe dropping to the floor.

She turned full circle, ultimately settling on Morgan. He felt a tension in him as she came closer. He was mesmerized by those tarnished eyes.

"My kind was the ultimate product of the geneticists' art," she said softly. "I was bred as a negotiator, as a leader, as an organizer. I can key into people's hopes and fears, then talk to them as they want to be talked to. I know what everyone in this room wants, and I know how to help them get it. I'm beautiful to look at, friendly when I need to be, firm when I have to be. I can talk to Governors and farmers alike. I can even talk to people who hate me. Watch. . . ."

She turned from Morgan, the loss of contact making him feel empty inside. She walked to Ona, the woman's eyes flashing at her.

"I've never done anything to you," Alicia said.

"It's not what you've done I fear," Ona replied tersely.

"Your children will be quite beautiful," Alicia said, her voice like a gentle mist on a hot day.

"C-children?" Ona replied.

"I sense two different life forces within you. Didn't you know?"

"Two?" Morgan and Ona said in unison.

Alicia reached out, took Ona's hand. "You are a strong and wonderful woman," she said. "You've followed your man into the wild and given your life over to him. You are fine and noble, and you will instill these characteristics in your children. Morgan is lucky to have one such as you around, luckier than he realizes."

Ona lowered her eyes. "Thank you," she said, and everyone felt the easing of her tension.

Dropping her hand abruptly, Alicia turned and stalked back to where Morgan stood, wide-eyed. "That is my talent," she said. "That is my gift."

Morgan walked closer to face her. They were eye to eye. "What has this to do with me?" he said.

"I have a plan," she said, "to give you what you want."

"What sort of plan?" Grodin asked, refilling his pipe.

She smiled a secret smile at him, and he felt as if they were conspiring together. "You will need a larger force than this to defeat your half brother," she said. "I think I know how you can get that force."

"You do?" Morgan asked.

"The Southern provinces will help you."

"That's ridiculous!" Grodin said, laughing.

Alicia wheeled to him. "Not so," she said. "Ramon Delaga hates the South and will run over it on his conquest of N'ork. If you could be sanctioned by the elders in Kipsie as the rightful ruler of Alb'ny, the Southern provinces would rally around you. Alb'ny has not had good relations with Kipsie for a long time. I think that, once alerted to the dangers of Ramon's expansion, they would gladly settle for you as an alternative to him. And who better to alert them than me?"

Morgan leaned against the door frame, deep in thought. "I see merit to what you say."

"I suggest that you and the People follow me to Masuria," Alicia said. "There we can use our factories and the talents of a Pure Blood Mech to equip your army as no army has been equipped in a thousand years. Then we will march to Kipsie and demand your birthright."

"I have the Mech," Morgan said, "and I have your plan. What need have I of you?"

"You're quite wrong," Alicia said, "about having the Mech."

She went to a small leather bag that sat by her place at the window. Opening the drawstring, she pulled out a black rock. She also had a small box with sticks in it. Laying the rock aside, she struck the stick against the side of the box. Fire sprang out, igniting the stick.

Morgan looked at Ona. The woman's face was deeply troubled.

Alicia picked up the rock and walked toward Nebo. Holding

the flame below the rock, she let it lick steadily against the edge of the thing. In a few seconds, the rock became gummy, then liquid, and it began to drip on the floor, forming a small, black puddle.

The effect upon Nebo was astounding. His eyes grew large, and his lips twitched. He tried to speak, but nothing came out.

"The Mech is mine," Alicia said, turning to Morgan. "His addiction will force him to follow me."

"Nebo . . ." Morgan said.

The Mech looked at him, eyes frightened, then returned his gaze to the dripping rock.

"There are large deposits of this near Masuria," Alicia said. "What is it?"

"Coal oil," Nebo whispered. "Fuel for engines. This opens up many, many possibilities."

"You would go with her?"

"I have no choice," the Mech said.

"You are a brave and fearless fighter," Alicia said to Morgan, blowing out her burning stick, putting the rock back in the bag. "You are a demon on the battlefield, but you know nothing of politics."

Morgan nodded, accepting the truth of her words.

"But you have the background," she continued. "Your birthright, plus my knowledge, can get us both what we want."

"And what do you want?" Ona asked.

"Power is my addiction," Alicia explained, sitting on her windowsill. "But being who and what I am limits me in my quest for it. Should Morgan of Siler and I form a bargain, I will want to share in the rule of Alb'ny. And, quite frankly, Morgan of Siler cannot accomplish his goal without my help. He will be as another leaf falling from the tree."

Morgan ran a hand through his beard. "And how could you know that you would actually get your half?" he asked.

She looked at him again, then at Ona. "I will secure power the way that women have always secured power in the society of males," she said matter-of-factly. "Morgan and I will have to marry."

XX
Sojourn

Morgan inched down the tree rungs just ahead of Ona. The woman moved slowly under the shifting weight of her bloated stomach, and he was ready to catch her should she lose her grip.

"Why don't you just leave me here?" she said. "Just abandon me and your child . . . children, while you go running off with that . . . sorceress."

"Would you calm down," Morgan said. "We haven't made any final decisions yet. Besides, even if we go through with the plan as proposed, the marriage would be in name only. Simply a convenience . . . a bargain."

"You think that makes me feel better?" she asked. "You've put me in the same position that your mother was in with Ty'Jorman!"

He reached the ground, lifting his arms up under her shoulders to help her down. "It's not the same at all."

She pushed him away. "I'll get down myself, thank you."

Ona tripped, her foot hanging in the final rung. She fell back, Morgan catching her. She jerked away from him.

"Why do we have to go?" she pleaded, turning suddenly to face him. "We've been happy here. We have everything we need. You don't know this woman, don't know anything about her."

"We were trapped here. I had no way of accomplishing my dream. Of course we know about the woman. We know what she's brought us and what she said. We know what Nebo thinks of her."

"Nebo's like . . . she is! Of course he wants you to go. We have our own dream here, yours and mine. The other is a fantasy."

"No!" he said, his voice charged with emotion. "I can do it. I owe it to myself; I owe it to the People."

She planted her hands on her hips and glared at him. "What about what you owe me? What about what you owe your children?"

"I owe them more than a bastard and a road agent for a father."

189

Morgan turned away, walking off through the confusion of the camp.

Everything was in motion around him as the People prepared for the trek to Masuria. He stood and watched a line of Woofers move slowly past, laden with supplies.

His decision to go had been made in haste, but not hastily made. For months he had known that life in Last Chance was an end in itself, that it would never lead to anything better. The Politico had been a breath of fresh air, someone who not only understood his passion, but shared it.

He had listened to her all night, listened to her own yearnings. That was the test. He understood exactly how she felt, and as that became apparent to him, he accepted her invitation.

"Morgan!"

Alicia, Nebo and Serge stood by the paddle machine that still wound itself out on the creek. The woman was waving to him. He looked back once to Ona, saw she was nowhere in sight, and moved toward the Genies.

He was attracted to the Politico also, an attraction that worked somehow deeply within him. She made him feel things that he had never felt for Ona, but he steadfastly refused to accept the feeling.

Serge was feeding Nebo large chunks of snake meat when Morgan walked up. Alicia was down on all fours, peering intently at the innards of the dynamo.

"You've done amazingly well," she said, her head moving slowly to look in this cranny or that. "With your handicap, your lack of qualified help and facilities. I'm impressed."

"Serge is qualified help," the giant said, and Nebo nodded.

Alicia stood, brushing the dust from her soft blue skirt. "Of course you are," she said sweetly. "And I apologize for that. You know, we have many big'uns in Masuria."

"You do?" Serge replied, perking up.

"More females than males in fact."

Serge's grin was about to crack his face. Morgan shook his head. The woman had an answer for everything.

"We should leave soon," he said, "before the day heats up too much."

She tightened her jaw. "My feelings exactly. With any luck we should be able to make fifteen or twenty miles today."

Morgan laughed. "Not likely," he said. "When the Sun gets hot, I rest the People and the Woofers until it cools down. I will be satisfied with ten miles today."

"That slow a pace will keep you that much longer from your

goal," she said curtly. "Every minute is of the essence at this point."

"When I lead the People, I lead them at the pace I choose. No matter what, I will not turn the decision making over to you. I want what you have to offer, but I can walk away from it if it jeopardizes my position with my own troops and my own feelings."

"You're telling me that you're in charge," she said.

"At all times," he answered emphatically, "right or wrong."

He looked at Serge. The big man was nodding to him. Nebo, for his part, simply watched the exchange, willing to go in whatever direction it dictated.

"Will you accept my counsel?" the woman asked him.

"If you'll accept that the power to act rests in my hands," he said. "Our partnership implies that faith runs in both directions."

"So it does," she said softly, and for the first time something close to respect seemed to rest on her face. "All right. I won't relinquish my right to grouse—loud and long if need be—but I will abide by your decisions."

"Good," he said, then began looking over the machine himself. "Should we take it also?"

"I don't think so," she said. "In Masuria, Nebo will have the ability to have anything made that his brain can think of. It would take much time to dismantle this."

Morgan nodded. "We'll leave it for the birds to figure out," he said.

"I have some things for you at the wagons," she said. "Will you look?"

He turned and searched out Ona again. She stood with Grodin a distance away. They were locked in deep conversation.

"Let's go," he said. Alicia led him away.

"Will there be trouble with us and the woman?" she asked, waving her arm to clear them a path.

"What sort of question is that?"

"You know what I mean."

He did know, but hated looking at Ona as an obstacle to be overcome. "She fears the marriage will shut her out," he said.

"Should I reassure her?" Alicia said with genuine concern.

"What could you say?"

She shrugged. "The truth wouldn't hurt. I would simply point out to her that the thought of a real union between you and I is unthinkable."

He stopped walking. "And why is that?"

She stopped and turned to him. "Well, I'm the genetic peak of knowledge and refinement. You . . . well, you're . . . you know."

"Are you saying I'm not good enough for you?"

She put her hands in the air. "You've got a woman," she said. "We're just business partners!"

He reached out angrily and grabbed her arm. "I'm man enough for you or any woman!" He pulled her to him, kissing her fiercely.

Reaching with her hands, she grabbed his face, tearing her chiseled red nails down his cheeks, drawing long streamers of blood.

She jerked away from him and stepped back, watching the blood drip from his face. "If you ever do that again, I'll kill you."

He looked around. Everyone had stopped, gathering near them, staring. He put a hand to his face and looked at the result of his anger and passion. Ona was also in the crowd, drawn by the commotion. When his eyes met hers, she turned and walked slowly away.

Two blood bugs were locked in deadly combat over the remains of the squirrel that Redrick had killed with a large limb. He had been standing rock still, a talent he had been studiously developing, and when the squirrel came over to investigate, he had flashed out with the bludgeon and crushed its head.

The small bugs, sleek black with large pinching mandibles, would never share a carcass. They would fight to the death over its possession, the winner then gorging itself on the victim's bodily fluids until it became the size of a man's fist and its color became slimy gray. Usually the blood bug would eat itself to death. If it didn't, within several weeks it would asexually reproduce thousands of its own kind.

Redrick divided his attention between the pincher to pincher struggle of the bugs and the activity on the roadway.

It appeared that the red-haired bastard was moving his entire campsite. All of his menagerie was there, resting under the trees by the road while that damned fancy woman watched her own bunch reassemble the big wooden machine that they had taken apart the day before.

What could the woman have said to him to make him up and move that way? He watched down the length of the uneven road. Morgan was no more than a good bow shot away. He leaned against a tree with his knees drawn up, some sort of tubelike object fixed to his left eye, which he seemed to be peering through. Redrick could kill the bastard right then, gut him with an arrow and end this, but it just didn't seem worthwhile if he couldn't be sure of getting away. Nothing wrong with self-preservation. Sacrifice was all right for the masses, but the elite needed to protect themselves so that there would be someone left to run things when the sacrificing was finished.

After a time, the big machine was once again whole. The bastard directed his people up. They were on the march, southward. Redrick glanced down at the bugs. One lay dead, the other victorious—but the price was great. The dead bug, in its final agonies, had locked a pincher grip on the other. The living bug, caught in the death grip, could only escape by pulling its head free from its own pinchers, an act that effectively condemned it to a living death. It staggered off into the brush.

Redrick turned and hurried back to camp, his field armor catching in branches and vines as he ran. Since he could only trust himself on watch anymore, he had now been two days without sleep.

His men were already breaking camp when he arrived. They were also fully dressed, the blessed restrictions of rank emblazoned on their tunics.

"Good," he said cheerily. "It appears that you've all finally come to your senses. We march immediately."

"Where?" asked the four-striped Constable with the scarred face.

"South," Redrick said, as he stooped to fill his own satchel with the personal items he had brought.

"Why don't we kill the red-haired man now, before he marches?"

Redrick stood and peered at the resolve in the man's face. "We can't," he said. "We must follow him . . . see what he's up to."

One of the others laughed loudly. "If you kill him, he won't be up to anything!"

Redrick swallowed back the words that were on his lips. "We march," he said resolutely.

"You're right," the Constable said. "We march. But not to the South. We march for home. We've had enough of this folly."

"That's insubordination."

"It's desertion," the man with the pig face said.

Redrick knew better than any of them what they were doing. He also knew his own fate should he go back without proof of Morgan's death or at least the pinpoint location of where he'd be.

"If you desert, I'll see to it that each one of you is hung for your crime. And don't think I wouldn't."

"We know that you would," the Constable said, and drew his sword. "That's why we'll have to make sure you don't go back."

The others drew their swords, forming a circle around him.

"I'll scream," he said. "I'll bring that whole crew down upon you."

"We'll take that chance."

With that, Redrick bolted. Swinging out with his right arm, he hooked one of them in the neck. Vaulting the falling body, he hit the jungle at full speed, his hands shaking, his legs pumping numbly.

They gave a halfhearted chase, but the thickness of the forest was a dark silent friend that enveloped the man from Firetree and gave him new life.

And, not for the first time, Redrick escaped the inevitable by running from it.

XXI
Stirring the Coals

The Schnecks were the best trackers in the whole country. They could flush Genies out of places where no one else would have thought anything could be hiding. In the space of four days the Schnecks had managed to round up over three hundred of them at Ramon's command.

The Genies were hanged now, all three hundred and twenty seven of them, from every horizontal overhang in the shipyard. Once-living creatures dangled like wind chimes, twisting and swaying in the southerly breezes. They had been hanged easily, gently, so as to die slowly, choke slowly.

The occasion had been caused by the untimely death of Hurtrain Nef, Mayor of Troy. His body had been found by the Governor, along with several other dignitaries in the Mayor's own quarters. He had been sliced up like so much rab meat and left to lie in a pool of his own blood. Beside the body, scrawled in blood was the word, "GENIES." The Mayor had apparently named his killers even as he died, although there were those who said that the Mayor could neither read nor write.

Ramon Delaga ordered up the retribution straight away, then "temporarily" installed himself as military commander of Nef's legions. When the round-up had been completed, Ramon ordered the executions in the shipyard and invited everyone to witness. Fifty thousand troops crammed the yard, for most their first look at the nearly completed ships that would carry them downriver. The executions stirred the complacency that had settled over the camp after the long months of waiting, and the sight of the boats further stoked the flames of passion of their cause.

Ramon stood amidships on the main deck of Nef's ship, just named *Avenger*, and stared down at the throbbing, pulsating crowds below. He could feel their tension, taste their anticipation, and he was glad. And the ship was pure white, radiant white, its figurehead was a giant eagle, wings spread, talons ready.

The Green Woman stood beside Ramon. He could feel her own excitement, something he had come to understand in her. He looked at her, a vision in blowing hair and pale light, his own eyes unfocused and dreamy as they most often were now.

All around milled the dignitaries of Troy in their white mourning robes with black arm bands, plus the other major provincial rulers. Ramon was at the peak of his power. What he didn't notice was the slow erosion that was taking place at the foundation of his leadership, an erosion that wouldn't become visible for quite some time.

"What becomes of me now?" the Green Woman asked, but her face didn't appear as troubled as her words.

"You will be taken into my employ," Ramon told her. "None of the Mayor's retainers will be turned away."

"You're too kind," she said acidly. "What will Pack think?"

"He will think nothing that I don't tell him to think."

"Don't be too sure."

Their eyes locked. "Perhaps I have . . . larger plans for you," he said. "Plans that even Pack will dare not think about."

The Green Woman made to speak, but was interrupted by a tall, white-robed Trojan. "Governor Delaga?" the man said.

Ramon turned to him. "Yes."

"I am Henri Darlow, cousin of Hurtrain Nef."

Ramon shook his hand warmly. "My sorrow goes with you," he said sincerely. "Your cousin will be sorely missed by us all."

The man smiled. "I want to thank you for burying Hurdy in your family tree," he said. "It was a grand gesture."

Ramon hugged the Trojan to him. "It was the least I could do for such a great man."

Ramon released the Trojan and turned back to watch the crowds. A dead Genie with large, furry hands swayed gently near him.

"Governor," the man said again. "If we could have words about the succession . . ."

"Not now," Ramon said curtly. "We'll not sully this solemn occasion with messy business." He never even turned to the man, who then wandered away.

"You know," the Green Woman said, "you'll need to appoint someone from Troy to take Nef's place on the expedition while his succession is decided at home."

"And someone like Darlow who is loyal to me might be just the person." Ramon said finishing her thought. "I think you have something there."

Above, on the next deck, Dixon Faf and the Lady Jerlynn looked down upon the proceedings.

"He stands so brazenly with the woman," Jerlynn said. "Has he no shame left at all?"

"She'll be his ruination," Faf said. He stood so close to Jerlynn that their legs touched. "There is talk that Hurtrain Nef died because of the Green Woman."

Jerlynn lowered her eyes, staring at the white wooden rail that she leaned upon. "I don't want to believe it of my son," she said quietly. "I can't."

"I believe she has him under some sort of enchantment," Faf said. "That's what I believe."

"His behavior has been . . . erratic lately. But, murder . . ."

Faf gently reached out and patted her arm. "No Genie did it," he said, "of that I'm convinced."

"It makes me wonder about . . ."

"Don't say it. Ty'Jorman is long dead. Let him rest."

They stood silently for a moment, enjoying their own closeness amidst the spectacle. Father Hus raged behind them, the boats in their moorings strung out around while humanity massed and swarmed wildly through some primal instinct.

"Look," Jerlynn said, pointing toward the gangplank. "Isn't that one of your friars?"

Faf looked. Frau Angelica walked up the gangpank as though he owned it, and with him, one of the monks he recognized from Techne Monastery.

"What's wrong?" Jerlynn asked. "Dixon? You look pale."

"My messenger from Techne," Faf said without inflection, "has just walked into the snake pit."

They watched as Ramon took note of the visitors as they were stopped by Castle Guard on the main deck. There was some commotion, and the Governor began to make his way over there.

"Let them pass!" Faf yelled through cupped hands. Ramon turned to stare quizzically up at the Programmer. "They're with me!"

Angelica saw Faf as he was passed on board and waved. Faf motioned them to the stairs that led to the deck. Ramon tried to intercept them, but was pulled back by the Green Woman who wanted to show him something below.

Faf watched the woman pull Ramon away, but when the Governor continued to gaze at the messenger, the Programmer knew this wasn't the end of the matter.

The men climbed the stairs and joined him

"I told you . . ." Faf said.

"I had no choice," Angelica said.

The messenger spoke immediately. "I insisted on this meeting," the man said. "I am called Hoblin. We have matters to discuss."

"Not here," Faf said.

"What is it, Dixon?" Jerlynn asked.

"Here," the man said sternly. "Now."

Faf looked behind him. "A cabin then," he said, and opened the nearest door. They walked into an unfinished cabin, the walls naked, the smell of pine nearly overpowering.

Jerlynn hovered on the deck, just outside the door, a look of puzzlement on her face.

"I think you should be here now," Faf said to her. "I can do no more without your consent. But I warn you, there could be danger."

Jerlynn stepped in without a thought, closing the door behind her. Faf smiled faintly, then turned to the messenger. "You jeopardize all of us by coming here this way."

The man returned his vehemence. "The Monastery is held hostage," he said evenly. "The lives of my fellows depend upon my quick return."

Faf's eyes narrowed beneath his bushy eyebrows. "What do you mean?"

"I had hoped you would tell me that!"

"Tell me your story," Faf said. "Quickly."

"The elders in Kipsie contact us through the box in Brother Clarence's office," he said. "There is a button that must be pushed to acknowledge that contact. Brother Clarence stopped pushing the button. Two months later, someone came to repair what they thought was a damaged box. Brother Clarence took the man into his office and closed the door. One hour later, the man emerged. He had . . . he had killed Brother Clarence."

Faf took the man by the shoulders. "Clarence . . . dead?"

Hoblin nodded sadly. "The man sent me to you, gave me seven days for the entire trip. I must confirm your leaving for Kipsie and report back to him. If I don't, everyone at Techne will die."

Faf turned from the man, pain etching his craggy face. He buried his face in his hands for a moment, then looked at Frau Angelica. "Take him to the hermitage," he said. "Feed him and give him our best Woofer." He looked at Hoblin. "Tell them I leave for Kipsie in the morning."

The Programmer shook his head. "I'm so sorry," he said. "I hope that whatever this is, it's worth our lives."

"How do you place a value on life?" Faf asked him.

Without another word, Friar Hoblin walked from the cabin, Angelica on his heels.

"Say nothing of this," Faf called after them.

"Dixon," Jerlynn said softly. "What's going on?"

Faf looked at her, then went on deck for a moment. When he came back in, he shut the door and leaned against it. Reaching into his robe, he came out with a folded piece of linen. "Read this," he said.

Jerlynn took the message and unfolded it. She read:

TO MY SON MORGAN:
I AM A WEAK AND FOOLISH OLD MAN. THROUGH RESPECT FOR JERLYNN AND LOVE OF YOUR BROTHER, RAMON, I HAVE KEPT THE TRUTH OF YOUR HERITAGE FROM YOU. BUT ON THE OCCA-SION OF MY DEATH, I FIND THE COURAGE THAT ELUDED ME IN LIFE.

I AM NOT HUMAN. NEITHER ARE YOU. I AM THE PURE BLOOD DESCENT OF A LINE OF WARRIORS BRED FOR LEADERSHIP. YOUR MOTHER, ZENNA, IS OF THE SAME STOCK. WE HAVE PASSED AS HUMAN FOR CENTURIES, AWAITING SUCH TIME AS THE AGE OF THE GENIE WOULD BEGIN. IT BEGINS NOT WITH ME. I MARRIED JERLYNN BE-CAUSE ZENNA'S EXISTENCE WAS NOT THEN KNOWN TO ME, AND ALSO BECAUSE I NEEDED THE ALLIANCE FOR MY OWN FOOLISH ADDIC-TION TO CONQUESTS. ZENNA WILL EXPLAIN THIS FURTHER.

YOUR BROTHER WILL GIVE YOU STATION.
SEARCH OUT SOMEONE LIKE YOURSELF TO MATE
WITH AND CARRY ON THE LINEAGE. PERHAPS
YOU WILL SUCCEED WHERE I HAVE FAILED.
THERE IS A GENIE IN THE DUNGEON NAMED
NEBO WHO MIGHT BE OF SERVICE TO YOU.

YOU ARE OF A GREAT AND POWERFUL RACE. BE
PROUD. I LOVE YOU.

                    TY'JORMAN DELAGA

Jerlynn was numb, dead inside, when she handed the note
back to Faf. "I've been touched by the unclean," she said, and
put a hand to her mouth.

Everything she had ever known, had ever believed, was
whirling around in her brain. She felt dizzy.

Faf took her in his arms and stroked her hair. "It's all right," he
said. "You didn't know."

"But I should have, I . . ." Her eyes widened and she looked
up at him. "But that makes Ramon . . ."

"I know," he said. "I know it does."

"Are you sure about this?"

He nodded slowly. "Many people have already died for this
information," he said, and he was thinking about Clarence the
Older. "It's real."

"Unclean," she said again.

"You didn't know," he repeated.

She hugged herself shivering. She had been too hard on herself. Ramon's actions had nothing to do with the way she had
raised him. He was of mixed breed, his problems congenital.
She was free of the responsibility of it. "What do you intend to
do with this?" she asked.

"Look at me," he said, and held her eyes. "Give me your
blessing. I want to take this message to Kipsie and present it to
the elders. Ramon is not of Pure Blood; he will not be allowed to
continue his rule. But you . . ."

"You would have me installed in his place," she said.

"If you're willing."

The idea rose within her, and crested. "Of course I'm willing,"
she said, "but we must make a condition."

"Which is?"

"Ramon must be allowed to live."

He nodded again. "I will do all in my power."

"Swear to me!" she said. "He is still my child. He must not be killed."

"I swear," he said. They embraced savagely, clinging to one another.

"I must make haste," he whispered in her ear after a moment. "I leave with the morning."

She took his hands. "That leaves tonight," she said. "Will you spend this night with me?"

Faf knelt, burying his face in the folds of her gown. "My lady," he said. "I would lay open mouthed in the rain to spend this night with you. I love you."

She pulled him to his feet. "Then hold me," she said. "Hold me with all the power that is in your arms."

He crushed her to him. "Do you love me?" he asked, the words strange and unfamiliar.

She answered with her lips and with the little moans down deep in her throat.

XXII
Masuria

It was still early afternoon when they reached the mud sea, but a bad North'r was rolling in on percussion thunder and the sky was so dark as to be nearly nighttime. The heavens groaned blue purple, and all the greens of the forest became dark and rich and heavy looking.

They had been traveling for five days, the last three of which upon hidden jungle roads and rab trails that humans were not aware of. Morgan sat on top of Alicia's machine with her, watching her Genie driver steer the huge contraption with a wheeled device, and listening to her tell him about life.

Morgan had some of the gifts Alicia gave him. Around his neck hung a large gold device called a clock—for telling time. Time, he had discovered, was a very important commodity to the Mechs. He had a telescope for seeing at a distance, a compass for determining direction. Stuck in the waistband of his trousers was a device called a gun that propelled pieces of lead at a high rate of speed.

The jungle was thick and tangled, and their narrow road closed up behind them as they moved.

"We're going to have to take shelter," Morgan said, hearing more than seeing the sky.

"Perhaps not," Alicia returned. "We're close to Masuria."

"How close?"

"There." She pointed, and he saw what appeared to be a large clear area ahead. "Beyond the mud sea."

Morgan looked down through the skeletal framework of the vehicle to the hammock that had been rigged for Ona in the frame. "Almost there," he called down to her.

She waved weakly. Ona was close to her time and the trip had been hard on her.

Morgan's troops stretched out in a ragged line behind the mover, many of them carrying poles between them from which swung the carcasses of a pack of wild canines, the ancient ancestors of the Woofer. These they were bringing to Masuria to feast upon.

The stiltwalkers moved easily through the ranks, pushing branches aside and conversing with one another. They had seemed silly to Morgan when he had first seen them on the road near Last Chance, but he had learned much since then. They moved well through mud holes, had no trouble with insects and the small, carnivorous rodents that thrived in the jungle, and were able to pick fruit from the high branches of the trees.

The machine led the way, F'brizi nearly always playing the steam music that, among other things, chased away any larger animals that might be lurking for an easy meal.

They creaked to a stop at the edge of the clearing that Alicia called the mud sea. It was spiced with fallen trees floating in the mud that seemed to be reaching out like grasping hands. The mud was gray green, a slimy concoction. A hundred yards beyond, the treeline began again, except, for the most part, the trees seemed bare and dead.

"Odd," Morgan said.

"Not at all," Alicia said smiling.

Morgan put the telescope to his eye. There was something in the trees, something solid that covered all of them, plunging them into darkness at all times.

Morgan put down the telescope. "I don't understand," he said.

"You will," Alicia said. "Have as many of your people climb on the mover as can fit. We'll transport them through the mud."

"Why don't we just march them through?"

"It's deep," she said. "No one could ever make it through there on foot."

He looked at her for a long moment. The sky rumbled loudly and the wind picked up.

"We must hurry," she said. "Even the mover won't make it through the rain."

He shouted the order through cupped hands, nearly a hundred of his people scurrying onto the device. When they were secure, Alicia gave the order—that Morgan quickly confirmed—for Merit, the Mech driver, to proceed.

They creaked forward, red robes feeding coal to the fire that formed the core of the steam engine. Morgan looked down at the People tree that fanned out below and all around him. They were like a large living organism, a machine of flesh jerking forward, reaching with hundreds of stretching arms.

They entered the mud, sinking quickly down nearly to the high axles, and Morgan immediately realized the purpose of the mover. The mud would come chest high on a man and was thick like old porridge. The mammoth wheels turned slowly in it, bringing up large gobs of the stuff as they wound their turn. It oozed down the wheels and onto the People in great claylike sections.

They moved slowly, but they moved. Nothing that Morgan could imagine, save that machine, could have gotten through it.

As they approached the treeline, Morgan got a good look at the covering.

"It's over everything," he said.

"A dome," she responded. "It keeps us from being slaves to the weather."

He brightened. "Then the mud sea was formed by the water running off the dome. It must cover an immense area."

She nodded. "It took them centuries to complete. It's made of ancient iron pieces welded together."

Morgan was impressed. "No water, no light. The jungle can't grow there."

She nodded. "No wasted time clearing it."

"And the runoff mud sea creates a perfect natural defense all around."

"That it does."

He looked at her. "And you run it."

She clucked her tongue. "All by myself."

He grinned broadly. "Until now."

Closing her eyes, she sighed heavily. "This is my city," she said. "I offer you my city for your convenience. Isn't that enough? I will continue to govern Masuria."

"We cannot operate that way, you and I," he said. The sky cracked loudly, a line of lightning striking the dome, dancing stringers of crackling light along its massive surface. "You want power, power only." She turned to stare at him. "I don't care about that," he said. "I love a good fight, but all I seek is justice—for myself and for the People. The power, and your desperate grab for it, seems more a sickness to me than anything. I have to know that I control things to my ultimate end. If I can't have that, I want nothing."

"You'd leave if you weren't satisfied," she said, incredulous. "Even now, you'd leave."

"Even now," he said. "I trust no one but myself. I trust no feelings but my own. I will let you run your city, so long as you clear all decisions with me first."

She shook her head. "I've never met anyone like you," she said softly.

"No."

They reached the far shore and Merit pulled the mover into a narrow corridor that just cleared the lip of the dome and was obviously made to fit the mover.

"Unload!" Morgan called down; the People hurried off the structure. Morgan climbed down through its innards to reach Ona's hammock. She was just sitting up when he reached her.

"How do you feel?" he asked.

"Put upon," she returned. "And my back hurts."

He helped her out of the hammock and to the ground. "We'll have you comfortable before long."

She stared at him, her eyes sad, her life energy depleted.

When they were completely unloaded, Merit backed the mover out of the dome and into the mud again. It took twenty trips to bring everyone across. On the first trip, they lost valuable time because Grodin had foolishly tried to ride one of the Woofers through the mud and had to be rescued. The Woofer panicked, and in its wild thrashing, managed to drown itself; Grodin cried like a child, and Morgan realized that once in Masuria, he was a virtual prisoner unless he knew how to drive the mover. He would learn as soon as possible.

The last load was brought across just as the rain came pounding down, making a nearly deafening drumbeat on the iron dome. They had to talk loudly just to hear one another.

"How far from the city?" Morgan asked as he stood before Alicia, his arm around Ona.

"Several miles."

"We'd best march then."

"We couldn't walk this."

"Why not?"

"You'll see. We'll take the tram."

They stood in near darkness. Morgan turned to the mud sea, but couldn't get a look through the solid curtain of rushing water that poured off the dome edge.

Alicia led them farther into the darkness. The terrain was uneven and craggy, all hills and gullies with exposed roots of dead trees sticking out of the ground like petrified hair.

They soon reached an area of light, a wooden building on stilts that had a long flight of stairs leading up to it. Alicia had Morgan's People line up in double files in front of the stairs.

They climbed the stairs and entered the building, one entire side of which was open. Cables that turned on huge metal wheels were creaking through the structure. In the distance, a large vehicle was riding the wire, moving slowly toward the house.

"They run continuously," Alicia told Morgan. "We'll take the first. My people will help everyone else on as their turns come."

The large wooden car bounced slowly into the building, Alicia stopping it with a lever. "Let's go," she said.

Ona grabbed Morgan's arm. "It's demon's work," she whispered. "Let's stay here."

Without a word, he took her by the arm and helped her onto the machine. If it was demon's work, he thought, then so be it. He would make pacts with a million demons if they would help him avenge Zenna and attain his birthright.

Everyone, including a sullen and depressed Grodin, climbed into the car. Serge, being too large to fit in the doorway, took his place on a large seat on the back built for those of his stature.

When everyone was aboard, Alicia released the brake and climbed on. They jerked once, then moved, swaying gently back and forth on the creaking wires.

The seats wound around the walls of the car just beneath the large, cut-out windows. Everyone craned their necks to look out at the land of the Mechs.

It was dark, but here and there along the dome line were lights like the ones Alicia had set up in Morgan's tree. They glowed just bright enough to cast the forest in a deathlike pallor. It was a foreboding nightmare landscape of collapsing dead trees and pitted ground that was never even—all gullies and hills and trenches. Here and there, water poured through tiny gaps in the dome, making a series of small storms that stretched out along Morgan's line of vision.

"Why is the ground like that?" Morgan asked.

"It was caused by the dome building," Alicia said. "Over the years, as they closed in more and more of Masuria, the unclosed gaps took the water drainage and eroded to the extent you now see."

"A horrible place to live," Grodin said, not caring who heard him.

"Don't condemn, human," F'brizi said angrily, "until you've seen."

As they rode, Morgan watched Nebo. The Mech sat absolutely still as was his nature, but Morgan could see an excitement just waiting to burst forth. The Mech sometimes exchanged glances with F'brizi, who usually did no more than nod in response.

"What's that?" Ona asked, pointing ahead of them.

Morgan turned to look. Thousands of lights were twinkling through the trees in the distance.

"Masuria," Alicia said simply. "Your new home."

"Alb'ny's my home," Ona replied.

"Of course," the Genie said.

"Oh my," Nebo whispered as they closed in on the city.

The lights were the first thing that Morgan noticed. They were everywhere, lining the trees and the tree buildings—bulb lights, pole lights, tube-gas lights. They burned in every color, some solid, others blinking. They lit up the city, light brighter than Morgan had seen even in the middle of the day.

It was an incredible clockwork city, full of rebuilt precision buildings that filled the dead trees, but weren't controlled by the trees. Time pieces hung everywhere, all reading 2:27. Huge clocks with exposed gears, smaller clocks with hundred-foot-long slowly swinging pendulums, all manner and size of clocks, all ticking together, all reading 2:27. Morgan looked at the clock that hung around his neck. 2:27. The city was bright and cheerful, painted in bright colors. Intricate woodwork covered all the tree buildings, and nearly everything was connected by small bridges with sculpted rails painted bright red and yellow. Mechanical platforms rose and descended under their own power, carrying Mechs of various brown hues up and down the trees. The ground around the trees had been cleared and covered with red brick. A multitude of strange-looking wooden vehicles putted along under their own power.

The city stretched out in all directions. It was large, capable of holding many thousands of Genies. It could easily accommodate a force the size of Morgan's. Mechs with large wings strapped to their backs floated from the treetops, swooping into the city to glide to their destinations. Several of them buzzed the tram, one landing on top. They wore brightly colored robes, a riot of color, a gaudy display of their mastery of the elements.

"This is incredible," Morgan said.

Grodin lit up his pipe. "It's frightening if you ask me," he said, but no one was asking.

In the center of the city was a large square. The dome had a hole in it here, the water rushing in torrents to the ground. But a hole in the ground accepted the water, splashing none into the city proper.

"It's our sanitation system," Alicia said before Morgan could ask. "The rain water churns through our sewer system below the city, flushing our garbage and waste out to the mud sea."

The Mech who had landed atop the tram climbed down to peer in one of the windows. His wings jutted out stiffly from his back.

"Honored one," he said, bowing his head to Alicia.

"We're back, Jeri," she said. "Is the extra housing prepared?"

"As you wished."

"You were certainly sure of your success," Morgan told her.

She looked at him and smiled. "I've never failed at anything yet."

The flying Mech poked an arm through the window space and patted F'brizi on the shoulder. "I worked out the crink in the angle trisection equation . . ." he started to say, then stopped when his gaze settled on Nebo. "Is he . . . is he . . . ?"

F'brizi nodded slowly up and down.

The Mech pushed off from the side of the tram, the car swinging back and forth in response. He swooped into the square, circling the waterfall. "Pure Blood Mech!" he screamed through cupped hands. "We've got a Pure Blood Mech!"

Morgan watched as Mechs and giants poured from the buildings, a large crowd of them assembling in the square as the tram jerked to a stop within the terminal above.

"You'd better go first," Alicia told Nebo.

The Mech moved to the door slot, Serge joining him on his right side. Morgan came out next. Nebo moved through the terminal to stand at the top of the outside steps. The square was already filled with Mechs, and when Nebo stepped through the outside door, a thousand of them screamed and cheered, waving their hands in the air. They were nearly in a frenzy.

Part IV

◇

PURE BLOOD

XXIII
The Rifle Range

Nebo used his long-necked screwdriver to make a minute adjustment to the calibration rachet on the back of his new left hand. His smooth face intense, he barely moved the tiny screw on the segmented black steel appliance.

"There," he said to Morgan, while opening and closing the hand rapidly to a series of clanks. "That's about as good as it will get."

Morgan studied the prosthetic device, confounded by the intricate engineering involved in such a project. The Mech always amazed him with his range of knowledge.

"You say these things will do everything a real hand could do?"

Nebo nodded, his eyes drifting to the other Mechs who were studying the rifles that F'brizi was handing out. "I don't think I'd like to juggle eggs with them," he said, arching a hairless brow, "but it's good to be able to feed myself again."

They stood in a natural clearing in the back forests of Masuria. A wide chasm separated them from the other Mechs and their new guns. Nebo had replaced a nearby dome light with a bright spot, bathing the entire area in brilliant white. Behind the Mechs, all the Woofers were tethered to the bare trees so that they could become accustomed to the sound of gunfire. Grodin was nowhere around, refusing to take part in this wrinkle in his animals' training.

F'brizi had a sour look on her face as she skirted the ditch and returned to Nebo's side. Morgan had often seen that look from her, and it was beginning to get on his nerves. She spoke directly to Nebo, ignoring Morgan.

"It is not good for the Mechs to learn combat," she said.

Nebo bent, clamping his hand on one of the discs he had designed. "Why not?" he asked, straightening to study the flat, circular object.

She put her hands on her hips. "Combat is anathema to a true Mech," she said angrily. "Mechs are bred to research, not savagery. Combat is beneath us. Besides that, we have no aptitude for it."

He let his eyes drift to hers for only a second. "A true Mech understands the nature of ego," he said, and her eyes flared in return. "A true Mech realizes the destructive nature of jealousy."

"Are you suggesting that . . ."

"A true Mech is able to adjust to whatever changes affect his life."

"What of her point of aptitude?" Morgan asked.

Nebo held up the discus. "This isn't combat," he smiled, "it's mathematics. Watch."

Stepping to the edge of the chasm, Nebo held up his hands. The Mechs immediately stopped what they were doing and turned their attention to him. His power over them was total, almost hypnotic. They were drawn to his knowledge recklessly, and Morgan was convinced that the Masurians would do anything Nebo asked of them.

"My friends," Nebo said quietly, as everyone strained to hear his words. "I present you with a problem in advanced physics: two vector quantities that must find the point of intersection."

He held the disc high in the air. "Your task is to calculate the speed and direction of this unit, taking into account the wind drifts that occur under the dome, and then intersect its path with the projectiles from your guns. Holding the rifles high on your shoulders, sight down the barrel to determine the path of your projectile. Once you have calculated the direction of the discus, simply lead the unit and find the point of intersection. Ready?"

The Mechs shouldered their rifles. Nebo twisted his body, flinging the disc to dance lightly through the air across the chasm. It floated for several seconds, then the forest exploded with the sound of thirty guns firing all at once. The noise reverberated back from the dome top, setting to flight legions of birds and small animals. The Bernards howled loudly, many of them breaking free of the tethers and charging off into the wood.

The disc was torn to shreds.

Nebo turned to smile at Morgan, who nodded in appreciation. They now had a corps of riflemen where once they had non-combatants. F'brizi, her face darkened by anger, turned from the scene and stalked off.

Nebo joined Morgan to watch the woman leave.

"I wish to take nothing away from her," Nebo said.

"I know," Morgan said. "I suppose it never occurred to her that she would lose her position when you came along."

They heard the sound of an engine and turned to look. Alicia, in one of the small wooden carriages, was picking her way through the dead forest toward them. She passed the exiting F'brizi, stopping to speak with her, then resumed her ride toward the firing range.

Morgan waved as she closed in. Skirting the chasm, she drove up beside them.

"The midwife sent word that your children are being born," she said without preamble. "I'll give you a ride back."

He stared at her in shock. "Did you say . . ."

"Hurry!"

He turned to Nebo, taking the Mech by the shoulders. "My children! My children are being born!"

Nebo put a mechanical hand to his ear. "I heard you," he said. "Can I get a lift too?"

Morgan jumped up on the boxy hood of the vehicle, then vaulted the windshield to land on the passenger seat. "Grab on back," he told Nebo, pointing to the flat cargo bed.

Leaning over, Morgan took Alicia by the head and kissed her cheek. "My children! Let's go!"

"Continue your math practice!" Nebo called out to the Mechs as they drove away.

The carriage bumped and groaned over the uneven terrain on the edge of the city, Morgan cursing every time they had to slow down to avoid hazards.

"Can't you go any faster?" he said impatiently.

"No," she said. "There's not a damned thing you can do except get in the way anyhow."

"I can lend . . . moral support."

"Drop me off at the lab," Nebo said. "I'm testing some chemical weapons today."

"What's that?" Morgan asked, turning to look at him.

A loud explosion charged the air, as the Mechs fired another volley at the range.

"Gases," the Mech replied. "Gases that make you vomit or make you die. Gases that attack the central nervous system and paralyze you or choke you to death. We've got many different kinds."

Morgan looked at Alicia. She returned his stare blankly.

"Chemical," he said, and the concept was distasteful to him.

"Where's the honor in a chemical? War is hot blood and flashing steel. Chemicals don't make men strong." He pounded his chest. "Only a good heart can do that. Death from gas . . ." He shivered involuntarily.

"Death is death," Nebo replied. "I only seek knowledge in whatever form it presents itself."

"Then let it present itself in some other form," Morgan said. "There will be no gases in my army."

"It seems foolish to limit our possibilities," Alicia said. "That is Grodin's way, the old way."

They had left the forest and were driving through the construction of the small refinery where they would convert the shale oil to gasoline. The mining of the shale oil was moving at full speed just near the refinery.

"There will be no gases in my army," Morgan repeated.

"You're making a mistake," Alicia said.

"What else do you not want in your army?" Nebo asked.

Morgan turned dark eyes to him. "Insubordination," he said in a low voice.

The streets were a bustle of activity: workers carrying materials to the construction site, Grodin training a class of assorted Genies in the art of the blade, the small assembly factories grinding out war materials.

Everything surged around their carriage, and the supercharged atmosphere shored up Morgan's level of confidence. They could never match Ramon's numbers or his combat training, but the equipment provided by the factories of Masuria could help to equalize the situation considerably.

"There," Nebo called, pointing to his private lab that occupied a wing of the rifle-assembly branch, a squat nondescript building in the midst of the factory complex. "Drop me there."

Alicia pulled in, scattering a group of playing giant children already larger than men. She screeched to a halt, raising a dust cloud that hung dully in the hot breezeless atmosphere.

Nebo climbed out. "I'll scrap the chemicals," he said with distaste, "and concentrate on my ultrasonics and microwaves."

"Nothing too impersonal," Morgan warned.

Nebo took a long breath. "Nothing . . . too . . . impersonal."

"And Nebo . . ."

The Mech waved the dust from his immediate vicinity. "Yes?"

"Congratulate me!"

Nebo smiled wide, moving to embrace Morgan. "Congratulations," he said. "If they're anything like their father, they will be great People indeed."

Morgan put his hands on the Mech's shoulders. "Thanks," he said, then turned, nodding, to Alicia.

She backed away from the building, then pulled onto the roadway again, the crowds parting to allow her passage.

"You can't stop Nebo, you know," she said. "His quest for knowledge is a pure thing. He doesn't place a value on his discoveries."

"That's what I'm here for," he said.

"You shouldn't condemn things that could turn a victory your way."

"I don't want a victory at the expense of my principles," he said. "Can't this thing go any faster?"

She turned to look at him, her red, shiny jumper glowing dully in the dome lights. "Are you willing to bet the lives of your army on your principles?"

"Yes."

They skirted the waterfall circle and pulled up in front of Alicia's opulent residence. Morgan was up and out of the carriage, running up the stairs, before it even stopped completely.

Alicia called to him, "Should I cancel the meetings you scheduled this afternoon?"

He stopped in his tracks. He had called a general strategy session with all the department heads and squad leaders. It would be the first chance to bring all the various elements together to form a viable campaign; it was an absolutely essential meeting.

"No," he said. "I'll be there."

"But, Ona . . ." Alicia began, then stopped herself.

"I'll be there," Morgan said, and hurried up the stairs and into the ornately filligreed, three-story dwelling. He knew what Alicia was referring to. It was Ona's absolute unwillingness to accept Morgan's mission. She put everything on personal terms, looking at any aspect of his work as merely something to take him away from her. The meeting would be no different, but it couldn't be helped.

The palace halls were wide and tall enough for giants to walk upright, their walls lined with prototype inventions, intricately rachetted contraptions of metal and wood, many of which served no function beyond their very machine-tooled existences. Masurians reveled in the joys of the machine age.

Morgan could hear Ona screaming all the way down the hall. A group of Genies was gathered around the hallway, anxious to witness the birth of a human.

He reached the crowd and took their congratulations and back slaps with sheepish pride. The door was partly ajar. He opened it all the way then ducked to miss the drinking crock that exploded on the wall beside his head.

"What the . . ."

"It's you," Ona said through clenched teeth. She lay on the bed, knees up and apart while Bara, the giantess wet nurse, loomed over her, one baby already tucked securely in her mammoth arm. "Keep those . . . monsters out of here."

He moved to the bed. "They just wanted to see. This is a big moment here. . . ."

"I don't care!"

"Push," Bara said. "Almost there."

Ona screamed, her face deep red from the exertion.

"The baby . . ." Morgan said to Bara.

The giant handed him the one she held. "A male," she said, impressed.

Morgan studied his son, already cleaned and wrapped. He was crying angrily, his tuft of bright red hair shaking as he yelled.

"Good lungs," Morgan said to Bara. "He's a fine boy."

Ona screamed again, the wet nurse bending to her.

"I'll call you Ty'Jorman," he said. "A name with honor."

"Here it comes," Bara said, taking hold of the second child. "Another male!"

"Two boys!" Morgan said. "I'm rich!"

The screaming stopped. Bara turned to show him the other baby. His pride swelled. Two heirs. All at once, two heirs.

He looked at Ona, her face now pale, totally drained. He moved to sit beside her on the bed as Bara cleaned the other child.

"Look what we did," he said, holding Ty'Jorman for her to see.

"Where were you?" she asked feebly.

"Busy," he said.

"The other baby?"

"Another boy. You'll see."

"I want them with me."

"Just as soon as Bara . . ."

"Now," she said. "I don't want any freaks handling my children."

"Ona . . ."

"Now!"

Morgan swallowed his anger and looked over at Bara. If the giantess was hurt by Ona's words, she didn't let on. She wrapped the baby in a tiny blue blanket and gave him to Morgan.

"Marek," he said. "We'll call you Marek of Masuria."

"Over my dead body," Ona said, reaching for the babies.

"Wait," Morgan said, standing out of her reach. "I want to show them to the People."

"To hell with the People," Ona said, "Give my babies to me."

"Just a minute," Morgan said. "They've waited for a long time."

He turned and walked toward the door, a baby in each arm.

"Morgan!" she said. He stopped walking and turned slowly to her.

"Give them to me."

He didn't move.

"You bastard."

He looked at her silently, the anger flowing between them wide and raging as the Hus. She said it again, hissed it. "Bastard."

"The People," he said and moved to throw open the door.

"Boy children!" he yelled to the assembled crowd, and the clamor of their response echoed up and down the great halls.

"No!" Morgan said emphatically, pounding his fist on the table to make the point. "I see absolutely no reason to put the riflemen under Nebo's direct control."

Alicia stared at him from across the room, from the window where she had been gazing out at the streets below. Her eyes were soft, her demeanor calm. She was in her negotiator mode. "Nebo would still be under your direct orders. It just seems simpler to make the obvious connection and let the Mechs have their . . . what, leader?"

"Try, God," Grodin mumbled.

"Instead of feeding their adulation," Morgan said, "we should just start getting them used to taking orders from me."

Alicia moved back to the table and took her seat opposite Morgan. Grodin sat as far from her as he could, the rest of the spaces filled by various Genie leaders. Nebo stood impassively near the door. Conspicuous by her absence was F'brizi, who refused to participate in any combat discussions.

"The Mechs will never be totally yours," Alicia said softly.

"They're not . . . made that way. Can't it be enough that Nebo has pledged himself to you?"

Morgan wiped at the sweat built up on his bare chest and turned to look at the Mech. "Do I have your total loyalty?" he asked.

Nebo turned blank eyes to him. "In all things physical, I am yours to command. My soul, however, belongs to the search for knowledge."

Morgan shrugged. "Knowledge is power," he said. "If I get the physical, then I can command the knowledge."

The Mech nodded. "I do not disagree with that assessment."

"Then we can't go wrong," Morgan said. "Nebo commands the riflemen under my direct orders."

"As you wish," the Mech said, nodding slightly. "I have a question about weapons research."

Morgan and Grodin shared a look of understanding about one of the few topics that they were in agreement over. "You're unhappy with the low priority given to new research," Morgan said.

Nebo spoke to the room. "Our knowledge has already far outstripped the crude weapons our factories turn out. If you'd let me convert even a few of the factories to new designs . . ."

"No," Morgan said. "The weapons we make now are deadly enough. What need of anything more?"

"How godless must we become?" Grodin said.

Nebo continued undaunted. "You said before you wanted to command my knowledge. Why do you hesitate on this point?"

"The honor . . ." Morgan began.

"What does it matter how you kill a man?" Alicia asked. "Whether by sword or gun or gas or sound waves, he's just as surely dead as if he'd fallen out of a tree."

"It matters to me," Morgan said, and as he looked around the giant-tall second-story room, no one seemed to understand his feelings. "If it matters how you live, it matters how you die. Nebo's knowledge is too . . . fragile. It builds its own structure, but maybe no one could live in such a fragile structure, maybe it would collapse around all of us if we didn't build a strong foundation."

"But who determines exactly what a good foundation is? "Alicia asked.

Morgan shook his head. "I won't play that game with you. While I'm in charge, I'll determine what's best."

"Do you then deny me research?" Nebo asked.

"No," Morgan said. "But I do insist that I be the final judge on the direction of your research. Besides, if we changed our factories every time you had a new idea, we would have a beautiful factory and no weapons."

"He's got a point there," El-tron said, and many around the table agreed.

"May we make arrangements to take a portable lab with us when we leave Masuria?" Nebo asked.

"To what end?" Grodin asked.

"So my research may continue."

"There's no need," Grodin said loudly.

Alicia stood again, moving, thinking on the move. "Are you saying we need nothing else to take N'ork from Ramon?" she asked Grodin.

Morgan leaned back and put his feet on the table. He watched the nervous twitching of Grodin's mustache.

"Ask me if a Genie army can ever defeat a force of Pure Blood humans," he said.

"Consider the question asked," Morgan said.

His old teacher looked at him with sad eyes. "I love you truly," he said and stared at the smooth-topped table. The room became desperately quiet. "I've watched your preparations for the dismantling of the world I know, the world I love."

"I love our world too," Morgan said.

The old man nodded, but didn't take his eyes from the table. "You've made weapons, deadly weapons. You've trained an army. I've helped you. You've even appointed ambassadors to the various Southern provinces to plead your case after you get the approval of Kipsie. Can you win? God help me, I hope not."

He rose to the startled exclamations of those around the table and walked, looking stooped and old, to the double-sized door. "Something inside of me keeps hoping that the South won't take up your cause, that every human in N'ork rises up and squashes you before you change forever the face of our world. I can't help my feelings."

"I know," Morgan said.

"You need to ask yourself a question: are you sure that what you want won't mean suicide for all of us, human and Genie? Are you sure you represent a better world, or just a world that will make you better by ruling it?"

With that, Grodin left. Morgan stared at the empty doorspace, listening to the old man's leather boots clicking down the hall.

"Well," Alicia said, returning to her seat, "that's the most positive reaction I've seen to our possibilities of success."

Nervous laughter followed her remark, but all eyes were turned to Morgan.

He knew he had to say something. When he spoke, it was with restraint. "I apologize for my friend's fears," he said evenly. "What other business is there to discuss?"

"My traveling lab," Nebo said.

"Approved," Morgan said.

"The matter of Genie recruitment and education," Alicia said.

"Good," Morgan said, but his mind was occupied by two new and contradictory feelings. One was that Alicia was right—Grodin's fear convinced him for the first time that success was a real possibility. The other was that his oldest and dearest friend was slipping away from him, inexorably and completely.

For Morgan, the world had already changed.

XXIV
Kipsie

Faf stood waiting in the darkened room. After nearly three weeks of painful traveling, he had arrived at the Holy City weakened with dysentery. His entourage of twenty had been cut by half on the road, several of those killed by the city custodians at the Kipsie gates. When he was finally authorized to enter, Faf was brought blindfolded, his company forced to camp outside the gates under constant surveillance. He had been within the gates for five days now and had seen nothing save a small room with a cot and an enclosed outside lavatory for the bloody discharges of his diseased body. Finally, he was brought blindfolded to a room, and made to stand in darkness for what could have been minutes or hours.

All at once, a brilliant light shone magically from the ceiling upon the unornamented floor. Faf, in the presence of a miracle, fell to his knees and covered his haggard face with his hands.

"Oh Ibem, forgive me my transgressions," he said.

"Programmer Faf," a disembodied voice said.

Faf looked up, fearful eyes searching the darkness. "Y-yes, Lord?"

"Step into the circle of light, please."

The voice was flat and listless, not at all what he would have expected from the throat of Ibem.

He stepped into the circle, fully expecting to be burned asunder by heavenly light. The light was hot, sweltering, but he did not burn.

He stood in the circle for several minutes, and couldn't shake the feeling that he was being studied, scrutinized by unseen eyes. Then, without a sound, the wall before him lit up with the images of three men.

Once again, Faf fell to his knees.

"Please," one of the images said. "Stand, please."

Faf nodded and stood, staring fearfully at the images on the wall. They appeared real, but they were flat as the wall. And the men were smaller, smaller than real men. He only saw them from the waist up and they all wore name tags on the lapels of clothing that looked much like what Pack the Physician wore.

The one named Rothman spoke. He was slim and spindly, like a spider. His skin seemed pale, nearly transparent. "You are Dixon Faf, Programmer of Alb'ny, issue of Techne Monastery?"

"Yes."

"Our condolences on the demise of Techne."

"Demise?"

"It unfortunately had to be . . . closed for good," the second man said. He looked old and tired. A white mustache drooped well past his chin. His name tag read "Penrad."

"And the novitiates?" Faf asked.

"It was a matter of contamination," the third man said forcefully. His name was Dycus. He was young, his face set and angry. He had chubby pink hands that he waved around continuously when he spoke. "Our monastaries must be clean . . . pure. This business tainted Techne, made it useless."

"You killed them?" Faf asked.

"Our field representative erased them at our request," Rothman said, his long face showing no signs of emotion.

Faf stared at the images, unsure of how to feel about them. They appeared in a vision, yet behaved like flesh and blood. He decided to ask a question to see what would happen.

"My men," he said. "They've traveled a rough trail to get here out of love for me. Might you offer them the hospitality of the Holy City?"

"That remains to be seen," old Penrad said, and the words were obviously an effort for him.

"I do not come uninvited."

"We'll take it under advisement," Dycus said.

"What does that mean?"

"You're out of order, Programmer," Dycus warned.

"Forgive me," Faf said, and it was an effort of will.

"The business at hand," Penrad said, wheezing.

"Yes," Rothman said. "We wish to speak with you about your allegations concerning Alb'ny."

"I make no allegations," Faf said. "I've simply stated the facts of the matter."

The three visions laughed.

"Programmer," Rothman said, still easing the smile from his face. "We decide truth, not you. All questions are allegations until proven to our satisfaction."

"I have served you faithfully for over forty years," Faf said. "I hope that you take that into account when you make your . . . judgements."

Penrad coughed. "Noted," he said weakly.

"Now," Rothman said. "About these claims of heresy on the part of the Governor of Alb'ny: you realize that the mounting of an expediton in and of itself is perfectly within the legal limitations of the Law?"

"Yes," Faf said. "But . . ."

"And you realize that the specified aim of the Governor's expedition is the eradication of Genies from the lands of N'ork, a perfectly acceptable and worthwhile motivation?"

Faf drew a ragged breath. "Yes."

Dycus spoke up. "And you realize that the Law allows for one Physician per province, and that the bringing together of many provinces naturally assumes any single province's autonomy in bringing its own Physician along?"

"They've built ships!" Faf said loudly. "Ships with cannons and explosives and metal sides. Ships with complicated steering devices and precision instruments."

"Hearsay," Dycus said.

"I've seen it!" Faf said. "With my own eyes I've seen it. And the Law doesn't allow for the combined knowledge of many Physicians under one control."

"You're going to have to calm down, Programmer," Penrad said. "Our ways are slow, but sure. You must trust us in this matter."

Faf forced himself to be quiet.

"We read the message," Rothman said, and held it up with

spiderlike hands. He moved slowly, rhythmically. "It seems to infer that the Governor of Alb'ny is not of Pure Blood."

"Yes," Faf said.

"How did you come upon this?" Rothman said.

"One of my . . . operatives removed it from Ramon Delaga's chambers."

"Is that within your jurisdictional authority?" Penrad asked.

"I do not know."

"In point of fact, you stole this letter," Dycus said accusingly, pointing his stubby finger at Faf.

"What does it matter how I came upon it," Faf said. "The fact is that it exists and is authentic. I'm not on trial here."

"No?" Dycus said.

"Don't you understand?" he said. "At this very moment Ramon Delaga may be sailing down the Hus with the largest force in our history. He intends to use the black arts to obliterate the South and lay siege to N'ork City. He is a half-breed who cares nothing for the old ways or Kipsie. He sets out to destroy our traditions and make himself King of N'ork. And given half a chance, he'll probably destroy you also."

The images laughed again.

"You are doing yourself no good with these insane ramblings," Rothman told him. "Isn't it enough that one Monastery has already been destroyed because of your loose tongue?"

"What of my petition?" Faf asked.

"What would you have us do?" Penrad asked.

Faf walked toward the images.

"Back to the circle," Rothman said.

"We won't speak to you out of the circle," Dycus said.

Faf returned to his place. "I would have you strip the half-breed of his title on the basis of the letter and put Alb'ny in the hands of his mother, Jerlynn Delaga, who is of proven Pure Blood. I would have you decry the expedition and demand that loyal provinces return to their homes. I would have you . . . erase the Physicians who have participated in communal magic."

"No, no," Penrad said. "I meant, what would you have us do with you?"

"Me?" Faf asked.

"Is your silence an admission of guilt?" Dycus asked.

"I've done nothing," Faf said. "My life is devoted to preserving the Law of Kipsie."

"We'll be the judge of that," Dycus said.

"Now what?" Faf asked.

"Now we check up on your allegations . . . and on you," said Rothman. "We authenticate every piece of information you've given us to determine what charges you'll have to stand accountable for."

"And what if you discover I'm right?" Faf asked.

"I hardly think we'll discover that," Penrad said laughing. "These allegations are unthinkable. There is no historical precedent for such flagrant violation of the Law."

Faf slumped, defeated. By the time they checked and rechecked their precious allegations, it would be far too late. "I thank you for your time," Faf said hollowly. "I'll be returning to my men. It's a long journey back to Alb'ny."

"You'll not be returning to Alb'ny," Rothman said.

"What do you mean?"

"You're not going anywhere, sir," Dycus said. "You're under arrest."

XXV
Above the Dome

Morgan and Ona sat on a wool blanket atop the Masurian dome, waiting for Alicia to return from her balloon trip into the clouds. The dome, glowing rust red, stretched out a patchwork as far as they could see, occasional limbs jutting up as if growing in metal soil. Twelve-week-old Marek lay quietly sleeping beside his father, while Ona nursed Ty'Jorman.

"I just don't want to raise the boys in this atmosphere," Ona said again. "That's all."

"This is our home," Morgan said, reaching out to touch her face. "These are our people. What better place to raise the boys?"

He leaned up and replaced his fingers with his lips on her cheek. She pulled away. "Because they are boys," she said with conviction. "They're human boys and should be raised with their own kind."

"We're all of a kind," Morgan said, "and that's all there is to it."

He lay down next to Marek, rolling on his side to watch the sleep of innocence on the baby's unlined face. He was looking at the future, at a mind that would never buckle to the prejudice which ruled the land he grew up in. Why didn't Ona understand that? Why did she insist on reinforcing such mindless hypocrisy?

"Alb'ny is my home," Ona said. Morgan rolled over to face her. He watched Ty'Jorman nursing on her pale breast, the light accenting the red fuzz that was growing on the boy's head.

"Your home is with me," Morgan said.

"Is it? You're betrothed to another."

He closed his eyes. Here it was—again.

"You know none of that means anything," he said.

Ty'Jorman fell asleep while nursing. Ona lay him down next to her and fixed the bodice of her shift. "I know that I want a father for my sons and not a crusader. I know that I can tell no difference between Morgan of Siler and that which he fights against."

He sat up, frowning. "You know what I am," he said. "You knew before you went with me. Why do you insist on trying to change me?"

"I love you," she said, reaching out a hand to cover his. "But I just can't live like this."

He looked at her face, trying to make his feelings flow to her. "I could never go back to the fields now," he said. "I've seen too much, learned too much . . . wanted too much."

She returned his gaze, and for a moment the flow between them was compatible; then her eyes hardened.

"You are a father now, with responsibilities," she told him. "Dreams are best left for sleep."

"No," he said.

He watched her eyes look past him, saw the shadow of hatred cross her face, and knew that Alicia had returned. Turning, he watched the hot-air balloon slowly descend to the dome, fifty yards distant.

Morgan stood immediately, his exposed chest lean and hard in the afternoon light. He bent to pick up Marek.

"Leave him," Ona said, pressing the button that would bring the dome vator back up. "I think I'll just take them back to our quarters and let them sleep there."

"Don't you want to say hello to Alicia?" he asked.

"I'm sure you can greet the Genie for both of us," she said listlessly, as she gathered the apples they had brought from hydroponics and the Genie-woven basket that was still large enough to carry the children.

Morgan took a few faltering steps toward the balloon. "I'll be down to check on you soon," he said.

"Of course," she said without looking at him.

He turned from her and ran toward the balloon. Ona's attitude bothered him considerably. If he couldn't convince her of the need for a united N'ork, who else would listen? His feet moved swiftly over the hot metal. As usual, he ran to Alicia, the only person who seemed to understand his quest the way he did.

He reached the wicker gondola attached to the huge red balloon just as it bumped gently to the dome. The variable wooden propeller turned lazily in the small breeze.

Alicia pulled the air mask off her face, her smile wide and compelling. "Have I missed anything?" she asked.

"Nothing I couldn't handle," Morgan said. They laughed.

She took off the cap which covered her ears and shook her fox hair out to glisten in the light. Then she removed the heavy coat and threw it to Morgan.

He grabbed it, putting it to his face to feel the coldness which still clung to the material. It was a sensation beyond his imagination.

Alicia climbed out of the gondola and tied it down while the air escaped from the balloon. She was dressed in a tight white jumper. "Feel my hands," she said.

He took her hands in his own. They were cold. He put one to his face, smiling at the sensation.

"Did you get above the clouds?" he asked.

She nodded. "It was beautiful—the sky like a clear crystal lake, and the Sun . . . brighter than fire straight overhead."

"So bright you couldn't look at it?"

"Always. Why don't you come sometime?"

"Me?" he said. "Up there?"

"Why not?"

He briefly considered the clouds. "I'll go when it is time to celebrate a victory," he said.

Leaving the equipment, they walked toward the elevator. Ona and the children were already gone. Morgan, in a burst of energy, tumbled forward to walk on his hands.

"Have you been to the factories today?" Alicia asked.

"Yes, production rolls along when we can keep Nebo in check."

"He's still changing things?"

"Every day he has new ideas," Morgan said to her kneecaps, "and wants to change production accordingly."

"It's the way of the Mech."

"He wanted to change the crossbows to light beams and the mortars to sound waves or something."

"How goes the food production?"

"Once Nebo came up with the energy chunks, he left the food alone." Morgan sprang forward to land on his feet. "Wouldn't you know that the one thing he could have made taste better, he left alone."

"I've had a lot of trouble with F'brizi. She seems to be jealous of Nebo."

They reached the recessed vator. Morgan pushed the button with his foot and they waited. "He stole her thunder," he said. "She was the top until he came along, and now she's nothing. I wish more of them were like her, really. The Mechs follow Nebo around like baby chicks. They listen to nothing but what he tells them."

"Sounds like F'brizi isn't the only jealous one."

The vator creaked up to dome level, pushing open the trap door to crash loudly on the dome. They stepped into the open framework and started down.

"We're going to have to move soon," he said. "If we wait until we have everything we need, we'll be here forever."

"I agree. I've been dreaming about Kipsie lately. It occupies my thoughts always."

"I've been dreaming about where we can raise enough men to fight my brother."

The vator lowered them into the silent city. No one was around, not even the children. Everyone worked in the factories and in hydroponics, not because they had to, but because the designing and production of mechanical items was the greatest joy in their lives, and because Nebo was their god of design and production. There were always plenty of new things to discover, and Nebo discovered new things daily.

When they reached ground level, a Minnie named Ratif came charging out of the tram terminal and down the stairs. He ran quickly to Morgan and jumped into his arms.

"How goes it little one?" Morgan asked, chucking Ratif under the chin.

"Symbiosis," Ratif said, out of breath. "Wide spectrum, no attenuation yet. Beep, whizzzzz." He gave Morgan a thumbs-up sign. "Copasetic."

"Good," Morgan said, and hugged the Minnie close. "You stick with me for a while, Little Bit."

The Minnie giggled, wrapping his tiny arms around Morgan's neck and nuzzling his long hair.

"What's he up to?" Alicia asked.

Morgan smiled. "Just a little job for me."

All at once, a huge explosion rocked the city, throwing Morgan and Alicia to the ground as pieces of building and dome came crashing down all around them. Within seconds, the whole area was filled with a dense smoky haze.

"The factories!" Morgan yelled, getting to his feet. Holding the Minnie under his arm, he started for the factory section, then stopped, thinking of Ona and the children. He turned to Alicia. "I'll join you in a minute!"

With that, he ran to Alicia's palace, barely finding his way in the smoke. He ran through the open front doors, avoiding the intricate wooden facade that had partially fallen and was swinging back and forth on one peg.

He found Ona, the children at her bosom, coughing in one of the smoky hallways. "I hate this!" she screamed when she saw him.

He ran to her. "Are you all right?"

"No, I'm not all right! What happened?"

Morgan had already turned from her. "Something in the factories. I've got to check." He started moving away from her.

"What about me? What about the children?"

"Take one of the small movers," he said, edging away. "Drive it to the forest and wait. I've got to go."

"You leave me now, and so help me I'll never forgive you."

"Can't . . ." he said, his steps faltering. "I've got . . . to . . ." He stood firm finally, returning her anger. "Do what I tell you. You're all right. There are others who need me."

He turned and ran from the palace.

"Freak!" she screamed after him. "Freak!"

He hit the streets full speed, Ratif still tucked securely under his arm. He ran for the dense area of smoke. It was coming from the coal mines. He ran past hydroponics, the lab's clear glass walls and banks of lights still intact for the most part. Mechs were busy moving around the greenhouses, sealing them against smoke damage.

The streets got more crowded the farther he ran, Mechs and other Genies pouring out of the production factories to see what had happened.

The way parted for him to continue moving.

It was the mines, all right, the most distant edge of the city itself. He reached the devastation uncomprehending. The destruction was nearly total. All the free-standing structures in the immediate vicinity were flattened rubble, as if a giant hand had come down to squash them. The refinery was gone. Its contents blazed with huge, licking flames and shot streamers of smoke blacker than the blackest night. A large section of the dome was missing, and the smoke poured upwards, catching fire again as it rose. Bodies lay everywhere, most either indistinguishable or twig stiff, smoking black as char.

The mines themselves seemed to have escaped damage, Worker Genies gingerly poking their heads out to survey the surroundings.

Nebo stood at the edge of the damage, along with F'brizi and Alicia. Alicia barked orders, while Nebo stood, silently watching, his new mechanical hands opening and closing, small puffs of gray white smoke squirting from the metal joints.

Morgan set Ratif on the ground and joined them. "It's the hand of God," he said in a hushed voice.

"Hand of God, nothing," Nebo said angrily. "It was the electrolyzer."

"The what?"

Nebo pointed, his mechanical hands locked into tight fists. "Do you remember the building that used to stand there? We made hydrogen in there to use in the refining process. I warned those tub brains not to smoke their pipes around the electrolyzer, because hydrogen is extremely volatile. They never listened. They didn't fear it because they couldn't see it. Idiots!"

The Mech moved into the wreckage, angrily kicking pieces of rubble out of his way. The Mechs left on their feet began gathering around him, flocking to him, and he talked to them in lyrical tones.

"No controls," F'brizi said to Morgan. "He tried too much without controls."

"Not now," Morgan told her, his mind still not accepting the devastation he witnessed, the monstrous fire that still raged in the background.

"We lost good Mechs in this disaster," F'brizi said. "Your Genies were safe in the mines."

"Search the rubble for survivors!" Alicia called to the Mechs, who ignored her and stayed with Nebo.

Morgan's walked toward Nebo's crowd, F'brizi grabbing his arm. "Morgan . . ."

He pulled his arm away. "We've taken risks on everything,"

he said. "I can't blame Nebo for this. Now pitch in and help with the wounded."

She put her hands on her hips. "I don't take orders from inferiors!" she shouted.

Morgan walked away.

Alicia heard the exchange and turned angrily to the Mech. "Do what you're told," she said, momentarily losing her always guarded composure, "or get out!"

Morgan waded into the sea of Mechs. "Move!" he yelled. "The wounded need help. Let's go!"

They slowly began to disperse, still hovering near Nebo, who was bent over, his hands clasping a broken gauge.

"Nebo!" Morgan said. "Tell them to help with the wounded."

Nebo stood. "Go," he said. "Help with the clean-up."

The Mechs scattered immediately and began pulling rubble off the fallen bodies of their comrades.

Morgan looked at Nebo. "Something we made did this?"

Nebo narrowed his gaze, the pools of his eyes showing depth but not sorrow. "Of course. Those fools blew themselves up."

Morgan turned and looked once more at the twisted metal and splintered wooden garbage that was even then still drifting in small pieces down from the sky. "But this is . . . too much. I never wanted us to make anything like this."

"What can I tell you?" Nebo said, throwing down the gauge belonging to the hydrogenation unit. His hand opened with a discernible clang and made a sweeping gesture. "This is progress."

Morgan watched his blank face and began to understand the nature of addiction.

"Morgan!" came a voice from behind.

He turned to see Grodin sitting atop a Woofer, his face set with uncontrollable anger.

"Where are the other Woofers!" Grodin said.

"We'll talk about it later," Morgan said, turning back to Nebo.

The Breeder jumped from his mount and ran to Morgan. "We'll talk about it now!"

Alicia moved near them.

"It looks like a total loss," Morgan told her.

"We've probably got enough fuel in storage anyway," she said. "From what I've seen we'll have to measure our physical loss in Mechs. Most of your people were down in the mines or on the production lines."

"The Woofers . . ." Grodin said.

"Perhaps this was a sign," Morgan said, still shaken over the extent of the devastation. Burned, moaning Mechs were being carried on litters made from debris. If he knew Nebo, the Mech would probably use the opportunity to advance medical knowledge.

Grodin drew his sword, resting it against Morgan's chest. "You will tell me where the Woofers are," he said, low and menacing.

Morgan returned his friend's glare and pushed the tip of the blade away. "I sent them off with the Minnies," he said softly.

"You did what?"

"I wanted to test the range of their mind link," Morgan said. "I sent them across the mud sea with El-tron to check at a long distance. Masuria was too small to use as a test."

"How did they get across the mud?" Alicia asked, eyes wide.

"On the mover," Morgan said.

"Without my permission? He doesn't know how to drive the mover."

"Yes he does; I taught him."

"How did you . . ."

"I told you!" Grodin said. "I told you that I wouldn't allow those little bastards on my Woofers."

"It wasn't your decision to make," Morgan said. "It was mine, and I made it." He turned to Alicia. "I taught myself to drive the mover so I wouldn't be trapped here at your mercy. I took the initiative on this issue because I'm in charge of this operation and I didn't need your approval to experiment. If you've got anything else to say, I don't want to hear it."

Alicia tightened her lips to a slash, but didn't speak.

"I warned you about this," Grodin said. "You're turning things around, turning life around. It's unnatural. You're surrounded by death and devastation, and still you can't see what you're doing is wrong. Maybe I should have left you to rot in the dungeons of Alb'ny."

Ratif ran to Morgan, leaping into his arms, his little face red and excited.

"What is it?"

"Beep, beep, beep. Interlock symby," he sqeaked, linking his fingers together. "Relay link-up, elec chain: mouthrunner. Input . . . input . . . input."

"The Minnies are mind-joined at a great distance north-

ward," Morgan said. "They've contacted our spy in Alb'ny on
the Southern Road." He held Ratif up so they were eye to eye.
"Scan input," he said. "Copy file."

Ratif nodded and closed his eyes tightly. When he spoke, it
was in a different voice, a low, large voice.

"Ramon Delaga and a force of sixty thousand have sailed today
in five ships. They travel south with the flow of the Hus."

Ratif opened his eyes, blinking several times. "Copasetic?" he
asked.

Morgan nodded, kissing him on the forehead before setting
him on the ground. "That's it," he said, and looked to Alicia. She
nodded grimly.

Morgan's voice rose to the workers. "Never mind the clean-
up!" he called. "We march for Kipsie!"

F'brizi glided smoothly over the mud sea, her wings bucking
the night breeze only slightly as she kept low, moving toward the
tiny light she detected in the treeline on the opposite shore.

The human who waited there was slow and stupid and consumed with self-importance, and she would be able to use him
as she wanted.

She had discovered him on one of her night flights several
weeks before, frightened and near death from the fever. He had
promised her riches if she would help him, and now she came to
collect on her promise, although the riches that she had in mind
were not exactly what the human envisioned.

She touched down easily on the far shore near the campfire.
Removing her wings, she folded them and carried them under
her arm. "Redrick of Firetree," she said into the brush so as not
to alarm him. "It is I, F'brizi."

"Come ahead."

She moved through the trees and into the small clearing
where his fire burned high to chase away the night creatures.

He was drawn and pale as death, his hook gleaming in the
firelight.

"How do you feel?" she asked.

"Better, thanks to your herbs," he said. "What brings you to
my vigil?"

"I have news for you," she said. "Important news."

He jumped comically to his feet, his face excited. "What is
it?" he asked.

"Calm down," she said. "Stop acting like a fool."

"Tell me."

"First the price."

"Name it. Gold? Gems? Plastic?"

She sat before the fire. "A favor."

He also sat, and she watched the firelight reflected in his eyes. He was a loathsome creature, devoid of abilities of any kind. She felt sorry for his inferiority, but had no compunction about using it for her own ends.

"I want someone killed," she said.

"Morgan?" he said, his voice climbing an octave.

"I don't care what you do with him. No, I want a Mech killed."

"Which one?"

"Nebo. The one with the mechanical hands."

Her eyes automatically traveled to Redrick's hand. He caught her eyes, then stared at the hook himself.

"Agreed," he said.

"You must also promise to let the Mechs go after you have defeated them. Allow them to return to Masuria. They will be no more harm to you."

He stared into the fire for a moment. "I will make this promise only if your information is worthy."

"Morgan takes his army to Kipsie," F'brizi said.

Redrick stiffened. "When?"

"Two days," she said. "Three at the outside."

"You're sure?"

"Absolutely. What about your promise?"

He nodded, smiling. "We have a bargain," he replied. "Come here and give me a kiss. That's the way humans seal their bargains."

She moved toward him. "That seems like a strange custom," she said. But then, humans were full of strange customs.

She sat beside him and offered her lips. He kissed her lightly, and she was just about to break the contact when the pain shot up and down her neck, the blackness overcoming her almost instantaneously.

Redrick twisted the hook back and forth in her neck until he was sure she was dead. Then he lay her gently on the ground, smiling at the glaze in her large eyes.

"Monster," he said, and spat on her unlined face.

He was happy, jubilant for the first time in months. With the morning light he'd leave to find Ramon, taking the information that would justify him before everyone.

Redrick was finished hiding behind bushes. From now on he would be someone to contend with!

XXVI
Choices

Twiddle listened to the tromping of feet and the clattering of equipment as the inhabitants of Masuria prepared to abandon the city of their birth and walk into the fog of history or obscurity.

He stood at an upper window of Alicia's palace, the palace she abandoned as easily as the snake sheds his skin. And he knew why; he understood her yearning perhaps better than she did. He also knew that the Mechs would leave without regrets. For Mechs existed for direction. Mechs were nothing without someone to tell them what to do. And the man with his hair on fire was just the one to tell them.

He knew something about the fire hair also, something that he wasn't telling. There was no hurry; the cycle would run itself out no matter what he said. That was the ultimate joke. Alicia had brought him out of the trees to use his mind's eye for the future—but the mind's eye saw only fleeting shadows in a world of substance, saw only the rushing stream of time. There was one thing Twiddle was sure of, and it was the reason he had allowed the Politico to bring him out of his tree for the first time in many years.

Focus.

At one point, his stream turned to solid ice. At one point, the shadows played solidly against a wall of rock. It all had to do with the red-haired man and his quest. In the insane confusion that had bludgeoned Twiddle's brain since the day he was born, there was finally a focus, finally something that he could grasp as real. Something monumental was going to happen in the lunatic miasma of life. Even the air smelled of change.

Twiddle intended to be there for it, as he always had been, as he always would be.

This was the reason why he hadn't killed himself years before.

This was the reason he stayed alive.

"Destiny," he whispered.

Morgan stood in the square with Serge, looking up at the eyeless man in Alicia's window. The big man was loading a large crate of ammunition on the back of a Woofer. Around them, the entire city was in motion. Preparations were nearly complete for the trek to Kipsie.

232

"Who is that?" Morgan asked Serge.

The giant followed his gaze, staring for a moment at the eyeless man. "He's a Genie holy man," he said. "Very special."

"Why?"

"He has the power," Serge said, and volunteered no more.

"He chills my blood," Morgan said.

The line of wagons extended from the waterfall straight down the main boulevard to the edge of town. A special tram hook-up had been rigged that would literally pick up each wagon and deliver it to the other side of the forest. Above, in the passenger trams, Morgan's troops were already being downloaded to the dome edge, while the Mechs were rechecking the packed wagons.

They had several cannon and mortar launchers, along with a series of bizarre and nasty personal weapons invented by Nebo and given life by his Mechs. There was a wagonful of wings with power boosters attached, along with the makings of two more large movers. There were small boats with motors and Alicia's balloon. The energy balls that Nebo invented were packed in all wagons to keep from losing the food supply in one mishap. The smell of snake meat drifted through the camp, the last meat meal they would have for a while, though that was no great loss to any of them. From here on, it would be fruit from the trees and energy balls.

Near the waterfall, Morgan spied a large pile of ammo crates not loaded. "Serge," he said. "Why hasn't that been taken care of?"

"The Woofers aren't here to load."

Morgan looked down the line of animals. They were short by nearly ten Bernards. "Where are they?"

"If I knew that . . ." Serge began.

Morgan held up a hand. "I know," he said. "Have you seen Grodin?"

Serge shook his head. "Not today," he answered.

Morgan thought about that. He hadn't seen the Breeder either. Alicia came walking out of the palace with a satchel slung over her shoulder. She had the eyeless man in tow. Morgan waved her over.

"Have you seen Grodin?" he asked when she walked up.

The Politico shook her head. "F'brizi's gone too," she said. "I haven't seen her for two days."

Morgan began to feel a tightness in his stomach. "Serge," he said, "go and check on Ona and the children."

The big man hurried off. Alicia and Morgan shared a look.

"What is it?" she asked.

"Something's wrong. He turned to the Woofer. He loosened the straps holding the crates on the animal's back. "The Woofers are gone, too."

"You don't think Grodin . . ."

"I don't know what to think," he said, taking the weight of one of the crates as it slipped down the Woofer's side. He barely got it to the ground. "But if he did take the other animals, I think I know how to get them back."

Serge came running out of the palace, a female giant running with him. "Morgan!" he shouted. "Ona is gone!"

"Damn," he said through clenched teeth.

The two giants hurried to join the group.

"We've searched the palace," Janna, the female, said. "She's gone and her gear with her."

Morgan stared up at them. "Get the other crates off this Woofer," he said.

"They can't have gone far," Alicia said. "You don't think Grodin would have taken the mover?"

"Not a chance," Morgan returned. "He wouldn't have learned how to use the machine had his life depended upon it."

"Now maybe it does," Serge said, as he lifted one of the crates and set it on the ground.

"Get others," Morgan told Janna, and he watched her and Serge smile at one another. "We'll form a search party."

They gathered all the help that could be spared from the packing, Mechs and Genies. Alicia even brought Twiddle along. When they were ready, Morgan reached up, winding his arm around the Woofer's neck, gently scratching its ear. The animal whined like a pup.

"Grodin," Morgan whispered. "Find Grodin. Find your brothers."

Its whine reached a higher pitch as it looked at Morgan with loving eyes. It shoved up against him to pet.

"No," he said. "Find Grodin."

With that, he slapped the animal on the rump. "Go. Go to Grodin. Go on!"

The Woofer got excited, jumping around, then trotted lightly in the direction of the factory mishap.

"Let's go," Morgan said, and they followed.

The Woofer led them through the city, past the rubble of the refinery and into the dead jungle on the back edge of Masuria.

They spread out on the rim of the forest and walked a broken line, keeping one another in sight as they moved.

It was rough going, over deep gullies and ground littered with dead branches. The exertion of constantly moving up and down hills soon left them sweating and exhausted. Morgan was just trudging up a steep hill when he heard a Woofer barking.

He hurried up the incline just in time to see the Woofer jump happily into a crater not far ahead. He felt the tightness again, knowing what he'd find in the gully.

He stood looking down into a deep cone-shaped hole. Grodin and Ona stood looking back up at him. She held the children in her arms. They were surrounded by ten Woofers.

The anger became a solid force within him. It tightened every muscle, every nerve of his body. It rendered him speechless, his eyes and Grodin's locked in a bitter contemplation.

One by one, the others joined the circle. Genies looking down at humans. The same divisions, always the same.

Morgan tried to force words out. They bottled in his throat, nearly choking him. Finally, he got the question loose. It came out in a frightening, strangled scream.

"Why?"

Grodin drew his sword. He spoke slowly, his words measured. "You know why," he said. "I thought I knew you once, you the pup I raised as my own with no question. But you turned, went bad. You fell in with these . . . creatures, let them turn your mind around."

"They're people!" Morgan shouted back. "Just like you!"

"No they're not," Ona said. "They're godless animals, sickening beasts!" She shook her head around. "God, how I've wanted to say that for so long. We stayed with you, tried to believe in you, but you've become more like them every day. You're no better than an animal yourself!"

"If an animal is what I am, then I am one with pride! The animals I live with don't set themselves up as lords of the planet. The animals I live with don't hide in gullies and talk of superiority."

"We are of the Pure Blood!" Grodin shouted. "We are the God-given masters of this land. You would have us mix with these creatures and tarnish our own blood. It's wrong, Morgan. Wrong!"

"My sons will grow up human," Ona said. "I will not raise them in a barnyard. I hate you! I hate you!"

"Your sons?" Morgan said.

"You leave my babies alone!"

"As your mother died," Grodin said, "I promised to look after you. I curse that promise. I deny it!"

"You were with Zenna when she died?" Morgan asked.

Grodin's face slackened, then resolved again. "Aye. Was me that killed her."

Morgan's scream tore through the forest and was heard even in the city. Without thought, the sword was in his hand and he charged down the sandy hill to Grodin.

They met in a tangle of Woofers, Morgan on the offensive. The old Breeder was no match for his skill, but defended boldly until he was finally backed against the edge of the cone.

Morgan screamed again, his father's sword slashing the air in a blur, severing the old man's blade at the hilt. Grodin fell back against the hillside, Morgan's swordpoint at his throat.

"Killer of my mother. Stealer of my children."

"Be done with it," Grodin said, his voice strong. "I don't want to live to see more of your perversion."

Morgan's swordarm quivered. He concentrated all his anger, all his hatred into the point of his blade, but still he couldn't do what needed to be done.

"Why do you hesitate?" the Breeder said.

Morgan locked gazes with him, saw nothing left there for either of them. He backed away.

"Get the Woofers," he said. The Genies trooped silently down the hillside.

Morgan backed several steps away from Grodin, then suddenly turned to Ona, his face still hard.

Her eyes became wide with fright as she hugged Marek and Ty'Jorman closer to her. She took several faltering steps.

"I did nothing to you," he said, his voice low and unnatural. "I asked only that you accept me. But you were weak, oh whore of my brother."

He walked up to her. "Perhaps he will want you now."

Reaching out, he snatched Marek away from her.

"No!" she screamed.

"You bastard!" Grodin said and tried to come for him again. Serge grabbed the man, pinning his arms behind him.

Turning, Morgan saw Alicia standing behind him. He handed her the child.

"Please give me my baby," Ona said, falling to her knees. "Please, God. I'll do anything, just don't take my baby."

"Marek stays with me," he said. "Ty'Jorman will be yours to

raise. But he will not stay with you forever. He will know his father, I swear it."

Ona bent at the waist, sobbing without control, rocking up and down. The babies, in response, started crying.

"We will bear both of you across the mud sea and give you provisions. From me you get nothing else." With that he strode up the hill, his mind turning over the failure of his Order. The others trooped silently behind, their own minds in disorder over the star they followed.

Waiting at the top of the bowl was eyeless Twiddle. He stood, serene and contemplative, the brightness of his focus dimmed not one bit by the events of the day.

XXVII
The Ruins of Catskill

It was only fitting that Ramon Delaga, Governor of Alb'ny and its provinces, would choose to hold his wedding amidst the carnage of attrition he was visiting upon the South.

Catskill, on the western bank of Father Hus, lay in smoldering ruins across the wide expanse of cleared harbor area. It had given itself over to the trees, had worked with them in a very fundamental way, wrapping a city and a way of life around the knotty branches of large pines.

Ramon and his warships had steamed without warning into the harbor, then mercilessly pounded the defenseless city with its big guns through an entire night. When the gray, hot morning arose, thousands of hungry troops disgorged from the bellies of the fire-spitting beasts and attacked the citizens who had come out in force to surrender. They had done the same to Hudson two days earlier, and the same to Athens three days before that.

The great ships lay at anchor now. Ramon's *Viper* first, then Nef's *Avenger* under the command of Henri Darlow, then old Reeder's *Graycloud* with its figurehead carved to a giant ax in remembrance that the old man was descended from a long line of land clearers, next Delmar's *Gentry*, its figurehead the torso of a naked man, and finally the *Gamecock* of Senator Murray, its prow finely chiseled to the features of a rooster's head.

But the commanders were not with their ships. They stood on the foredeck of *Viper*, gathered amidst the wispy smoke and the rape of Catskill. They gathered to witness the union of Ramon Delaga, magnificent in his polished armor, and the Green Woman, who wore a sheer gown as light and wispy as the remnants of the Catskill fires. Beyond them, on the piers and open beaches, the army of Alb'ny sacked what was left of the city, raping its women and putting all to the sword eventually. It was destruction on a massive scale, and its immediacy added an edge of excitement to the ceremony aboard ship.

Jerlynn stood, forgotten, her back to the wooden snake, and watched with sadness as her son prepared to make an even greater fool of himself. She had been brought on the expedition despite her protestations. Ramon had told her that he wanted to be able to take good care of her, but she was locked in her cabin most of the time, and never allowed out without supervision.

Ramon didn't trust her, he had stopped trusting her the day the messenger had arrived from Techne.

She watched the others on the ship, never turning her eyes to the horror that was wrought on the Southern cities, as if she could deny it and it would then systematically disappear, never having happened. Matters became less reversible every day.

She closed her eyes and leaned her head back against the thick wooden scales of the ship's mascot. Where was Faf? If he would only arrive with the proper authorization from Kipsie, they could still halt this madness. The bloodlust of the soldiers would surely be sated with three dead cities. Surely with Faf's arrival, they could all return home satisfied.

"Thinking about your holy man?" a voice said.

She opened her eyes to Ramon. He stood before her, a giddy smile on his face, his demeanor relaxed, almost slovenly. Ramon had always been high strung. This newfound behavior made absolutely no sense to her.

"You can't intend to go through with this . . ."

"Say it, Mother," he said, smiling. "Marriage, Mother. Marriage, marriage."

"This is no marriage," she said. "It's a vile exhibition, some manner of perverted display designed to show how little respect you have for life or its sacred institutions."

He nodded. "That's the kind of support a bridegroom wants on his wedding day. I can always count on my mother."

"What do you want from me? You have your godless Physicians to perform the ceremony. You marry a woman who has tatooed her entire body green and has no name. Then you pledge the renewal of life through sacred vows in the middle of a human slaughter. And now you've got the audacity to ask me to sanction it!"

He stared at her with unfocused eyes. "In time of war, one marries where one has the opportunity. The reason Pack is performing the ceremony is that our Programmer ran off when we needed him most and has not returned."

"He was called away by the Lawgivers," Jerlynn said, realizing he was trying to put her off balance. "You know that."

"What I know is that when I need my mother's support the most, she rejects me."

She watched his sad eyes, nearly taken in by their contrived depth. "Oh, you're a sly one," she said, looking away.

"I learned my lessons well, Mother."

Jerlynn looked at him again, and the Green Woman stood before her. Jerlynn's insides shook with the tension that was always upon her in the presence of this strange creature. What a fitting place for her to be, upon the *Viper*, for her eyes were snake eyes, betraying the consummate evil which made the reptile so inherently repulsive to humanity.

"Will you give us your blessing, Mother Delaga?" the woman said, the venom in her voice sweet poison.

"I will not," Jerlynn said, her throat constricting.

The Green Woman cocked her head. "Oh, have we done something to hurt your feelings." The woman looked at Ramon. "I told you we should have come to Mother Delaga before we announced our plans. I'll bet she feels left out."

"Stop it," Jerlynn said. "I don't know what kind of a spell you've put on my son or what kind of evil plan you have in that caldron of a mind, but you'll never make it work. Never!"

The woman's eyes widened. "But I love Ramon," she said, patting Jerlynn on the head. "And I love you too."

"Get away from me."

"Mother . . ." Ramon said angrily.

"Maybe she's not feeling well," the Green Woman said. "Why don't we just get on with the ceremony."

Ramon wound his arm around her. "Whatever you say, my love."

He turned, the blur of his consciousness taking a few seconds to catch up with his movements. He was drifting through a euphoric cloud of pastel color and dissonant cacophonous sounds, the air itself a thick physical thing, all sweet taste and gelatin wiggles. There was life going on around him, life that he participated in, but his role was only as an interested spectator, giving orders and watching the results. On the deck was a marriage party; below, outside the boats, his soldiers danced around to unheard music while smoke drifted lazily through the proceedings like ground-hugging clouds.

It was a grand spectacle for his marriage. He hugged the Green Woman closer to him, unable to actually feel his arm on her waist. She had given him a needle this morning, something she called, "a shot." It was from her vial of 'dorphins, but was more than she usually gave him. The shot only hurt for a second before the bliss washed over him like a hot wave.

They moved across the wide, rolling foredeck, to where his commanders stood happily. They were all excited. After more than a year of waiting, they were finally getting to bloat themselves on war, raining death and destruction on the heretics and cowards of the South. He had no doubt that he could conquer N'ork City just as easily.

"Let's get on with it," the Green Woman whispered in his ear. "Can you walk all right?"

He winked. "You just watch me," he said, and pulled away from her.

"My friends!" he said, extending his arms and turning a complete circle. "I am pleased and delighted that all of you, my loyal compatriots, could join me on this most joyous and happy occasion."

The assembled applauded loudly, including the Physicians who usually showed no outward emotion.

Ramon held his hands up for silence. "When our dear friend and colleague, Hurtrain Nef, was torn from us so ingloriously, I made a vow to keep his memory and holdings alive."

He reached out for the Green Woman, pulling her roughly to him. They wound their arms tightly around one another. "I didn't know the reward that awaited my altruism."

With that, he kissed her, their mouths and bodies grinding together, their hands roving freely over one another. The crowd began to hoot. They reluctantly broke the embrace.

"That will give you something to think about in your beds tonight!" Ramon said.

He saw movement out of the corner of his eye. His mother was skirting the group, moving back toward her cabin.

"Stop that woman!" he said, pointing.

Two of his knights grabbed Jerlynn and drew her to the wedding party.

"And now my Physician, Pack, will perform the ceremony."

Pack drew forward reluctantly. He was hurt when Ramon took up with another Physician, and furious when Ramon began seeing her openly. So much of the war, their conquests, had germinated in Pack's own mind and been brought to fruition through his efforts. For Ramon to form a union with another Physician was unthinkable to Pack, the greatest insult he could ever be dealt. He would have to do something about it—and soon.

He stood before them, Ramon and woman embracing and fondling one another again. He began without preamble.

"Friends and honored guests, we are gathered here today to witness the union of this man and this woman. It is more than simply a marriage, though. It is the union of statesmanship and technology, the reconciliation of politics and science."

Ramon had his hands on the Green Woman's buttocks and was pulling her to bump against him.

"After a thousand years of darkness, we once again walk into the Light. Behold the dawn of the Second Age of Man!"

His words were the signal to the relay messengers to the other ships. Upon those words the big guns on all the boats fired at once with a deafening roar, two hundred heavy guns spewing noise and death all at the same time.

The crews cheered, as did the troops, who stopped the pillage long enough to raise a toast to Ramon's marriage. And as they cheered, the shells struck home, lining both shores with red orange bursting flowers of destruction, raining splinters down upon the land of N'ork in a display that would not soon be forgotten by anyone involved.

On deck, Pack continued the ceremony. "Today we begin the reign of wisdom and put behind us the reign of fear. We are the future of N'ork. We are the spawn of salvation. We are the masters of Heaven and Earth!"

The cannons fired again, and there were those, even among Ramon's inner circle, who thought that perhaps the Wizard had gone a bit too far in his marriage proclamation. But their voices were too small and quiet to be heard amidst the tumult of the celebration.

Pack hurried to complete the ceremony, for Ramon was trying to pull off the gown of his betrothed even as the words were being said.

"By the authority vested in me by the Government of Alb'ny and the Land of N'ork, I pronounce you husband and wife, scientist and statesman, bound legally by all the covenants and conventions of the Province of Alb'ny and the Lawgivers in Kipsie."

Cheers resounded once again on the deck, as Ramon successfully removed his wife's gown. Pack looked on in disgust as the Green Woman shamelessly allowed the men on deck to gaze upon her body.

Ramon grabbed her again, the lust a primitive force that tore through him without control. He pulled her to him, his hands moving over her body as the crowd looked on.

"My Lord," came a strangled cry from outside the circle of guests. A commotion was being raised.

Ramon forced himself away from his wife, angry at the intrusion. He turned as the crowd parted to see a filthy, emaciated beggar being led by two of his knights.

"My Lord," the beggar said, bowing low.

"What is this . . ." Ramon began, then somewhere in the back of his fogged brain he recognized something—a hook.

"Redrick?" he said. He had forgotten where the man had even been.

Redrick hurried to him, kneeling on the deck to kiss his feet. "Please. Your forgiveness for my interruption, but I have important news."

"Stand," Ramon said, trying to determine what possible news this pitiful excuse for a man could have for him.

Ramon looked at him, the man's eyes darting. He suddenly became self-conscious about his own eyes and put on the dark glasses that were in his ditty bag.

"I have news of Morgan of Siler," Redrick said.

"What? Say it then!"

Redrick nodded, his filth-smeared face drawn and pale. "The red-haired man has made alliance with a Mech city called Masuria. He marches even now with a force of several thousand Genies toward Kipsie."

Old Councilman Reeder stepped forward, his lips sputtering. "Why Kipsie?" he said, and Ramon realized that the bastard's jailbreak had affected everyone more than he wanted to admit.

Redrick took a deep breath. "He goes to Kipsie to align the other Southern provinces against you."

"But why Kipsie?" Reeder persisted.

"He tries to have the Lawgivers declare him rightful ruler of Alb'ny."

Pandemonium broke out on deck, while Ramon assured everyone that such an event could never take place. Jerlynn listened with a heavy heart, knowing that Faf was caught in the middle of everything.

Ramon stood while everyone raged around him. They feared Kipsie, he could tell. Despite everything that had been said and done, the old ties were too strong in many of them. An idea came to him.

"My friends," he said, holding up his hands. "There is no need for alarm. This means nothing."

Count Delmar stepped forward, his brocaded silk ground-length coat a riot of swirling color. "If the South unifies against us with the Genies, we will have a full-scale war on our hands. One that we may not win."

"Though I don't accept your conclusions," Ramon said, "I note your concern and have made plans to alleviate it. Tomorrow morning, the *Avenger* sails immediately for Kipsie to intercept and destroy the heathen forces."

There was a commotion on the main pier. Ramon glanced over to see the Schnecks had impaled a large number of Genies on long pikes, and were parading the still living, agonized creatures around the deck as a wedding present for Ramon.

The Governor of Alb'ny smiled. "The *Avenger* will be manned by a crew of Schnecks under the command of Captain Henri Darlow. My personal representative and expedition leader will be . . . Redrick of Firetree—" he put his arm around the decrepit man, happy over his own internal sense of justice, "—the brave and courageous man who ferreted out the villains single-handedly and made their plans known to us at great personal peril."

No one could argue with that, so they all applauded. Redrick bore up well under the adulation of the crowd. Command at last! Now he would show everyone what real soldiering was all about.

He watched as Ramon carried his naked bride over his shoulder to his cabin. "Darlow!" he snapped to the man who would be commanding his ship.

The man walked over to him quizzically. "Yes?"

"You'll come to attention when I address you!" Redrick said.

The man straightened reluctantly, looking all around as he did.

"You will begin gathering the crew immediately. I will want to see the manifest within the hour."

"I'll . . . uh, try," Darlow said, confused at how to handle the man. He started to walk off.

"And, Captain," Redrick said. "You can deliver those to me in your cabin."

"My cabin?"

"Yes. You'll be moving out of it this evening and into one of the guest cabins."

With that, Redrick of Firetree, expedition leader, sauntered off the *Viper* and onto the *Avenger* to familiarize himself with his command.

XXVIII
The Cornfield

Morgan sat with his back against the huge china elm, sweat dripping from his beard. Marek lay upon his lap, naked except for the wide straw hat tied under his chin to keep away the filtered sun.

The People were tired from days of walking, tired of the unending jungle. They had seen nothing else for four days. When they came upon the cornfield and their first uninterrupted view of the sky, they decided to stop there for a time.

No one bothered Morgan of Siler; in his loss of Grodin and Ona, Morgan had become unapproachable. Their departure had seemed inevitable. Still their leaving reduced the human side of Morgan's dream by two thirds.

Alicia approached through a stand of white pine trees, stopping to let a squat phylabo wander by with a mammoth ear of corn tucked under his muscled arm.

Her face was grave as she sat cross-legged in front of Morgan, her white traveling cottons crisp and clean, as if her clothes mirrored the perfection of her person.

"You don't sweat," Morgan said.

Alicia smiled without humor. "My body is a balanced union of muscle and body fat, my metabolism geared to keep me at a certain peak. I've nothing to sweat out."

Morgan's mouth pulled into an involuntary frown. He was angry at her, angry at the world, and didn't know why. "Don't you ever get sick or hungover or tired?"

"I have a genetic resistance to most germs," she said, an edge to her own voice, "I'm immune to alcohol. Yes, I do get tired."

"Me too," he said, watching Marek yawn wide, his little double chin pulling the hat strap tight. "I get tired to death."

"How long are you going to feel sorry for yourself?" she asked.

"As long as it takes."

"As long as it takes to do what—get all your people killed? We've nearly reached Kipsie, and you have a responsibility to the People to get yourself together."

"I'm tired," he said. "Worn out."

"Nonsense," she said harshly. "You failed with Ona and Grodin, so now you're going to sulk like a child."

He stiffened. "So what if I am?"

She stood. "I won't mince words with you," she said, gold eyes flashing. "Either get yourself together or get out."

He jumped up to face her, the quickness of the movement scaring Marek, who began crying loudly. "You'd be nothing without me!"

"At this point, we're nothing with you," Alicia said, then turned and stalked away.

"Alicia!" he called to her. "Come here!"

She ignored him, moving into the thick trees. He started after her, then realized he had nothing to tell her. Instead, he lay Marek over his shoulder and walked to the cornfield.

It was a wild field of genetic hybrid that stretched fifty feet into the air and covered an area of several square miles. The stalks were thick as young maples, the ears the size of a man's forearm. Morgan pushed into the field, large leaves swish-crackling as he moved past, pale green glowing dully in the afternoon light.

He walked a distance; he was drowning in an ocean of corn. Then he closed his eyes and spun around, much to Marek's irritation. When he opened his eyes, he was totally without direction.

He held the baby out in front of him, watched his son's face under the hot shade of the hat. "You've lost a mother and brother," he said. "And I've lost a little more. All that was close to us is gone."

Tears he thought had long dried welled up in his eyes. "I don't know if I've ever done the right thing. Your mother didn't understand, neither did Grodin."

Marek giggled, his little arms reaching out for Morgan's beard.

"I loved them both, and I love your brother as I love you. But I love the People too. I love them with a fire that burns deeper than any love I can feel for any one person, any . . . family."

He choked out the last words, the tears finally running unashamedly down his cheeks. "Why does such a curse lie with me? I never asked for any of this. I was a simple farmer. I wanted nothing more than daily bread and the love and respect of those close to me. Now, I've deliberately denied myself those treasures. I can't blame Grodin and Ona for feeling as they do; I denied them the part of me that they loved and gave it to those . . . freaks."

He said the word, but it stuck on his tongue, leaving a bad taste, like tarnish. His lip quivered and he cried again, hugging Marek close to his breast.

When he came away, the child had hold of his beard and was tugging furiously.

"Wh-why, you little monkey!"

He had the baby by the sides, shaking him around with his hands. Marek laughed, finally releasing the beard to pull at the fingers tickling him. Morgan found himself laughing too, his depression easing despite himself.

And he knew why Alicia had been so hard on him at camp, knew that it was the only way to make him face up to himself.

"Up you go!" he said, and tossed Marek high in the air, catching him on the way down.

The baby laughed and Morgan did it again. On the third toss, the child suddenly reached out in mid-flight and grabbed a corn stalk, breaking his own fall.

Morgan looked up at him in astonishment as he dangled, laughing from the bending stalk, his little legs flailing the air.

Morgan gazed in wonder at the three-month-old infant. Zenna had told him similiar stories about himself when he was that age, but seeing it —*seeing it*—was something else again.

He stuck his arm out straight and looked up at the baby. "Come on down here, Marek," he said. "Show your papa what you can do."

The child looked down, his little eyes fixed in concentration. He swung back and forth on the stalk to build momentum, then kicked out, letting go of the stalk.

He fell several feet, the smile never leaving his face. As he passed Morgan's outstretched arm, he grabbed hold, bringing his legs up to wrap around it too.

Morgan grabbed Marek and cuddled him, the two smiling together. A vague feeling was building within him that he had yet to give definition to.

All he knew was that life had to move on. He had lost much, a loss perhaps beyond consolation. But he still had much. The child in his arms told him that without saying a word; the People told him that by sticking with him. And he still had a dream. He was a rich man who had lost part of his fortune, but who was still rich. Instead of dwelling on the loss, he would count the blessings he had and go on.

He turned and faced the way he came, his sense of direction unerring. He and Marek hurried back to camp. There was much to do before they reached Kipsie.

XXIX
Among the Lawgivers

Morgan and Alicia rode the lead mover up the long paved road to the Kipsie gates. Each had been uncommonly quiet during the trip from Masuria, their thoughts occupied with their expectations of the future and their assessments of the past. Marek lay upon Morgan's knees, bouncing with the rhythm of the creaking wheels, sleeping blissfully with the easy motions.

One of the giant women had given birth several weeks before Ona, and she nursed the child as her own. Marek, if he knew the difference, kept it quietly to himself.

There was an unease between Morgan and the Genie, an unease that neither of them could explain. When Ona had been there to act as a buffer, the relationship between the two had been obvious and businesslike. Suddenly, they were man and woman, facing one another across the open ground of emotion, and neither wanted to admit that there was any ground to cross. They were to marry, and all at once it was as if both of them were awakening to the fact.

The ruins of an ancient city stretched out around them, although this one wasn't overrun with foliage. The ground was barren and dead. Nothing grew. The ruins were nicely kept with signs and plaques indicating certain landmarks. Ahead, the gates gleamed shiny gold, uniformed troops moving into position to stop their approach.

"Nothing grows," Morgan said.

"They've defoliated," Alicia said. "I'd heard that they still practiced many of the old ways. It's unfortunate that they've chosen to not be selective enough about what they practice."

"I don't understand."

"They use chemicals to kill the growth. But the chemicals get into the water supplies and kill everything else as well. I'll venture that the citizens of Kipsie die young for the most part."

"And what of the city?"

"A museum, I think, for the pilgrims who come here. A glimpse of the old world."

Morgan pointed to the troops ahead. "Looks like we'll have to fight our way in."

"No," Alicia returned flatly. "We won't."

"Sure of yourself," Morgan said absently, his fingers tracing softly the hilt of his father's sword.

"You're thinking about Ona and Grodin," she said.

He set his jaw as if he weren't going to answer. Instead, he softened and looked at her. "Can we really talk?" he asked.

She rested a hand lightly on his arm and fixed him with the gold of her eyes. "Yes," she answered simply.

"I mean really talk," he said. "Honestly. No Politico sugar-sweet."

"We can't afford that between us now," she said, and there was something new and frightening about her own demeanor.

"I thought people would understand my dream, how right it was, and flock to it. Maybe I'm wrong, or . . . crazy."

He stared down at Marek. The child had Ona's face, at least everywhere except the eyes. He continued. "But Grodin and Ona, they were both so close to me, I worked on them so hard— but they never understood any of it."

"There is an old proverb," Alicia returned, "about a prophet being without honor in his own home. You were too close to Grodin and Ona; they were too much a part of your own past. When you began your new life, it was necessary for you to begin with new people. It is a strange fact of life, but true." She smiled. "If it helps, I believe in your dream."

"You only believe in the power," he said.

She shook her head. "You've always been wrong about that; and it was convenient for me to let you go on believing it. But there's a connection you don't understand. Yes, I'm addicted to the power, but the real seat of my addiction is in the disposition of that power."

"I don't understand."

She stopped and thought for a moment before going on. When she did, it was slowly, as if she were specifically choosing each individual word.

"I care for the power but not for the symptoms of power. Not the glory, not the riches, not the prestige, not the control—only the power. I want nothing from the power, save its successful operation. That's the beauty of the Politico. You see, power tied to greed or ego is totally self-destructive. It eats itself away and collapses under its own weight. The only government that works is the government that exists for the benefit of the governed. When the people are satisfied, they give back to the power and increase it. Power flourishes in a healthy environment."

He looked at her, half smiling. "So a government that is fair to all the people, human and Genie, is one that will become even more powerful."

"You're beginning to understand," she said happily. "I love the People as much as you do, for that love feeds my power addiction."

Morgan made the final connection, his mind clearing with it. "That means that my dream . . ."

"Is the same as my dream," Alicia finished. "And that's why I came to search you out in the forest."

"You do believe in me!"

She nodded vigorously. "I believe in very little else."

Morgan leaned back on the bench, his eyes staring at the gray, rolling sky. A weight had been lifted from him, a weight that had pulled him down more than he had realized. Suddenly, it all seemed possible again. He wasn't a lone voice crying out against the blackness of the night. There were other voices, others who believed as he did.

The mover jerked to a stop. They had reached the gate. Morgan straightened and looked at Alicia. She nodded slightly, and for once, there were no controls, no demands in her eyes. For once, honesty passed between them, honesty and affection. For once, he felt he didn't have to ask himself what she really was thinking.

Bara, the giantess, climbed to the top of the mover and silently took Marek, who awoke, screaming. They all smiled at one another, and Bara climbed back down to take the child to the rear and safety.

"I want you to know," Morgan said, as he watched the massed troops prepare to fend them off, "that at this moment in time, there's no place I'd rather be in all the lands of all the world, and there's no one I'd rather be with."

She leaned across to him, kissing him on the mouth. "Nor I," she said.

Morgan jumped up, his body a coiled spring. He turned to the rear, to his troops in the next mover, and lined out long behind.

"Prepare for Destiny!" he yelled, and thrust a fist into the air. They answered him with a rousing cheer.

He turned back. Alicia was already climbing down, her long gown of blue velvet hitched up around her waist to facilitate her movements. He hurried to join her.

Troops in dark blue uniforms with silver badges on their chests were massed at the gate. There might have been a hundred of them, but Morgan doubted there were too many more. From the looks on the troops' faces, they were not prepared to repel an armed invasion.

The gates, wide and gold, were attached to a high stone wall that wound around the entire complex. Inside, Morgan could see the Holy City. It was a one-block street filled with ancient buildings in perfect shape. It was beautiful and inspiring, a testament to the arts of a civilization long dead.

He raced Alicia to the ground, hurrying directly to the gate. Spears and arrows were pointed at him, but no one used them, afraid of the consequences.

"Good afternoon," Morgan said, when he strode up to the gates.

"Leave this place," a gruff, clean-shaven man said.

"I've come a long distance to speak with the Lawgivers," he said.

"No visitors," the man said, brandishing his sword. "You must go now."

"If you don't let us in," he said as Alicia walked up, "we'll force our way in, over your bodies if we have to."

The man took a breath. "We are prepared for that."

"So be it," Morgan said, drawing his sword and pistol.

Alicia put a hand on his arm. "Let me," she said.

"They won't listen."

"Morgan of Siler is the rightful heir to the throne of Alb'ny," she said. "As such, he is legally and spiritually bound to the Lawgivers. It is necessary that he present his grievance directly to them."

"The Lawgivers speak in their own time," the man answered, eyes roving, fearful of Alicia's eyes. "Our orders are to let no one within the gates—ever."

Alicia smiled. "I quite understand your predicament," she said. "Let me ask you this: has this ever happened before?"

"No ma'am," the man said, and his eyes finally got sucked into hers. "This is the first time since I've been here."

"Don't you think it would perhaps be worthwhile to you to ask your supervisor this one time, just in case?" Her voice was friendly, concerned. "If you're making a big mistake with this, the first thing they'll ask you is if you talked to your supervisor about it. If you do, it's on his head."

The man thought about that. Finally he turned to a bluesuit who hovered near him. "Get Captain February," he said.

As the man scurried off, Alicia turned to Morgan and winked. "It may take a bit of time," she said, "but we'll get in."

The second man showed up moments later. He wore a blue suit and a khaki coat that reached the ground. He puffed lethargically on a huge corncob pipe.

"What seems to be the problem?" he asked, lips smacking on the pipe stem.

"We respectfully request an audience with the Lawgivers on a very grave matter of State."

The man nodded thoughtfully. "We are the arbiters of what constitutes a grave matter," he said. "We see nothing grave connected with your visit, save the inordinate amount of heathen Genies in your party."

Alicia smiled and motioned the man closer to the gate. "If we are to save your city," she said, "we'll take our army where we can find it."

The man backed away, his eyes confused. Taking the pipe from his mouth, he knocked a bowlful of still-smoking ash onto the ground. Then he banged it against the bars to make sure it was clear.

"What makes you think our city is in danger?"

"A pretender sits on the throne of Alb'ny," she answered. "Even now he conquers the South. He also will try to conquer you."

The man pulled a long nail from his coat and proceeded to scrape the pipe bowl, periodically dumping the resin onto the ground. "We don't allow anyone from the outside in here," he said. "This is Kipsie. No one would dare attack us. It simply isn't done."

"We could attack you," she said. He looked up, startled. "I mean, if we wanted to."

He cocked an eyebrow and began refilling the pipe from his coat pocket, tamping the tobacco down with his thumb.

"If we wanted to," Alicia said, "we could march right through those gates and kill every one of you. And all we have is an army of Genies. If we could do it, anyone could."

The man pointed his pipe at her. "But you haven't done it," he said.

Alicia just stared at him, smiling.

He watched her for a moment, then looked around for a light for his pipe.

"Here," Alicia said, removing a match from her gown. She struck it on the gate itself and pushed her arm through the bars. Captain February arched an eyebrow as he bent forward to light his pipe.

"I'd better talk to my supervisor."

Two hours and five supervisors later, the gates were opened and for the first time in Kipsie's history, outsiders other than prisoners were allowed into the gates.

Morgan and Alicia walked down the center of the street surrounded by armed guards. The People, however, waited outside the gates on the roadway.

The city was a massive shrine to the ancient ways, reinforcing the love/hate relationship that all N'orkers had with the Old World.

The buildings were in perfect order, upheaval apparently never reaching there. Everything was precise and meticulously clean. Windows all had glass. Colorfully painted signs with words and pictures on them hung from buildings and lampposts. Flowing, ornate words were painted on the windows. Cement walkways wound around the buildings. People in ancient attire continually cleaned the buildings and grounds—men and women on their hands and knees in the streets, picking up dead leaves or tiny scraps. Shiny ancient carriages moved past from time to time. They were painted bright metallic colors, and had wheels of some strong yet pliable material. They were drawn by teams of stark white Woofers, whose reins went through tiny holes in the front carriage windows. The carriage drivers were all young novitiates.

Morgan and Alicia passed a building with a glass front. Within were a series of large boxes with glassed-in fronts. Old men with flowing beards and colorful robes sat cross-legged on the ground with the boxes covering their heads. They talked continuously, their heads showing through the front of the boxes.

Farther down the street were family dwellings. Each house had its own plot of dirt in front over which men and women in short-legged pants pushed strange churning machines or stood with flexible lengths of pipe from which water poured, muddying the dirt.

"What's wrong with all the people?" Morgan asked as they walked toward the large building that dominated the end of the block. "They seem so . . . strange."

"Many seem retarded . . . deformed also," Alicia said thoughtfully. "I think we're looking at a result of all those chemicals they use to kill the trees."

Gangs of children were following them. Many of the children appeared grossly deformed. He had seen few adults as deformed as the children, and it made him wonder what happened to the bad ones.

They reached the end of the block, and stood before a large building. It was wide and went straight up as tall as a tree. The building was made of cement; it was painted a flat, dark green.

"The temple of Ibem," Alicia said.

Morgan knelt on the ground, bowing low.

"They tell me that's a good way to get your head lopped off," Alicia whispered.

Morgan looked at her in consternation, then got slowly to his feet. "Do you profane my religion?"

"Your religion's inside of you," she said. "This is merely a building."

They were taken into the temple, its halls dark and hot. The smell of incense wafted gently; everywhere was a solemnity that made Morgan feel it necessary to whisper when he spoke.

They were ushered into a totally dark room and left alone. Morgan had relinquished his weapons when he entered the gates. This closed-in room made him wish he had done otherwise.

"I don't like this," he said, turning a slow circle.

Alicia lit a match, its glow showing a room bare except for a black box that hung suspended from a corner. A glowing red light blinked on the box's bottom.

She dropped the match before it burned her finger. "This won't do," she said quietly.

Then, a blinding light shone from the ceiling and a voice said, "Step into the circle of light."

"What is it?" Morgan asked, voice quaking.

"Take it easy," Alicia said, stepping into the circle. Morgan followed her.

When they took their places, the three screens lit up on the wall to reveal Rothman, Penrad, and Dycus. Rothman's face glared righteously at them.

"You dare to disturb the deliberations of the Council of Law-givers?" he said.

"I'm here to do you a favor," Alicia said casually. "But you'll have to meet me face to face to get it."

"Silence! We ask the questions here!"

"You may ask the questions," Alicia said, "but we've got all the answers."

"What answers?" Penrad asked.

"Face to face," Alicia said.

Dycus reddened noticeably, even through the screen.

"We are the power and the glory! We are the living embodiment of the soul of Ibem. You will answer us!"

Alicia smiled. "Let's sit down, let some light in, and talk with one another like people."

"We'll have you killed," Rothman said.

"Your prerogative," she said, "but I'll have to warn you that if we don't go back to our troops, they'll burn this whole city to the ground and you along with it. And by now, you probably know that they're Genies, so you can't scare them with your mumbo-jumbo."

"You have one more chance to answer our questions," old Penrad said, fingers nervously tugging on his droopy mustache.

Alicia shook her head and stepped out of the circle of light.

"Back in the circle. Back in the circle."

"No. And this is your last chance to sit down with me before I have the rightful Governor of Alb'ny put his fist through your television screens. That would be an awful waste, wouldn't it?"

Penrad left, followed quickly by Rothman. Dycus sat quietly glaring for a time before he too disappeared from view. The spotlight went off immediately.

"What are you doing?" Morgan asked.

"Just bear with me. Everything's under control."

"Thanks for telling me," he said.

The door opened and more guards came to take them to another room. They were marched down a hall to a brightly lit room with windows all around and a large table with many chairs in the center. A large man in black robes sat at the table. He had fiery eyes and tangled beard and hair.

"You!" he said, coming to his feet when he saw Morgan.

Alicia looked quizzically from one to the other. "You know each other?" she asked Morgan.

"Dixon Faf," he said, eyes locked with the man. "Programmer of Alb'ny."

Alicia moved to sit across from him at table. "My name is Alicia," she said, extending an ignored hand. The man looked pale and weak, as if he were just recovering from a severe illness. Perhaps she could use that. "What a coincidence that we should all meet here. What brings you to Kipsie?"

"You conspire with the bastard of Alb'ny," Faf said.

"Not exactly true. A bastard has no father. I think we both know better about Morgan."

"How did you get here?" Faf asked.

Alicia reached across the table and patted his gnarled hand. "If I tell you that, will you tell me why you're here?"

He fixed her with his burning eyes. "Be you a sorceress?"

Alicia laughed, shaking her head. "I'm just a little girl from out in the woods trying to improve myself. How about you?"

"I'm a child of God," Faf said.

"Well, that's a club we all belong to," she said. "You know, I wouldn't be surprised if we were all here for the same reason."

Just then, the door opened. Rothman, Penrad and Dycus entered. Each carried an umbrella in one hand and a leather case in the other.

"We will either work this thing out," Rothman said, taking a seat, "or you will all die here this afternoon."

Lizzie lay prone on the back of the sleeping Woofer, far up-river from the excitement of Kipsie. She lay with her little eyes tightly closed, breathing in sync with the short breaths of the animal. The roar of the river by which they lay was in her ears, the feelings and visions she shared with her brothers and sisters filled her mind's eye.

Her mind went no further than the Kipsie gates, where Rhiner had posted himself to await the outcome of the conference with the Lawgivers.

The mood of the Minnies was expectant, yet that was mostly a reflection of the feelings of the rest of the People, since neither Lizzie nor the others were able to connect seriously with complex feelings and relationships. They loved Morgan and knew he was looking for a safe home for them, yet beyond that the auras got complicated. Intricate patterns of physical realities, chains

of action and reaction, all were easily understood on a fundamental level; but the gray area of emotion, the complex inter-
woven threads of shifting moods and feelings dumbfounded her
and the others.

That's why they loved Morgan so—his aura was clean and
pure, his emotion straightforward and linear.

The Woofer began crying in his sleep, whining painfully.
Lizzie shivered and sat up. The others, a full day away, turned
their minds to her.

The Woofer came awake slowly, unwillingly. It was the hottest
part of the day, the time for shade and sleep. She shook her
large, shaggy head and howled low.

"Glitch?" Lizzie said, leaning over, and the animal turned its
big head to look at her for sympathy, a moan still issuing from the
Bernard's throat.

Then Lizzie heard it too, and shook her head. A high-pitched
howling sound drifted through the forest, scattering birds, making the animals uneasy. Lizzie put her hands over her ears, as
did the others in Kipsie.

The Woofer sat up, Lizzie sliding off her back. Raising her
head to the sky, the animal howled loudly at the heavens, the
high-pitched sound driving her crazy.

Then it was there.

The boat came rapidly down the Hus, far larger than Lizzie
could have imagined. Thousands of ugly, deformed humans
crammed the decks full. They were screaming!

Lizzie put her arm on the Woofer's back and they watched the
warship pass just fifty yards from them. The men on the deck
still screamed and it was for the pure enjoyment of it that they
raised such deadly cries to their gods.

Schnecks, she thought, the horror of the word rifling through
all of them. *Schnecks. Schnecks.*

XXX
Blood Conference

Alicia faced the Lawgivers, sizing each one up as she looked,
trying to find the wedge that she needed to reach them all.

"You've wormed your way in here," Dycus said, and she could
tell that he was more interested in looking at her than in any-

thing she had to say. "But there really isn't a thing in the world that you could possibly have to say to us."

Alicia's eyes caught his; she let him drown in them for a moment. "Honored sirs," she said, still staring at the young one. "I offer you nothing less than the salvation of N'ork in the person of Morgan of Siler."

"The land of N'ork was saved a thousand years ago by the power of Ibem," old Penrad said. "That salvation is served by continual elimination of the impurity that you have brought with you to this Holy City. We have nothing to talk about."

"Will you not even listen?" she asked.

Rothman stood up and opened his leather bag. He removed a small machine from it that connected to a power source in the table. "We will listen," he said, "because we have Genies at the gate who threaten our immediate safety."

"We're here to help you, damn it!" Morgan said.

"Let me handle this," Alicia said softly.

"We're wasting time," Morgan said. "Ramon is on the march. If you don't organize against him you're finished."

"He's left Alb'ny?" Faf asked.

"A week ago," Morgan told him.

The Programmer covered his face with his hands, an act not lost on Alicia.

"Ramon of Alb'ny hunts your kind," Penrad said. "A perfectly acceptable practice for an honorable Governor."

"Ramon lays waste to the South," Alicia said.

"He wants everything!" Morgan shouted. "Can't you understand that? He's not afraid of you."

"Blasphemy!" Dycus shouted back, his face reddening.

"Wait!" Rothman said, raising his hands. "We are the instruments of Divine Will. Listen to the voice of Ibem." He punched up something on the keyboard of the box. Static crackled through the room. "Ready?" he asked.

A mechanical voice droned: "READY."

Morgan and Faf exchanged wide-eyed looks. Alicia, with a bemused expression, walked around the table to the box, making sure she brushed against Dycus as she did so.

"A working computer," she said. "Amazing."

"It is the voice of God," Rothman said, then spoke to the machine: "Ibem. We seek audience."

"FILE NAME?" Ibem asked.

"GodProj," Rothman said reverently.

"PASSWORD?"

"Restabilization."

The machine churned a moment, then it spoke again. "YOU HAVE CALLED ON GOD FOR ADVICE. WHAT IS YOUR QUESTION?"

"We have Genies at the gates of Kipsie," Penrad said. "What should we do?"

"DO NOT EXPOSE YOUR GENES TO THEIR CORRUPTION. KILL THEM ALL WITHOUT MERCY OR EXCEPTION."

"But there are more of them than there are of us."

"THEN KILL YOUR WOMEN AND NEGOTIATE."

"Negotiate what?"

"THE SALVATION OF HUMAN THOUGHT AND IDEAS IN EXCHANGE FOR YOUR SUICIDES."

"That doesn't leave a lot of room, does it?" Morgan said, shaking his head.

The Lawgivers stood blankly, their faces drained of all color.

"We don't want your lives," Alicia said. "We want to protect you."

Rothman pressed on. "The Genies say they want to protect us from humans who are attacking the South. Could this be true?"

"HUMANS ARE OF PURE BLOOD AND HENCE ARE THE PEOPLE OF GOD. ATTACK SIGNIFIES WAR. WAR SIGNIFIES THE PROTECTION OF PURE BLOOD, AND THEREFORE IS IN THE BEST INTERESTS OF ALL HUMANS."

"There, you see?" Penrad said. "Ramon of Alb'ny only seeks those who are not of the blood. It's very simple."

"No!" Faf said. "I've seen with my own eyes, heard with my own ears."

"Ah," Alicia said casually. "We *are* here for the same reason."

Faf's face strained under conflicting emotions. "Ramon seeks the rule of perverted science and the fall of Kipsie."

"I agree," Alicia said. "We're on the same side."

Faf sputtered. "I never said . . ."

"Ibem does not lie," Dycus said. "Why do you persist in this fabrication. We know all about you."

Alicia walked to the box. "Do men ever fight other men?"

"IT HAS HAPPENED."

She nodded. "Of course it has. For what reasons do men fight?"

"HUMAN MEN?"

"Yes."

"That's enough," Rothman said. "Only Lawgivers can speak with Ibem."

"GREED. SELF-INTEREST. SELF-DEFENSE. EGO GRATIFICATION."

Alicia moved quite close to Dycus, their bodies almost touching. "Ibem had admitted human greed," she said sweetly and caught his eyes again. "Could that not be Ramon's motivation?"

"Stop," Penrad said. "Ibem has already spoken about Ramon's expedition."

Dycus wiped a line of sweat from his forehead. "It wouldn't hurt anything to ask a few more questions," he said. Alicia smiled at him.

There was a loud knock on the door and one of the Kipsie bluesuits came in without waiting for response. He was struggling with a large sack that wriggled in his grasp.

"What is it?" Rothman demanded.

"Terrible unease at the gates," the man said. "I had to bring this one."

He dumped the contents of the sack on the table. It was Charl, one of the Minnies. The little man shook his head to orient himself, then scurried to Morgan, leaping into his arms.

"Schnecks!" he said, terror contorting his face.

"How far away?"

"Polarized Hus relay from Lizzie."

"How long ago?"

Charl glared at the bluesuit. "Beep, beep. Maxtime delay. Bad circuits."

Morgan stood. "A boatload of Schnecks is heading this way. I'm bringing some of my people in here to give orders."

"You'll do no such thing," Rothman said. "They're looking for Genies anyway. You'll not get our protection."

"I don't need your protection," he said. "It's you I'm going to save." He looked at Charl. "I want El-tron and Squan in here right now."

The Minnie nodded, thinking to the gates.

"Should we stop them?" the bluesuit asked.

"No," Rothman said. "Get a delegation together to meet with the men from Alb'ny. We'll explain this unfortunate misunderstanding to them, then let them have the Genies."

"You're making a mistake," Alicia said. "This is the spearhead of the invasion force. Side with us now. Help with your own defense."

"If we sided with Genies," Penrad said, his mustache twitching, "we'd be denying everything we held dear."

Alicia leaned down to him, for he was too old to even stand without assistance. "Morgan is Ramon's half brother. . . ."

"We know about Morgan," Penrad said wearily.

She turned to stare at Morgan. He shrugged in return.

"They have warships on the waters," she continued. "Warships outfitted with the tools of science." She turned her head to the box. "Science!"

"SCIENCE IS THE KEY THAT UNLOCKED THE DOOR OF GENETIC HORROR."

"Ramon practices the black arts. Morgan is older. Declare Morgan rightful ruler of Alb'ny and we can rally the South to Ibem's cause, and stop this madness before it infects us all."

The Lawgivers began to laugh.

"Are you people crazy!" Morgan shouted, driving Charl away, hands on his ears.

Penrad flapped his hands. "Show him the letter," he told Dycus.

The young man with the pudgy hands looked apologetically at Alicia before pulling the linen from the breast pocket of his suit and handing it to her.

She glanced at it quickly, then turned to Morgan. "Can you read?"

"Yes," he said. "Nebo taught me."

She slid the linen across the table to where he stood. "Then grab hold of your rear end and look at this."

Morgan took the paper, reading in his slow, faltering way.

"Where did this come from?" Alicia asked.

"I brought it," Faf said. "Ty'Jorman Delaga left it for Morgan, but Ramon changed the message."

Morgan read the words with a wash of understanding and relief. So much, so many things, made sense now. O Father, he thought, our bond is stronger than death. A new and frightening world was opening to him, was overwhelming him. They all turned to Morgan. His face had paled deathly white and his hands shook like birch leaves in a Northern gale.

"Well?" Alicia demanded.

"I never suspected," he said.

"So you ask us to appoint a Genie as Governor of Alb'ny?" Rothman asked shrilly.

The door burst open, Squan and El-tron hurrying in. The Lawgivers shrank from Squan's cat face.

"The Schneck boat is anchoring by the long pier," El-tron said. "They've sent a delegation to meet it."

"I feel others," Squan said. "Nearby. In pain."

"Others?" Alicia said.

"Refugees, I'll venture," Morgan said. "Refugees from Ramon's attacks farther North."

"It's begun," Faf said sadly.

Morgan moved to Alicia, put an arm around her.

"What do you think?" he said.

She smiled. "It's wide open," she said. "I've already chosen my side."

He took her eyes in his, no longer fearing the power there. Understanding and respect tied them to one another. The old excitement built within him. "Well, let's have some fun with it."

"You're the boss."

He spun quickly to El-tron. "Dig in outside the gates," he said. "Let's see if we can save their damned city for them. Keep the big guns low. I want to take some Schnecks out with us."

Schnecks swarmed the decks like soldier ants, screaming out their insanity to the hot gray skies. Smelling Genie flesh in quantities they'd never seen in one place before, they became mad Woofers straining at the leash that Redrick pulled tighter and tighter. The man from Firetree stood in the wheelhouse with Henri Darlow and the other humans who ran the ship. He had somehow acquired a coat of shiny gold wool that was literally covered with braids, and wore it continuously, though it made him sweat to near dehydration. He carried with him a large flagon of river water that he drank from time to time.

"I've never seen the like," Darlow said, watching the fierce insanity of the Schnecks.

"Beautiful, isn't it?" Redrick said, his eyes fixed on the small delegation that marched resolutely down the pier toward them.

Darlow looked at him, took a breath. "I wonder what they want?" he said of the delegation.

"Doesn't matter. They're harboring Genies and will share their fate."

Redrick's hair was slicked to his skull, the sweat running in sheets from his face to drip onto his heavily latticed front. His eyes jumped, never resting in one place.

"This is Kipsie," Darlow said. "What do you mean, share their fate?"

Redrick turned to him, jaws clenched tightly. "I spoke clearly,

Captain," he said without moving his mouth. "I intend to level this city with our guns before moving in."

"You can't!" Darlow said.

Redrick brought a sweat-coated hook up to press against the man's throat. "I can do whatever I choose."

"Master of the vessel!" a voice called from the pier.

Redrick looked through the cut out window down at the three men in blue suits. Several hundred yards distant, he could see the red-haired demon's men scurrying around the ruins of old Kipsie.

"I am Redrick of Firetree!" he said, "Commander of this expedition! State your business!"

"We bring you greetings from the Lawgivers of Kipsie!"

"My greetings in return! Would you care to come on board?"

"You're most gracious, Commander Firetree! We wish to discuss disposal of this Genie population to our mutual satisfaction!"

"Lower the gangplank!" Redrick called to the Schnecks below. The decks writhed with them, moving, twitching, screaming. They shoved the gangplank down and the bluesuits reluctantly climbed into the hive.

Once they reached the deck, Redrick grinned. "I bring you the best wishes of Ramon Delaga, Governor of Alb'ny!"

The men waved up, trying to shove their way through the slithering decks.

"Schnecks!" Redrick called. "Whet your appetites on these bastards!"

The Schnecks cheered wildly, then grabbed the screaming bluesuits, ripping them to pieces with their hands, as was their custom.

"PURITY OF THE SPECIES MUST BE PRESERVED," Ibem said. "THERE IS NO GREATER LAW. FOR MANKIND TO SURVIVE THOSE OF IMPURE BLOOD MUST BE ELIMINATED."

"It's clear," Rothman said. "There can be no misinterpretation."

"Things have changed in the last thousand years," Alicia said. "Adjustments must be made."

"Status quo," Penrad said. "We maintain the status quo."

"Everything must change," Alicia said. "That which doesn't change, dies."

"That which does change, dies," Rothman said, jabbing the air with an index finger. "That's the lesson of Ibem."

A steady stream of bluesuits and Genies moved in and out of the room, jabbering things to confusion as Alicia continued to hammer her points.

A bluesuit ran in, out of breath and announced to the room, "They've killed our greeting party," he said, panting, "killed them without even talking to them."

"See what you've done?" Penrad said.

Squan was right behind the man. "Refugees," he said, "seeking sanctuary in large numbers."

"There is no sanctuary," Morgan said. "Put weapons in their hands."

"They're sick and exhausted."

"They'll kill those who murdered their families. Have you gotten any idea of their strength?"

"Ten thousand," Squan said, whiskers twitching. "At the very least."

"Now do you believe us?" Faf asked, suddenly reviving from his depression.

"Circumstances seem to indicate a misunderstanding," Rothman said.

"I urge you to implement my plan of putting Jerlynn Dalaga on the throne of Alb'ny."

"Over my dead body!" Morgan yelled across the room.

"She's of Pure Blood," Faf said. "And is no stranger to the administration of that province."

"Who would lead your army then?" Alicia asked. "We would not sanction such an arrangement."

"Someone in the South," Faf said. "You must have strength in the South. Perhaps in N'ork City."

Penrad looked quizzically around the room, at the confusion that flowed around him like a river. "The South is peace-loving," he said. "And N'ork City . . . We have no contact with the Jewel of the East."

"No contact?" Alicia said.

Serge appeared at the door. Too large to fit inside, he knelt in the hallway, poking his large head through. "The People are nearly ready," he said. "What of the Woofers?"

"Hold them in reserve," Morgan said. "Pick a squad to ride them." He pulled the gun from his belt, checked to see if the chambers were loaded. "Save Murdock for me."

Rothman moved to Ibem. "Humans are fighting humans," he said. "What should we do?"

"NEGOTIATE A SETTLEMENT," Ibem replied. "PURE BLOOD MUST BE PRESERVED."

"A settlement?" Dycus said.

"It doesn't matter," Penrad said. "Humans would never attack Kipsie. Perhaps we will have the time to negotiate."

"No!" Faf said. "If it must be so, choose Morgan. But you must not wait to decide."

"Well said," Alicia added.

"I think they're right," Dycus said. "Perhaps Ibem doesn't realize the gravity of the situation."

"Humans will never attack the Holy City," Penrad said.

Just then, a huge explosion rocked the temple, showering them with plaster dust and chips of ceiling. The windows to the outside cracked, several of them breaking outright. There were more explosions. Through the windows, they could see the streets filling with screaming, frightened people running in all directions, trying to escape the whistling doom that surrounded them on all sides.

"It can't be!" Rothman screamed, running to stare out the windows. A shell went off just outside, its concussion knocking the Lawgiver back, his face cut from fragments of broken glass. Dycus threw himself over Ibem in a protective gesture. Old Penrad opened his umbrella to shield himself from falling plaster.

"I'm coming out!" Morgan yelled to Serge, as swirling smoke plunged the room into semi-darkness. "Have Nebo meet me at the gates."

The giant hurried on.

The room was total confusion, coughing bluesuits and Genies picking themselves up from the floor and turning back and forth in the confined space. Morgan found Alicia in the miasma and took her in his arms.

"I've got to go," he said.

She nodded. "I'll stay here and keep after it. You watch out for yourself. I pride myself on picking winners. Don't make a fool out of me."

Another explosion shook the room.

"A few thousand Schnecks never bothered me," Morgan said laughing, then got serious. "You be careful too. I don't want any of this without you."

She looked surprised. "You mean that, don't you?"

He took her face in his hands. "God help me, I do," he said.

A tear came to her eye; she blinked it back. "I don't want it without you either," she said, then kissed him quickly.

She released him, stepping back. "Not bad for a Genie."

He grinned wide, pulling back his long hair and tying it with a blue bandana.

Faf moved up to him. "I'm making choices," he said, and stuck out his hand. "You have my wish for luck if you want it."

Morgan took the Programmer's hand. "Neither of us will regret this moment," he said, then pulled away and hurried out the door.

"This is the seat of our faith!" Darlow yelled to Redrick over the roar of the cannons. "You can't destroy it!"

Redrick's teeth were chattering with the pounding excitement of the guns. With every orange burst of destruction, he felt a thrill rifle through him. He'd show them all what he could do. "Leave the bridge," he told Darlow. "Place yourself under arrest and stay in your cabin."

"Ramon wouldn't want this!" the man pleaded. "Don't you understand? No one in the North wants the end of Kipsie!"

Redrick couldn't stand Darlow's whining any longer. He had given the man more than ample opportunity. Drawing a dagger from within his coat, he turned quickly and gutted the Trojan, the man sinking to his knees.

He flared around to the other humans who cowered on the bridge. "Who else?" he said. "Who else can't follow orders?"

They stood for several seconds, then a man turned and ran from the bridge, the others following quickly behind. Redrick watched as they shoved through the Schnecks on deck and dove overboard to get caught in the swift-moving current.

Redrick didn't need them. He didn't need any of them. This was going to be his victory alone, and he would direct it from the wheelhouse, the way all generals did.

"Prepare to attack!" he yelled down to his troops.

Morgan moved through his defenses, crumbling stone walls and rusted carriages looking out upon an expanse of open beach. The cannons and mortars were the first line. The cannons were being loaded with grapeshot: stones, chains, bits of metal. Next came lines of riflemen, Mechs who could dispassionately pull triggers at a distance, but who had no belly for fighting up close. The human refugees worked grimly beside the Mechs reloading the cannons. The Genies stood armed and ready to do battle with their most bitter enemy. His people were outnumbered tremendously, but Morgan never thought any further than the moment itself. Defeat, if it came, would leave nothing to worry about, for there is no greater solitude than the security of death.

Nebo walked behind as Morgan hurried through the lines, shouting encouragement.

"I don't understand," the Mech said.

"Anything," Morgan said. "Any tricks, anything you've been working on that we could throw in here."

"I brought along some chemicals," he replied. "Nausea gas that you would never let me test."

"Gas," Morgan said, turning his eyes to the giant warship. Of what value were his principles in the face of total extermination? When it came right down to it, he would take whatever progress he could get. "Load it into the mortars."

"I've also been doing some work with microwaves . . ." Nebo began.

"I don't want to hear about it," Morgan said. "Just use whatever you've got." He hurried away before Nebo came up with any other ideas.

He moved down a wide stone street, demolished buildings on either side. He looked at the clock on his chest. Four o'clock, only three hours of usable daylight left.

The street curved away from his defenses, away from the shelling that the boat with the eagle prow was dealing out. His Woofers waited at the end of the street, and for the first time he wished that Grodin were still with him.

"What do we do?" Dycus asked. "The city is in danger!"

Ibem replied. "IS THIS UNIT IN IMMINENT PERIL?"

"Yes! Yes! Everything is in peril!"

"IN THE EVENT OF AN EMERGENCY SITUATION, THE FOLLOWING MUST BE DONE IN THIS ORDER: EVACUATE THIS UNIT AND ITS POWER SOURCE; EVACUATE THE PARTS DEPARTMENT; PROTECT THE REPAIRMEN AT ALL COSTS; PROTECT THE SYSTEMS ANALYSTS AT ALL COSTS; PROTECT THE PROGRAMMERS AT ALL COSTS."

"Where are the repairmen?" Penrad asked.

"I sent a bluesuit to get them underground," Dycus said.

"We must get Ibem underground . . ."

"Not yet you don't," Alicia said. "We're not through negotiating."

Faf agreed. "If you don't settle this, there's no reason to get underground."

"I don't . . ." Penrad began.

"Listen to them," Dycus said. "We must evaluate our own data, make our own decision in this matter."

"What is the third law?" Alicia asked Ibem.

"PURE HUMAN BLOOD IS HOLY—IMPURITY OF BLOOD IS AN ABOMINATION BEFORE IBEM."

She persisted. "What is less holy, impure human blood or pure genetic blood?"

"What are you getting at?" Rothman asked.

"PURITY OF BLOOD IS ALWAYS THE IDEAL."

"There you have it," Alicia said. "Morgan of Siler may be a Genie, but he is of Pure Blood. Ramon Delaga is a half-breed, impure in all senses."

Rothman stroked his chin. "Ibem said it. I heard it."

"What guarantees do we have," Penrad said, "that Morgan of Siler will not destroy the society of humans should we give him this sanction?"

"Morgan only wishes to provide a homeland for himself and others of his kind. Conquest is not his imperative."

"We have no guarantee of that," Rothman said.

"Listen," Dycus said. "Listen!"

They all stopped talking.

"I don't hear anything," Penrad said.

"Exactly," Dycus returned. "The shelling has stopped."

"Is it over?" Rothman asked.

Alicia shook her head. "It's just beginning," she answered.

Morgan sat atop Murdock just behind the row of cannons. "Don't fire until I give the order!" he called up and down the all-too-short line of artillery.

There was quiet, deathly quiet. All sound had stopped, even on the Schneck ship, and Morgan had a moment to wonder just who was in command of the vessel.

Nebo worked his way along the rows of mortar, topping their pyramids of shells with his gas cannisters. Morgan looked back, surveying his troops. Faces lost in their own form of contemplation stared back at him. Mech faces, weary human faces, distorted faces, animallike faces—and he was a part of them all.

He shared the breadth of his heart with every one of his mismatched army, human and Genie alike. And if they died today, at least they died as one mind, one heart.

He turned to look back at the ship several hundred yards distant. All was silence.

Then the screaming began again, low, like a distant thunder, building in intensity. Schnecks, tiny in the distance, charged down the gangplank.

They were a trickle, then a river, then an overwhelming flood. They charged, screaming down the pier, filling it, overflowing. There seemed no end to them.

The front ranks reached the beachhead and scattered, more behind them, always more.

"Steady," Morgan said. "Hold your fire."

They just kept coming, their screams a frightening emotional intrusion.

They drew closer, still pouring from the ship. They were a hundred yards distant. Fifty. Twenty-five.

"Morgan!" Nebo shouted, a cone-shaped object in his hands that was attached to a small generator strapped to his back.

"Wait . . . wait . . . wait . . ." And when he was close enough to the Schnecks to see the horror of their lopsided heads, he gave the order.

"Fire!"

The cannons roared pointblank into the advancing lines, grapeshot shrapnel decimating the front ranks, tearing the Schnecks to pieces. The mortars went off farther down the beach; clouds of nausea gas floating gently through the madness.

Morgan turned to the riflemen. "Fire!"

And the guns exploded, human reloaders working on the simple mechanisms as back-up weapons were passed to the riflemen. The mortars continued to pound away as the cannons were reloaded. Fire and smoke filled the beach, the pier disintegrating under a heavy barrage. Nebo leaned into the fighting from his position with the riflemen, his weapon humming loudly, all who it touched falling in seconds, their insides bubbling out of their mouths and ears as they cooked from the inside out.

And still the Schnecks came, oblivious to their own multitude of dead and the scores vomiting on the ground.

There would be no retreat.

* * *

"Morgan of Siler will swear a blood oath if necessary," Alicia said, pounding on the table, the sound of distant fighting a continual presence in her mind. "What more can he do?"

"The idea of turning a province completely over to a Genie doesn't sit well," Rothman said, "despite our acceptance of your argument."

Alicia pointed toward the front gates. "He's out there at this very moment, sacrificing soldiers for you. What more do you want from us?"

"A human claim," Penrad said.

"What?"

"Jerlynn Delaga," Rothman said, "has prior claim."

"You sanction the right of succession," Alicia returned. "It means nothing without your approval."

"We will not negate the prior claim. Human claims always take precedence."

Alicia folded her arms on her chest. "And we will not accept such a proposal. We would not let Ramon destroy you and the South first, then take what we want from Ramon."

"Perhaps a joint rule could be arranged," Dycus said.

"Jerlynn Delaga would not find that acceptable," Faf said, "but there is a condition under which the Lady Jerlynn would relinquish her prior claim."

Alicia looked at Faf, saw something turning in his brain. He was tired; he was ready to make a deal.

"Go on," Penrad said.

Faf cleared his throat. "The Lady Jerlynn entrusted me with a mission," he said. "Her priority centers on one issue, the life of her son. If we could extract Morgan's promise to spare Ramon's life, Jerlynn Delaga would abdicate her prior claim to the throne of Alb'ny."

Alicia took a breath. "Ramon had Morgan's mother killed," she said. "He lives to extract the just vengeance he deserves."

Faf showed her empty palms, grit and dried blood covering his hands. "It's the best I can do. I also have my duties."

The Lawgivers conferred briefly while Faf and Alicia looked at one another across the debris-covered table.

"This is our decision," Penrad said at length. "If Morgan of Siler promises to spare the life of Ramon Delaga, and if he further promises to not seek further conquest beyond the province of his birth after his defense of the South is finished, we will declare him rightful ruler of Alb'ny and urge the support of all the provinces loyal to Kipsie."

"What about his just vengeance?" Alicia asked.

"You have heard our proposal," Rothman said. Dycus shrugged sadly. "There will be no other."

"Are you qualified to speak for Morgan?" Penrad asked.

Alicia nodded.

"Then the decision is yours."

She thought for a moment, running possibilities through her mind. She could see no other recourse but to bind the agreement with her promise, the one thing a Politico would never undo.

"We accept your terms," she said.

"Get on the radio," Penrad told Dycus. "Call every monastery and relay the news. They will spread it from there. Have all the Southern provinces and delegates here immediately."

Faf and Alicia were both moving toward the door, toward the fray.

"Make no mention of this to Morgan yet," she told the Programmer. "I must find my own time to tell Morgan."

"You will do this thing for me?" Faf asked.

"You have my word of honor," she said, feeling caught in a trap of her own devising.

Morgan charged into the fray upon Murdock, leading his squad of Woofers at the vanguard of his footsoldiers. The boar's head was in his hand, as he hacked away at the misshapen faces that snarled and screamed all around him.

Murdock growled, teeth flashing. He ripped off arms and heads, going up on his hind legs to slash with his long claws at the monsters on all sides.

The Woofers cut through the ranks, running over anyone in their way. Behind, cat men and pickers and big ears and L-shapes and giants bounded into the fray while crossbows sang metal bolts into soft Schneck flesh.

Cat men jumped upon Schnecks' shoulders, raking long claws to scratch out eyes, while the giants used the half-breeds as bludgeons and Minnies worked as units to bring down the screaming vermin of the North.

The sheer numbers of Schnecks were overpowering, their ferocity pushing the Genies back, though time after time Morgan regrouped his squads, inspiring them with his own bravery and fierceness.

And the ground was soaked red and littered with bodies until the Woofers charged over a landscape of skin and bone, Genie and human and half-breed all made of the same fabric.

The laughing madness was on Morgan, as he hacked away until his blade dulled to nothing and his arm numbed and he was sprayed red with blood. When Murdock tired, Morgan leapt from his back and somersaulted into the thick of it. When his blade no longer cut, he sheathed it and used his hands. When they realized he couldn't be stopped, the Schnecks ran from him, leaving him wandering the battlefield alone, only the dead daring to come near.

But it wasn't enough. The Genies were driven back a foot at a time by wave after wave of relentless Schneck savagery. They had been pushed back past the first line of defense, being forced to abandon the big guns, and the riflemen were threatening to rout. Only the humans were keeping them at their posts, while Nebo, his weapon spent, sat on the ground and tinkered with his generator, totally engrossed.

Morgan flared around, his flower-printed shirt in tatters, his white britches stained red. The Genies had been broken into small groups, all fighting for their lives. They were faltering badly, threatening to collapse at any moment.

In desperation, Morgan looked to the movers. They were still parked on the road to the gate, still heavy laden with ammo and extra fuel.

"El-tron!" he called into the thick of the crowd. The Genie had his long fingers wrapped around the windpipe of a Schneck dressed in patches. Morgan shoved through the crowd to him, fist slamming necks and chests. "The movers!" he shouted. "We'll rally at the movers!" The two Genies fought their way through the bloodtide, breaking free to the road.

"Take the back one!" Morgan said.

"We don't have time to get the boilers up," El-Tron said.

"I know. Take the brakes off, we'll drift."

Morgan jumped onto the rigging of the first mover, then climbed into the storage shelves for a satchel of bombs and a can of fuel.

He caught movement out of the corner of his eye. Someone was climbing the framework. Alicia!

"We had the same idea!" she said to him.

He threw the satchel over his shoulder, then grabbed the gas. It was heavy. He strained up the framework through the middle of the machine, reaching the top just as Alicia slid into the driver's seat and kicked open the brake levers.

"I thought you were going to handle this!" she said over her shoulder.

"Everything's under control! What about negotiations?"

They began rolling down the road toward the fighting, picking up speed as they went.

"We're in! You've been declared legal ruler of Alb'ny. Congratulations!"

"Thanks!"

Morgan pulled the bag off his shoulder and pulled out one of the smooth bombs. He tripped the fuse and looked down at the battle that raged ever closer.

"Genies!" he yelled. "Genies! Rally to me!"

He cocked his arm and chucked the buzzer deeply into the Schnecks' ranks. It flared bright orange, kicking Schnecks high in the air.

The mover churned into the fighting, the huge wheels rolling over the living and the dead. Morgan turned back to see El-tron right behind, Genies jumping onto the mover and fighting from there.

Morgan threw another bomb, then another. Genies and Schnecks were all over the structure now, swarming it; the ground below looked like a writhing snake pit. And the giant wheels turned on the ground of flesh, dredging up gore the way it dredged up the mud sea.

Others began tossing bombs, shaking the beach, darkening it with the fog of cordite. The mover was alive with activity, its framework now the battleground.

"We can't hold this much longer!" Alicia said.

"I know!" Morgan said, grabbing the gas can. He started emptying it onto the framework, gas raining down on the combatants.

"Get off!" he yelled to Alicia.

"You too!" she said, sliding out of the chair and climbing down.

"I'll be there!"

"Here!" She held out a handful of matches.

He moved over to take them, winking as he did. "Beats the farm!"

She shook her head, laughing, and resumed climbing.

The Genies, smelling the gas and remembering the refinery explosion in Masuria, were jumping from the platform. The Schnecks, unchecked, climbed toward Morgan.

He emptied the gas can just as a Schneck breeched the top of the mover. Morgan swung out hard with the can, knocking him back onto his fellows.

Several others found the top. Morgan struck one of the matches on the driver's bench and dropped it straight down.

The mover went up like tinder. Within seconds, the whole structure was ablaze, high flames shooting into the early evening sky as Schnecks screamed and fell, their bodies charred like the night.

The flames surrounded Morgan. There was no way to climb down. Through the waves and heat and the smoke, he saw Serge far below on the ground watching him.

"Serge!" he called. "Catch!"

He jumped without fear or thought. Serge, fortunately, was waiting for him and snatched him from the inevitable.

The battle moved away from the burning movers. And though the Schnecks still had the numbers, the nightmare had turned against them until finally, with painful slowness, the tide washed back upon itself. The rows of Schnecks seemed to ultimately snap at once, breaking, charging back toward the churning river of life.

Redrick watched in growing disbelief as his huge army was wiped out by the red-haired demon, and when the Schnecks charged back toward the boat, he knew he had to save the vessel.

"Weigh anchor!" he yelled. "Let's get out of here!"

Then he realized that there was no one on board but him. The crew had all deserted.

The Schnecks were coming; the Genies were coming.

He was alone.

Charging out of the wheelhouse, he ran the length of the upper deck, taking the steps down as quickly as he could.

The Schnecks had reached the water and were wading through the current to reach him, Genies right behind. Charging across the deck he reached the great spool of the anchor, its thick rope pulled taut. He grabbed one of the turnstiles, but was unable to budge it on his own.

He looked over the side. The Schnecks had reached the ship and were trying to find ways to scrabble aboard. The remnants of the gangplank dangled down to the water line and they were massing there.

Taking out his sword, he began hacking on the anchor rope. His arm rose and fell, the tight rope giving a little more each time. Looking once more toward shore, he saw a curious thing. Dixon Faf, Programmer of Alb'ny was walking the beach among the Genies, picking his way through the stacks of bodies.

"His fault," Redrick said, nodding. "The holy man's responsible for this."

The rope gave, its anchor side pulling quickly off the deck. The *Avenger* began immediately to drift. Redrick ran back to the wheelhouse, but the boat was already turning sideways when he got there. He spun the wheel hard, but was unable to control the actions of the large vessel.

The boat turned completely around, back end pointed downriver. Within moments, it ran aground with a jerk that threw Redrick violently to the floor.

The man rose, dazed, and left the bridge, the terror on him like maggots.

XXXI
Dinner

Grodin squatted on the porch of Morgan's old treehouse in Last Chance, his sword jammed into the wood before him. It stood straight up, and reflected the candlelight from inside.

He watched the light play up and down the contours of the blade and tried to sort out his life. Love, loyalty, honor, and duty swirled around in a confusing mist of Pure Blood and breeding.

"Food in a minute," Ona said from inside the house.

"Coming," he said listlessly.

He had wandered through sixty-two years knowing, absolutely knowing, what it all meant. Now, he felt blank, as blank as the child who lay sleeping within the house.

Ona appeared at the doorway bearing a green sapling with a carp stuck on the end. "You're thinking about him, aren't you?" she said.

"Yes."

She handed him the stick and squatted beside him. "He's crazy," she said, "as crazy as the rest of them."

"Maybe."

He brought the fish to his lips, the steam reaching him before he bit into it. He moved it away to cool.

"This doesn't end here," she said, and the hatred that twisted her face made her ugly. "I'll never rest so long as that bastard has my son."

"It's his son too."

"No!" she said, standing. "I'll not accept that. I'll never accept that!"

She turned and walked quickly back into the house. "I'll find a way to set this right! I'll do anything it takes!"

He let his eyes fix on the blade again and concentrated on his breathing. It was as though the whole world were caught in a monstrous flux that tore the emotions from each individual and gave them back all twisted.

He could hear her crying from the back of the house. It was something she did quite a bit of.

Redrick of Firetree hobbled slowly along the riverbank, eating raw the small lizard he had hooked for his supper. He was heading downriver, figuring to find the closest Southern settlement and rest there until Ramon brought his armada.

The South was noted for its hospitality, and he decided that it wouldn't hurt to sample some of it before it all came to an end. He laughed at the thought of people who would be so stupid as to feed and house their own executioner.

Meanwhile he would have time to work out exactly what happened at Kipsie. He had done everything right, of that he was sure. It must simply have been the ineptness of the half-breeds coupled with the duplicity of the Programmer.

There'd be plenty to tell Ramon about, all right. But there was no hurry. Southern hospitality was the order of the day. He had worked hard. He deserved a little rest.

Ramon's mind had completely slipped away. It was as if he were outside his own body, watching as it sat around the campfire with the circle of Physicians. He sat cross-legged, but couldn't feel his legs. His whole body was numb, only his mind worked—but it was disembodied.

It wasn't unpleasant.

It was quite pleasant.

One of the Physicians was poking a needle in his arm. The 'dorphin liquid glowed in the barrel of the needle, sparkling in the firelight.

"So dark," he heard his own voice say.

"Never mind, dear," the Green Woman said, patting his leg. He couldn't feel her hand. "You just sit there quietly."

"What Genies we don't kill can be put to work in the labs," Scab said. Ramon sighed deeply as the initial rush flushed through his body.

"They can be useful," Dunbar said, twin campfires reflected

in the smoked glass covering his eyes. "Will we have any trouble keeping them?"

"Let me handle that," the Green Woman said, looking into Ramon's face. "Isn't that right, dear?"

"The Jewel of the East," he said, and wondered why he said it.

"That's right," she said. "We'll get it for you."

All the Wizards laughed, and Ramon laughed with them so they wouldn't know that he didn't understand what was funny.

He was looking at dirt.

"Come on up here," his wife said, and hands pulled him back into a sitting position. "You had a little accident."

"Do you love me?" he asked.

They all laughed again.

"We'll need the space to experiment," feather-suited Jerico said as his squirrel ran up and down his arm. "And no interference from the powers that be."

"Times are changing," the Green Woman said. "All by themselves the powers that be are seeing to the fact that they will soon be the powers that were."

"Here, here," Scab said.

Something struck Ramon as odd in all that. "W-what?" he asked. "What did you . . . say?"

The Green Woman leaned over and kissed him on the lips. "Nothing, my love," she said. "You just take it easy."

And Ramon felt a small prick as she stuck the needle in his arm again, pushing the magic fluid deeply into his pulsing veins.

And in the shadows of the ruins of Catskill that stretched out around them, Pack sat hidden, listening with a vengeful heart.

They performed the ceremony upwind from the pyres on the foredeck of *Avenger*, Morgan's newest acquisition. Dixon Faf raised his arms to heaven and invoked the Spirit to smile in favor upon the marriage of Morgan of Siler, Governor of Alb'ny, and Alicia of no fixed surname.

On the beach, monstrous fires incinerated over twelve thousand, lighting the area to near daylight. The yellow-orange glow of the pyres bathed the deck in radiant light and gave an otherworldly presence to the ceremony.

Fewer than two hundred of Morgan's People remained, but now they were a good mixture of human and Genie, a mixture that truly understood the purpose of Morgan's dream—of their dream. They were the solid core he wanted, the beating heart of the organism of his soul.

And when Faf was finished, the People cheered. Ravaged and war weary, they found happiness and hope within themselves and opened their hearts with love for the couple who were their material and spiritual leaders.

Morgan smiled at the brightly lit faces around him, solidifying himself even more in the righteousness of his vision. He saw the Minnies standing on the edge of the crowd, hopping madly up and down.

He laughed, holding his arms out to them.

"Morgan!"

They ran to him, jumping all over him like baby Woofers on their mother.

Everyone else crowded in then, offering congratulations.

"My friends, thank you," he said, reaching out to put an arm around Alicia. "You've made us happier than you realize with your support."

"This is truly a new beginning for all of us!" Alicia said, and they cheered again.

Everyone crowded in, Serge taking both Morgan and Alicia in his arms at once and lifting them from the ground. El-tron and Squan offered their good wishes. Someone handed Marek to his father, and the crowd cheered again as Morgan held the infant high in the air for them to see.

They had a future.

Steaming trays of rab meat were brought on deck, a present from the Lawgivers who attended the ceremony with Ibem, who was hooked up to a portable power source on wheels.

"Eat, my friends," Morgan told them. "You deserve full bellies and bright spirits!"

As everyone went for food, Faf found his way over to Morgan and Alicia, who were greeting the last of their well-wishers.

"It was a beautiful ceremony," Alicia told him.

"My pleasure," the Programmer said. "I wish you much luck and happiness."

"Where do you go from here?" Morgan asked, as he bounced Marek on his arm. "You are more than welcome to travel with us if you choose."

Faf stroked his beard. "My thanks," he said. "But my place is with the Lady Jerlynn."

"You go back to Ramon?"

Faf nodded gravely. "I go to look after her. And who knows, perhaps I can do some good for our cause working behind the scenes."

Morgan moved Marek onto his shoulder and stuck out his hand. "Good luck," he said, "and be careful."

Faf shook his hand. "And you also."

The men embraced quickly, Faf turning to disappear into the crowd just as Nebo worked his way over to them.

"All is in readiness," he told Alicia, then nodded to the remaining Mechs who huddled together on A deck. "They also send their regards."

"What's this?" Morgan asked.

"Your wedding present," Alicia said. "Come with me."

"Wait," he returned. "I have something to say first. Serge! Serge!"

The giant made his way through the crowd, his yellow robes glowing brightly in the flickering light.

"Put me on your shoulders," Morgan said.

The giant took Marek and pulled Morgan to kneel, then stand on his broad shoulders.

"My friends!" Morgan called to the crowd, then waited while the noise died down. "We stand here together tonight, Genies and humans, the founders of a new age. No more will the yoke of breeding and Pure Blood hang from our necks. We are free to be what we are!"

The crowd cheered Morgan's pronouncement, and his heart swelled with the grandeur of their accomplishment.

"You did it, every one of you. With the blessing of the Lawgivers, the union of human and Genie has taken place. We are one People, our dreams of freedom are reality for all, our sacrifices here today the cornerstone of a new and better world. Congratulate yourselves!"

He applauded the People, human and Genie, as they applauded themselves. And he knew that something far larger than himself had sprung from his conflict with his brother, something far better.

"I want you to do something for me," he said. "I want to solidify our purpose. I ask you to make love tonight. I ask you to share the intimacies of your bodies, and I ask you to do it . . . outside of your own species."

They stayed quiet, looking at one another.

"Mate with any except your own kind tonight. Do it for me. Do it for yourselves. Do it for the dream we all share!"

They applauded, reluctantly at first, then with growing enthusiasm. They did accept the dream.

"I take my leave!" he said, and they shouted their best wishes to him.

Morgan climbed from Serge's shoulders and walked off with Alicia, passing old Twiddle who smiled, nodding knowingly. Neither spoke until they were amidships, away from the commotion.

"We've wed," he said nervously.

"I'm thinking of your final command," she said. "Are we of a species or not?"

"We don't count tonight," he said, "unless you . . ."

"Unless I what?"

"We had a bargain," he said. "Business only. I'll not hold you to anything else."

She took his hand, a look of devilment in her fire-reflecting eyes. "Come with me," she said.

She led him to the stern. There, sitting on deck was her balloon. It was filled with air and straining against the ropes which held it to the deck. From time to time the flame beneath the balloon would light, making the whole balloon glow red.

"What's this for?" he said.

"We're going up," she told him, "to see the stars."

He made to speak, but she put a finger on his lips to silence him.

"No excuses," she said. "You're going."

He smiled and nodded, let her lead him into the wicker gondola.

"First this," she said, pulling a rab cape off the floor. "Here is your sign of office."

He put the cloak around him.

"Governor of Alb'ny," she said.

He opened the cloak for her to enter it also. She moved up close to him.

"Lady Governor of Alb'ny," he said, and closed his arms and the cloak around her.

"I didn't trust you at first," she said into his ear. "I didn't believe a human could dream the way you did."

"I'm not human."

"I didn't know that. Anyway, I learned to respect you, then . . . to love you."

He kissed her deeply, feeling the surge of emotion that ran like an electric current from one back to the other. The passion rose in both of them and he pulled her closer.

"I love you," Morgan said, his hands moving up and down her back.

"Wait," she said, moving away from him.

Going to the sides of the gondola, she unfastened the ropes that held them, and the balloon rose shakily into the clouded night sky.

"Are you sure . . ." he began.

"Come here," she said, and pulled him down to the floor of the gondola. He took one look over the side looking down at the boat far beneath them, seeing the orgy taking place on deck. He knelt before her.

"I have given myself before to others," she said. "But I have never felt as I feel right now."

The blue velvet gown came up and over her head and she wadded it up to use as a pillow. She lay naked on the gondola floor, more beautiful than Morgan could have imagined.

They had risen into the cloud bank, grayness closing them in its protective shroud. Morgan shrugged out of his robes. Alicia pulled him down to her.

They made love, the rab cloak going over them as the temperature got colder. They were slow and tender together in marked contrast to the brusqueness of their daily lives, and he got lost in her, their rhythms pushing his senses like an external heartbeat. The cold washed over him and the heat of his loins, and he became a creature of sensation. When the air got thin, she put the oxygen mask on his face and he breathed, perfectly happy.

When the swirl of sensation was finished, he lay beside her drifting like the balloon, the rab cover tightly bundled around them, the oxygen passing from one to the other.

"Look around you," she whispered between breaths of bottled air.

He sat up, realizing they had lost the cloud cover. The carpet of the sky was black, but tiny pinpoints of brilliant light poked through everywhere. It was beautiful.

They stood together, shivering in the rab cloak, sharing the air. The stars stretched out to infinity in every direction, twinkling, their light reaching across the chasm of eternity to touch them. And the Moon—a big, bright crescent whose glow bathed the balloon in simple radiance—dominated the starfield more numerous than trees, and conducted the celestial orchestra that played its greatest concert for an audience of two.

Morgan pulled Alicia closer to him.

He felt small and very large at the same time.

ABOUT THE AUTHOR

MIKE MCQUAY began his writing career in 1975 while a production line worker at a tire plant. He turned to writing as an escape from the creeping dehumanization he saw in the factory and gradually worked himself out of Blue Collarland and into Poor-but-happy-starving writerism.

His first novel, *Lifekeeper*, was published in 1980. Since then, he has published twelve novels, ranging from juveniles to mainstream horror, with the emphasis on science fiction.

Pure Blood is his seventh novel with Bantam, following *Escape from New York*, *Jitterbug*, and four books of the Mathew Swain detective series.

McQuay lives in Oklahoma City with his wife and three children. He is an Artist in Residence at Central State University in Edmond, Oklahoma. He watches too much television and adamantly refuses to eat fried okra.

MEL White
9/5/82

Coming in August . . .

The gripping sequel to **PURE BLOOD**

MOTHER EARTH

by Mike McQuay

The epic battle between Ramon and Morgan
comes to a thrilling conclusion in N'ork City.

Read **MOTHER EARTH**, on sale in August,
wherever Bantam paperbacks are sold.